ALSO BY CHRISTOPHER PANICCIA

THE GRIDIRON CONSPIRACY SERIES

Gridiron Conspiracy

Chasing Shadows

Redemption

THE HAVEN SERIES

Heaven's Gate

Rise

RISE

BOOK TWO OF THE HAVEN SERIES

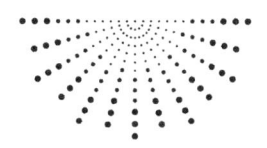

CHRISTOPHER PANICCIA

GRIDIRON PUBLISHING

Gridiron Publishing

Copyright © 2019 by Christopher Paniccia

Cover art by Andrew Paniccia

Cover Model: Baylee Curran

All rights reserved: This book or any portion thereof may not be reproduced or used in any manner whatsoever without the expressed written permission of the publisher except for the use of brief quotations in a book review.

This is a work of fiction. All the characters and events portrayed in this book are either products of the author's imagination or are used fictitiously. Any resemblance to real person's, living or dead is purely coincidental.

Rise: Book Two of the Haven Series

Printed in the United States of America

First Printing: January 2019

If you purchased this book without a cover, you should be aware that this book is stolen property. It was reported as, "unsold and destroyed," to the publisher, and neither the author nor the publisher has received any payment for this, "stripped book."

❦ Created with Vellum

CONTENTS

Chapter 1	1
Chapter 2	9
Chapter 3	15
Chapter 4	21
Chapter 5	27
Chapter 6	35
Chapter 7	42
Chapter 8	49
Chapter 9	56
Chapter 10	63
Chapter 11	70
Chapter 12	79
Chapter 13	88
Chapter 14	96
Chapter 15	103
Chapter 16	112
Chapter 17	121
Chapter 18	129
Chapter 19	137
Chapter 20	143
Chapter 21	151
Chapter 22	159
Chapter 23	167
Chapter 24	176
Chapter 25	184
Chapter 26	190
Chapter 27	198
Chapter 28	206
Chapter 29	213
Chapter 30	221
Chapter 31	229
Chapter 32	236

Chapter 33	243
Chapter 34	252
Chapter 35	259
Chapter 36	266
Chapter 37	272
Chapter 38	279
Chapter 39	286
Chapter 40	293
Chapter 41	300
Chapter 42	307
Chapter 43	314
Chapter 44	322
Chapter 45	329
Chapter 46	336
Chapter 47	343
Chapter 48	350
Call to Action	357
About the Author	359

DEDICATION

*For all those who reach for the stars,
look within yourself for the power that shines through.
The star that shines brightest is you!*

CHAPTER ONE

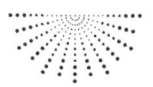

Haze filled Peter Sullivan's mind. He struggled to recall where he was or what he was doing at that moment. A strange sensation came over his body as though some unseen force led him. The hum of vibrating energy jostled his eardrums. Blinking his eyes and moving his head from side to side, he tried to focus to see what laid ahead of him. His sight failed him, causing a state of panic. Gel in his eyes prevented him from seeing vivid images. Only vague outlines in the form of shadows were in front of him.

Although limited in sight, he gained control of his other faculties and listened to his surroundings. At first, he could only hear the shallow breathing of his own body. As if he were in a state of meditation. This struck him as odd because if he were walking, he should at least be breathing a little heavier. The slow rhythm reminded him of a person sleeping. If this were a dream, why did it feel so real to him?

Peter tried to listen to anything around him that would give him a clue to what was happening. Concentrating harder, he let his feelings search his surroundings for recognizable sounds. At first, nothing happened, but as he let himself calm down some more, he heard footsteps. He heard the shuffling of others walking with him and from time to time, he could make out the crunch of gravel underneath his feet. He was with a group of people, but the number and their whereabouts remained a mystery.

Continuing to concentrate, he tried to smell for anything that might give him a clue as to where he might be. The smell of stagnant air filled his nostrils, along with a whiff of pungent moisture filled with mildew. Peter tried to place these two smells, and he recalled his trip to the ice caves with his grandfather Jerry Sullivan one summer. The thought of his grandfather brought him out of his haze and his mind focused.

Jerry Sullivan, grandfather, father, leader, and mentor groomed Peter to take over his legacy. He did this without alerting Peter about much of what he would be asked to handle soon. Mr. Sullivan was the typical grandfather to Peter as he would spend a great deal of time with the boy. Peter didn't think much of it, as his grandfather taught him to think on his own. He would make Peter work on puzzles and solve all types of critical thinking problems. Peter was into codes and secret languages from an early age, which made his mother laugh. A huge fan of astronomy, Peter always felt someday he might visit the stars. To everyone else, he was much the everyday sort of kid, growing up with a doting grandfather.

His best friend Jake noticed Peter might not be what people saw from the outside. Being Peter's best friend, he was with him all the time and was much more observant than most people. He saw Peter do things normal boys shouldn't be able to do, such as move things with his mind. Jake Andrews didn't say a word but took it upon himself to be his friend's bodyguard and confidant. The two boys grew to be inseparable, bothering Peter's grandfather together many times.

The older Sullivan never minded and treated Jake as family. As a matter of fact, unknown to Peter, his grandfather was a close friend of Jake's father, Derek Andrews. Mr. Andrews was a decorated Navy Seal and developed a steadfast relationship with Jerry Sullivan. Since the two boys were together always, neither thought it weird that Mr. Andrews spent so much time talking to Peter's grandfather. The fact that Mr. Andrews was a Navy Seal was never lost on either boy but especially Jake, who followed in his father's footsteps.

Jake loved to learn even though many of his teachers thought he was a space cadet because he would get his work done, only to think about some other subject. Once he learned something, he moved on to conquer the next task. His love of military history and tactics impressed his father, who constantly tested his son until Jake surpassed even him in this type of knowledge. Mr. Andrews responded by finding his son more to learn.

Outward appearances gave people a different picture of Jake as he was extremely athletic and muscular. He fit the mold of a fine-tuned athlete with his broad shoulders and his long, lean body. One would assume he was an athlete of the highest order. Although he enjoyed playing sports and performed well, it frustrated people that he just did it for fun. No, he was into working out at home and hanging out with his odd best friend.

Peter's grandfather thought to himself many times, what an odd couple the two were. As his grandson was an awkward young man, he noticed other children shy away from him. All except for Jake, who seemed determined from early on to watch over Peter at every turn. He sensed Peter would develop into someone special but right now, confidence and grace weren't his strong suit. Mr. Sullivan trained his grandson as he would any other student but without him aware of the purpose of the training. He didn't want to overwhelm the boy with what would become a fight to save the world. Peter finished his lessons always with a smile on his face, which brought an inside warmth to his grandfather. He wanted so badly not to take his grandson's innocence, but the day was coming fast where he would need to become what destiny had preordained for him.

He showed Peter the precious journal many times, but really didn't explain too much about it, always thinking he would have time to continue to tutor his protégé. Evil forces had other plans and intervened, coming for Peter after his grandfather's mysterious and untimely death. Now, without the guidance or protection of his grandfather, Peter would be on his own to face the huge preordained destiny awaiting him. Peter fled with the wondrous journal and his best friend Jake in tow at the behest of a beautiful, mysterious woman. Using the teachings of his grandfather, he unlocked the secrets of the magical journal and gained entrance into a hidden civilization. Through uncounted run ins with Nazi soldiers along with a race of reptilian soldiers, he and Jake managed to get to their Antarctic destination unscathed, only to be captured by those they thought to be their friends.

Being the leader of his group, Peter relented and allowed himself to be captured, along with his friends, so they might gain entrance into a long-secret ancient city under the South Pole. This thought, along with the love of his grandfather, brought Peter back to reality. He heard the footsteps of those around him, but now things came back to him. Without further thought, he let himself be led but took his mind to another place, thinking of Rebecca. Rebecca Beals was a beautiful young lady who warned Peter of the evil following him. At first, the young woman communicated with him by coming to him in his mind and through glowing balls of energy. At her request, Peter began his long difficult journey to the continent of Antarctica.

Rebecca, unknown to Peter, was a member of a long-forgotten royal family of the very ancient civilization that lay hidden under the frozen nothingness of Antarctica. Peter discovered the journal wasn't just a family heirloom but a much more important part of the overall picture. Rebecca assisted Peter, only to be captured herself, halting her preordained meeting with Peter. Peter finally reached his destination, opening a secret entrance, only to be captured himself. All these thoughts flooded back into his head at once, and he felt anger building inside. He felt the power rise inside him, only to hear a calming voice enter his head.

"Peter, I know this is something terrible I've asked you to do, but please understand my people have watched over your people for millennia. We've tried not to interfere with you and allow you to live your life. Our nemesis, the reptilian people, followed us to this planet. We thwarted them after many long years of battle, imprisoning them inside the earth for what we thought would be forever, but you know as well as I, nothing lasts forever."

The voice was so calm and soothing, Peter relaxed his mind and responded, "Please tell me we'll be okay?"

"I can tell you this, I'll give my last breath to make sure you and your friends are looked after. We're almost to the city. You and your friends have nothing to fear. We were sent to retrieve you but as I said, you still have to be brought before the high council before being granted asylum."

Everything came back to his mind—the trip, the danger, the intrigue, and Rebecca. He almost lost the connection but blurted out, "Rebecca! Where is Rebecca?"

"That, my fine friend, is something I'm concerned about! Something tells me she isn't in danger though. Call it a feeling, but I think Rebecca is all right. Trust me, I've known her since she was born, and one thing is for sure. I could always tell when she was in trouble. We share a connection almost as strong as the one you share with her!"

Peter mentioned, "My connection to her is unlike anything I've ever felt! It's as if we're somehow joined! How can that be? I've never actually met her!"

The voice laughed. "Trust me, Peter. I've asked myself the same question, but there's something about you. I cannot put my finger on it, but you're definitely more than you appear to be."

Peter thought about this statement, and he couldn't disagree. During this whole ordeal, he continually learned more about himself. The power he discovered during his journey grew inside him. Though he couldn't understand the power itself, he could make it work in his favor.

"This power I have, is there anyone who can help me control it and learn how to use it?"

"A magnificent question, one asked by the young lady you yearn to see. I was Rebecca's teacher and if you will have me, I would be honored to be yours as well!" Holly Cheric's voice came back.

Holly Cheric, a high-ranking member of the very council due to sit in judgement of Peter and his friends, was sent by the secret Antarctic people to bring Peter to them. She could only smile inwardly at Peter's question. She never even thought of who would see to the boy's training and only worried about getting him to the council safely. All her efforts were focused on seeing him in the council chambers. Now, when the question was asked, she could only see herself mentoring the boy.

Peter thought about her response. "Any teacher of Rebecca's would be most welcome! I would be honored to be your student. The sheer lack of control I have at times is very scary!"

Holly knew his plight. "Yes, Rebecca has similar issues despite being taught for many years. The two of you have a power unseen among our people and is unmatched. I have a feeling I'll teach you many things but, much like Rebecca, you will continue looking for others to help you along the way."

Peter added, "Holly, what will actually happen once we arrive? If protocol is so important to your people, what happens if they don't accept me?"

Holly laughed. "Peter, we have watched you from afar since your birth. No, Peter, they all know who you are. The issue isn't you; it will be the council itself and what it should do from this point on."

Peter hadn't given any thought to what the council would do if they couldn't agree on a straight course of action. The only thought that consumed him was finding Rebecca. Holly reassured him they would find her, but they needed to get him safely to the city first, where they could protect him. Not that long ago, he would have thought someone crazy for suggesting such an adventure as his. The more he thought about it, he knew the adventure was only beginning.

"Holly, what should I expect?"

"The council will be welcoming but guarded. We've chosen to be hands-off for a long time, and many of us are at odds as to what to do next. If we offer too much assistance, does that harm your society, and if we offer too little, does that destroy us both? Trust me, Peter, this isn't an easy issue. We would gladly stand with you, but I think the council will need a push to get them to be unanimous. I only hope seeing you will convince them of our plight. My hope was to present you and Rebecca together. Trust me, when they see you two together, they will know as I do. You two are the future!"

Peter, a little nervous, asked, "Holly, what if I'm not what they're looking for? What if they're disappointed? I am only a teenager. Not only that, I have no clue what to do with this power or what my grandfather had in mind for me once I got here."

Holly couldn't help but chuckle. "Yes, it's quite the predicament, that's for sure! Peter, your grandfather was an important man. He would be extremely proud of you and from what I can see, he trained you very well, even if you cannot see his handiwork. I understand all this is a bit much, but in a little while, we will sort it all out."

An image of Jake popped into his mind, causing anxiety. "I cannot have anything happen to Jake! He's a terrific bodyguard, and one day will make a wonderful soldier, but he's loyal to a fault. If something happens to him, I'll avenge him!"

Holly calmly stated, "Nothing is going to happen to either of you. It's a matter of what our role will be in all this. We have lain hidden for so long, it's now at the precipice of destruction, we come out of our cocoon. I, for one, hope we come forth in glory and remain hidden no longer!"

He couldn't help but feel a renewed energy with Holly's last statement. He felt her determination and hoped the entire council would as well. Still, he couldn't help feeling a sense of helplessness when it came to Rebecca. He felt as if he should be focused on finding her. With Jake and Alex in tow, he also felt the responsibility of others beside himself weighing on his mind. These friends followed him but if anything happened to either of them, he would never recover. Jake, his best friend, and Alex, his grandfather's best friend, he felt the added pressure.

The closer he came to the city, he felt warmth touch his face. Ice cold was the only way to describe the feeling in the cavern, but his whole body felt warm. He knew they would arrive soon. Again, nervousness took hold of him. Only the image of Rebecca's face calmed him, as if he could reach out and touch her but since they connected last time, he couldn't regain communication with her. His mind raced as he thought about helping Holly's people and searching for his beloved.

CHAPTER TWO

Rebecca shot straight up in her bed, screaming! Rage in her eyes, she jumped out of bed, only to see the gentle face of her Aunt Grace running to her side. Startled and unaware of her surroundings, Rebecca blinked her eyes furiously to focus. Her aunt met her halfway across the room, engulfing her in a huge hug. Although nothing more than a hug, Rebecca felt warmth enter her body, along with a peaceful feeling seeping into her body. Looking up into her aunt's face, she saw pain cross her face and watched as her face returned to normal.

Still unsure of what to make of her long-lost aunt, Rebecca backed away slowly, nodding a look of thanks in her direction. The two stood for a moment, looking at one another, neither willing to speak in that moment. Stillness and awkwardness filled the room while the two women stared at each other. Rebecca's thoughts returned to what woke her from her slumber. A vision of Peter captured came into her dreams. She saw him bound with some unseen force, being led against his will. The thought of Peter in the hands of the enemy infuriated her, and the rage built again inside her, threatening to overtake her.

Her aunt spent a lot of time and energy attempting to help Rebecca control her power. According to her aunt, Rebecca's power was unlike any seen by her people and unless checked, could consume her. Fear of losing Peter, along with her present situation, made her feel so useless and helpless. Peter was out there somewhere being taken who knows where, and she was here playing in groves of ancient trees. Standing in the middle of the room, she felt the rage inside her build. Heat rose from her feet and worked its way upward until her face felt as if it were on fire. Her eyes blazed with a mixture of energy and rage. To the unsuspecting eye, she would resemble a demon waiting to attack.

Once again, her aunt strode forward to intercept her student, only to feel her body become like stone, and she could no longer move. Panic overtook her as no one ever with power before. There would be no telling what Rebecca was capable of at this moment. Unable to move, she closed her eyes and tried to contact Rebecca. At first, nothing happened as Rebecca glowed and lifted off the ground about a foot with her head arched back. To Grace, Rebecca seemed to be sucking in more and more energy from everything around her as even the lights flickered. Grace knew if she didn't breach Rebecca's field, she would unleash all that power unchecked.

Calming her mind, she let her own empathic power build in her body and sent it to envelop Rebecca. Once the connection took hold, Grace felt rage swirling around Rebecca. It took Grace's breath away, and she thought it would tear her apart. She tried to calm herself and let her special gift take hold of all that rage. Grace's brow beaded with sweat, and pain filled her head, but she sucked up all of Rebecca's rage. Although she felt as though she would be sick, she concentrated on how much she loved her niece and her family.

Much like Rebecca, Grace needed to find out where she fit into her society, and her power made it extremely difficult to fit into everyday life. Try as she would, no matter what she did, people looked at her as an oddity. Holly, taking pity on her sister, sent her on a mission for the city to try to reconnect with one of the other ancient Zarillion cities. Altogether on the planet, the Zarillions had originally seven huge cities but over the eons, because of greed and expansion of the humans, the cities became deserted. Holly received information that one of the cities may still yet strive although, according to her information, the city lay underwater.

Grace used Holly's information to locate the ancient city and establish diplomatic relations with its inhabitants. She quickly found that she was unwelcome and, despite sharing a kinship with these people, became a prisoner. While in captivity, one of her guards accidentally slammed his arm in her door while closing it. Grace immediately went to him and took his pain away while the other guards tried to bind the man's wounds.

Other guards arrived, only to find Grace soothing the pain of their fallen comrade. She was brought before the council and interrogated about the nature of her power. Grace shared her knowledge and, by sheer force of will, brought the council to tears over the current plight of her own people. A tall woman came forward out of the shadows into the lights, and Grace fainted. The woman looked exactly like Grace's long-dead mother. Without a word, she strode up to Grace and placed her hand on the younger woman's face. Immediately, Grace felt the power surge through her, and an immediate connection to this woman filled her mind.

Once the strange woman broke the connection, Grace could look at her in the light and although the resemblance was uncanny, this wasn't her mother. She searched her memories and blinked quickly, looking at the woman. "Aunt Renie?" The woman was indeed Grace's aunt and like her, was an empath. Renie was furious no one could see this was indeed one of their own. The council immediately released Grace into the care of her aunt. Much like Rebecca, Grace needed a teacher and Renie took her under her wing.

During her training, Grace learned that attempts to reconnect with the other cities was unsuccessful. They were doing all they could to remain hidden from the humans because of the ancient edict that allowed the humans to live on their own. Unlike Grace's people, however, they didn't have the specter of the reptilian people looming over them. They did indeed have many other issues to face, including not only how to stay hidden, but how to deal with the changing climate affecting all the surrounding water. The sealife, now in grave danger because of temperature change to the water, threatened the very existence of the Atlantians.

Seeing the plight of her kin, Grace decided to stay with her aunt while training and helping these people. Unknown to her though, her time underwater affected her telepathic ability, and she could no longer contact her home. In time, she saw the importance of her work and training, allowing her to justify her stay. Alongside her aunt, the two became a formidable duo and used their powers to benefit the underwater people. Although she missed her own people, she had purpose, and her power was a blessing here, not a curse.

All these feelings came back to her as she struggled to help her niece during this time of turmoil. Grace redoubled her efforts and sent another calm message to Rebecca. This time, something came through because Rebecca's breathing normalized, and Grace observed her body relaxing. The glow and heat coming from Rebecca's body subsided while she came to rest on the ground in a heap. Her unseen prison broken, Grace ran to her student. She knelt, putting the young woman's head in her lap, caressing her hair.

It took a few moments for Rebecca to regain consciousness. Looking up into the azure eyes of her aunt, she saw love and worry looking back at her. Rebecca pushed herself and hugged her aunt, apologizing for her behavior. Her aunt hugged her back and felt all the conflict swirling in Rebecca's mind. She understood the connection to Peter through Rebecca. This was something preordained, and these two were destined to be together in more than one way. It was as if these two were vessels for larger forces. For the first time, she saw why Rebecca needed to find Peter.

She released her niece and helped her to her feet. Looking at her with determination, she spoke, "Rebecca, you're right! We need to find Peter, and I feel there's no time to lose. We will need special permission to leave the city. I've been here a long time, and permission hasn't been granted to leave as long as I know!"

Rebecca rose with a frightened look. "You mean we're prisoners here!"

Her aunt placed a hand on her shoulder. "No, we aren't prisoners, but it will be a delicate matter to receive permission to leave. Let me do the talking."

"Will you be going with me?" asked Rebecca.

Grace smiled. "I've waited my whole life for you! I feel it in my soul, and I know I was meant to be your teacher. Yes, I'll be going with you! It's time for the seven kingdoms to be united and vanquish our foes for good this time!"

Rebecca reached across and embraced her aunt. The amount of love pouring from Rebecca entered Grace's body and almost took away her breath. She knew this was the key to her life, assisting this young lady. When the two broke the embrace, Grace explained to Rebecca that much like the council in her own home, the Atlantian council was very rigid. Rebecca laughed and told her aunt she would gladly allow her to do the talking. One thing she wasn't, as she explained to her aunt, was a diplomat.

Grace smiled and told Rebecca she would teach her the tricks to diplomacy as well. Rebecca never would have thought that important, but something told her she would need to become an expert. Grace moved forward, grabbing Rebecca's hand and pulling her behind. She guided them through the maze of hallways until they stood before Grace's chambers. Stopping to make sure no one saw them, Grace quickly thrust Rebecca inside.

Rebecca almost laughed as she had been with her aunt for several weeks and never visited her aunt's private quarters. Grace always wanted to meet Rebecca at the ancient tree. Not that Rebecca minded as she loved the grove and trees, but she thought it odd not knowing where her aunt lived. Once inside, Rebecca was in awe as it wasn't a typical bedroom, but an entire house. From the outside, no one would ever guess Grace was afforded such luxury. Grace saw Rebecca's eyes and told her that being a member of a royal family did have its advantages. She apologized for the secrecy but told Rebecca she didn't want anyone to know.

Grace explained that much like the Zarillion stronghold, there was a distinct hierarchy among the gentry. The council allowed her to live in this home because it was a little-known, and rarely used, getaway for the top officials. Although being kin and a member of the royal family, the chancellor thought it wise not to announce that to anyone else. Long ago, there was a huge rift between the leading families for control over all the kingdoms. This rift was sealed when Rebecca's ancestors won control of all the kingdoms and squashed the rebellion. Grace didn't argue and focused on her studies with her Aunt Renie. Grace told Rebecca that they even lived together here for some time.

When Rebecca asked about Renie, Grace's face went dark. She told Rebecca that Renie suddenly disappeared without a trace. Grace couldn't contact her or find her. According to the official investigation, Renie left the city, and that was all the information they were willing to give Grace. Rebecca saw the hurt in Grace's face and apologized for asking. Grace smiled and told her they could locate both of their loved ones. This brought an immediate smile to Rebecca's face.

CHAPTER THREE

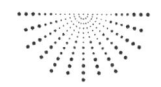

High Commander Zosa, ruler of the reptilian people, dreamt of this day his entire life. Even with his specially designed helmet to protect him from the sunlight, he walked undaunted into the blaring rays of the afternoon sun. Despite warnings from his lackeys, he chose to walk free into the frozen wasteland unaccompanied. Aware of the desolate frozen wasteland awaiting him, he continued forward, letting his feet feel the crunch of ice and snow beneath him. His scientists, planning for this moment, developed an entire suit that resembled a spacesuit to protect the reptilian people from this harsh environment.

Through the special lenses, the sun invaded the commander's eyes, causing them to tear and his vision to become blurry. Rather than stop as he was aware his subordinates were watching, he walked forward, not missing a step. He blinked his eyes rapidly to clear the tears and looked around to see he was alone out in the bleak landscape. Even with his new protective suit, the unrelenting cold hammered his body, causing him to shiver. The commander knew he couldn't stay out in this weather long but after waiting eons to reappear from his earthly prison, he didn't want to turn around.

In a move of defiance, he reached up and tore off his helmet and let the cold air blast against his exposed reptilian skin. The icy air felt like knives entering his skin, and his eyes teared at the harshness of the invading sun's light. Raising his fist to the sky, he let out a primal scream that would have shattered the ear drums of his enemies were they in hearing distance. Now both arms raised, he looked at the demon sun and cursed it.

He felt his skin freezing and quickly donned his helmet. Cold seeped deep into his face, making the rest of his body feel very weak. He knew it was time to return to his once prison for the time being. With a new spring in his step, he turned and walked briskly back into the cavern. Once in the cavern, he saw the smirking face of Colonel Whilhelm, the leader of the Nazi forces his people were aligned with from humanity. Though the commander would love to melt this man's face right off his body, he needed him more than ever. Having felt the harsh reality of the environment that awaited them once outside the safe confides of their underground lair, he knew there was no choice but to work with these creatures.

Unexpected, the colonel walked right up to the commander, grabbing the commander's arm in a gesture of welcome. Initially, the commander's first thought was to strike the man, but he looked into his eyes, only to see a welcome look. He looked down at his arm and saw the colonel hadn't shaken his hand yet clasped his arm halfway up his forearm. When the colonel released his hand, he immediately snapped a salute toward the commander.

Commander Zosa snapped the salute back quickly. "Well met, Colonel!"

"Commander, now that you're free, are we going to speed up the timetable for our enemy's demise?" sneered Colonel Whilhelm.

The commander couldn't help but smile. Here was a man who hated the humans as much as he did. Once in the safe confides of the bunker, he took off his suit and waved the colonel to follow him. With the force field down fully, he could talk to the colonel face to face. The colonel followed warily behind. The party entered a small conference room resembling what one would find in any office situation. Commander Zosa took a seat at the head of the table and motioned for his guest to do the same. Colonel Whilhelm followed his host's lead and sat across from him, eyeing him carefully.

Sweat formed on the colonel's brow as he felt the blast of heat emanating from the vent overhead. Nausea crept into his head and stomach. The commander sensed his guest's struggle and raised his hand to talk into a communicator, asking someone to turn the heat down. In a few moments, the heat leveled off, and the colonel breathed regular. Still quite warm, the sweat built up on his brow.

He looked at his guest with embarrassment. "I apologize, Commander. I've spent so much time in the cold during my time here, any type of heat is too much for me!"

The commander laughed. "Colonel, I know exactly how you feel. Going out into that cold was just as uncomfortable. I have to admit as much hatred I've harbored against you all this time, is much tempered by my freedom!"

The colonel turned and looked proud. "Commander, we're allies. We may never be true friends, but I hope now that you're free, we will be able to work for a common goal."

Commander Zosa cackled. "The destruction of those human insects!"

Colonel Whilhelm laughed. "They will never know what hit them! They are all weak and entitled, pathetic scum!"

"Colonel, now that we're able to meet like this, it will be much easier to plan and share information. I know it was difficult, always trying to carry out my orders with half of what you needed. You've indeed proven yourself. Together, we will be unstoppable and as a team, the humans are in for a rude awakening."

Both men looked across the table at one another with mixed emotions. They spent so much time hating one another, now the tension dissipated. Taking one another in, the commander acknowledged the colonel was very well put together. His uniform was impeccable, and his body, even for his age, was in top physical form. Likewise, the colonel took in his rival. The commander's corded muscles were imposing in person, but it was his height that overall was the most intimidating. The colonel, himself well over six feet tall, looked up to the commander, who stood at seven feet at least.

The commander began, "Let us focus on the business at hand. We need to strike while they're still unsure what's happening with the force field. They too knew it would be down soon but until they are, we should attack now. Honestly, Colonel, that's why I had you attack them so often lately. They would think of this as another probing mission."

Colonel Whilhelm stated, "Your Excellency, everything you asked for is ready. We did have a small issue due to the heat vents, but we've recovered nicely, thanks to your assistance. We stand ready to take the fight to the Zarillions. Once they are dispatched, the humans will fall with little resistance."

"Colonel, I love your confidence but don't get ahead of yourself. The Zarillions are a formidable foe and won't be defeated so easily. It just so happens that this plan will allow us to breach their city and make them feel like captives for once."

With a nod, the colonel leaned forward. "All I meant is that once inside, the Zarillion people will have little time to react."

The two men sat back in their chairs, thinking about the upcoming campaign. Though both were veterans of many a battle, the nervousness at the beginning of each battle never went away. Much of the afternoon was spent going over strategy and when the colonel stood to leave, he walked over to the commander, offering his arm. The commander reached out and grabbed the man's arm with a viselike grip. The colonel walked back out of the cavern feeling as though his plan was ready to implement.

Commander Zosa watched as the man walked away, and he felt a kinship to this man, having met him face to face. This made the commander feel much better about using the Nazi forces in the campaign. If nothing else, he knew they were excellent fighters having watched them in many battles over the years. With his technology and their fighting skills, he knew the Zarillion people stood little chance against the coming invasion.

He took one last look as the door to the bunker closed, collecting the last of the daytime sunlight. All his life, he hated that huge ball of gas but today, feeling its warmth on his face, he reevaluated his feelings. Being such a historic day, he allowed his men to celebrate before the invasion. He would allow them one day of celebration and then lead them to the destruction of the Zarillion people. Without looking up, he smiled knowing for the first time, he could remember he was free to go and do as he pleased.

This newfound feeling allowed him to concentrate more on the task before him. Entering his office, he closed the door behind him and turned on the huge screen on the wall. Before him, he saw various winter scenes from hidden cameras dispersed throughout the known Zarillion entrances. He needed to admit that Colonel Whilhelm was indeed very handy. The amount of intelligence the colonel gathered was invaluable. Although the last attack was considered unsuccessful, he knew that entrance was the key to breaching the city.

He also knew the Zarillions couldn't fix the damage left behind. Even though the colonel barely escaped with his own life, he alerted the commander to the fact it might be a fake entrance. Further exploration revealed it was indeed an entrance imploded to prevent breach. The commander laughed at this; rock was no deterrent for his technology. His weapons could easily melt the rock that awaited them. The Zarillions, unaware of their release, wouldn't expect this technology. Also, the commander ordered both his men and the colonel's men to be outfitted the same! The Zarillions would never know what hit them until it was too late.

With the press of a button, he ordered his generals to meet him in HQ within the hour. Commander Zosa stood to his full height straight and with pride as his lifelong dream was about to become reality. He shed what was left of his spacesuit and donned his uniform to be presentable for his generals. His strides were extra-long that day, and he arrived well before any of his leadership. While seated waiting for his subordinates to arrive, he couldn't help but think of what it would be like once his people had the freedom to choose where to reside on this planet.

Colonel Whilhelm described many places over the years that he thought the reptilian people would be comfortable, but they needed to choose themselves. The thought of coming and going as one pleased was very comforting to the commander at this point. As the first of his leadership arrived, he knew he must focus on the task at hand. They were all too close to their goals to let anything get in their way at this point. The room filled, and the commander looked at the determined faces before him.

When the entire table was filled except the final seat, the commander thought to himself, who was missing? He was in thought when a tall, shadowy figure walked into the room. At once, the commander's guards rushed to intercept the stranger. A wave of unseen air slammed into the guards, causing them to crash into the wall. The entire room was a mass of activity as they all were ready to come to the aid of their commander. With a flourish of his hand, the chaos that was HQ suddenly stopped. All the senior leadership stood in suspended animation before a confused Commander Zosa.

The commander still didn't move but looked at the figure warily as he stepped from the shadows. A sneer came across the commander's face as the figure took a seat across from him. The heat sent toward the two figures would burn anyone between these two rivals. They took each other in for a few moments.

The commander spoke first, "Michael, what's the meaning of this? I should kill you where you stand for this intrusion!"

The tall, lanky man laughed. "Commander Zosa, did you not see how I laid waste to your ring of protection? If I wanted you dead, it would already be accomplished. See, Commander, you fail to realize something. Now that the force field is down, you're also vulnerable to attack!"

CHAPTER FOUR

Michelle Sullivan shook her head, trying to clear he mind. Blinking rapidly, she turned her head quickly from side to side to gain her bearings. The familiar surroundings of Derek Andrews' living room made her heart slow down a bit, but she couldn't remember coming over to visit her friend. Michelle carefully stood still, feeling as though she were in a dream, and walked to the kitchen calling for Derek. The house remained silent as she searched from room to room without finding a living soul.

Derek, like Michelle, lost her spouse to a mysterious accident which made the two fast friends right away. Of course, the fact their boys were like brothers made it even easier. Although nothing romantic ever materialized between them, they still always had a little tension that some thought might turn into something. She, like her son, held the key to many secrets, and although her outward appearance was one of an every-day woman, she too was extremely powerful in her own way. Knowing this power could be the demise of others close to her, kept her at arm's length when it came to relationships with others.

Peter's father won her over with his persistence, always asking her politely to have coffee with him. She finally one day agreed to spend some time with him, and she was hooked. They dated shortly before deciding to marry. Her father, Jerry Sullivan, surprised her when he gave his permission to Joseph Randle blessing the union. Joseph was a large man at six feet three inches and looked the part of protector. To Michelle, however, he was a gentle giant and won her father over quickly.

When Peter was born, the pride in Joseph's face was enough to make anyone smile. He immediately took on the role of father, protector, and provider. To the neighbors, they were the perfect normal family. As Peter grew, the close relationship of father, grandfather, and Peter made her feel her boy would grow up well cared for and loved. Growing up with her father, she always knew he was more than he showed others, and when she first started showing signs of her own power, he taught her without question. One day, when she was ten, their dog was being very mischievous, and she was very frustrated, yelling at the dog. The dog wouldn't listen, and she told herself she wished the dog would behave. Playing, she raised her hand and, in her mind, told the dog to behave. Much to her surprise, the dog obeyed and came over to her, standing by her side.

Her father explained that she could enter people's minds and communicate with them. He further went on to tell her to be careful because putting thoughts into people's minds was extremely dangerous business. She listened carefully to his counsel and worked hard to control her gift, using it only when necessary. Still, her father told her little about himself and what was yet to come. He would meet with many people over the years that she knew not who they were. He did explain to her that he was a guardian of sorts and that someday soon, things would be explained. That day never came as he died before sharing the secrets with her.

One mystery her father shared before his untimely death was a spectacular ancient wooden rod. The rod was highly polished and made from the wood of an ancient tree as described to her by her father. Smaller than a staff, the rod looked as though it should be in the hands of a king as a scepter. With a smooth highly polished finish, it looked indestructible and mysterious, with strange runes running up and down the length of the entire shaft of the rod. Her father gave her little more detail about the strange rod but made sure to hammer home to her that when Peter came of age, he must be given the rod.

Michelle didn't question her father but kept the rod in a safe, secret place, awaiting her son's day of taking possession. She didn't handle the artifact much throughout the years but just after her father's death, she took the rod out to look at it. The shaft was smooth and cool to the touch. She let her fingers run over the carved runes, feeling the indents of each carving. Something in the back of her mind told her to place the artifact in another safe place. The feeling of warning sent chills down her spine, but she listened and placed the rod into a secret nook in her bedroom.

She and her father lived in this house for years, and they were always redesigning the home, adding little special places out of the way of prying eyes. Her father loved woodworking and designed a special vanity for her with all kinds of special hidden doors for her to put precious things. One space was in one of the legs, which was hollow. Inside this leg, she put the ancient rod until it was time to give it to Peter.

The thought of her son cleared her head, and she looked around, trying to figure out how she arrived at Derek's home. Then, like a bolt of lightning, she recalled waking up in her own home after what could only be described as a home invasion. Her entire house was destroyed with the front door blasted into oblivion. At this point, a couple of Derek's friends came through the door, whisking her away with little explanation. She demanded to know what was going on, but they said Derek would explain. Michelle thought this odd, but she knew the Navy Seal to be cryptic at times.

Once safely at Derek's, she was asked to wait for his arrival and to stay out of sight. She was also instructed to stay away from the windows and not to go outside. She offered little resistance and made herself comfortable on the couch, only to feel the weight of exhaustion and fell into a deep slumber. Here she was at this moment, waking from a prolonged sleep, trying to make heads or tails out of the last twenty-four hours. The passing of her father still fresh in her mind, and the knowledge that her son was with Jake going on a school trip, left her feeling very much alone.

She looked briefly toward one of the kitchen windows, only to see it was quite dark outside. This told her she had slept for quite some time and was incredibly nervous. Derek should be home by this time. Michelle searched for any clues as to the whereabouts of her host. Her journey led down to the basement. It looked much like any finished basement with simple furniture and a comfortable nature. Something pulled her in the direction of a closet off to the side, and she opened the door, clicking the light overhead to get a better look. Looking quickly, it seemed like a normal closet with clothing hanging, but she looked slightly past them, only to see the closet was much larger than appeared from the outside. Curious, she pushed past the clothes and stood in front of a cement wall.

As she was about to turn around and go back the way she came, a distinct click sounded in front of her. Michelle swung around to see the wall part, leaving an entrance for her to walk into the wall. At first, she almost ran the other way, but something held her fast as she knew her friend to be an active Navy Seal. Pushing aside her fears, she walked into the secret room, only to have the wall close quickly behind her, making her a captive. Fear gripped her until she heard a familiar voice come from somewhere across the room. Derek's voice came from a computer monitor on one of the tables close to where she stood.

Quickly, she rushed to the computer screen, only to see a laughing Derek Andrews looking back at her. He laughed a little. "Well, Michelle, it took you long enough!!"

She barked back at him. "Derek, this isn't funny! What the hell is going on here?"

The hardened man's strong jaw straightened as his face became more serious. He said, "Michelle, sit. We need to talk."

She could tell by his serious tone that something wasn't right. Without another word, she sat in front of the computer screen, taking in Derek's image. The typical stereotype of a soldier was on the screen before her. Derek's hair was cut into a flat top, and his square jaw added to the stark look. His uniform looked impeccable, and she thought he looked quite dashing. Michelle sat waiting for Derek to start but noticed the man was having a difficult time knowing where to begin.

He looked at her. "First, both boys are safe!"

She rose from her chair, practically tearing the screen to her face. "What do you mean the boys are safe? You told me they were doing something for school!"

Derek winced. "I needed to come up with something quick after we found you and the shape of your house. I didn't want you worrying!"

"Worry! Why would I worry, Derek? What aren't you telling me?"

He looked at her. "Your father gave me orders! I took care of them! They're in a safe place."

She didn't look convinced. "Why would they have to be in a safe place, Derek? Spit it out! Now!"

Derek went on to explain how her father gave him specific instructions regarding the boys and where they were to go. Michelle listened graciously as Derek outlined the entire scenario. He went into detail about why the boys needed to be brought down to Antarctica. She sat back when Derek finished explaining to her that her boy was the key to saving the world. Overwhelmed, she just stared at the screen.

After a few moments, she spoke, "Derek, you knew about this the entire time and didn't feel I should know this information?"

He looked hurt. "Michelle, I'm sorry. Your father gave me specific instructions not to involve you, for your own safety. If these people believe you're not involved, you would be safe! I couldn't bear to see anything happen to you!"

This last statement caught her off guard as the two were fast friends, but this caused her to think more about her relationship with Derek. She saw he was struggling with the decision to leave her out of the loop. Here was the ultimate soldier showing his weakness—the two boys. Over the years, Derek acted as a second father to Peter. Especially after the loss of her husband, it seemed as though Derek was always there helping either her or Peter with something. She never gave it much thought as the two boys were as close as brothers. Michelle watched as he, instead of shirking his responsibilities as a father, this military man stepped up to the plate to be an even better father and friend.

Rather than yell at her friend, which she felt like doing, she thought for a moment. Her father always told her they were preparing for something big and that she needed to be ready when it was time. Although it didn't quench her anger, she tried to understand her father and what her role was in all this. She sat up and looked back at the screen.

Through gritted teeth, she started, "Derek, what did my father have in store for me?"

Derek looked relieved. "Believe me, if so much wasn't riding on this, I wouldn't hesitate to share everything with you. Right now, you and I have our own mission. The way your father described this mission, it's as important as what the boys are doing right now!"

Lifting her brow, she spoke, "What mission?"

He smiled. "The good news is we're on our way to see the boys! The bad news is, to get there, we need to go right into the middle of enemy territory. We need to steal something particularly important!"

"Steal something! From whom?"

He shrugged his shoulders. "The Nazis!"

CHAPTER FIVE

The veil of sightlessness melted away from his eyes, and he blinked rapidly to focus. At first, he could just make out blurry images but, in a few minutes, he saw the images take on solid shape. In the dim light, his eyes also needed to focus to make up for the lack of light. As the images gained more clarity, and his eyes became more accustomed to the light, he noticed a grand wooden gate reaching high into the huge cavern in which they stood. On the gate, he saw many of the runes he came across back at the doorway in the ice cave. His eyes brightened when he saw the largest shape on the door. The starburst shape reached out to him.

Holly noticed this. "Yes, Peter, in time, you will learn the significance of the starburst! For now, please follow me and say not a word."

He turned to his side to make sure Jake and Alex followed. Jake gave him a warm smile and punched him in the shoulder. Alex came up to him and put his hand on his shoulder for reassurance. When satisfied his friends were well, he looked to Holly. In the dim light, she glowed with power and majesty. The more Peter looked upon her, the more regal she seemed. She smiled and strode forward, reaching out her hand and placing it on the starburst pattern. Her hand glowed along with the starburst pattern, and he heard locks unlatching. The door creaked open slowly.

Within moments, armed guards surrounded them. General Giles, the Supreme Commander of the Zarillion people, stepped into the light and commanded his soldiers to form a wall around their small band of friends and escort them into the gateway. Once inside the gate, Peter felt a wave of warmth as he looked up into what could only be described as a small sunset. Being far below the surface of the earth, he couldn't understand how this was possible as the warmth radiated down upon his face. He moved his head to look at the plush vegetation everywhere around him. Coming from the stark-dead cavern into what he would describe as sheer paradise.

Peter and his friends stood in awe of such a magnificent sight. Holly strode forward at a brisk pace, and he needed to nearly run to keep up with her as she was quite a tall woman. She peered back at them, telling them there would be time for sightseeing. Right now, they needed to hurry. They all quickened their pace as they passed from the beauty of the wooded area into a more village-like situation with cabins and small homes. As they continued forward, the scene changed into a stone mason's dream.

The dirt and gravel trail gave way onto a beautiful, stone-paved road with large stone buildings on either side. Gone were the tall trees, and now it was a large cityscape. With each step, the buildings became larger and taller. Peter couldn't believe the expanse of the city as he could look in every direction and see nothing but huge, stone buildings. The roads at first large and wide became narrower. Peter felt the weight of the buildings bearing down on him, and the fresh smell of the secret wood gave way to a pungent mixture of smoke, cooking food, and animal smells. He was surprised the smell wasn't more unpleasant in such a large city, considering they were underground. Peter noticed that even though the city was hugely stone, there remained many large trees and growth between buildings.

Holly didn't stop but pushed them faster until they felt the ground pitch upward. As the incline became steeper, Peter peered upward. The sight was truly breathtaking. It was the largest, most ornate castle he had ever seen. To him, it was a sight straight out of a fairy tale. The climb became steady and more strenuous. Now full of sweat, he said nothing but followed as close to Holly as he could. He realized it was quite a long time ago in which he ate his last meal. With his stomach growling, he struggled forward, trying to maintain the same pace. He saw Jake right next to him, keeping pace with Holly with little trouble. Jake was such a mystery to Peter this way. He looked so mild mannered but sometimes, Peter thought his friend was made of steel.

All at once, they came to an abrupt stop before another large, ornate, wooden gate. There were no runes, but carvings of people dug deep into each door. Peter looked carefully. The ancient doors were weathered, and the once-crisp features of people were smoother outlines. Peter couldn't help but wonder who these important people were to have their likenesses carved into these doors.

Holly didn't need to open the doors. Opening on their own, more soldiers appeared but these wore decorative armor, with a large starburst symbol on their breastplates. A billowing cape flowed behind each of the guards, and Peter could tell these men were important by how Holly deferred to them, as they replaced their more common escort of soldiers.

General Giles went to the head of the guard and led the way, falling right into formation while marching in step with his men. Even without the armor or cape, the general was cut from the same mold as these men. With each step forward, the general became more regal, and Peter glanced over at Holly to see her prideful look at the general. Once again, Peter felt out of place, sandwiched between such powerful and important people. Without another word, he followed quickly as they maintained the frightful pace.

Peter tried to catch a glimpse of the castle as they made their way forward, but the sheer size and height of the structure made it extremely difficult to see much. The one thing he noticed was the architecture didn't differ much to that of some of the castles on the surface. He would expect such an ancient civilization would have different architecture and building techniques. Upward they raced and, for the first time, Peter felt exhaustion creep into his bones. He wasn't sure he would make it and now stumbled, only to have Jake prop him up and keep him close.

All he could do was offer a weak smile and try to keep up. As he was about to stumble again, they came to a halt. Peter could hardly breathe and was sweating profusely. He leaned against a wall with his hands on his knees. Jake placed his hand on his back to check on him. Peter thought of Alex and turned to look for him as he was much older than they. He was close by and leaned against a wall much like Peter, but he looked intact, if not a bit weary. Holly instructed them to wait here as she and the general went to announce their arrival.

Taking a seat on the ground, Jake, Peter, and Alex leaned with their backs against the stone wall with their heads slightly forward, trying to gain energy to finish the journey. They looked up to see the ring of steel still around them. The guards didn't look upon them with disdain, but they were there to keep them under control. Rather than complain, Peter struggled to get up and straighten his body to its full height. He looked around him to see more growth. Not wooded as when they first arrived, but there were quite a few trees and off to the right was a gorgeous garden.

Unable to find an entrance, he was disappointed with being kept from the garden's beauty. He turned to walk back when he heard a rustling coming from the garden. He saw the once-blocked garden open before him, revealing an untended and overgrown path. Curiosity overtook him as he leaned forward slightly to peer into the opening. Feeling a tug on his mind, he strode forward, only to be met with the breastplate of one of the guards blocking his way. He stopped and looked at the guard.

He was the tallest of the guards and the most regal. "You may not enter the royal garden! As a matter of fact, no one has entered the garden for many lifetimes of men. I don't know who you are, and I don't know why the garden opens for you, but you will stand fast!"

Peter turned to join his resting friends but stopped in his tracks, feeling the pull of the garden deep within his mind. Once again, he walked toward the garden, only to be intercepted by the guard. This time, the guard placed his hand on Peter's shoulder to refrain him.

Jake, now at his side, grabbed the man's hand and bent it, causing the guard to go down to one knee. Alex ran, yelling for everyone to stop, only to have the other guard strike him in the chest. Seeing Alex go down, Peter's rage swelled until he released it on both the unsuspecting guards. Both men were lifted into air and sailed into the large wooden entryway.

Jake raced to Alex to help him up, but the man was already on his feet. Jake shook his head as he realized the older man was made of some very sturdy stuff. Alex and Jake moved over to Peter, who looked as if he were about to be grounded by his mother for some huge offense. The guards struggled to their feet when the door opened, revealing Holly and the general.

Holly rushed out, "Peter, what's the meaning of this?"

"Holly, you tell me I'm important! You tell me I'll be welcomed by your people! Well, I'm not impressed by your welcome! You treated my friends as criminals, rushed me here, and left me on the doorstep to be accosted by these thugs! Now, you stand in judgement of me when I've done all that has been asked of me without question!"

Holly stood in embarrassment as she knew the young man to be true in his assessment. She ordered the guards to stand down and asked the general to see to the boys. As she grilled the guards about the incident, she peered over their shoulders to see the garden still open before them. Without another word, she turned and rushed over to the boys.

She towered over Peter. "This is the Royal Garden of Admor and will only open for a member of the royal family. This itself isn't puzzling, but the fact that the garden has chosen to open itself to you is rather curious."

Peter looked dumbfounded. "What are you talking about? I thought I used my power to open it by mistake."

She laughed. "No one has opened this garden in the memory of anyone living in the city. As a matter of fact, we have only two recorded times in our history here when it was open at all. No, this is an omen!"

"I didn't mean to hurt your men, but they hurt Alex, and I cannot let that stand! The garden just opened and as soon as the entrance showed itself, I felt a huge tug on me to enter. I felt as if I were being drawn in, and the guards barred my way rather forcefully."

Holly smiled. "They can be rather zealous at their job! Then again, that's why they're here. I apologize for their actions. As for the garden, I don't know what to think. If you go in, you must go alone. It's the law!"

Peter looked to Jake, and they shrugged their shoulders. After a few moments, Jake nearly pushed Peter toward the garden. Holly looked as if she were about to stop him but backed away. He looked toward the now-parted overgrowth giving way before him and inched forward. When within a foot of the entrance, he felt heat emanating from the garden and a presence watching him. Despite his misgivings, he couldn't stop himself and stepped forward.

He peered into the opening to see what awaited him, seeing an overgrown path off to his right. He then turned to see Jake, who waved him on. Peter knew Jake to protect him at every turn but here, he sent him off into the unknown. Catching Holly's uncertain look made him stumble as he didn't lift his foot to avoid some roots. Tripping a little, he caught himself and stood tall as he entered the calling garden.

The garden looked as one would expect, with plants and flowers of all kinds surrounding him. The air inside the garden was fresh and pungent with various smells from the numerous flowers. Peter looked to see if he could recognize any of the flowers. To his great surprise, he saw many types of roses, lilies, and wild flowers he would see in his mother's own garden. The lush scene before him became even more inviting with every step forward.

Without thinking, he turned to look to his friends as he was a good six feet into the garden. The doorway he entered was a different color as he viewed his friends. It seemed to Peter, an energy field covered the opening. He squinted his eyes, and he thought he saw a slight yellowish ripple where the doorway stood. Jake stood ready to run in if needed, and Holly stood with anxious nervousness.

Warm air brushed against his cheeks and again the fragrance of the garden called to him telling him to move forward, as though the garden wanted to show him something important. He was nervous but didn't feel any sense of danger as he turned. As he turned, he heard the same rustling he heard when the garden first opened for him. He swung his body just in time to see Jake running for the entrance, only to be repelled. Peter saw Jake's angered face as the once-inviting opening was closing fast.

As the thick branches covered the opening, he thought they might come forward and imprison him. With furious hands, he tried to pry the branches apart so he could escape to his friends, only to feel the tough, thick branches scrape his fingers. When his hands were raw, he stopped and stepped back to look at his destroyed hands. Large scrapes, cuts, and abrasions left his hands a mess and with pain starting to take hold panic rose inside him.

The once-inviting garden taunted him forward. Despair caused him to let anger enter his mind. Feeling the power build he rose his hands to unleash everything into the growing boundary barring his exit. As he straightened his hands to let loose the power, he saw his wounds heal on their own. He brought his hands down to look at them and sure enough the wounds were closing.

A new rush of fresh air crossed his face as if someone were caressing his cheek. Once more, the danger passed, and the garden seemed inviting. Of course, to Peter nothing about any of this trip and his many encounters made and sense so why should a magic garden be any different. Looking at the growing wall before him, he turned and saw the path calling him. At first, the path looked dim and unused but with each step forward, the light grew.

Peter strode forward, knowing the only way to go was forward. Much like everything he faced recently he didn't have a choice. His thoughts wandered to the loss of his grandfather. The entire journey southward danger lurked around every corner gave him pause. Each leg of the journey tested him in ways he never thought possible. Even without his grandfather's he managed to successfully find the hidden civilization. The path brightened as he followed it carefully. Making his way into the heart of the garden, he saw it was built as a maze.

This made Peter smile a bit as his grandfather always made him work on mazes. Always good with his sense of direction, he followed his instincts into the garden until he stood in the very center, looking at a huge, ancient tree.

At first, this didn't seem too odd as he was inside a large garden, but then Peter didn't recall any other large trees inside the garden. Something about the tree felt familiar, but he couldn't quite place it in the back of his mind. Moving away from the garden itself into the grassy opening surrounding the ancient tree, he felt as if an energy was reaching out for him. The closer he came to the tree, the warmer he felt, and the air grew more charged with static electricity.

The hairs on his arms and hands stood straight up. His hair on his head felt as though it would all stand and looking down at his feet, there was a definite glow building around his body. Although the electricity surrounded him, he still didn't sense as though he was in any danger. With each step toward the tree, he felt a sense of pride reaching out to surround him.

When he was within a few feet of the tree, he looked at the gnarled roots, digging deep within the earth. At first glance, Peter could tell the roots were thick and strong, but then he caught sight of something that made him do a double take. Some of the roots had faces on them. Peter peered closer and indeed saw eyes staring back at him. He almost jumped back until he caught sight of something that made his knees buckle.

Peter stood frozen as from behind the tree, an image strode forward to meet him. This was too much for Peter, and he collapsed to the ground. While on the ground with his head swimming, he looked up to see the welcoming branches of the tree covered in what he noticed for the first time as golden leaves. He still felt dizzy and couldn't raise himself from the ground. Sleep took him as he struggled to keep his eyes open. He looked up just in time to see the figure bend down and smile at him.

The figure reached out and touched his cheek with great pride and reverence. "Sleep now, my boy! You've done so well. Beyond all expectations. I'm sorry to say, this is only the beginning!"

CHAPTER SIX

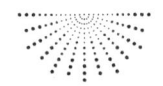

Rebecca, with excitement overflowing, couldn't contain herself and let out a high-pitched squeal. Her Aunt Grace looked at her and shook her head. Now that the decision was made to find Peter and Renie, came the difficult task of convincing the council to release them. Grace led her giddy niece through the ornate hallways of the Atlantian government building. Like every other building Rebecca viewed during her stay, this was no different. Although made with many materials, the buildings seemed fluid and natural. Her eyes were always drawn to the many windows that offered a spectacular view of the undersea world surrounding them.

She found herself sorry that she would be leaving soon. This was such a beautiful place, it was a shame she needed to go this soon. Though short, her stay ignited a great love for learning. She pestered her aunt about every aspect of the Atlantian society. As her aunt whisked her through the hallways, she thought she saw some other rooms with just as beautiful furniture. It wasn't long before Grace turned to Rebecca, instructing her to wait for her while she announced their arrival.

The large, wooden door shut with a thud and echoed in the

rotunda in which she found herself. In silence with her thoughts, she thought of Peter and what he must think of her not coming for him as she promised. This thought made her furious until she realized how this was just as important. An odd thought crossed her mind as she stood before the council chambers, and she couldn't recall meeting one member at all during her lengthy stay. She knew her aunt to be cryptic when it came to this council, but Rebecca, being of royal blood, attended many of her own people's council meetings in the past.

Rebecca didn't have to wait long before her aunt reappeared with a tall man that reminded her of General Giles. Obviously a military man with a strict look to him, Grace waved for her to follow, as he kept a close eye on Rebecca. She felt his hard eyes on the back of her head. The uneasiness continued for the rest of the trip to the council chambers as the man spoke no word. Rebecca hurried behind her aunt and followed closely to avoid bumping into the soldier.

Once in the council chambers, Rebecca nearly fell over laughing. The inside of the chamber mirrored the one of her own people. Every detail down to the scroll patterns on the arms of the council chairs was identical to that of their surface brethren. Still smiling, she was forced to stop in front of the center chair in which sat a tall woman who also reminded Rebecca of another council member back home, that of her cousin Nora Beals. The woman didn't smile and almost looked disgusted at being disturbed.

The woman scowled. "Would someone please tell me why this council meeting is being interrupted by an exile and a little girl?"

Rebecca looked quickly to her aunt who waved her hand to stand down. Grace walked forward with a straight back and a regal look of her own. Rebecca saw she was a woman of power and deserved her namesake, Grace. Despite the woman's scowl looking down on Grace, her aunt walked to within a foot of the foul woman. The rest of the council was indifferent to the intrusion, but their leader wouldn't relent and glared at Grace.

Grace stood tall. "Council members, thank you for adjusting your busy schedule to hear my plight. As you know, some time ago, my Aunt Renie was found to be missing from the city."

The leader stood with her hands straight out, holding herself up, and looked ready to jump down upon Grace. "Your aunt is a criminal! I should have arrested you the moment she was found missing!"

Grace didn't take the bait. "Yes, my esteemed colleagues, a very unfortunate incident of which I'm sure my aunt deeply regrets. Which brings me to my point, and I'll be brief."

She was interrupted, "Yes, brief it shall be! Quickly before I do seize you both!"

"Yes, Chancellor, I'll be quick with my request."

The Atlantian leader sat back down, still not looking happy. The other council members looked relieved as they weren't happy with their leader's handling of this situation. Grace took a step forward and gathered herself for the next salvo. Rebecca felt her own anger rising as she watched her aunt being treated with such disrespect. Her aunt, sensing, this peered over her shoulder and winked at her niece. This made Rebecca feel a little better, but the chancellor's face was still quite angry.

Grace began, "Chancellor Newhouse and esteemed members of this council, I come to you today with a heavy heart. As the chancellor has already alluded to, I am indeed an exile of my own people, but I feel I've become a valuable member of your community. As part of your community, it's respectful to ask permission when one must leave the protective confines of this great city."

The entire council erupted in debate amongst themselves. Grace waited until the murmurs died down before beginning anew. "Council members, as much as I feel I am a part of your community, fate has intervened and brought my own niece to me. In this time of great uncertainty, I, along with her many gifts, are needed elsewhere for the benefit of all people.

The chancellor laughed. "The benefit of all people, now that's a funny notion!"

Grace continued, "Yes, we come before you to ask permission to leave your wonderful city to help the plight of all that live in this world. The time has come for the world to come together lest it perish. You know as well as I, the evil that could very well be free this very moment to wreak havoc on this peaceful world."

"Peaceful! I don't know if that's the way I would describe this world, more chaos than anything!" the chancellor spat.

Grace looked serious. "Chancellor, you know as well as I that the humans have been left to fend for themselves while we live in the shadows under the guise of not interfering. The fact remains that we're safe because they insulate us and quite frankly, it should be us insulating them!"

Once again, the council spoke to one another quickly. They went back and forth until one whispered something in the chancellor's ear. The chancellor looked alarmed. It took a moment for her to put the words together. Everyone in the room waited to see what would come next.

The chancellor straightened out and began, "It seems as though we do have some decisions to make. I've been informed that our mortal enemies, the reptilians, have been freed from their earthly tomb!"

Rebecca rushed forward. "They are free!"

Again, the chancellor smiled. "Well, child, you have a tongue after all! I still don't know what your role in all this is, but my spies tell me a lot of people are looking for you. It might be better politically to hand you over and be done with it!"

Rebecca took a cue from her aunt and stood tall. "Honored council members, the reason I'm here is simple. I am a diplomatic envoy sent to ask for your assistance in the coming conflict that sits at our very door!"

Again, the chancellor laughed. "My dear, that's noble, but the conflict is as you put it, at your door."

Rebecca continued, "True that it is my people are in danger, but one of the fantastic things about reconnecting with my aunt is that I've been lucky enough to reconnect with your people as well. Once, we were close and, as a matter of fact, people in this very room, there are those with kin in my city as well. There comes a time when we must face and vanquish a common enemy. That time is now! When our enemy is routed, let us look to one another as we did in the past as family and not strangers!"

The power of her words made the eyes of council sparkle. Smiles broke out on every face, all except the chancellor herself who didn't look all that impressed. She sat back on her seat and looked at this young lady, interrupting her meeting with disdain. The other council members talked amongst themselves, waiting for their leader to address this current issue.

She sat back. "True that there was a time our peoples were familiar with one another, but that time is one few remember. The seven cities are either destroyed or overrun by enemies, and we sit here alone, surrounded by more enemies. You would have me let you leave so you could bring more of your people to us to destroy us!"

Rebecca carefully proceeded, "Madame Chancellor, the danger on your doorstep isn't from my people or the humans, but your mortal enemy. I don't have to remind you that once they are finished with us, they will come for you. Stand for a while yourselves maybe but in the end, you will fall. Stand with me, and we will destroy them all!"

Again, the council couldn't believe the power behind her words. Even the chancellor looked unsure of herself at that moment. Rebecca was in control, but she felt the power growing in her and used all her aunt taught her to keep her emotions in check. Her aunt stood beside her and though her aunt was slightly taller in the light, the council members could tell the regal nature of this young woman.

Once again, the chancellor rose. "Stand with you. Who are you, my dear, that you should order us to your side as though we were common foot soldiers? You're addressing in me the Chancellor of Atlantian people, the closest we have to royalty left in the city!"

Rebecca stood her ground. "Madame Chancellor, you're being addressed by two members of the royal family here and now! Yes, I may be young, but I know protocol and if you will excuse me, I don't have time to mince words. Time is against us all! I don't order you but plead with you to join us to protect the world we have come to call home."

The council members stood. "Royal family?"

Grace moved in front of Rebecca. "Yes, my friends. Due to all the hostility, it was determined that this information was kept as a guarded secret so it couldn't be used to fuel any other disputes."

The chancellor spoke, "Yes, that's true. Grace could stay if her identity remained a secret. I didn't bring it to the council because in times of crisis such as this, I needed to act quickly and in the best interest of the city."

The council members looked offended and again talked amongst themselves. Once finished, they sat back down, all except a tall, older-looking gentleman. He was a stoic-looking man, one who in his early years would be quite the intimidating figure. His lined face and graying hair made him look more distinguished than intimidating. He remained standing and looked at the two ladies before him.

He started, "Ladies, first, forgive us! We knew not who you were. Indeed, protocol is important to us, especially when addressing members of the royal family. With all due respect, Madame Chancellor, you would have us treat these ladies as common criminals. As a council, we've decided we should listen and offer advice. I'm not sure we're in a strong position to help all that much, but what help we can offer, we will. Madame Chancellor, what say you?"

Her face softened for the first time since the ladies entered. "If this is indeed the will of the council, I'll abide by the decision. Bear in mind, this may very well lead us to war!"

Rebecca broke in, "Madame Chancellor, war is upon us whether we want it or not. With the reptilian people free, it's only a matter of time before they attack. While we sit here and debate, they may already be attacking my city. I welcome any help you may offer, but please allow us safe passage to help those outside this city. I would say to all of you that this is a historic day. A day of renewed kinship, allies, and strength. Let us go forth and show these evil beings we will be free, and we won't be ruled by tyrants!"

Standing strong, the chancellor looked down. "You shall have safe passage from the city but as for your request for assistance, in the defense of your city and the humans, that's a matter for another day. I'll say this, you've earned my respect this day. You're strong beyond measure and stood with grace in the face of great adversity. Rebecca and Grace, you will always have a place among our people. Safe journey and may you never want for freedom!"

Strangely, council members applauded the two ladies. Rebecca and Grace bowed low and retreated to the back of the room. Grace put her hand on Rebecca's back and looked at her with great pride. She could also see the power sparkling in Rebecca's eyes and knew they were leaving just in time. Grace escorted her to her quarters and told her to get some rest; she would come to collect her in the evening to prepare for the trip.

Rebecca closed the door to her chambers and bolted the lock. She walked over and poured some water to refresh herself, looking around the room cautiously. Something wasn't right as everything seemed more quiet than usual. Carefully, she walked over and turned on the light. As she turned, she saw a seated figure. To her surprise, it was the chancellor.

She spoke quietly, "Now, my dear, let us speak frankly!"

CHAPTER SEVEN

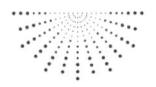

Michael sat with an arrogant smirk on his face while addressing Commander Zosa and his leadership. Commander Zosa looked as if he would jump over the table at any moment and slice the man's throat. During his long life, the commander faced off many times against this nemesis seated across from him. Much like the colonel, he found himself aligned with this jackal. Michael, in one way or another, continued to best the commander through the years, so he decided another plan was needed. When Michael approached him with his own plans to gain control of the council for himself, the commander was ready to assist in any way possible.

Still watching this smug weasel chirping at his prideful men about how they lacked the fortitude to finish the job, he only thought of ending the man. When Michael was finished tongue lashing them, he turned to the commander, waiting for him to say something. Commander Zosa rose to his full height and walked over to Michael, staring down upon him the entire way. The two glared at one another as eons of hostility drew them to near blows. Cooler heads prevailed, and the commander swung around and looked over the table at his hand-trained soldiers.

Without another thought, he began, "We stand here at this moment in history on the brink of a monumental victory. Our prison is no longer but as our esteemed colleague points out, we need to keep our guard up. I agree that we need to be smart about how we proceed. Our captivity definitely has us at a disadvantage to our enemy who is used to the surface and knows its defensible positions." Murmurs rose amongst the leadership as he continued, "Our enemies definitely outnumber us, but we're a stronger, a more skilled fighting force. This will even the score as we decide our course of action. Michael, you're obviously here for a reason. What is it you really want?"

Michael smiled and turned to his lifelong enemy. "I knew I came to the right person! I've come at the right time. Now that you're free, the time for action is at hand. Despite all your best-laid plans with the Nazis, you still stand no closer to your goal of entering the secret city."

The commander tightened his lips. "Michael, you don't know our council, and we will be in that city within days!"

"Ah, yes, the boy and the girl! That is your master plan. I assure you, those two, when brought together, will be your destruction. You, sir, have faced off against the boy, and he still knows not what he can do. Trust me, Commander, those two are a force unlike any this universe has ever known!"

"Michael, they are children! Yes, the boy and I sparred, but he's still unaware of his strength. They won't have a chance to combine forces. Right now, the girl, Holly, and the general are prisoners. When I have the boy, I'll keep them apart!"

"Keep them apart!" Michael spat. "Nothing in this universe can keep them apart! No, Commander, you need to find a way to bring them onboard with you or perish."

The commander paused. "Yes, Michael, this is definitely in my thoughts. Imagine having such powerful entities by our sides."

Michael stood. "Commander, I know your lust for the destruction of all people not your own but take a moment to look at what your hatred has done to your people. They were prisoners for eons! Your people are scattered among the cosmos. It may be time for another approach. I know your pride may not let you see this but right now, you're a conquered species!"

Commander Zosa stood frozen as for the first time, he realized Michael was correct. In his hatred and fight to get out of his prison, he never thought of his people's plight. One wrong move and what was left of his people would be destroyed. Not wanting to show weakness was paramount, but Michael was correct in his assessment of the reptilian's need for assistance. For the first time in his life, there crept in a little uncertainty about moving forward.

He looked at the faces of his leadership to see them staring back at him with stern faces, awaiting his commands. Now that freedom was theirs, he wouldn't have them snuffed out because of his own wants. He thought carefully about his next communication. After a few moments, he stood proud and addressed the table.

High Commander Zosa stood tall and proud. "As the leader of our people, I am caused many times to make decisions with far-reaching implications. This decision will determine the course of our history to come. I for one would see our enemies bow before us in utter destruction!"

This brought a surprising round of applause from his usual stoic group of leaders. He noticed the group was thinking much the same and would see their will, along with his own, done. The thought of being imprisoned won out, and he would see them all destroyed. There was little doubt he would be smart about his plans going forward, but his people would rule this world. Once this world was brought into the fold, he would turn his vision toward the universe.

Michael held his hands up and waited. "I can appreciate your angst and loathing of those who imprisoned you, but do you really intend to fight everyone again? Might I remind you, it didn't go so well for you the last time and look at your numbers. Last time you waged war, your numbers were so much greater and your overall power tremendous. Commander, you're a shell of your former glory!"

"Again, I ask you. Michael, why are you here?"

Michael looked at the leaders before him. "I've come before you to give you what it is you desire. I would see your enemies driven before you and dispatched. I alone can deliver that to you!"

Commander Zosa cackled. "How do you propose to get us into the city? By now, they are alerted to your betrayal."

Michael smiled. "I've been at work from the inside for a long time, and I assure you the city and council are in complete upheaval. I wouldn't be surprised if my people are completely in charge by now. No, Commander, you will be in the city before the week is out, and your enemies will bend to your will."

The commander faced the scrawny man. "When that doesn't happen, what makes you sure I won't dispatch you as well?"

Michael offered a sly smile. "Commander, first, you cannot destroy me. You, my friend, will need my help with Rebecca. I know her very well. When this is all over, all that I ask is you allow me to rule over the city and Rebecca as a gift."

Commander Zosa eyed the man suspiciously. "What do you want the girl for?"

Michael's eyes lust betrayed him. "She will be mine! Once, she was my protégé, and I will have her!"

The commander relented, "Fine, you may have the city and the girl. Now, tell us what you propose. I'm weary of this conversation and want to dispatch my enemies forthwith."

Michael continued, "It is quite simple. I'm going to walk you in the very gate they destroyed on you, and you will take the city in a day."

"Michael, how do you think we're going to get an army in that gate?"

Michael retorted, "I already cleared it under the ruse of an escape route if needed. Do you forget I control the finances of the city? Rest assured, you will be in the city with little resistance. By the time they realize what's happening, it will be too late!"

Thinking about this proposal, he sat and pondered if this was a trap. He knew the jackal across from him would sell out his own mother but selling out his own people was altogether different. Conversations took place around him as the room erupted into a wave of different ideas about what to do next. The commander leaned forward, holding up his head in thought. If he followed the council member, and he led them into a trap, they were finished.

He couldn't help but think that Michael wouldn't go through all this trouble and put himself in harm's way if he weren't telling the truth.

The next decision made would plot the course of the next chapter in his people's history. One wrong move, and they would be imprisoned or worse. History would judge him as a leader, not a pawn. His course decided, he rose to address his peers. Waiting for quiet, he looked around the room. Immediately, silence took over the room. The leadership looked to their commander and awaited his orders.

Commander Zosa began, "We have waited a long time to decide our own future. That future will be written by the deeds of those in this room. If we're to perish, it will be as free people and by taking as many of our enemy with us as possible!"

Michael's face brightened. "Commander, you shall not perish!"

"Michael will get us into the city, and we will take it from there. Make ready for the invasion!"

All the soldiers rose to their feet and applauded loudly. He dismissed them all and waved Michael to stay. When the soldiers were gone, he sat across from his mortal enemy. Looking at the wraith, he couldn't understand how one appearing so meek could be so powerful. Looking into Michael's eyes though, he witnessed a confidence and power unmatched by anyone else.

For a few minutes, both opponents looked at one another, waiting for the other to make a move. While the other soldiers were in the room, the commander remained diplomatic but strong. Now, he would find out the true nature of this smug being. Reaching out under the desk, he slid open a few inches to see the contents of the drawer before him. When satisfied what he was looking for was within his reach, he carefully closed the drawer. Once again, he looked to this would-be ally and paused.

He began, "Michael, if you deliver what you say, you will indeed have everything you want. I'll tell you this though. If this is a trap, I promise you I'll take you with me before I perish. You have my word on that!"

Michael calmly replied, "I've put this plan into place over a long, calculated period and would see it through without you, but it is nice to have allies. No, my dear Commander, you will be happy to see the ease with which you will take the city. The general spends so much time defending the gates, he spends little energy on the actual defense of the city itself. He claims to be an important part of the council but in truth, he's just a figurehead. You've assured that with your constant attacks on the gates."

Commander Zosa straightened in his seat. "Yes, our attacks on the gates cause great damage to only the outside though. We need to get inside the city. That is the only reason I'm considering your plan. You must tell me, Michael. What's really your endgame? This is your people you're betraying!"

"Commander, my reasons are mine alone, but I will say I'm looking forward to their demise. The entire council looks down upon me with loathing and disrespect. To see their faces as their precious council crumbles will be reward enough for me. Yes, Commander, I do want more, but that's a discussion for another day. For now, let us get into the city and take control. Once that happens, we will make further plans. Trust me when I tell you, this is just the beginning."

With eyes raised, he viewed the man cautiously. "Michael, if you're a man of your word, once the council is in my hands, we will definitely look to other plans. As you say though, one step at a time. The gate is cleared of all the rocks and rubble? What about the defenses there?"

The lanky man answered, "Yes, all is clear. The entrance is very weakly defended because they have yet to replace all the destroyed weapons. Also, they don't yet know the field is down, so they cannot know you're coming. The element of surprise is in our favor right now. This is the opportune moment to strike!"

He pushed himself up in his seat. "All right, Michael, let's proceed quickly. As you say, we have surprise on our side. My men can be ready within the hour. It will be dark, and they will be wearing their special suits to handle the outdoor temperatures."

Michael looked relieved and rose to cross the room. "Commander, you won't regret this, and we will be in the city by morning!"

He walked across the room to meet his newfound friend and went in for a handshake to seal the alliance. As he reached forth to shake the commander's hand, he felt a metal strike his wrist and before he knew it, both wrists were bound. He tried to break the hold of the cuffs, looking with great rage at his captor.

His rage barked out, "How dare you! What are you doing! I came here to offer you what you've been looking for your entire life, you idiot!"

With a large smirk on his face, he sneered. "Michael, you cannot expect me to take you at your word, can you? Do not try to get out of those either because they render your power useless. You will deliver as you've promised and once in the city, I'll release you. You have my word that I'll give you as we agreed, but I cannot put my future and those under my care in the hands of a traitor."

CHAPTER EIGHT

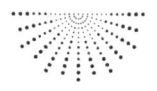

Michelle Sullivan peered out the small plane window, watching the landscape change. For many hours, every time she looked out the window, all she saw was an ocean view. The thought of all that water unnerved her a bit, but Derek Andrews sitting next to her droning on about the culture in Buenos Aries kept her mind occupied. As she focused her eyes, she saw land forming through the clouds below. At first, all she saw was dense, green growth and some rolling hills.

The small cabin of the private jet was comfortable and during any other time, she would love the luxury. Her mind could only think of her boy alone doing who knows what right now. In her hand, she held the precious bundle with the mysterious wooden rod. She held the rod carefully and wouldn't let it out of her sight. A part of her father's legacy, she couldn't help but feel curious as to the importance of the rod. Derek said little about what she carried and updated her on their progress. He laid out their plans carefully and assured Michelle she would be safe.

During their descent, Michelle noticed a desolate area with nothing around it. The airport itself was an isolated runway with one building in the middle. As the small plane taxied to a stop, Michelle saw out her window a lone jeep waiting off the runway. She carefully placed the rod into a wooden box made for fancy pool cues and stowed it in her backpack. Derek took charge of the luggage and made ready to step out of the plane. Their flight attendant, a perky blonde woman opened the door and said goodbye to them with a bright smile.

Michelle walked out onto the first step and held up her hand to block the strong, burning sun. The temperature difference hit her like a blast of heat from an open stove, and she immediately felt her brow moisten. Looking down, she saw Derek already on the tarmac, speaking with a young soldier standing alongside the lone jeep. She cautiously made her way down the steps and breathed a sigh of relief to feel the solid earth. Not that she was afraid of flying, but she always felt better once on the ground again. Michelle scurried to meet up with Derek and his mysterious new contact.

Derek turned slightly and gave her a warm smile before looking back the young soldier's way. She moved over to Derek's right and waited while the men conversed. Her eyes scanned the area for signs of life. Off to the left, she noticed a hillside about a mile or so away and to the right, only dirt with sparse grass. Other than the airstrip, she saw no other manmade structures as far as the eye could see. Being so out in the open made her uncomfortable, and she moved closer to Derek without stopping her scan of the overall area.

Derek motioned for her to get into the jeep, and she wasted little time jumping in the backseat. He quickly followed and after tossing their possessions in the front, Derek reached over and put his hand on her shoulder reassuringly. Michelle smiled back at him, breathing more regularly. As intimidating a man as Derek could be, he could disarm a situation with a wink or a nod. Michelle always felt comfortable and safe when around him. Though there was nothing romantic between them, their connection was more than friendship. Spending so much time together with the boys, they developed a close-knit relationship and leaned on each other many times.

The jeep sped into the unknown and yet, Michelle saw nothing but a road leading nowhere. Her backpack on her lap, she felt for the box holding the rod, making sure it was safe. She found it easily and went back to her vigil of watching the roadway. Derek gave her a quick update, telling her they were going to a contact's home outside Buenos Aires. He alerted her to the fact they were going into the lion's den. According to Derek's information, where they were going was a small, hidden Nazi state. After World War II, the Nazis escaped to this area and set up shop in the hopes to bring back the Reich. The allies kept tabs on them and rounded up many of the top brass to keep them from causing trouble.

The allies also rounded up all the scientists and used them to their own advantage, helping to create the space program. What the allies didn't count on was the sheer number of Nazi sympathizers in South America. The gigantic network remaining in place to immigrate fleeing war criminals to the new Nazi state still baffled investigators to this day. Derek went on to explain some of the missions he was sanctioned to carry out to bring back some of these aging war criminals. He further described how the locals defended the Nazis as heroes, and it was extremely difficult to get them to talk.

Michelle sat in exasperation. During her lifetime, she was told the Nazis were vanquished and ruined from existence. Something in the back of her mind couldn't believe it though, as she watched over the years as her father spoke about ancient cultures. The ancient Germanic tribes were prideful and strong, giving rise to the notion of bringing back that nationalism, along with its strength. The Nazis took things to a whole new level, bringing the world to the brink of destruction, only to be bested by the allies. Here, Michelle was told the Nazis were still going strong, causing all kinds of mischief.

Michelle could no longer contain herself. "Derek, you mean to tell me our government knows about this network and allows it to still exist?"

Derek winced. "It isn't that simple. After World War II, a better part of the world was destroyed. As far as people were concerned, the evil was vanquished, and people wanted to focus on recovery and rebuilding."

"This is the Nazis we're talking about, Derek!"

Again, he winced. "Yes, Michelle, but you also have to realize the Soviet threat became the more immediate concern with the advent of the Cold War. We almost traded one form of evil for another. The nuclear age took hold, and both sides were ready to push the button."

She shook her head. "I understand, but this is the Nazis!"

"That's right, the Nazis, and they're on the verge of launching their largest campaign ever. This war will make the World Wars look like playtime if they have their way."

Michelle sat stunned. Not only was Derek telling her about the existence of a viable Nazi state, he was going into detail about their credible threat. How in the world did the government keep this under wraps with today's instant internet news? Looking into Derek's eyes, she saw the truth, and she thought of the boys on their own. Her boy on his own, caught in the middle of this whole situation, and she was thousands of miles away. All the information swirled around her mind, overwhelming her as she lay her head back on the seat.

Derek nodded. "I know, I know! As a military member, they tell you a little here and there but over the years, operation after operation, you see the big picture. I'll tell you this. Peter is in Antarctica. Things are turning in our favor. Michelle, your son is an amazing young man who is realizing his place in all this. The only thing that scares me is the amount of destruction these evil men will cause before Peter takes his rightful place."

Michelle gave him an odd look. "Rightful place? What are you talking about?"

He grinned. "You still don't know? He's the key to this entire situation! Your father was grooming him for greatness! You raised him to be a gracious, humble young man, but your father raised him to be a leader of men."

She turned, facing him. "My boy! Derek, he isn't ready! Who will he lead?"

"He will lead whatever is left," he said solemnly.

"Whatever is left?"

Derek nodded. "Michelle, a war is coming! We have thwarted it time and time again, but the Nazis have a powerful ally. We have an ally of our own, but things will come to a head soon, and the meeting will be catastrophic!"

Michelle couldn't believe her ears. Her life to this point was a normal, everyday sort of life lived in peace. Here, her life was being turned upside down, and so many unsuspecting people were about to be affected. Always the one to think of others, she couldn't help but feel distraught over the loss of human life about to take place. Still, she couldn't grasp fully how her own son fit into this complete puzzle. Peter grew up before her eyes as a compassionate and gracious young man. She couldn't be prouder of the man he was, and he was about to become something more. Not sure how she felt about all the responsibility to be heaped on her son, she sat up straight in her seat.

She looked seriously at Derek. "Are we prepared for this?"

He looked her in the eye and winked. "We're prepared but like anything else, there are many things that can happen. I tell you now! Evil won't stand!"

"Why is it I always feel so safe with you?"

"Could it be the fact I feel safe under your care?"

This stunned Michelle. "Safe with me?"

Derek laughed. "Yes, Michelle. Safe. You, like your boy, are much more than you seem! I would follow you anywhere!"

She knew not what to say at that moment and stared at her friend in disbelief. Here was one of the baddest men on the planet, telling her he would follow her. She thought about all her conversations with her father over the years about her own power. Michelle knew she held this gift for a reason but never knew when it was to be used. Now here, things came into focus. She and Peter were meant to be a part of events yet to come. She again held the box in her hand tighter and turned back to Derek.

Derek looked down and nodded. He told her they would meet a contact of his outside the main city. He instructed her to let him do the talking and not to get too upset if they looked at her suspiciously. She assured him she wouldn't interfere with his negotiations. They sat silently for the few remaining miles, and she leaned over to look out the window, seeing more houses and cars. The sight of life made her feel more comfortable. The houses looked simple with small gardens and well-tended yards. The picturesque scene lightened her heart as they continued down the road.

At last, the jeep stopped in front of a small home with several fields of various growing crops surrounding it. As Michelle stepped out of the jeep, she dealt with the powerful sun hitting her. It took a moment before she could focus and by that time, Derek was already knocking on the door of the house. There were very few windows in the home and none on the door. She could hear someone calling something from behind the door. As Derek responded, the door opened a crack. When Derek spoke again, the door opened more, and he waved them to follow him.

The inside of the house was pleasant but dim, with a comfortable living room including several chairs and a nice couch. Derek sat on the couch and motioned to Michelle to do so as well. She joined Derek and looked at her host. The man before them was in his eighties but held a lot of life and smiled at Derek. He sat before them on one of the chairs as Derek informed him as to the nature of their visit. The mood in the room changed as if the air became sucked out of the room.

Without another word, the man rose and went to his door, flinging it open and yelling at Derek to leave. At first, Derek maintained his position, but the man became more animated, yelling even louder. Not wanting to announce their arrival, he moved toward the door. Derek grabbed Michelle's hand, leading her toward the door. As they were about to leave the house, Michelle let go of Derek's hand and stopped in front of the red-faced man, waiting for them to leave. The man looked as if he would forcefully escort her out the door, but she looked into his eyes.

Michelle held her stare for a few moments, not saying a word. The man stopped and invited them back into the house. Derek looked at Michelle with a confused expression on his face. Michelle winked and grabbed his hand, leading him back into the house. The military man did as he was told, following her back to their same seats. Once seated, the man smiled again and asked Derek what he wanted to know. Derek informed him they needed access to an old underground German bunker.

The old man looked as if he would go off the rails again. "Derek, you cannot go there! That's a place of great evil! No one goes there! Not even the Nazis!"

Derek remained calm. "Just point us in the direction, my friend, and I'll take care of the rest."

With a twisted face, he looked to Michelle, who nodded to the man. "Derek, I can show you what's left. They destroyed the entrance so no one could ever get in there again."

The man sprang up and ran to the lone window in the living room, peering outside. He turned toward them and announced they would leave at dusk. Without another word, he disappeared into the kitchen, only to return a few minutes later with tea and biscuits. They all sat and had a drink while the man quizzed Derek about his dealings over the last few years. Derek discussed his work with the new computer systems and kept things generic. The man seemed in good spirits, but Derek kept looking to Michelle, who shrugged her shoulders while munching on a biscuit.

CHAPTER NINE

Jake jumped forward, ripping at the growing vines and branches before him. His hands grabbing and tearing, he made a small hole in the garden wall, only to have it grow in as fast as he could tear. Fear gripped him as he tore at the branches and only stopped after he saw the branches getting so thick, he couldn't even move them. Pain tore through his hands at that moment, and he looked down to see his ravaged hands. Deep cuts and blood covered his hands. He turned to see Holly running toward him. She immediately grabbed his hands.

Before he could pull away, a wave of warmth entered his injured hands. He wanted to back away, but he couldn't stop looking into Holly's eyes, which at this moment, danced with electricity. Jake's pain faded as the warmth continued up his arms, and he calmed himself. Holly released his hands, and he looked down to see they still showed dried blood, but the gashes were no longer. His eyes shot up to Holly with a look of gratitude.

This look didn't last as he spun to gaze at the garden imprisoning his friend. Quickly, he ran to his pack on the ground, grabbing a can of lighter fluid and a lighter. As he approached the garden with the incendiary material, the guards met him, standing in his way. Though a large young man, sturdy in his own right, these guards were seasoned and more than his match. Holly ran to intercede, moving between the boy and the guards. She quickly told Jake they were under orders not to let anything happen to the garden. She explained it was a sacred place and was treated and guarded as such.

Jake, frantic about the loss of his friend, stood in disbelief. "I promised to be his guide and always watch out for him!"

Holly smiled and embraced the young man. "Jake, trust me! He's quite all right and well taken care of. I might not be able to get in there, but I can read Peter. He's quite safe! He found something he didn't expect, but it's a good thing! No, my friend, he's safer than we are now. We need to move inside. Too much time has already been spent outside, and we need to see the council."

Jake stood tall. "I should wait for him to return!"

Again, she smiled. "Jake, he'll be in there for quite some time. It's his destiny to be here, and he's learning about that destiny. We can help him more by paving the way for him to return. Jake, when he does come out, everything will change in this city, and there are those who don't want to see change. It'll be up to us to prepare his arrival."

The way Holly spoke, things here in her city were more unsettled than she let on, but she spoke the truth. He relaxed his muscles and moved toward the now-open door as more guards streamed out to meet them. They surrounded Jake, Alex, and Holly, leading them into the door and closing it swiftly behind them. Jake looked back at the garden before the door completely shut, still feeling apprehensive about leaving Peter. The door closed with an ominous clang, and the guards urged them forward.

Jake took notes of every corridor, door, and person he passed on the way to the council chamber. His father would be proud of the amount of detailed information he compiled by the time they were announced before the council chambers. Much like the door to enter the complex, the council door was two huge, wooden structures. Carvings covered the wood, and the doors were a nice, warm, red color. Though the door was ancient, the high-gloss covering the door gave it a more modern look. Jake couldn't help but laugh at the large carving making up the middle of both doors.

Standing in front of both doors, Jake saw a large starburst symbol as the centerpiece of the doors. Jake smiled and thought of Peter. This symbol meant more than Peter could figure out to this point, but he knew his friend would crack the code. The doors opened slowly to reveal a warm, bright glow of light coming to greet them as they walked into the chamber. Jake was in awe of the size of the chamber. The ceiling was easily one-hundred-feet high and vaulted. Worn but detailed paintings covered the ceiling. Subject matter was difficult to see from his vantage point, but he observed battles and triumphant scenes.

Bringing his eyes back down to floor level, he looked between each huge column he passed and saw more paintings covering the walls, as well as multiple sculptures. Again, the paintings depicted epic battles and historical scenes. Jake stopped in midstride as he saw a painting that made him gasp. Without asking permission, he strode over and stood within a foot of the large painting. He couldn't believe the image before him. It was Peter or his twin. The painting showed Peter coming from what looked to be a doorway with stars all around it. Another painting next to it showed Peter defeating a group of what Jake could only describe as reptilian people.

Jake moved down the wall, looking at each subsequent painting, chronicling the exploits of the image of Peter. Jake couldn't digest as each image showed the importance of Peter grow. Holly joined him and instructed him to follow. She promised she would explain everything but speaking to the council was of the utmost importance. She also stated they needed to find out more about the garden. Holly rushed him forward to stand in front of an extremely large, lavish, round table of what looked to be made of one solid piece of stone. It was highly polished and shone multiple colors of the stone with small facets of light bouncing everywhere because of the brightness of the above lights.

Holly, Alex, and Jake stood before three individuals that looked extremely serious. A large man with the sternest face stood and addressed his guests. The door opened, and the general joined them. The man asked if Holly and the general would like to return to their own council seats. Holly looked at the general, and they refused, and Holly asked to approach. The man waved her forward.

Holly waved her hand while turning slightly sideways to introduce her guests. "Andrew and honored council members, I have the honor of bringing before you Mr. Jake Andrews and Mr. Alex Collins. They have traveled through unknown miles and dangers to be here in our presence. I ask the council to render a decision on their freedom as quickly as possible. My friends, I don't have to tell you how important these people are to our cause. I've brought them before you, as is our law. Please judge them justly."

The large man stewed for a moment. "Holly, you're right that I don't have to be reminded of their importance, but I do recall there was supposed to be another young man with you. I'm looking, but I only see the two. Where is Peter?"

"My Lord, the garden has claimed him!"

Andrew stood gripping his chair. "The garden? Holly, the garden hasn't opened itself to anyone in memory and only then, it will only open itself to a member of the royal family. Are you sure?"

She walked over to her friend. "Andrew, the garden opened, and he entered. From what I can read of his experience, he is quite safe and is being taught many important things by an unlikely teacher. The boy is in good hands and safe. It is us that I'm worried about. Did you capture Michael?"

Andrew's face grew red. "That traitorous bastard evaded us. We tracked him right to the enemy's doorstep. I have no doubt he is in concert with our enemies as we speak."

Holly approached closer and leaned in. "Andrew, he must not be allowed to contact them!"

"Holly, as much as I agree with you, there's little that can be done right now unless we try to invade our enemies' encampments. No, we must focus on more important matters. If the garden let Peter in, we have no telling how long he will be in there and whether or not it will even release him."

Holly brooded, looking at her colleague with questioning eyes. He was right, of course, and they did in fact need to focus on their current situation. Now that the boys were safely in the city, they should plan their next step in the defense of the city. A city that no doubt would be under attack soon, as all intelligence concluded that the reptilians would be clear of their force field any day now. Holly knew this meant all-out war and many deaths. She turned to look at Jake who stood next to the general and looked every bit the soldier as the general himself. This image made her step back and think of this scene as one she recognized, but she couldn't place where.

Alex, on the other hand, just kept wandering around the room with his eyes drinking in the entire scene. Holly forgot here was a man who gave his life in search of this glorious city, and here he was, standing in the very council chambers of said city. Holly smiled at the look of awe on his face as it reminded her of her first time on the surface, taking in a magnificent sunrise. The thought of seeing something amazing for the first time and the feeling of wonder at that very moment gave her a warm feeling.

The feeling was gone in a second as Andrew waited for her next statement. Without another thought, she turned to the remainder of the council and searched for her words carefully. Those in this room were about to change the course of history, and she needed all her faculties to make the correct decisions. Standing to her full height, she matched the leader of her people in stature and grace. She strode forward back to her original position with Jake, Alex, and General Giles before speaking.

Holly's face hardened. "Our mission of bringing the boys to our fair city is complete and yet, there's so much left to accomplish. I ask the council to allow Peter and his friends to move free about the city as honored guests. What say you?"

The three remaining members of the council stood as Andrew proclaimed his judgement. "Holly, as is our law, all outsiders must be brought before the council to be judged. You honor us with your respect of the law. The judgement was made, however, when we made the decision to go after the boys in the first place. As we've discussed before, the time has come to look beyond our borders to the larger world."

Holly stood silent as Andrew took a moment to decide how to proceed. He was a very measured man and wasted little time mincing words. She couldn't help but smile inside as she saw her friend and leader standing tall, pronouncing judgement. Holly grew up with Andrew and knew from an early age, he was destined for greatness. Again, she looked up to see his steely eyes ready to speak further.

Andrew continued, "Jake Andrews and Alex Collins, you will be granted leave about the city. Considering what we're about to face, I must insist, however, that you be always accompanied by guards. Not out of trust but out of safety for you. I welcome you, my friends, to the capital city of Oberon. May its borders protect you and guide you to what you seek. Now, is there anything I may do to accommodate you further?"

Alex said nothing during Holly and Andrew's exchange. He strode forward, standing tall. The older man straightened his clothes and faced the council members with reverent pride. He seemed a bit choked up as to what to say to these people he just found for the first time who existed right under the humans' noses.

Without further hesitation, he asked, "My Lords and Ladies, thank you for the kind welcome, but you and I know what's going on out there. We need to band together or else perish. The world outside as you may have known it doesn't exist anymore. The reptilian people are at our doorstep, and we must reign true, or evil will inhabit this world along with all others. We're the dam holding back the storm, and we need help. Please allow me access to your library so I might learn all I can to help all people!"

Andrew smiled. "An honorable request! Done!"

Andrew looked at Jake and couldn't help but know he recognized his likeness but couldn't place it now. Jake moved in front of Alex and stood at attention as his father taught him. His flexed muscles and strong stance made the general smile. Andrew took the boy in and immediately knew what to do with him. He walked down to the boy and stood in front of him motioning the general to come forward. Both the general and council member stood in front of Jake.

Andrew began, "Jake, welcome and well met! As for your request, I think I may have an inkling of what you may ask, so let me venture a guess. You would like to train with the vaunted general here, am I right?"

Jake nearly laughed. "Sir, that would be absolutely amazing and yes, I would accept that any other day, but my friend is a prisoner inside the garden. I cannot accept anything until he is released."

The Zarillion leader smiled. "A true friend and soldier indeed! General, you need to take care of this one. Something tells me he will become one of the finest soldiers this world has ever seen. Yes, Jake, I share your concern. I will say this, if Holly can read Peter and see he is in no danger, then rest assured he is safe. Might I suggest that while Alex is researching, he could start with the garden itself and in the meantime, I would be honored if you trained with General Giles."

Jake moved forward and reached his hand up and saluted the men before him. "It would be my honor, sir!"

General Giles returned the salute. "Jake, we will worry about training tomorrow. I'll take you both and find suitable quarters first. Then we can sit and eat a nice meal together. I don't know about you, but I cannot remember the last real meal I had to eat. Follow me, gentlemen, and don't worry. I'm sure Holly will be able to contact Peter and check on him."

The general turned and bowed to the council members and winked at Holly as he passed by her.

Andrew turned to Holly. "Michael is going to be a big problem! We need to capture him. If the enemy is allowed the use of his gifts, we're in more trouble than we realize."

Holly nodded but said nothing.

CHAPTER TEN

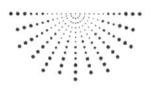

Rebecca sat nervously with her hands cupped together, waiting for the chancellor to speak. The room was empty, and the silence threatened to suck up what life remained in the huge room. For the first time, Rebecca noticed the lines on the face of chancellor who from a distance, looked flawless. The glow surrounding her at the head of table gone, revealed a more human and aged person sitting across from her. Again, she looked into the timeless eyes of her host and waited for a response.

The chancellor then surprised her as facial features softened, and she even offered a tight smile. Without a word, she rose to her feet, taking Rebecca's hand in the same motion. Rebecca let herself be led through the hall and into a room off the back of the large hall. At first, she thought it another office, but a closer look revealed a front as the chancellor strode to the far side. Once standing before a large portrait of some long-lost hero, the chancellor reached up and pushed something behind the painting. The large painting swung outward to show a hidden tunnel.

Rebecca stood frozen, not knowing what to do as this was the woman who moments ago, seemed ready to throw her into the dungeon. The chancellor, sensing her plight, nodded before entering the tunnel, first leaving Rebecca standing alone in the strange office. Something tugged at her mind, pushing her forward, and her legs followed her mind. She struggled to see the chancellor through the dimly lit tunnel. Keeping as close to the chancellor as possible, she ran into an outcropping or two before their journey ended. The tunnel itself showed moisture everywhere, and Rebecca noticed a type of moss growing in the rocks that gave off a glowing light.

This glowing light guided their way, and the chancellor moved at a fast pace, looking back often to see if they were being followed. The air in the tunnel, despite their location, was surprisingly fresh. Rebecca marveled at this as she knew them to be deep below the surface. Rebecca breathed freely and deeply but sensed something unfamiliar in the air but said nothing. The chancellor continued their march to nowhere, and Rebecca felt a change in the atmosphere of the tunnel as the temperature sharply changed. Perspiration beaded on Rebecca's forehead and with each step, the temperature rose.

Unsure of the length of time in the tunnel, Rebecca came to a halt, nearly running into the chancellor as she stopped fast. The chancellor turned and placed a finger to her lips, telling Rebecca not to make a sound. The sight before them shocked Rebecca, who nearly ran back up the tunnel. The chancellor grabbed her arm and clapped on it like a piece of steel and indicated her to wait. Rebecca felt the sweat building on her lips and forehead as the temperature was quite high. The light was a little brighter in the cavern before them being lit by a more typical bulb lighting system.

Rebecca looked at the immense cavern rising to swallow them whole. The cavern was a natural formation, but the modifications made her freeze in fear. She turned to the chancellor and was about to speak. Again, the chancellor looked at her and pointed back toward the cavern. For the first time, Rebecca saw movement down below as their vantage point was some twenty feet above the cavern floor. At first, her fright almost won out, but the clapped hand of the chancellor kept her in place.

Coming into view were a few reptilian soldiers carrying boxes of what appeared to be weapons of some kind. The chancellor pulled her closer and pointed in another direction. In the ebbing light, Rebecca discerned large caches of weapons stacked many feet high, littering the floor everywhere. Rebecca couldn't help but scan the entire area, and the sheer number of stored weapons made her gulp. Watching from their perch, they were careful not to come totally out of the shadows of the outcropping and stayed for a few more minutes, watching the progress of the soldiers.

The chancellor pulled her back into the tunnels and again said nothing but ran her back through the maze until coming to another, smaller cavern. Here, she stopped and swung Rebecca around to look her directly in the eye. The stone-faced woman showed great concern and seemed unsure what to say next. She placed both hands upon Rebecca's shoulders, holding her at arm's length.

The chancellor sucked in a deep breath. "As you can see, my dear, we're always on the edge of danger! Those repulsive beings aren't just a menace, they're on our doorstep."

Rebecca croaked, "How is it they're unaware of you after all this time?"

"Well, originally, my people needed to lure the reptilians down into the earth to trap them, and we needed an exit strategy. This was our exit strategy. Pretty clever really as we used the earth's own magnetic fields to create an energy field that would enclose the reptilian people. Our scientists said it would last as long as the earth's own fields, but they were incorrect. The field weakened and, in many places, it's down already. It won't be long before the entire reptilian people will come forth for vengeance."

The chancellor took another breath. "The outcropping I showed you is cloaked and looks like the side of the cavern but still, I wouldn't take a chance of being seen. We can cloak the entrance easily, but our scientists have been unable to duplicate the energy field needed to keep the reptilians captives. They will come for us! Some may already be on their way. True, they don't like water and won't travel in or on water, but if it was ever discovered they could attack us underground, we would be in a lot of trouble."

Rebecca stood shocked. "You knew this was going on and yet, you chose to keep all this to yourselves?"

The chancellor winced. "Yes, my dear. Our cities haven't communicated in a long time. Some of us weren't sure if your city was still a viable location. We lost contact with your city and the remaining cities long ago. When we discovered the reptilians were making use of that cavern, it was much too late to do anything about it. For thousands of years, that cavern remained empty, and we assumed they would never find it or use it. Now, of course they're on our doorstep."

Rebecca rubbed her forehead. "Chancellor, we must alert the others! Do your own people know about this approaching danger?"

"Rebecca, the council is aware of the cavern, and our people are aware of the reptilian people's captivity ending. What we cannot do is create a panic. Our military is preparing to fortify that area as we speak, and there's one more entry into those tunnels, which is guarded every moment of every day. Until now, I needed to see for myself without a military escort, but I'll alert the military of that secret entrance as well."

The chancellor frowned. "I so wish you visited us during peacetime! This is a place of amazing beauty and peace. Should we win the day, please promise you will come back and spend some time with us?"

Rebecca bowed low. "It would be my honor, My Lady, to join you once my task is complete."

The chancellor smiled and patted her on the shoulder, leading her back into the tunnel. Snaking their way backward, Rebecca was relieved to feel the temperature level out and become more comfortable. When they returned to the office and placed the painting back so no one could see anything was disturbed, they took a seat at the chancellor's desk. Both ladies showed signs of their trip as each other's dress were soiled at the bottom and grime mixed with sweat covered their faces.

Both women looked at one another and broke out laughing. The joy was short lived as a knock on the door paused their moment. The chancellor walked briskly to the door, standing slightly to the side as to not show the intruder her full self. She opened the door, slightly peering out and whispering to the intruder. The door closed as soon as it opened. She turned to Rebecca and indicated she follow. Rebecca, without a word, followed her into the council chambers, staying close.

A large guard dressed in an impressive uniform pulled up to the right-hand side of the chancellor, and Rebecca stayed behind. Again, the chancellor nearly ran through the chambers and into another tunnel, not saying a word. Struggling to keep up, Rebecca lagged. As she felt her legs give way, they entered another large room. This room looked exactly like the headquarters of her own city. Rebecca saw military and civilian people rushing around, giving orders. The amount of activity told Rebecca something was about to happen.

A red-faced chancellor turned to Rebecca. "They have attacked your city! News is scattered, but I believe the reptilian people have breached the city!"

Rebecca held her stomach, feeling as though someone punched her directly in her gut. When she could stand, she saw the chancellor's face red with anger. She turned and barked orders at her people, and the entire room exploded with frantic activity. Rebecca watched as the chancellor moved about the room, telling her people to launch the fleet of submarines immediately. Rebecca watched the screens as the submarines were underway within minutes. She couldn't help but think about her peaceful people struggling for their lives against a great evil.

Grace appeared from out of nowhere and ran up to Rebecca with a look of sadness. She grabbed Rebecca. "We have to go! The city has been attacked! We must go and help."

Rebecca looked over to Chancellor Newhouse for guidance. The tall woman came to their side. "Go now! I'll send you in my personal submarine. When things are more settled, send word, and we will be there to help your city. My forces are yours!"

Rebecca ran forward and hugged the startled woman. Grace bowed low and thanked the chancellor. Rebecca and Grace followed two guards that were assigned to the ladies. They walked at a trot and found the trip to the submarine uneventful. The guards helped them onto the walkway to the submarine. They shuffled the ladies into their quarters and asked them to stay put while the sub got underway.

Grace tossed her backpack onto her bunk and laughed at Rebecca. Rebecca turned and glared back. "What?"

"What the hell happened to you? I leave you with Chancellor Newhouse for five minutes, and you look as though you went to battle."

"Aunt Grace, you cannot even imagine what the chancellor showed me. I'll tell you on the way but for the moment, let's discuss what our plan will be once we arrive home. Holly doesn't even know you're alive!"

Grace stopped for a moment and swung around to face her niece. "I never even gave a thought to what to say to my sister and now, what would I say as her city is under siege?"

The two women sat on their bunks and looked at the floor, wondering what to say or do next. As events unfolded around them, they found themselves deeper and deeper amid trouble. Humming of engines told them they were underway, and they looked into each other's eyes to see energy dancing. Rebecca felt the anger raging inside her but remembered her aunt's teachings and calmed herself, focusing her energy on Peter.

For some reason, she couldn't see Peter, but she could make out what looked to be a grove of ancient trees. Standing in the middle of a grove surrounded by grass, a massive tree reached into the sky to unseen heights. The tree seemed recognizable, but she couldn't place where. Then from behind the tree stepped a man. Rebecca immediately recognized the man but almost choked as he shouldn't be in her mind any longer.

She felt herself step forward. "This shouldn't be! You're dead! Where is Peter?"

A wide smile came across the man's face. "Worry not, my child. Peter is well. Quite well actually. Just as your aunt needs to train you before her time is done, so do I have a task to perform before moving on."

Rebecca, again, felt her emotions telling her something wasn't right. Her anger built once more. She raised her head to face the man. As she was about to raise her hands toward the man, she felt every muscle in her body stiffen.

Once again, the man smiled. "Your Aunt Grace is a good teacher, but you still are very raw. When you learn to truly control your power, our enemies will be in a world of hurt. That's what you must focus on at this moment, your training. When you come to the city, make your way to the Royal Garden as Peter and I will be waiting."

She peered up. "The Royal Garden? To enter is to sign your death warrant! Besides, no one has entered in a thousand years. Also, only a member of the Royal family may enter."

A sly grin crossed his face. "Exactly, my dear! Worry not. It is yours and Peter's time. The garden will open for you. I'll explain when you arrive, but don't tell anyone. Holly knows Peter is here but as you know, she and the general are mounting defense of the city. Hurry, there may not be much left when you arrive."

Again, her anger nearly took control at the thought of her precious city under attack. "If the city is under attack, how am I expected to reach you? Won't our enemies burn the garden?"

He laughed. "Those fools have no power over this garden! Just as they have no power over you or Peter. No, child, we will teach them the true nature of power. They may win a battle, but in the war to come, they have no idea what's in store for them and their people."

CHAPTER ELEVEN

Sweat rolled down their backs as swarms of bugs flew around their heads. In the sweltering heat and dense brush, it became harder and harder to see what lie in front of them. Through sweat-covered eyes, Derek Andrews, Navy Seal and a veteran of countless incursions behind enemy lines, kept his head pointed in the direction of the Nazi bunker. Michelle spoke not a word and kept close to Derek, occasionally swatting and failing as the nasty bugs biting her on the neck. She marveled at the old man guiding them as he seemed not bothered by the heat or the bugs. He guided them skillfully through the dense undergrowth, and they soon came to a break in the jungle.

Stepping into the clearing, Michelle's eyes needed a moment to adjust to the glaring sun blazing down on top of their unprotected heads. Wiping her brow, she strode forward to move to within a foot of the old man. He turned to her with a small smile and waved to Derek to follow. Again, the spry elder man sprang forward at a brisk pace, and they were forced to double time it behind the man. Derek smiled to himself and caught up quickly peering over his shoulder to make sure Michelle was still with him.

Seeing Michelle right behind him brought a bright smile to his face, and they followed the older man in silence the rest of the way up the hill that lay before them. The landscape was much different here, and the growth on the hill was less dense and lusher as if water were more prevalent in this location. They ascended quickly, and Derek stopped halfway up the large hill and motioned them to hide behind an outcropping of rock. The old man looked at him quickly, but Derek spoke not a word but uses his hand to show them they needed to scan the area.

He pointed to his eyes and back out across the open area. The man understood and scanned the area, looking for any other signs of life. Michelle, catching her breath, looked down the hill at the path they just travelled up but saw nothing. Derek, with a much more trained eye for these types of situations, investigated the path, the side of the hill, and the clearing where they once stood. Once satisfied they weren't being followed or watched, he motioned them to continue up the hill.

They set out at a fast pace, wanting to reach the bunker before noon. Now, the path before them was well defined and easy to follow. Even though travel was easier, the hill was much higher than they first thought, and it took them much longer to get to the top than anticipated. Derek led the way with the old man whispering things to him occasionally. Before long, the path gave way to a rockier openness with a nice breeze hitting their faces.

As the old man was about to take another step forward, Derek grabbed his shoulder hard, keeping him in place. The man turned in surprise to look at his friend, only to see Derek pointing to the ground a few inches from where he was about to step. To an untrained eye, it looked like another small rock sticking out of the ground, but Derek easily noticed the glint of glass. Derek got down on all fours to get a closer look and saw another rock on the other side of the path. He knew beyond a shadow of a doubt, this was an infrared motion detector.

He jumped to his feet and brought his friends to a flat, rocky area off the path. Derek sat on the rocks, joined by Michelle and the old man. The cool breeze felt wonderful, bringing goosebumps to

Michelle's neck as she waited for Derek to tell them what he found. At first, Derek remained quiet as if not sure how to proceed, but then his face brightened. The military man adjusted his hat and wiped his own brow with the back of his hand. Michelle marveled at how collected he seemed and though she saw sweat on his brow, it wasn't pouring down his face.

Derek looked up and began, "My friends, it seems as though this bunker isn't as off the radar as we thought. Those rocks are a motion detection system and when someone walks between both points, an alarm will go off inside."

He looked at the old man. "I thought you said not even the Nazis came here?"

The old man just shrugged. "Honestly, Derek, no one ever comes here. As far as I know, no one has been here in years. Occasionally, some brave teenagers will trek up here for fun, but they have never reported seeing anything or anyone."

Derek pondered this new mystery and stood. Without another word, he brought his friends around the secret eyes and continued up the hill until they stood at the very top. The view was stunning, and they could see in all directions for miles. Though the sun blazed above, a now-brisk breeze brushed their faces. The old man pointed to the huge pile of broken pieces of concrete that lay in front of them. Derek noticed that the man was right, the Nazis destroyed the entrance. He wasn't fooled as quickly as he knew the Nazis were notorious for destroying one entrance, only to have other secret ways into places.

He turned to the old man and spoke in hushed tones to him. The man nodded and quickly walked back down the hill, leaving Derek and Michelle by themselves. Michelle looked questioningly at Derek, but he waved her forward. Carefully, he combed over several areas away from the main pile of rubble for clues to another entrance. Michelle asked what next if they could find nothing, but Derek assured her they would find what they were looking for, and it was a matter of getting in the bunker. Both combed the rocky side of the hill, working their way back down the hill, being careful not to miss anything.

Soon, they came to a ledge that overlooked the village below, and Derek threw himself to the ground. Michelle quickly joined him and looked below where he was looking. At first, she saw nothing but at a second glance, she saw the glare of glass along with the blinding flash of the sun pointed their way. Derek told her someone was down there with either a camera or a looking glass of some sort. She looked around where the flash of light came from but saw no sign of human life. Derek said they were in the right spot. He wormed his way to the very edge of the ledge and peered over the side. He let out a hearty laugh before pushing himself back to Michelle. He grabbed her hand, and they moved back to grassy area off to the side, away from sight of the ledge.

Michelle pushed him in the shoulder. "Well?"

He laughed again. "The door is right there in the open! No wonder someone is keeping an eye on the entrance from below."

He sat up and peered above his head, taking note of the sun's location. "It definitely took us more time getting here than I anticipated, and it's late in the afternoon."

Michelle nodded. "What next?"

Derek winked at her. "We wait until dusk and slip in using the shadows to cover our tracks. In this blazing sun, it's easy to detect movement but in the shadows of dusk, it's hard to see things."

She got a serious look on her face. "Derek, you've dragged me across continents in search of something I have no idea what we're looking for. I'm not moving another inch until you tell me what we're searching for!"

His face looked a bit hurt. "Michelle, I'm sorry. I don't want to give you too much information in case something happens. That way, you really don't know anything."

Michelle swung across her body and punched the man square in the shoulder. "Derek, at this point, I'm in this just as much as you! Tell me!"

A look of amazement on his face at the strike, he smiled and told her of the artifact in which they searched. According to his description, they were looking for an ancient medallion that made the wearer impervious to magic. Derek further described it as an unknown metal, slightly larger than a silver dollar with an intricate starburst pattern on the front. Derek further explained that the Nazis took the medallion during a raid of a Zarillion science outpost on one of the Antarctic islands during World War II. No mention of the artifact was heard for seventy years until the U.S. government intercepted a transmission describing the artifact here in Argentina.

Michelle's eyes widened. "The government knows what's going on?"

Derek laughed aloud. "For quite some time, my dear. For quite some time. The issue has always been what to tell the public and how. Most people aren't ready to share the planet with other humans, let alone other humanoid species. The fact is we're at a large precipice, and humanity is about to fall off and be sucked into the abyss unless we stop it."

Michelle didn't know how to respond to this latest revelation. Just then, an image of a young man appeared in her mind's eye. Focusing her mind, she saw two images. She saw another man with her son but couldn't believe it. She was brought awake by a hand on her shoulder. As she turned to see Derek, she came back to reality but couldn't bring herself to tell him what images she saw in her mind. He pointed to the sky and for the first time, she noticed it darkening.

Without a word, she followed him to the ledge. The shadows were lengthening, and it was getting harder to see. The military man swung himself down onto the ledge below and helped Michelle down as well. They stood in front of what was another dead end. She saw the rocks that made up the side of the hill and looked at her companion with questions. He smiled and strode forward, grabbing in front of him. Michelle watched as his hand wrapped around a mesh fabric and pulled it back slightly to reveal a modern metal door.

She stood in surprise, and he laughed. "You need to know what you're looking for. Come on, we have to get the artifact and be gone before anyone knows we're here."

Reaching forward, he used a small knife and jiggled the door a little until it opened. Michelle was surprised to see so little security surrounding the door and the door itself. Once inside, Derek locked the door and wiped down all traces of his touch. Inside the hill, they could smell a musty yet dry environment. Looking at the amount of dust on the floor, it was obvious no one entered here in a long time. They strode forward cautiously until they came to a more modern tunnel as the rock gave way to tile flooring.

Artificial lights came on, surprising them, and they spun around, looking for people who might be coming to capture them. Looking around the room, they found no one and surmised the lights to be on a motion detector. The room itself resembled a nurse's station at a hospital with a large desk area and tables and computers everywhere. Still to this point, they saw no sign of human life. They followed the hallway until they came to a large glass door. Looking through the door, they saw it was a laboratory of some kind.

Various science experiments in different stages were going on, and the lab tables were full of computers. Still, they saw no one monitoring these experiments. Derek moved toward the door which automatically opened before them. Walking quickly, they entered the room, noticing all the scientific activity. Derek kept them moving forward until they came to a door with a small window in it. He peered into the window and smiled. Grasping the handle, he pulled the door open and walked into the next room.

Michelle followed behind and gasped as she walked into the room. Large tanks filled with a clear liquid stood before them. Inside, the tanks contained people in a sleep-induced stasis with face masks resembling those of divers, covering their eyes, noses, and mouths. Derek didn't even look at the suspending humans, muttering something about case healing chambers. Instead of stopping, he sped forward and stopped before a natural cave-looking entrance. He quickly grabbed a flashlight from his backpack and went into the blackness. She grabbed his shirt and followed him quickly. Once inside, the musty smell took over, but now there was a hint of moisture in the air.

Through the darkness, they crept until Derek stopped, holding up his hand for Michelle to stop as well. He flashed the light in front of him and in the dim light, they saw what amounted to an elaborate display box with the ancient medal resting on a lush velvet fabric. Derek looked around, still nervous at the lack of human interaction. He fully expected to fight his way in and out. He turned to Michelle who was already standing in front of the case, marveling at the artifact. Indeed, as Derek described, it was the size of a silver dollar, but she couldn't place the metal which looked like a brushed golden color.

Derek looked around the room for signs of alarms or security devices and shook his head. He went up the case and carefully opened the glass door. Again, peering inside looking for an alarm, he reached in carefully to grab the medallion. At first, everything seemed fine, until the medallion glowed in his hand. A shout of pain, and he released the medallion, causing it to clink onto the ground. Derek held his hand as though he was burned. Michelle ran over to him, but he said he was fine, just a little shocked.

The lights popped on, and a cackling laughter came from behind them. "Well, we've been expecting you!"

Both twirled around to expect a host of men surrounding them, only to see a shimmering image of what appeared to be a German scientist smiling. The man stood about six feet with a slight build and a full head of blond hair parted to the side. He smiled and shimmered as they could tell the image wasn't a real person. They looked around for others coming to capture them, but no one else came forward.

Again, the man smiled. "Mr. Andrews, you cannot handle the medallion. Only a member of the royal family can do so. We have special tools that allow us to look at the medallion and experiment on it but so far, we cannot use it in any way. Mrs. Sullivan, would you be so kind as to try your hand at the medallion."

Everything in Michelle's head screamed don't touch the metal, but it seemed as though her body was already in motion and before she knew it, the medallion was safely in her hand. Without knowing what she was doing, she placed the medallion over her head and pulled Derek close to her for protection. The scientist, no longer smiling, spoke into a communicator on his wrist and disappeared, only to be replaced by a grotesque reptilian humanoid.

The figure glared at them. "Well, Mr. Andrews, well met. Mrs. Sullivan, an honor!"

Derek stood straight. "Who are you, and what do you want?"

"Interesting question. Let's just say I'm the owner of that medallion, and I would like it back."

"You and I know that isn't true. The real owner of the medallion has it on her neck, and there it will stay!"

The image became furious. "Yes, it seems as though I underestimated her power. Your father did a wonderful job of hiding you from me, but your secret is out. No matter, there's no way for you to escape, and I'll come for the medallion soon enough."

The military man flexed his muscles and taunted the figure. "Why don't you come and get it! I'm sure you'll find it not as easy as you imagine!"

The figure nodded. "I doubt not your prowess! As a matter of fact, down the road, I may have use of such a soldier as you."

Derek spat, "I'll never join an evil creature such as you. You're a scourge on this planet, and I'll see you expelled from my world."

"Your world! My dear boy, this isn't your world. It may be your home, but that wasn't always the case. You're right though, this isn't my world and soon enough, I'll return to my own. Not before I destroy yours, of course!"

Derek and Michelle looked at each other, standing their ground. Derek spoke, "I think you will find our world harder to conquer than you imagine. We fight for freedom and life. What do you fight for? Fear and death!"

Again, the image cackled, "Yes, your kind always sees yourselves as the freedom fighters, but it was your kind and others that imprisoned me here on this planet. We're free now, and we will devour you and your planet! Enjoy your small victory because when I finish with your boy, I'm coming for you!"

Michelle's rage took control of her, and she felt electricity build in her. "You won't harm my son! Trust me when I tell you that you have no idea who you're dealing with."

The image looked at her. "True enough, but the boy is just coming into his power, and he's still a child. I'll be sure to train him in my image. Rest assured, I'll take care of him!"

Cackling laughter filled the small cavern as the image disappeared. The cavern was once again dark, and Derek snapped on the flashlight, grasping Michelle's hand and leading her out. They fled through the halls back the way they came until they came to the large glass doors. The doors were closed. Again, the image of the scientist materialized before them.

He looked at them. "There's no way out. You might as well make yourselves comfortable until the commander comes for you!"

CHAPTER TWELVE

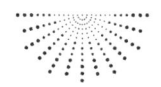

Under the dark of night, Commander Zosa stood on the deck of his all-terrain vehicle alongside Colonel Whilhelm and the traitor, Michael, watching the computer screen for signs of the enemy. To this point, they went along unmolested and made great time toward the gate. Michael gave them directions to a little-used gate but assured the commander they could penetrate the city undetected. He explained that he used the entrance on multiple occasions, putting his own plans into motion.

All seemed too quiet for the commander's liking, and he scanned the computers, waiting for the hammer to fall. He leered at Michael, knowing that at any minute, his chance to get into the city could be snuffed out by a double cross. To his great surprise, they arrived at the location of the gate with the enemy yet to be heard from. The commander felt excitement build in his body as he stood to his full height and barked orders for the invasion to begin at once. The colonel saluted and grabbed Michael, pushing him outside. The snow was high here, and the commander's men, not used to the terrain, had difficulty making their way toward the gate.

The commander noticed the struggles of his men but made no comment, in hopes they would adapt quickly. Watching the slow progress of his men tramping through the high snow, he felt the nervousness come back. He plowed through the snow toward the front lines. The snow flew around him and in his face, but he wasn't daunted, quickly taking the lead. His men, seeing his enthusiasm, quickened their steps and forgot their difficulty, falling in behind their leader. Even the colonel was impressed by the commander's resolve and followed behind quickly with his own troops.

Michael, despite his bonds, glided over the snow and stayed close to the commander, gently guiding him toward the gate. He couldn't help but smile and would feel vindicated when he saw Andrew's face while he was placed in irons. The smile widened as the gate loomed unguarded before them, and he asked the commander to come forward with him. At first, the commander thought it a trap but relented, following his new ally. To the commander, the gate was a simple cave and as they entered, he grew more nervous, not seeing his men any longer. Michael reassured him, and they proceeded forward until they stood at what looked to be a sheer rock wall.

Before the commander could complain, Michael held up his hand and placed it directly onto the rock wall. For a moment, nothing happened but then, the commander noticed Michael's hand glow, and he heard a click. A snap and the grating of rock as the rock wall moved slowly outward to reveal a small entrance. The commander was at a loss for words as he waited what seemed to be a lifetime to enter this accursed city. With Michael's hand still glowing leading the way, he waved the commander onward. Without another word, he disappeared into the darkness behind this loathsome creature.

He felt the earth squeezing in around him, and the nervousness returned. For countless years, he dreamed of his release from his earthly prison, and here he was, inside what he thought might be his tomb at one time. He felt the heat grow, which made him feel a little more comfortable, and stayed close to Michael, making sure not to lose sight of the man. They walked for a few minutes until Michael stopped abruptly and held the commander back from continuing forward. Standing motionless, he peered around the corner to see why Michael suddenly stopped. The hallway was full of guards making their way to another part of the city, preparing for the siege they knew was coming.

Michael scooted backward and motioned the commander to follow him back. The commander did as he was instructed, and they made their way back to their original place at the entrance. Before going back outside, he stopped to take in the entrance. It was much too small to get his troops in great numbers into the city for a siege, but he would have to adjust his strategy and make enough havoc to open one of the larger gates. He strode outside with a triumphant look on his face, which didn't go unnoticed by his men.

Commander Zosa spoke with his top officers and told them of his wishes. He explained to them that although not a perfect situation, they could get enough of a force inside to see his will done. The officers listened and went immediately to their troops to explain the new strategy. Soon, the specialized troops the commander requested were assembled before him for inspection, before carrying out their orders. Proud and excited, the commander stood before his men and viewed his best and most skilled fighters. He saluted them and ordered the engagement to begin.

The men quickly filed into the cave and flew through the rock doorway. The commander was pleasantly surprised by how little time it took for the small force to infiltrate the entrance. In the meantime, Michael explained to the remaining officers where the larger gate was and assured them it would be open inside the hour. He further explained that most of the enemy troops were assembling at the main gate and didn't expect this smaller gate to be attacked. Listening intently, the commander's troops readied themselves for their part in the attack. With their orders confirmed, they all marched toward the other gate, which Michael assured them they could get to in about twenty minutes marching. He advised this to keep the element of surprise as at this point, the fleet of vehicles would draw too much attention.

Commander Zosa viewed this as sound advice and agreed to the plan. He ordered his vehicles to remain at the ready for once the gate was open, they would pour in and finish the job. He watched his troops disappear into the darkness and all he could do was wait for the signal. The commander thought things over quickly and barked orders to his second in command before grabbing Michael by the scruff of the neck and pushed him toward the entrance. He announced to Michael that he would be joining the mission so he could keep an eye on him. Michael nodded and let himself be led.

Inside the entrance, he quickly found his men assembled ready to attack and were surprised to see their lord with them. Again, the men straightened and looked proud to have their commander with them. Commander Zosa waved them forward as he felt like a young officer leading his first engagement. Excitement filled his body, and he still gripped Michael with a vise-like grip pushing him forward. They stopped at the corner where Michael first stopped and peered around to see if the soldiers were still there. Luck was with them as they encountered no one, and they moved into the larger hallway fanning out to be ready for any resistance.

As excited as the commander was, he still knew from experience that the battle would be difficult to win. He understood even though surprise was on his side, his enemy would be fighting on their home turf, making things extremely difficult on his soldiers. The commander kept up a quick pace and under Michael's guidance, came to a large hangar full of different types of military vehicles. He gave quick orders to stay in the shadows around the hangar. After conferring with Michael, he understood that they needed to cross the hangar and make their way to the gate just beyond.

He readied his troops, and they moved forward into the hangar, no longer having the shadows to hide them. Soldiers working on the vehicles immediately engaged them, and small skirmishes ensued around the hangar. As soon as the first encounter took place, the alarms screamed throughout the entire hangar. A much larger force of fighting men ran into the hangar, toward the commander's awaiting troops. Fighting became fast and heavy. The commander knew things were too easy up to now, but he had great confidence in his men.

Now, the entire hangar was a mass of fighting men, most of which was close quarters, hand-to-hand combat. It seemed as though the enemy didn't want to damage any of their vehicles. Good strategy in his mind, but he knew there weren't enough of his men to hold this hangar or to move forward at this time. The commander watched as more and more enemy troops filed into the hangar. His victory looked bleak, and he knew if he retreated, he would never get another chance such as this again.

Thinking quickly, he ordered his men to place ordinance on some of the vehicles and retreat to the main hallway. Fighting continued, and he knew he would lose a lot of men if this plan worked, but what choice did he have if he wanted to get to the gate? Grabbing Michael, he and the rest of his men backed off into the main hallway. The commander gave the order, and the men blew all the ordinance with deafening explosions everywhere. The commander knew this type of devastation as he experienced a similar tragedy in his own armory recently. Explosion after explosion rocked the hangar and when he could hear no more, he ordered his men to make for the gate.

Running as fast as they could through the smoke-filled room, trying not to get burnt from the many unchecked fires, they inched toward the gate. Enemy troops rallied, in hot pursuit of the commander's men. Commander Zosa swung his head around and was astonished to see so few of his men still with him, but they were too proud to stop. Pressing forward, his much smaller group crossed the large hangar within view of the huge waiting gate. Now, he saw for the first time, another force at the gate waiting for them. His men quickly engaged the new force and kept moving toward the gate.

Feeling a quick slice cut into his arm brought the commander to his senses, and he knew he would have to fight for his life. Spinning quickly, he came face to face with a large muscle-bound soldier wielding a long sword. The two men squared off and metal struck metal, sending sparks into the air. Both men, very seasoned in sword fighting, danced in and out, swinging while ducking to avoid each other's blade. Commander Zosa parried and spun, trying to catch the man off guard, only to have the move countered. He could appreciate a skilled soldier, but this had gone on far enough. With a quick fake, he worked his way inside the man's defenses and struck the man in the side.

His enemy, with surprise in his eyes, went down to one knee, holding his side. The commander didn't have time to finish the man off and ran again toward the gate. He quickly glanced around, and his once-proud force lay on the ground scattered around the hangar. A handful of his finest men remained and rallied to his side as they ran forward. Once again, they were met by enemy forces, and the commander smashed into two soldiers, sending them flying. He saw a small force guarding the control panel, waiting for them.

Fighting his way forward, blood covered his sword, and he felt blood all over his face. The commander came to a skidding stop as one soldier lashed out at him with his own sword, and he quickly dispatched the young man. Raising his sword, he pointed to the leader of the waiting force guarding the gate. The man took the bait and reached behind him with both hands, revealing double swords. Normally, the commander wouldn't be impressed, but this man handled the swords he knew he was in for a fight.

Both men squared off, and the clash of swords rang out in the hangar. The commander was vaguely aware of little sound besides that of his sword ringing out. After a few minutes of slamming into one another and using all known moves, it became apparent the commander couldn't defeat this man alone. He attacked, only to be repelled time and time again. Taking his attention off the man for a second, he caught Michael out of the corner of his eye. A feeling of slicing flesh ripped through his leg and pain shot up his side. The commander fell to one knee and raised his sword just in time to block the kill strike headed his way. He pushed the enemy sword up in the air, and rage filled him as he rose to his feet.

As he was about to swing his sword to attack, he felt a wave of energy whiz by his body, almost taking him off his feet. Again, out of the corner of his eye, he saw Michael moving forward. The gaunt man moved with a speed that surprised the commander. Michael always seemed so frail and weak to him, but he knew there was much more to this man than met the eye. He watched as Michael moved toward the door.

The wave of energy struck the soldiers guarding the gate, scattering them everywhere. A few were back on their feet quickly, looking for a fight. Michael again raised his hand to release more energy when the commander heard a booming voice yell, "Michael, stop!"

Everyone in the entire hangar stopped as the commander turned to see the origin of the voice. He looked into the face of a rage-filled Holly, followed by the general and another large force of soldiers at his back. The commander couldn't believe his luck. He was so close to his dream of seeing these scums pay for their transgressions. He turned toward Michael who stood calm and full of confidence.

Michael came forward to address Holly. "Your reign is over, and mine is just beginning! I suggest you leave with your life or die here and now!"

Holly towered over the slight man. "My reign! You're a madman! I don't reign. I serve, a concept you have no grasp of. The only one you serve is yourself, and that's going to be your undoing. Back away from the gate, and I'll let you live!"

The gaunt man cackled and turned, spitting as he spoke, "You speak of serving myself but what have you and the council been doing this whole time! Allowing our people to become soft and our arch enemies to infest this world. No, Holly, it is you who is guilty! I'll rebuild what you destroyed, and we will be the strongest people in the cosmos!"

She ran up to him and grabbed his neck, lifting him high in the air. "You fool! You of all people know what my seat on the council has cost me personally! I won't have you sit here and spout evil in such a fair place. What happened to you? You were someone I respected and looked up to!"

For a moment, the man looked unsure before gaining his bearings. "Holly, it's over! You're a lost cause, along with your council. Enjoy what I have in store for you!"

As he said the words, he sent a bolt of energy into Holly's chest, sending her flying across the room. The general, seeing his beloved treated so, immediately ran forward with sword in hand, raised to strike. His swing was met by another blade in mid-swing. General Giles seethed as he turned to square up against his nemesis, Commander Zosa. The two towering warriors waited a lifetime for such a contest and turned to each other, taking measure of their opponent. Circling each other, neither seemed ready to make the first strike.

Commander Zosa looked at the general, noticing his knotted arm muscles and the way he gripped the sword. His hand held the sword tight, but it looked like fluid in the seasoned warrior's hands. To show dominance, he raised his hands quickly and swung over his head, coming down toward the general's head. General Giles moved quickly to the side and swung to meet the falling blade, letting it glance off his own. Turning in a spinning motion, he thrust his blade out before him to end the fight quick, hoping to slip into the commander's defenses. Slipping to the side, the commander let the thrust meet nothing but air and swung upward to deliver a blow of his own. Once more, the general's blade met mid-strike the large sword of his opponent, creating a large scraping noise.

Both men backed away slightly to reevaluate their strategy. General Giles noticed the gash on the commander's leg and another on his arm. Blood saturated the commander's pant leg and sleeve. This gave the general an idea, and he renewed his attack as fast and furious as he could, swinging, thrusting, and spinning in a blur of action. The reptilian leader was taken off guard and tried frantically to keep up with the new attack. He met every strike but for the first time since the fight began, he felt his strength leaving him. Now, his sword felt very heavy, and his movements became labored. The general sensed his struggle and kept coming with wave after wave of moves and strikes.

The huge reptilian leader faltered and slipped on a fallen soldier, tumbling to the ground, and losing his sword as his hand struck the stone floor. He immediately rolled to spring up, only to come face to face with the general's glaring face with blade bearing down on the commander's head. Before he could move, the blade was at his neck, and the commander knew he was finished. General Giles, with eyes red with rage, went in for the kill when he heard another voice cry out.

He looked up to see a bloodied Holly held by the neck, still on her knees with a dagger across her neck. Michael took matters into his own hands and bent her head back, telling the general to back up. At first, the general stood fast, but Michael pushed the blade into Holly's neck enough to draw blood. He backed away from his fallen foe and strode forward to face the new threat. Michael held up one hand in warning.

He flashed an evil smile. "Enough of this! That gate is opening, and I don't care who I must kill to open it. Now you can open it, or I slit her throat and open it myself!"

Gritting his teeth, he continued forward as he saw Holly wink at him. In seconds, she flipped Michael over, leaving him looking up at her as fists pummeled his face. Holly grabbed him by the neck and threw him against the wall. The evil man slumped to the floor motionless. General Giles ran over to Holly to see if she was all right. Looking into her eyes, seeing energy dancing gave him the answer he sought and hugged her with a big embrace.

As they broke their embrace, they heard laughter. "Now the end begins!"

They turned to see the gate rising and in rushing enemy troops.

CHAPTER THIRTEEN

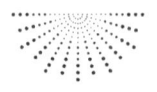

The fragrance of a fresh spring day with pungent flowers, freshly mown grass, and newly made food struck his nose before even opening his eyes. Peter breathed in deeply the wonderful smells which reminded him of home before the realization of what happened to him returned. Shooting up with his eyes wide open, he nearly jumped out of the plush bed he found himself lying. Supporting himself with his arms, he looked around the room nervously to figure where he might be located. Natural light filtered in from two normal-looking windows but as he looked around the room, it seemed foreign.

The walls were a type of horse-hair plaster and were painted with subdued earth tones. Furniture resembled that of something he might see in a fairy tale; everything was hand carved. He turned quickly to look at the headboard and nearly laughed. Staring him in the face on the hand-carved wooden headboard was the strange starburst cross. The cloth curtains gently moved as a soft breeze entered the room. Again, the natural scents entered his nostrils, making him think back to the tree he encountered when he first came to the garden. Turning away the comfortable blanket covering him, he swung his legs over the edge of the bed, preparing to lift himself.

A small scratching noise alerted him to someone turning the door knob to enter. Nervousness entered his being, and he didn't know what to do. In a quick thrust, he was on his feet but needed to steady himself on the nearest bedpost. As the door opened, he readied himself for a fight. When the person walked in, he nearly passed out. Blinking rapidly, he tried to refocus many times, thinking his eyes were failing him. The man walked right up to him with a warm smile and gently put a hand on his shoulder. He felt the hand, but something was different as if it wasn't a solid substance.

Again, he shook his head, trying to clear his mind and rapidly blinked some more. Without a word, the man sat on the bed and motioned for Peter to join him. Still uncertain if events were real, Peter slowly sat on the bed, not taking his eyes off the man. Once comfortable, he turned to the man who remained smiling widely at Peter. Several times, Peter tried to say something, but the words were stuck in his throat. The man eyed him with sympathy and seemed ready to begin the conversation.

He took a breath and spoke, "My dear boy, I know this is much to bear, but I'll do my best to explain. Just know I'm with you always! We don't have much time for reunions. The world outside is ready to implode on itself."

Peter, with a look of shock, blurted out, "You've been alive this whole time?"

The man returned a sad look at the young man. "Peter, I'm not what you would call living. I guess you could call it life but, in my state, it's more like pure energy or my essence."

Again, Peter looked confused. "So, I'm imagining you here and now. How is it I can talk to you?"

Sadness spread across the man's face. "My job isn't done. I've been given time to perform my task and then, I must move on as all beings do eventually."

"Grandfather, what task?"

Hearing the word grandfather perked up the man. "You, my boy, you! You're my greatest task and joy! My love for you and my family wouldn't let me fail, so I'm here to finish what I started. I'll see you trained, and I'll be sure to help you meet your destiny."

Peter nearly reached over to hug the man but stopped. "Grandfather, why when you touch me, could I barely feel you?"

Again, sadness crossed his eyes. "Peter, as I said, I'm more energy than man. It's that energy I must teach you to manage so you can join Rebecca and take control of your destiny."

"Destiny, everyone keeps talking about destiny, but I'm a normal boy and no one special. I'm just your grandson."

The man stood and turned in front of Peter. "That's right! You're my grandson, and you're far from normal. I, along with your mother, raised you as a normal boy to help you grow and learn the beauty of life. There will come a time in the not so near future where your love of life will save many!"

Peter's eyebrows raised. "Jake always said things like that to me. He always knew something I couldn't see myself. I was always so worried about being a normal kid, struggling with school, chores, and not disappointing you."

A broad smile came across the man's face. "I'm far from disappointed in you! I couldn't be prouder. Just arriving here intact is an amazing feat. The armies of darkness are everywhere! No, my boy, your path is just beginning. The evil surrounding us can only see what's right in front of them, but those with vision can see much more to come."

Peter sat, unable to say anything else. He watched his grandfather be buried and mourned him. Sitting back against the headboard, he thought over the events leading him to this moment. So many things he believed were shattered during his journey, so why should his grandfather appearing to him be any different? Hands on his head, the overwhelming feelings going through his mind clogged his thoughts. Rebecca lost, his mother with Mr. Andrews, Jake who knows where, and now his grandfather was all too much to handle. He tilted his head back and let out a wail.

The entire room shook, and he felt himself drawing more power. Again, he felt a sense of calm reach out for him, and the vision of his grandfather came into his mind. Jerry Sullivan stood quietly, reassuring Peter things were all right. The calming presence was enough to bring Peter back to reality and then, he sat on the bed. Both looked at each other and knew the relief of having time together.

His grandfather rose. "Follow me. We haven't much time. The enemy is on the move and may already be in the city!"

Peter jumped to the floor and followed quickly. Both walked briskly through the small, ornate, woodland cabin. If time allowed, Peter would love to spend time here. The calm, warm nature of the wooden beams, furniture, and walls called to him. He felt a deep connection to his surroundings as he emerged from the door into the lush garden. With each step, Peter felt the energy of the garden reaching out to mold every step forward. Peter's grandfather walked him through a maze of hedge to a place in the middle. To Peter, the bronze medallion coming from the ground made him laugh.

Covered in a few places by the encroaching growth of the untended garden, he discovered the famous starburst cross. Without a word, he strode forward and fell to his hands and knees as if being called. As if a magnet took hold of him, he reached out and placed a hand in the middle of the starburst pattern. Immediately, the pattern turned bright yellow then blue, before sending a wave of energy into Peter. At first, he felt stuck to the medallion as though it would never release him. A ringing in his ears almost caused him to pass out. When the ringing stopped, he opened his eyes to find himself in the middle of a battle.

He barely jumped out of the way of a spear whizzing by his head. The sounds of battle surrounded him, and he kept turning to see where he could escape. As he spun, he caught sight of a kingly looking man on a horse. This great warrior sat on his horse with a sword raised, waiting for someone to engage him. Even with the battle raging around him, nothing touched the king as an aura engulfed him. His beautiful, powerful steed sat ready to enter the fray but stood as regal as the king. For the longest time, the king went unchallenged. Out of the chaos, he ran another man with a sword.

Peter thought him just another soldier, but a shiver went down his spine as the man came into the light. Peter noticed a reptile's eyes and sharp teeth baring down on the king. The soldier stood eye level with the horse and was well muscled. The soldier, in the blink on an eye, swung up and punched the horse in the head. The regal horse took the blow in turn, but its head snapped back, and it went down on its front knees, causing the king to fall forward. The enemy didn't wait for the king to get up but rather, grabbed him by the back of the collar and picking him up in one swift movement and threw him to the ground.

Peter saw blood streaming from the king's nose, but he managed to lift himself from the ground with rage in his eyes. Peter recognized that look as the energy danced from eye to eye. For the first time, he saw in the light, a clear image of the king. Peter gasped as he looked at himself. Shaking his head in the hopes to wake, he was unsuccessful, and the scene continued. The king released a bolt of energy directly into the soldier's chest, sending him flying, landing ten feet away with a thud. Now, it was the reptilian soldier's turn as he released his own bolt of energy in the direction of the king. Peter winced as the horse stepped in front of the bolt, and it burned into the horse's flesh. A moment went by, and the horse fell to his knees then onto its side with a crash.

Rage overtook the king, and he wielded the sword over his head with its blade gleaming bright white. Again, the reptilian soldier sent another death bolt toward the king, only to have it deflect off the blade harmlessly. Running at full speed, the king reached the soldier and swung the blade with all his might. The king's sword was met by one of the soldier's own, and the two locked into a desperate fight for life. Move after move, the two supreme warriors matched blow for blow. Neither could break down the other's defenses as the battle raged on around them. After a few minutes, even the battle stopped to watch the two combatants.

A large ring of men surrounded the two warriors, including men from both armies. Time seemed to stand still as the blows fell. These two magnificent warriors battled to a draw as they backed away from one another. Each breathed hard and looked at one another, not ready to end but knew there would be no victor this day. Now, the reptilian soldier turned toward Peter, who saw for the first time who the soldier was, and it shocked him. The warrior was none other than Commander Zosa.

Peter didn't know what to do as the commander stared right at him. Then, a blast went off, and the commander and Peter looked toward it. They saw the king fall forward as smoke appeared behind him from a sneering reptilian soldier's weapon. The king landed on the ground, sprawling in the blood-covered grass. The commander went crazy, killing every reptilian soldier within his sight. Seeing their king go down renewed the fighting, and the Zarillion forces, out for vengeance, tore the reptilian soldiers apart.

As the battle ended, it was apparent the Zarillion forces held the day, and the reptilian forces were in full retreat. The commander knelt beside the now-upright king and grabbed his hand. Anyone watching wouldn't know what was transpiring, but Peter saw the commander lean in to say something to the king. The king nodded and looked like he was fading. With a quick movement, the reptilian commander moved to leave, only to have the area around him light up in a huge blaze.

Out of the glowing fire walked a tall, statuesque woman with fire dancing in her eyes. Her beauty overwhelmed Peter but in her state, she was terrifying, and the fire danced around her. She raised her hand to finish off the commander but stopped mid-stride as she looked down to see the king with his hand raised. The fire immediately abated, and the reptilian, seeing his chance, escaped down the hill.

Zarillion forces surrounded the two huddled figures of the king and the beautiful woman. Walking closer, Peter couldn't help but have tears in his own eyes. The woman leaned back a little to look at the king, telling him to hold on so she could heal him. With a bloody hand, he reached up and gently caressed her face, leaving a trail of blood. When the strength left him, his hand fell to his side, and Peter noticed for the first time who the woman was and gasped. Staring back at him was the face of his beloved Rebecca. The king whispered something to Rebecca, and the woman reached down, handing him his ornate sword. Rebecca backed away slightly as the king took the sword and, with the last of his energy, used the sword to stand.

Soldiers everywhere applauded as their king rose, but the praise quickly waned as they saw the state of their king. Blood covering him from head to toe, he was a grisly sight. Sword in hand, the king walked gingerly to a circular stone sticking out of the ground and raised the sword high. Again, the sword glowed but this time, it was a brilliant orange. With all the effort he possessed, the king spoke, "Victory is ours this day!"

The king waited for the applause to die down. "Victory is bought at a terrible price of lives from both people. This will be the last war I fight, but it's just beginning. There will come a day when Earth will need a champion and, on that day, he will rise a king!"

Nearly falling forward, the king caught himself as Rebecca steadied him and watched as he fell to his knees. Kneeling before the strange, circular rock, he still held the orange glowing sword. Reaching forward, the king placed the still-glowing sword onto the surface of the rock. Immediately, energy sparked everywhere and orange, red, and yellow light mixed with the glowing sword. As the energy subsided, the strange stone still glowed many colors, but the sword was no more.

The king, still with his arm outstretched, touched the stone, but he was almost expired. Rebecca turned him over to help him. Tears streaming down her face, there was little she could do for him. His hand still glowing, he reached up one final time to touch her tear-stained face. Time stopped as all the soldiers took one knee and removed their helmets.

Rebecca took his hand. "My love, there must be something I can do!"

The king smiled. "Don't you know you've done all for me as you're my everything! Be not sad, my love. We will meet again! There will come a time when we'll be needed! On that day, we will truly Rise! Farewell for now, my love."

The king's hand fell limp to the ground, and Peter knew he was gone. Rebecca wailed uncontrollably, and the soldiers bowed their heads. Still folded over her fallen love, Rebecca didn't see the rock. Peter moved over so he could see it, still glowing. This time, it was a pure white light. He moved closer, only to see the rock and sword were gone and, in its place, stood a metallic medallion. In the middle, the sword shone in a bright, white light, but it looked more like the starburst Peter was so accustomed to seeing. The light faded, leaving just the metal medallion in the ground.

CHAPTER FOURTEEN

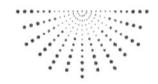

Air shot into his lungs, and he coughed frantically to regain his breath. Hands outstretched, head down coughing and knees bent, Peter blinked through watery eyes to see the ground before him. His arms still shaking, he struggled to push himself upright. Still looking with his eyes down to the ground, he realized something was in his hand. The fingers in his right hand were wrapped around a circular, metallic medallion. Cautiously, he turned the medallion over to inspect it. He shook his head as his eyes focused on the image cut into the face of the medallion. Again, the mysterious starburst pattern stared back at him.

The medal felt warm, and Peter thought he felt a vibration coming forth. Gone were the lights and colors, but Peter felt the sheer energy in the precious item he held in his hands. Still unsettled, he looked to find his grandfather. He found the smiling older Sullivan peering at him with raised eyebrows. The two looked at one another for what seemed like an eternity, until the medallion's vibration intensified.

As if by instinct, Peter held forth the medallion, ready to hand it over to his grandfather. His grandfather took a knee and bowed his head, leaving his grandson holding the medallion in an outstretched hand. Confusion overtook Peter until the vibration in his hand caused him to nearly go to one knee himself. The medallion flashed with a bright white light, and Peter turned away for fear of burning out his eyes. When the vibration stopped, he opened his eyes and looked to his hand.

No longer a small medallion, Peter's hand held a gleaming sword, reaching to the sky. The brilliant sword still glowed with white light, and he turned to his grandfather for guidance. The older gentleman, still on his knee, looked up with reverent pride at his grandson but didn't leave the ground. Peter, still shocked by the sword, thought back to the vision of the gallant king. He looked back down at the sword, feeling the energy still moving up and down his arm. A warm flow of energy moved up his arm and reached out to every part of his body.

With his body feeling on fire, he stood as the sword became a highly polished silver, and the ornate scrollwork showed all over the blade. When the tingling in his body subsided, he felt his strength renewed and turned to his grandfather. Still yet to stand, he nodded to his grandson. Peter finally brought the sword down and placed it into a beautiful leather scabbard. He shocked himself as he had no recollection of the scabbard showing up. Once the sword was safely tucked away, he stood to his full height, feeling somehow taller.

His grandfather finally spoke, "My liege! What's thy command?"

Peter looked surprisingly at his grandfather. "Grandfather? It is me! What are you talking about?"

Slowly, the man rose. "No, Peter, you're no longer just my grandson. You're the one we've waited for! In many ways, I hoped it to be true, but until the garden allowed you to pass, I was unsure. Now, the sword is yours, along with all it entails. No, Peter, your destiny is revealed."

"Grandfather! What destiny?"

The man came up to him and smiled. "Peter, you're the leader our people have searched for throughout the centuries. It was said you would return, but many of us thought the power was lost and wouldn't return, allowing evil to triumph. You are the counter to evil, and you're the light in the darkness!"

A feeling of weakness took his knees, and he lowered himself on a nearby fallen log. Looking up, searching his grandfather's eyes, he could tell the man spoke the truth. If he didn't see the vision, he would have believed himself crazy. Thoughts swirled around his head. Then, the eyes of Rebecca came into his field of vision. At first, he only saw the outline but then, her eyes became bright and energy filled. The vision was fleeting, and he couldn't understand what she was saying, but she wasn't in danger.

When the image whisked away, his grandfather smiled. "She's all right, Peter, and she's on her way! We must prepare a path for her. She will soon be at your side, and you will rule as was preordained by destiny."

Peter looked panicked. "We must help her!"

His grandfather shook his head. "Right now, the way you can help her is to focus your own energy on training to control your own power. You're far behind your enemies. They're much more experienced than you and although your powers alone are stronger than anything the enemy possesses, you are raw."

Peter stood. "What do you need me to do?"

His grandfather rose to meet him with a wide smile. "My boy, you never cease to amaze me! The world falling apart around you, and your first thought is fulfilling your duty!"

"Grandfather, I'll do what needs to be done to get to Rebecca! Nothing else matters! I know saying that aloud doesn't sound right, but I have to make sure she's okay!"

The older man nodded. "I understand. There are more forces at work than the two of you wanting to be together. Trust me, son. Rebecca is going through the same training. If history has shown us anything, you two are destined to be together forever!"

Peter's face grew serious. "Grandfather, you keep mentioning training. What training are you referring to?"

His grandfather's face lightened. "Have you ever heard the expression, with great power comes great responsibility? Well, my boy, you have the greatest power in the known universe, yet you have no idea how to wield it. That makes you beyond dangerous!" He waved Peter to follow him. "Come now. We have much to do in a short time. I want to take you somewhere special. Stay close though as it's getting dark."

Peter did as he was told and followed closely behind his grandfather as they moved farther into the garden. He watched as the plush garden gave way to a rockier, sparsely vegetated area. The surrounding area seemed uninviting and hostile, but still his grandfather moved forward. After an hour, they ascended a steep, rocky hillside. Darkness moved in around them, yet the older Sullivan didn't slow. Finally, at the top of the hill, they found an ancient, worn path and followed it through twists and turns in the dim light. All at once, Peter's grandfather halted and turned to look at his grandson.

Peter could barely see his grandfather. "My boy, I can go no further. Just stay straight, and you will find what you seek. I'll be here when you return."

Peter detected sadness in his grandfather's voice. "What is it I'm looking for? I cannot see anything."

He heard a chuckle. "Not everything will you see with your eyes, Peter! Trust your senses. Good luck, my boy, and listen carefully."

Peter wanted to ask so many questions, but he couldn't bring himself to bother his grandfather any longer. In the dark, he felt a tug on his mind as he peered into the darkness. As if on command, he moved forward in the direction of the tug. He felt every pebble under his feet as he strode through the pitch dark. After a few minutes, he felt the tugging subside but could still see nothing. All at once, he felt the air around him growing very cold. His breathing became more labored, and he saw the mist coming from his breath even in the darkness.

Along with the cold, Peter felt as if he were being watched. Instinctively, he called out, "I'm here as called upon!"

At first, nothing happened, and he almost turned back, but, at the last minute, he heard a click ahead of him in the dark. A harsh smell of stale air mixed with rotten material met his nostrils. He froze as he felt someone standing before him, although he couldn't see who lay ahead. A strange glow filled the air in front of him as he glimpsed a strange figure appearing out of the darkness. The glow built, and Peter gasped as the figure came into view.

The figure cackled at the face Peter made. "Not what you were expecting?"

Peter cringed. "Sorry, this whole situation is a bit much to take in all at once. My grandfather sent me here, but what am I really doing?"

The figure strode forward with his eerie light surrounding him. "Peter, you have much to learn about the power you possess. While your grandfather is correct that you need a teacher, only time will truly teach you the lessons you need. We have little time, and that's why you're here, so I can speed up your training as much as possible. You surprised the commander the last time with your attack but trust me, that won't happen again!"

At the commander's mention, he shook his head. "He'll pay for what he has done! I know he's the reason my grandfather is no longer with me in person, even though no one wants to admit that."

The figure smiled and moved forward. "Yes, the commander has been responsible for much evil, and he will be punished, but, right now, you have much more immediate problems to solve. Your focus needs to be the safety of this planet and its inhabitants. That will be a daunting enough challenge for you now."

Peter stood straight. "Who are you really?"

A smile passed across the figure's face. "Peter, I am who you see! You! Or one version of you. Don't worry, I'm your ancestor, not actually you, but we're connected by more than blood. I've been called forth to instruct you to use your power in the correct way."

Peter looked puzzled but felt very tired. He sat on a pile of rocks and stared at the wraithlike figure. Confusion swirled in his head about the safety of the planet and the people here. How could he as one person do anything against the rage of evil growing all over his world? He always knew of the struggle between good and evil, but now, these forces dueled for control of his world.

As if the figure could hear his thoughts, it responded, "Yes, Peter, you're one person, but even the smallest can be the difference between light and dark. That will be my most important lesson I'll share with you. Even the best of intentions can become evil. Many people fail to listen to their peers in situations where great power is needed to solve issues. The more power someone gains or uses, the less they listen to others. It's all about balance. In nature, everything has a balance point. People are no different. Good and evil are two universal forces always vying for supremacy.

"The key is to listen, to others, teachers and especially yourself. If you listen, the power won't take over your life. Rule the power and not the other way around. The power is a gift to be used in the service of others, not for your own gain. So many before you were unable to grasp that fact."

Peter sat back, thinking of the last statement. "I've felt the power and can do just about what I want with it. To me, that's scary."

The figure chuckled. "Yes, you can certainly do anything you wish with the power, which is why we're here. You are indeed right, it's scary. Again, listen, and you won't be alone. In the end, that's why good remains while evil fails every time. In the end, evil always makes it about themselves rather than for the common good. You, Peter, are a rough gem, and you'll need to become a finely sculpted stone to defeat your enemies."

He couldn't fathom the completeness of what the figure shared with him, and he thought deeply about the shared information. Much of what the figure said, he knew to be common sense, but he met many people in his short life who had little in the way of good sense. Surrounded by his thoughts, he seared into his brain the lesson of listening. He nearly laughed as his grandfather spoke these same words his entire life. There was no doubt of the importance of this lesson, and he would heed the lesson.

Without another word, he rose and walked within a few inches of the strange figure. "My King, what would you have me do?"

The figure looked admiringly at the boy. "I have to tell you, Peter, in this age of selfishness, you surprise me. Your nobility is refreshing. Keep in mind, you're my ancestor and as such, you bow to no one! Have you not figured out you're my successor yet?"

Peter stood in awe. "What, your successor? I am not noble or a king. I'm a plain-old boy looking to become a man!"

The figure smiled again. "That is exactly why you'll be a fantastic leader for our people—your humility! Every leader needs to know what it's like to struggle, what it's like to follow. You, Peter, know what it's like to fight for everything you have. You earn your way every step of the way, and you'll lead by example, not by right. Trust me though, you lead by right. Tomorrow, we'll begin your training but know you have everything you need to accomplish anything already deep inside your person."

Peter relaxed. "How long will I be here?"

The figure started, "You won't be here as long as I had hoped, but I'll train you as best as I can for now and hope you'll return. Tomorrow, we will focus on the power itself and the sword. One thing, never let that medallion out of your sight. Not that anyone else can call upon the sword but while it is in this form, anyone can use the blade, which can kill just as easily as any power. Rest now, and we'll begin in the morning."

Peter felt himself being lifted off the ground and floating into an unknown opening in the hillside. As sleep took him, he thought he saw a comfortable room passing. In a moment, he felt himself come to rest on a plush bed and sleep swiftly moving in. He lay back and let the sleepiness take control. The last thing he saw was the smiling face of Rebecca.

CHAPTER FIFTEEN

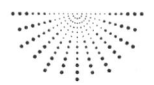

Panic set in as Michelle and Derek stared at the clear glass wall. Derek spun to turn back down the hall they just came from, only to see a similar glass wall at the end of the hall. He turned quickly and grasped Michelle's hand, looking at her without a word, telling her she would be all right. Without another word, he reached behind himself and withdrew a large hunting knife and raised it to strike the glass wall. Swiftly, he brought the sharp instrument down in an arcing motion to hit the glass door.

The impact was terrific with sparks flying everywhere, but the door remained intact without signs of damage. Derek's face grew red with rage as he backed away in disbelief as he looked at the unmarked glass door. Looking down at his hand, the blade still looked strong and sharp, but Derek needed another weapon for their escape. Again, they heard the cackling laughter and turned, scowling at the evil image.

He laughed. "I told you! You are mine! Make yourselves comfortable! It won't be long now! The commander will wrap up his conquest immediately and travel here to collect you."

Derek's face rose in full anger. "When the commander arrives, he will be dealt with accordingly! Don't worry though, I'll take care of you as well."

The image blinked in surprise. "Mr. Andrews, yes, the consummate soldier. We will see who will defeat whom. In the meantime, sit tight."

Derek went to raise his knife but felt a calm hand reach up on his shoulder. He turned slightly to see Michelle's eyes dancing with energy and the medallion around her neck glowing. She walked past him calmly and touched the glass. At first, the glass seemed unfazed but after a few moments, Derek sensed and heard a harsh vibration building. The vibration grew, and Michelle's body glowed even more. The vibration reached a fever pitch, and the glass door exploded outward, leaving an empty space where the door once stood.

The evil image was gone, but they heard the nervous voice scream, "Impossible!"

Michelle peered over her shoulder, speaking to the phantom voice, "You haven't a clue who you're dealing with! True, my son is untrained, but I'm not! You will find me a very formidable opponent."

With one last glare back into the void, she strode purposefully forward, grabbing Derek's hand and leading him out of the compound. Eyes aglow, she walked out into the fresh air, raising her head toward the stars, and nodded, moving forward to a smooth area on top of the hill. She spun to look at Derek, who still seemed bewildered as he kept blinking at Michelle. A smile broke across her face, and she clasped his hands, reassuring him. Derek watched as she took something out of her backpack and unwrapped it. To his untrained eye, it looked like a metallic rod of some kind. Michelle said nothing but motioned him to stay put.

Derek peered through raised eyebrows as his friend rushed forward with the rod in hand. When she reached the entrance of the compound, she raised the rod above her head. Once more, he heard the vibration sound, and it reached its climax. She smashed the rod into the ground, and the shockwave that ensued knocked Derek off his feet.

When he could straighten himself, he saw Michelle glowing with power dancing around her, and the vibration continued. He felt the ground cracking beneath him and moved several times to a safer location. Feeling frightened for his friend, he wanted to move forward to help but each time he did, another crack opened before him. Finally, he could only watch as she released a final barrage of energy into the ground. The ground in front of her disappeared into small particles, yet she stayed unmoving.

At last, Derek saw the power dissipate in her eyes, and the glow dim around her. She pulled the rod out of the remaining ground and turned to Derek, who could only look with his mouth wide open. This didn't go unnoticed as Michelle walked to him around cracks in the earth and reached up, gently closing his mouth, letting her hand caress his face. Derek shook his head still in disbelief as this was Peter's mom who never seemed as though she could hurt a flea. With a large smile, she grabbed his hand, leading him back down the hillside.

Derek watched further as she reached up around her neck and rubbed the medallion. He said nothing and followed, unsure what to say at that very moment. When down the hillside, Derek went to turn toward his friend's place, only to have Michelle stop him. He turned and looked at her determined face.

He blinked. "What is it? We cannot help your friend! They have him! We must go now!"

He shook his head once more. "The Nazis?"

"Yes, now, let's move! They aren't far behind. The commander hasn't arrived, but it's a large enough force we cannot take on alone!"

He looked at her. "Then lead the way, My Lady!"

She turned and nodded slightly before walking briskly in another direction. They continued down the hillside through dense growth but moving steadily, keeping watch around them for signs of pursuit. They made good time and were about to come out of the tree line into an opening at the bottom of the hillside when Derek grabbed Michelle, pulling her quickly behind a tree. Both hugged the tree with their back as Derek peered around to see several military transports with men surrounding the vehicles. He watched for a few minutes, assessing the situation. Michelle was correct; there were too many for them to handle at this point, and they needed an exit strategy.

Off to the right, he saw a tree ready to fall held up by some vines. He gently touched Michelle's hand and pointed to the leaning tree. She nodded and stayed put as Derek snuck between trees. Michelle watched as he took his hunting knife out and placed it between his teeth. With surprising quickness, he gripped the tree next to the broken one and climbed up the trunk until he lay outstretched on one of the higher branches leaning over the vine-held tree.

With great nimbleness and quickness, he broke through the vines with little noise. Even from her secluded position, she heard the broken tree crack more until it came crashing down upon two of the large military transports. Derek was already scrambling down the other tree and making his way over to her. Chaos in the camp ensued as soldiers ran around, trying to figure how such a large tree could fall out of nowhere. While the soldier's attention was on the fallen tree, Michelle and Derek made their way around them under cover of the tree line.

They quickened the pace as the trees became sparser, with the danger of being seen more prevalent. Now, they heard fewer signs of the soldiers behind them. The light was dim in the evening sky, with darkness rapidly approaching as they saw signs of civilization. They ducked into an alley behind a drugstore. Huddling behind a dumpster, they took a moment to breathe and assess their situation.

Derek whispered, "Well, my friend, you're going to have to tell me some day how you were able to do that!"

Michelle smiled. "Training, Derek, training! My family is what you would call Knights of the Cosmos!"

This statement confused him further. "Knights of the Cosmos?"

Barely able to see Michelle now, she said, "Yes, Derek, knights! My family has been protectors for much of known history. My father, Peter's grandfather was the Grand Knight, the finest, strongest knight ever known. I know we seem like the typical family from next door, but that was for protective purposes. Our enemies needed to be unaware of Peter's presence."

Derek blurted out, "Yes, I know about Peter and your father. I just had no idea you were involved."

She laughed slightly. "So, what are you saying? You don't want to protect me anymore?"

He snickered. "Not sure. I might need you to protect me!!"

Again, she laughed. "It would be my honor and duty! Fear not though, my military training is nothing compared to yours and here in this terrain, I have much need of you. Now, in the cosmos, that's another story, but I'll always have need of a military leader and more importantly, a friend."

Unexpectedly, she leaned over to kiss his cheek. "Besides, Derek, you're more important to me than you could possibly imagine."

Derek was speechless, which was surprising because he always knew what to say or do in most situations. He accepted the kiss and gently clasped her hands in his. The two sat unmoving and in silence for a few moments. Michelle moved first and motioned for him to follow, whispering in his ear that soldiers were still in the area. She also told him they needed another route back to the docks and their vessel.

Renewed by the few moments of rest, they made their way out of the alley. As they were about to emerge, they saw a row of dark figures blocking their way. In the dim light, they couldn't make out the nature of the men and as they came closer, they noticed weapons in the hands of the human blockade. Derek immediately reached behind and grabbed his hunting knife and positioned it in front of himself for the oncoming assault. He put his hand out, warding Michelle, and she cautiously stayed behind him. At first, no one seemed ready to advance on one another until another larger soldier joined the ranks of those blocking their escape.

The new soldier towered over the other dark shapes, and Derek noticed the man was about seven feet tall. The other soldiers parted, allowing the larger soldier to make his way toward Derek and Michelle. As he moved closer, Derek caught sight of his face and was repulsed. Even in the dim light, he could make out reptilian features, and the creature's fangs shone in the dark. The soldier's build was substantial and would be a tough opponent, but he moved forward anyway.

The large soldier stopped a few feet from Derek, letting him see his prowess in the near darkness. The creature's eyes glowed in the dark and again, the fangs threatened to grow larger with each step forward. At seven feet, the soldier was quite the specimen as his corded muscles bulged under his uniform. The soldier, seeing Derek's knife, reached behind, pulling forward his own long, dangerous blade. A wicked smile formed on the soldier's face. Both men circled one another, thinking strategy and measuring the other. After a few passes, the larger soldier stopped and pointed his blade directly at Derek.

Stopping in his tracks, Derek looked at the soldier. "Your move, fang face!"

Smiling, the soldier pointed the blade at Derek. "Little man, prepare to meet your doom!"

Derek retorted, "Come and get some!"

The soldier advanced, immediately raising his arms in a two-handed thrust at Derek's head. He dodged the knife and turned to the side, quickly using the soldier's momentum against him, and kicked him in the back, causing the man to stumble and fall. With resounding speed, the man was up with a more calculated assault. This pass, he turned the blade so it was against his forearm, and used it as an extension of the forearm itself. He dove inside to slice Derek quickly, moving to one side while doing so. Derek met the slice across his stomach, blocking it and coming up with a thrust of his own.

Both men backed away from one another to regroup, each trying to gain an advantage. Derek quickly thought to himself that for a large man, the soldier was lightning quick and extremely strong. His adversary thought much the same and was surprised by the strength Derek possessed. They quickly reengaged and hacked away at one another for the next few minutes until one of the other soldiers near the back took a swipe at Derek with a knife of their own, causing a wound to the back of Derek's leg.

The reptilian soldier saw this and went into a rage. He leapt over Derek and shoved his knife from underneath directly into the man's skull who interfered with the fight. The soldier, with a surprised look on his face, slumped as the reptilian soldier yanked his knife out of the man's skull. He quickly turned and faced Derek who, despite the cut on the back of his leg, stood ready to continue the battle. Again, the large soldier dodged forward in the hopes of catching Derek off guard. Derek calmly dodged and weaved between the thrusts and hacks.

Minutes passed with no clear victor, but Derek's leg hampered him as he couldn't stop the bleeding. He felt the moisture of his own blood leaking down his damaged leg. He saw nothing in the darkness but the flash of steel and the glowing of the creature's eyes. Once again, they broke from the assault and looked at one another.

The large soldier spoke, "It's a shame I still have to kill you! You're by far the greatest warrior I've faced. You're honorable and fight with bravery and conviction. My orders are clear, you aren't to be left alive! Now, the lady, well, I can do with her what I wish!"

At that last remark Derek could only see red and swiftly drove the shaft of his blade upward at blazing speed and pierced the man's chin with the blade going directly into his brain. The reptilian creature stood convulsing for a moment until Derek pulled the blade out. Sliding to the ground the large soldier slumped and fell to the ground in a heap. Despite gasps of surprise from the surrounding soldiers, they didn't take long to move in around Derek.

As the soldiers surrounded him, Derek heard a high-pitched vibration. He quickly glanced back over at Michelle to see her eyes dancing with electricity and the rod in her hand. She strode forward, holding up her hand to stop the soldiers from their advance. At first, the soldiers, seeing her eyes, stopped and didn't know what to do until one brave soldier stepped forward to intercept her. He was quickly repulsed by some unseen force and flew backwards into a brick wall.

Once again, the other soldiers stopped, unsure of themselves seeing their fallen comrades.

Michelle took charge and continued her own advance standing within a foot of the first few soldiers. They cautiously stood their ground but still knew not how to proceed. Michelle saw her window and sent another soldier flying with ease. The soldiers grew angry at the treatment of their fellow soldiers, and they came at Michelle at full speed. She held up her hand and stopped the men in their tracks. This time, however, the soldiers seemed paralyzed.

Michelle came within a few inches of one of the frozen soldiers. "This will stop now! You have no power over us, and we will be leaving. Now, you can choose to walk away under your own power, or I can leave you here in stasis for someone to find later. What shall it be?"

She waved her hand, allowing them to speak, "Well?"

One of the more brazen soldiers spat out, "We will do nothing for you, witch!"

"Witch, that, sir, cannot be further from the truth. No, I'm no witch. I'm a knight, and I use powers granted to me by the universe to defend it against evil scum such as yourselves. One more chance, gentlemen!"

In unison, they all called together, "Go to Hell!"

Michelle shook her head. "Have it your way, gentlemen. I will say this, however. I know each of you now and if ever I see you again, I will kill you!"

Again, she waved her hand, and they returned to their paralyzed state. She motioned Derek to follow as she walked right by the frozen soldiers. He limped slightly as the cut on his leg burned, and he felt fatigue set in from the loss of blood. This didn't go unnoticed by Michelle who stayed back to help, but Derek waved her on. The two walked out of the alley and saw one of the soldier's vehicles standing ready for use. Without another word, they got in the vehicle and turned toward their destination.

As they came closer to the docks, Derek suggested they pull off the road as to not drive right into the dock. Michelle did as instruct, and they walked the rest of the way winding their way through old pallets, machinery, and debris. They came within sight of their waiting vessel, but Michelle held Derek's arm telling him to wait. Peering out from behind their secure spot behind some old oil drums they couldn't see anything wrong, but they had a distinct feeling of dread. Derek looked at his watch and nodded to himself as he knew dawn would be here in a matter of moments. They decided to wait until light to see what lie in store for them.

CHAPTER SIXTEEN

Holly, bloodied and exhausted, leaned heavily on General Giles, watching the huge wave of enemies coming straight for them with murder in their eyes. Holly straightened herself and pushed away from the general to face the threat as the general himself held his sword upright to cut down the first soldier who swung a weapon his way. He quickly glanced around to see if the commander stayed to lead the battle. Through the building smoke, he saw his own troops rallying around him, but the commander was no were to be seen.

A familiar sight did greet his squinted eyes, that of the dreaded Colonel Whilhelm. The colonel's stoic gaze held fast as he moved toward the breached gate. He immediately saw the general and with a smirk, he ran forward to intercept the Nazi leader. Covering the space quickly, the general ran right by the colonel, swinging his sword to the side in the hopes to hit a swift cut to the colonel's side. The veteran Nazi countered with a sword drop of his own and spun to swing his blade up toward the general's face. Ryan moved his head back quickly nearly losing his balance, only to see the blade coming at him again from the side.

With a swift spin, he avoided the strike and gathered himself for a counterattack. The combatants circled one another, trying to determine strategy and weakness. Both warriors were well versed in each other's style of fighting and knew the winner would need something special to break the stalemate. General Giles could wait no longer and raised his sword above his head, while running forward in hopes of delivering a death blow. At first, the colonel looked befuddled but warded the blow, barely falling to one knee in the process. Ryan jumped up, swinging his blade down again at the head of his enemy. This time, the blade got through, coming down on the colonel's ear, slicing it clean off.

Screaming in anger and pain, the colonel popped up, not even grabbing his bleeding head, facing the general with eyes red with rage. As if taken by madness, the colonel launched a barrage of moves and strikes the likes the general never faced before. As skilled as the general was, the blows took their toll, even though none hit their mark. The general took a knee and saw the blade swinging toward his head just in time to fall to the ground and roll away from his enemy.

As he prepared to push himself up, he saw a glint of steel coming again toward his head and lifted his own blade to block the weapon. He swung his leg around, causing his body to rise just in time to block another blow, but this time the advancing blade slid through his defense, nicking his arm. Though not a large or deep wound, the reality of the commitment of his enemy doubled his resolve to dispatch the Nazi. Blood gushed down the German's face, making a horrific sight along with his red eyes. The general just shook his head and advanced.

Again, both men met each other with a few different parries and thrusts with the blades, only to have no movement in who might win the battle. In the back of the general's mind, he knew the German soldier couldn't continue much longer as blood oozed down his face, making the front of his shirt soaked in his own blood. The general decided to end this game and reengaged the enemy with renewed purpose. As the general anticipated, the colonel's reflexes slowed slightly. He spun one way, only to spin back the other, catching the Nazi off guard, and he felt the blade slice into his enemy's side.

Colonel Whilhelm backed away, grabbing his side, looking in disbelief at the Zarillion general. Lifting his hand away from his damaged side, he saw his own blood and looked at the general with even more loathing. He went to lift his blade, only to stop mid-strike as the pain in his side wrenched the blade back down. Quickly switching hands with his blade, he again advanced on the general. Ryan knew there would be no surrender or quarter given in this situation and rose to finish his nemesis. He ran forward to strike, only to see out of the corner of his eye Holly walking to the middle of the doorway.

He ducked the swing from the Nazi and countered with a thrust straight in front of him. The colonel blocked the shot, only to have the blade slide off to the side rather than a square chest shot. Again, the already slick blade found the colonel's flesh. A scream of anguish came from the German as the blade ran through his already damaged side. Pain shot through his body as the general pulled his blade out and turned to finish him.

Through blood-filled eyes and blood oozing out of his mouth, he sat up to face his end, only to see the general flying away from him. Images around him were blurry, and he could barely make out the imposing shape of the commander making his way toward him. He tried desperately to say something, but his mouth was filled with blood, and the words came out in a gurgle. The images grew darker, and he felt his body start to go. As he was about to pass out, he felt large hands lift him up, and he saw the angry face of the commander looking down at him as darkness took him.

As he pulled the blade from the colonel's side, he swung it up for the death blow, only to feel a force slam into his own side, sending him flying. He controlled his landing, slightly rolling onto his side while popping up to face this new threat. Feet planted firmly apart, he peered through the mounting smoke to see the large form of the commander walking away from him with the body of a soldier in his arms. In an instant, he ran to meet the commander, only to see Holly stand between the two with her hand up.

She looked at the general. "Ryan, we cannot hold this gate, but if we don't do something, the city will be quickly overrun!"

The general scanned the battlefield, only to see the reality of Holly's statement. All around them, the battle raged, and the general's defenses took heavy losses, being beaten back. He looked out into the dimming light of the outside world to see waves of enemy soldiers heading their way. All his planning and training of his troops came down to betrayal of one of his own. He looked to Holly who nodded and walked forward, standing in the middle of the doorway. Enemies all around her fell to ash as she moved to position, and she knelt on one knee with both hands touching the ground.

At first, the general thought about joining her until he saw the first soldiers turned to ash, and he backed up to make sure no one came at her from this direction. He looked at Holly as she glanced to the sky as if calling someone's name. Power gathered all around her, and more enemies came for her, only to be disintegrated as they approached. Even from his distance from his beloved, he felt the heat of the power surrounding her and shielded his own face and eyes.

The wave of released energy pulsed outward, lashing out at the advancing army was devastating. The blast worked its way out onto the frozen landscape, destroying everything in its path for a radius of quarter mile. Although the energy was sent outward, the backlash still sent the general flying backwards into several other soldiers. He pushed himself just in time to see Holly collapse. Running, he slid to the ground to reach his beloved.

Holding her limp head in his hands, he called to her, "Holly, my love, you have to wake! We must go!"

No movement came from Holly, but he could tell she was still breathing. He lifted her onto his shoulder to carry her away. Before turning to go, he beheld the destruction his loved one unleashed on the world. Everything within view was either dead or blasted into nothingness. The once-bright, clean snow and ice were a mixture of blood spray along with scorched earth. To behold this scene of destruction gave him a chill up his spine as he looked down at the woman he loved, realizing for the first time how dangerous this precious creature was.

Sweeping Holly up into his arms, he leaned her gently against his chest and moved swiftly away from the destroyed gate. Ryan knew within minutes, reinforcements would arrive and continue the onslaught toward his home. Looking over his shoulder, he couldn't believe the devastation around him. Without another thought, he broke into a trot, cradling his love close as he swiftly made his way through the maze of natural rock tunnels. With the gate destroyed, the enemy would soon swarm all over these tunnels. The general quickened his pace and used little-known paths to reach the council chambers ahead of the enemy.

Bursting through the hidden chamber door, he came to a complete halt as the gruesome sight of slain guards and council members alike. The Zarillion general placed his beloved carefully on the ground, hidden behind a large column, and slid his sword from its scabbard. The metallic ring echoed in the seemingly empty council chamber. With trained eyes, he scanned the chamber as he inched forward, turning this and that way as to not be taken by a hidden enemy. He saw Andrew face down on the ground in a pool of his own blood, unmoving. As far as the general saw, the entire council was dead.

General Giles moved into the main hall of the chamber with his sword out in front of him, ready to meet any unknown challenger. Turning slightly, he brought the sword back with one hand in a striking pose, leaving his free hand to ward off an attack. His eyes grew wide as he took in the figure seated in Andrew's council seat. Ragged, covered in blood, and haggard sat a smirking Michael. Even more shocking to see was the prone figure of Helena Beals with a leash attached to her neck being held by Michael.

The wraithlike creature in the chair cackled. "Well met, General Giles. I see you noticed my handiwork. Don't worry, you and Holly will soon follow your fellow council members to their graves. My plans are flawless and while you were so worried about the outside world, now your own home is in shambles."

Ryan placed his large sword point down onto the marble floor, leaning both hands on the pommel. He then looked up at Michael with venom in his eyes. Seething, searching for the words, he straightened himself and glared at the former council member turned traitor. Rage burned within his body, but his military training came through, and he calmed his inner storm. Composing himself, he closed his eyes momentarily and focused his eyes on his enemy. When his eyes opened, he saw the smirking Michael and the traitor alone.

Still leaning on his sword, he spoke, "Well, Michael, I knew you were capable of dangerous things, but I never imagined you would slaughter your own friends and people!"

The tattered figure sprang from the chair, yanking on the chain around Helena, forcing her to fall over. Looking down, he yanked again, causing Helena to turn herself over. Helena looked at the general and nodded. The general knew Helena might not live through this and nodded an okay to him to do what he must. Michael now moved down the steps toward the general, practically dragging an injured Helena behind him. The already weak council member fell to her knees and caught herself with her hands.

Without moving, the general continued his vigil, leaning on his sword and waiting for this scourge to make a mistake. He watched as Michael stopped within a few feet of the general. Still not moving a muscle, he looked the figure up and down. Although much of the blood covering Michael was others, the general found multiple wounds, causing pain to the former council member. Although unhinged, the general noticed winces of pain as he moved.

Michael now stood within grasp and spat, "You arrogant jackass! Look around you! Your pompous nature caused this tragedy. I warned you all what was coming. I constantly told you we couldn't turn back the tide. Now, this is all on your heads. Your precious society is in ruins, and the humans will soon follow suit. If only you chose us over them, we would still be the ultimate power in the universe!"

The general barked, "You fool! You're so power hungry, you chose evil over your own people. You tell me to look around me but look yourself. These people were your friends and countrymen. You slaughtered countless innocent people today, all for what? What did the reptiles promise you, power? You do realize that they share power with no one, including among themselves."

Michael retorted, "Power, ha! I have plenty of power, much more than any of you ever knew of. Well, Helena's daughter knew. Where is my little beauty? Now that I have her mother in tow, I'm sure you will produce her right away. We have much to discuss, the young lady and I. If she wants her mother back in one piece, she will become my wife. When she produces an heir for me, I may let her go. That is minus her power."

Ryan shook his head. "You truly are delusional. Honestly, Michael, as smart as you claim to be and yet you know not who Rebecca really is, do you? Trust me, if you survive the day, I'll let Rebecca have you, and you will wish I took your life!"

Michael looked uncertain. "Rebecca is just a young girl! She has no power over me!"

Laughter filled the room from the general. "You really are an idiot! Rebecca is the most powerful being this universe has ever seen! When she gets a hold of you, I don't even want to know what she will do to you."

Michael took a step back. "Her power is untapped and raw! She doesn't know how to control it, and it will be her undoing. No, General, she won't survive long enough to come for me."

With a wide smile, the general growled, "She won't be alone, you ass! You cannot fight fate. Peter and Rebecca were ordained by the universe! Their power will sweep this planet and many others, bringing peace and prosperity."

"You hold much faith in destiny, Ryan! The thing about destiny is that one wrong move or turn, and everything changes. The two have yet to meet and trust me, their meeting will never take place!"

Michael faced the general, focused on the defender of the realm; he didn't notice Helena now behind him with chain in hand. Without a sound, she flicked the chain over Michael's neck and yanked as hard as she could. Michael, caught completely off guard, tried to turn, only to have the chain constrict even more. He went to one knee as he tried to reach the chain and yank it away from Helena. She moved to the side and kept away from the crouching figure. The air dissipated, and he reached for his neck in hopes of releasing the chain.

General Giles, now on the move, raced to assist Helena. The struggling figure was now on his knees gasping for air and with fear in his eyes, knew he would be finished. Ryan now stood with his sword ready to strike the viper struggling on the ground. Helena raised her hand to stop him. She looked at the general, and he knew she wanted to interrogate the man herself. His death should be swift, and it would rid the world of a great evil, but Helena was right to question him. They knew little of the enemy's actual plans and how much damage Michael really caused.

With eyes bugging out of his head, the general watched as Michael's face turned blue. The general eyed Helena, but she kept the pressure on the chain until Michael's eyes rolled into the back of his head, and he lost consciousness. The limp body fell to the floor, and Helena released the chain and immediately knelt by the body. She motioned the general to get the collar from her neck. The general complied, and she put a hand on Michael's head, bringing him back to life. Breath came back into his lungs, but Helena now controlled his mind and caused him to go into a trance-induced sleep.

She turned and put the collar onto Michael's neck and used the loose chain to bind his hands. Helena touched his forehead and commanded him to walk. Michael, now completely under Helena's control, moved forward as the general moved to her side, and she led both men out of the destroyed council chamber. General Giles scooped up the still-limp Holly and followed Helena. Moving to the left side of the chamber, she brought both men to a sarcophagus in the corner, which looked to house some long-dead council members. Helena reached out and touched the head of the pommel of the stone figure's sword, pressing down. With a click, the huge stone coffin moved to the side to reveal a set of stairs leading downward.

The woman led the two men down into the dark stairs. Once on the bottom of the stairs, she turned to a symbol on the wall and placed her hand until the symbol glowed, causing the coffin to cover the hole above them and leaving them in complete darkness. General Giles still held his sword out in front, waiting for any intrusion. Suddenly, he saw a glow some two feet from him. One by one, globes on the wall lit up until the entire corridor shone in an eerie light.

He looked down the corridor to see many places of burial. As many years of service as he was a part of the council, he never once remembered this place. Cut into the walls were places with the bones of long-dead people, and the tunnel seemed to go on forever. Helena alerted him to the fact their enemies couldn't sense them here, and this place was powerfully warded against intrusion. A blast of air rushed around them, and the general felt as if a force were testing him with each step forward.

Helena led them forward with steel determination and wouldn't be daunted by the presence of death surrounding them. The general, a veteran of countless military incursions and used to death, still felt uneasy walking forward. Michael now looked as though he were a zombie in the eerie light. Moving at a steady pace, they passed grave after grave, and the general marveled at the size of the catacombs. They finally entered a massive cavern. Ryan saw the stone coffins everywhere. He let his eyes take in the huge burial ground, and his eyes fell upon the memorial in the middle. To his eyes, the memorial looked like a small castle.

He stopped and reached out to touch Helena's arm. She stopped for a moment and looked at Holly, touching her forehead. Closing her eyes, she winced with pain for a moment, but Holly's eyes opened. Ryan still held her tight, but Holly sat up and tried to reach the ground. Carefully, the general set her on her feet and waited for her to be sure enough to stand. Helena said Holly was still very weak from using so much power, but she wasn't in any danger.

Holly looked into Helena's eyes. "Helena, why have you brought us to the burial ground of our ancestors?"

Helena responded, "My dear Holly, our home has fallen, and we'll need all the help we can get to stem the tide of the evil that's to come!"

CHAPTER SEVENTEEN

Rebecca held her breath as she pulled herself through the energy field, separating the chancellor's realm from the reptilians. She felt the electrical charges flowing through her body, causing her fingers to tingle as she entered the damp awaiting cavern. Looking over her shoulder, she saw Grace appear out of nowhere as she too squeezed through the protective field. For good measure, she tried to push back into the Atlantian Kingdom but was repelled by an electrical shock. The chancellor warned Rebecca this was a one-way trip and if she were ever to see her again, it would be through the water entrance.

Crouching low and using her hands to guide her down the steep embankment, Rebecca kept her head up and listened intently for any signs of life. Her heartbeat slowed as she heard only the dripping of water coming from above their heads. Though dark, there still was some residual light coming from a tunnel leading away from the cavern. Grace kept close to Rebecca but seemed comfortable with allowing her to lead the way. The two continued along the outer edge of the cavern, making their way toward the lighted tunnel but still heard no signs of life.

She stopped at the mouth of the tunnel and peered out, taking in the expanse of the cavern that was visible to her. The thought of her mortal enemies being this close to another free people disgusted her, yet she quelled the rage building in her to focus on the task at hand. Reaching around behind her, she grabbed Grace's hand and pulled her forward into the dimly lit tunnel. Grace let herself be cautiously led while still looking behind them to be sure they weren't being followed.

Rebecca continued forward and when she saw no one in sight, she grew bolder and quickened their pace. Each step caused the echo in the tunnel to sound ominous and still, they saw nothing but rock and a few dim globes on the walls. The tunnel seemed never ending and wound around a few corners until they saw signs of civilization. Walls once hewn rock were now made of cement bricks, and the globes were much brighter. She flung herself against the wall to let her eyes become used to the newfound light. After blinking for a few moments, her eyes identified the changes to the environment.

Both women stood against the wall, looking to each other for their next move. Rebecca's heart raced, and she thought this was justice for the reptilian people invading her home. She would make them pay dearly for their intrusion. Despite her confidence, Grace couldn't help but wonder if they bit off more than they could chew with this adventure. The chancellor didn't offer any assistance in the way of military or otherwise.

Sensing Grace's uncertainty, Rebecca looked at her and offered a confident smile before moving forward. The lights made travel much easier, and the rough cement tunnel soon gave way to a more finished, well-painted, and lit hospital-style hallway. The floor now became smoothly polished tile, and the ladies noticed doorways on either side as they continued their journey. All remained quiet as they strode forward. Grace peered into a few of the rooms, only to see empty furniture and tables. It appeared to Grace that this was a newly formed area and was yet to be inhabited. Rebecca investigated a few, only to agree with Grace that the owners weren't moved in yet.

As they rounded another corner and peered into an odd-looking room, Grace felt herself being tugged through the doorway. Rebecca practically dragged Grace into the uninhabited room. She walked over to the corner out of view of the doorway and sat to look up at Grace. Grace peered quickly over her shoulder but relented and sat in a chair next to Rebecca. The two looked at one another, trying to decide what the best course of action from here would be at this time.

Rebecca whispered in Grace's direction, "We know nothing of this compound, and we're in enemy territory. This is going to be rather tricky to get out of here!"

Grace laughed. "You think so?"

With a nod, Rebecca began, "The chancellor knew what she was doing when she showed us this entrance! If we're successful in our attempt to find out what the enemy is up to, then great! If we're captured, the chancellor washes her hands of us. In either case, she wins."

Grace's face took a serious look. "You think she actually sent us in here thinking we wouldn't make it?"

It took a moment, but Rebecca responded, "I think she's a very calculated ruler and is used to playing both sides of the fence."

Grace nodded and looked around the room. The office-style furniture looked brand new, and the floor didn't have a mark on it. The sterile look was made worse by the stark-white walls glaring the bright LED lights in their eyes. Even in the hospital, there would be artwork on the walls but here, just the white walls looked back at them. Even the bookshelves looked lonely without volumes taking up their space on the shelves.

Grace took the lead, determined if someone would see anyone, they would see her first then Rebecca. They found themselves moving at a quick pace down the hallway. Doorways passed by, and they didn't stop to examine any. Within the next twenty minutes, the environment changed to an older, more established section of the reptilian's kingdom.

Around the next corner, they found a supply area off to the side and made their way behind the large wooden crates stacked on top of one another. From their dark vantage point, it would be easy to see the comings and goings around them without being discovered. They peered out to see a reptilian soldier walking by taking his turn at watch. He stopped a moment and looked down toward the new hallway but went no further and turned, walking back the way he came. The ladies waited until he was out of sight and crept from their hiding spot to follow the soldier.

Rebecca and Grace kept far enough back to not make any noise or give the soldier any cause to look their way. The farther they moved down the hall though, they knew they would need to make a move to find a way out and report back to General Giles their findings. Grace grabbed her from behind, only to see how close they were to the soldier. They stayed back slightly, allowing the distance between them to increase.

Panic struck Rebecca when she heard multiple voices coming in their direction. Quickly looking around for a place to duck into, she saw a room off to their right. She pushed Grace in front of her as they burst through the door, only to come face to face with a startled reptilian soldier walking in their direction. Grace, quick on her feet, struck the soldier in the face with a metal tray that laid on the table next to her. The impact was devastating as the tray connected with the creature's face, and Rebecca heard bone crunching. The soldier fell to the ground, writhing in pain. He looked up at the ladies, only to have Grace strike him on the side of the head, knocking him out cold.

Rebecca smiled as Grace looked at the tray then Rebecca. Unthinking, she flipped the tray back toward the table, making a terrible clanging noise. Both ladies scrunched up their shoulders, waiting for soldiers coming in from everywhere. To their great surprise, no one came, and they lifted their captive to a sitting position, hoisting him up into a chair.

Grace held up the soldier's head and touched her fingers to his temple. The soldier stirred, blinking his eyes, resembling that of a snake, and glared at the ladies before him with hatred. Unfazed, both women glared back, waiting for the creature to say something. When it was obvious the soldier was trained not to speak, Grace took matters into her own hands. She quickly grabbed the metal tray and, this time from the side, drove it straight down into the serpent's knee.

Again, a howl of pain broke the silence, but the soldier, true to form, spoke not a word as blood trickled down the side of his face from the previous head shot.

A few more strategically placed shots to various body parts yielded the same results. The women were impressed with the soldier's resolve, but they needed information and needed it now. Rebecca felt her anger building inside her and on cue, Grace placed her hand gently on Rebecca's wrist reassuring her that she had the situation under control. Rebecca stood down and let the power go, watching Grace move to the front of the soldier. Grace smirked and reached out with both hands grabbing the creature's head firmly.

The serpent's eyes rolled back into his head as she saw the concentration on her aunt's face. Grace held onto his head for a few minutes before releasing it. The reptilian soldier looked exhausted and leaned heavily forward against his restraints. Grace straightened herself to full height, taking a moment to compose herself, and turned to Rebecca, telling her to follow closely. As Grace left, she picked up the tray and swung it with all her might, hitting the serpent's head. With such force, the neck snapped.

Without a word, Grace placed the tray down on the nearest table and strode from the room with Rebecca in tow. Grace led the way through a maze of hallways, rooms, and caverns to get them to one of the lesser-known gates. Rebecca couldn't help but be amazed as Grace knew every place to hide from the view of suspicious eyes. As they approached the gate, they stepped into a larger cavern full of weapons of all kinds. Though the cavern wasn't huge, it was full to the rafters with things capable of destruction. Grace continued toward the exit, but Rebecca stopped and looked at the weapons with disdain. Grace knew Rebecca couldn't leave the weapons there for soldiers to use on her countrymen. She moved over to the control panel to unlock the gate so they could escape, and a look of panic came over her face as she looked behind Rebecca.

A squad of soldiers entered the cavern, coming to this armory to load up for a mission. They looked at the intruders in surprise but kept their military bearing and ran forward to intercept. Rebecca quickly grabbed energy from around her and released a blast into the heart of the squad, sending them flying in all directions. Soldiers scrambled, landing on the floor and up against the wall. Some were up again to continue the fight, but many didn't have the ability to rise. Rebecca felt her anger build, but this time, she calmed her inner storm and looked at Grace with a wink.

Grace, with the message received, flipped open the control panel and punched in the code as the large door opened. A blast of cold air flew into the cavern as the door reached its apex, revealing another tunnel. As she turned to get Rebecca to follow, she felt her throat constrict, causing her to fall to her knees, grasping at her neck as she tried to breathe. Rebecca saw her aunt go down and looked around to see her assailant. Out of the shadows, she saw the largest Reptilian she had ever seen. He was well over seven feet tall and very muscled. As he came into the light, Rebecca recognized him right away as Commander Zosa.

The commander came into view and cackled. "Well, what do we have here? Now, this is an interesting development. I've been looking for you, Rebecca, and here you are, delivering yourself to me. How very accommodating of you!"

Rebecca allowed energy to build within herself yet keeping herself calm. The commander couldn't sense any aggression, so he moved forward, thinking the young lady feared him. She let him keep coming as the energy threatened to tear her apart. With a wide smile, she looked up at the commander as he was now a few feet from her with a smile of his own.

Rebecca kept the smile on her face as she spoke, "Commander, you invaded my home so I thought I would return the favor!"

The commander sneered. "All by yourself?"

Rebecca again smiled. "You don't think I'm enough? Well, let us just see about that, shall we?"

She raised her hand in front of her and allowed a small amount of the energy to blast into the soldiers leftover from the attacking squad. This time, not one soldier made it back to their feet. The commander looked around at his fallen soldiers unimpressed and turned again to the young lady with a sneer. This time, he raised his own hand and squeezed his fist together, causing Grace to fall to her knees, struggling to breathe.

Rebecca remained calm and allowed another stronger blast of energy to soar toward the commander. The commander easily moved his arm and deflected the blast sending it into the wall next to hit sending chips of rock flying behind him. Although it didn't harm him, he did have to let go of Grace to protect himself. Grace struggled to her feet and scrambled out the door into the tunnel. A few more blasts Rebecca sent at the commander, only to have them continually deflected.

Each time the commander sent the blast into the rock caused a great deal of damage. This gave Rebecca a wonderfully devious plan to stop the commander. This time, she grabbed even more energy and blasted the rock face next to him, causing rock shards to blast away from the wall catching the commander off guard. The shards entered the reptilian's hard skin, causing great gashes, and the commander recoiled in pain. He turned to see the still smiling young woman looking proud of herself.

He gathered power of his own to release into Rebecca to finish her once and for all but could hear his advisors screaming in his head that she must be taken alive. This nearly cost him his life as another blast caught him in the chest unaware, causing him to sail into the rock wall with great impact. Dazed, the commander struggled to his feet. In his long career, he couldn't remember ever being bested by any of Rebecca's ancestors, but this young woman showed great resolve. Standing to his full height, he now let the anger inside him build for a death strike. He wouldn't leave this upstart to finish him off.

As he was about to unleash his own energy, he felt a wave of heat building all around him. Usually heat wouldn't bother him, but he looked around at all the flammable weaponry around him and knew exactly what the woman was doing. Without another thought, he turned and ran back toward the tunnel at the back of the cavern. He felt the building heat almost overwhelm him as he tried to get to the tunnel.

Rebecca still maintained her composure and took in as much energy as she could hold onto safely. As the commander made his way back to his feet, she was ready. She watched as the commander felt the heat around him build. Emanating wave after wave of vibrations causing immense heat, Rebecca sent it out in a semi-circle in front of her. When the commander figured out what was going on, she couldn't help but laugh to herself. She knew he was too late, and she thanked her aunt inwardly for teaching her control.

Now, the weapons, caches, and vehicles glowed with such heat building in the cavern. She didn't need to set off the whole cavern, but she knew the front needed to go first. With a nice backward pace, she neared the gate. With a push of a button, she started closing the gate. As the gate was about to close all the way, she sent one last blast of energy to ignite the already heated weapons. The effect was devastating. The entire cavern blew up in one large fireball, sending flames shooting in all directions down all the tunnels like a flame thrower. Nothing in its wake survived.

Rebecca ran to catch up to Grace but stopped momentarily and stated, "That's for my city!"

CHAPTER EIGHTEEN

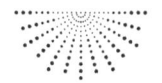

Sword still in hand, Peter looked the blade up and down, taking in the scrollwork along the blade. He looked at the craftsmanship of the pommel and hilt with admiration. Though the power no longer flowed through his body from the blade, he still felt the residual energy in his fingertips. Gripping the hilt a little tighter, he reached over with his free hand and grasped the sword in two hands as if awaiting an unseen attack. As he faced his mirror image, the figure smiled to see the boy handling the sword properly.

The kingly figure glowing with light now turned dark and a sword appeared in his own hand. Without another word, he glared at Peter and attacked, raising the sword over his head and arcing it down upon the unsuspecting young man. Peter, though not a seasoned warrior, knew enough to dodge the strike and spin to one side with his own blade ready to deflect another blow. A blow that came swiftly and this time from the side. The king now swung the blade to the side in hopes of landing a strike to Peter's unprotected ribs. Instinctively, Peter blocked the sweeping blade and felt a rage of his own building.

Again, a warmth built in his arms, and the blade glowed a white light. Peter, feeling the power grow in him, wanted to flail at his attacker, but something in his mind told him to calm his emotions. He took a breath, brought his blade back in front of him and refocused his attack. This time, he was the aggressor, but he calculated his movements and strikes. He wasn't hacking away at a tree here but facing a skilled warrior. Peter brought his blade around in a sweeping motion and coming over his right shoulder, headed for his opponent.

The king warded the blow and swept his own blade quickly upward to try to catch Peter off guard. Again, Peter smartly deflected the blow and spun to deliver another of his own. Power flowing directly from his body to the blade made it feel a part of himself, and the weight of the blade felt minimal. He swung with power and fluid motions, matching blow for blow with the experienced King. Peter, surprised by his success, decided to turn up the pressure and launched a series of quick blows to catch his opponent off guard.

Again, the king had little difficulty meeting each blow with a counter of his own, but Peter felt his strength waning. He backed off a moment to catch his breath, and the king took advantage of this lapse, attacking Peter anew. The king moved much more quickly than Peter expected, and he jumped out of the way to avoid a fast blade making for his head. Landing on the ground, he turned quickly on his back, only to see the king's blade coming straight down on his head. Peter moved his blade to deflect the death blow and was successful, seeing the king's blade hit the rocky ground near his head.

He rolled quickly thrusting himself up to his feet, only to have his legs swept out from under him by the king. His blade came loose from his grip and landed with a crisp clang on the ground. Before he could grab it, the king, in one fluid motion, grabbed the fallen blade and now faced Peter with two blades. Again, without a word, he attacked the unarmed boy with full force. Peter darted out of the way and frantically searched the area for anything that might resemble a weapon. Finding nothing, he ran behind a nearby tree for some protection. He peered around the tree to locate his attacker and saw nothing. Carefully moving to the other side of the tree, he looked out to see the king coming for him.

Without thinking, he jumped up and grabbed one of the low-lying branches, pulling himself up into the tree. He scrambled up the tree away from the spinning blades of the attacking king. Once safely nestled in the crux of some of the larger branches, he peered down to assess his current situation. He barely saw the blade whistling past his face and sticking into the branch next to him. Peter's emotions took hold, and rage filled his body. Pointing at the king, he let the flow of energy release and sent it into the body of the king.

Seeing the energy come his way, the king dove out of the way. He landed on the ground but still held onto his own blade. Standing, he brushed himself off and calmly smiled up at the furious Peter. Looking down at Peter's blade, he held it upwards toward Peter, indicating it was safe to come down.

Peter climbed cautiously down the smooth bark of the tree until his feet were safely planted on the ground. He moved within a few feet of the king and picked up the blade he tossed down after prying it from the tree branch. Walking to the king, he handed the blade back to him. With a nod, he graciously accepted it back and handed Peter's blade back to him as well.

The blade felt good in his hand as if it were one with his arm and again, the weight felt minimal. He let the blade swing and arc through the air a few times to see it was truly his blade. When satisfied it was the true blade, he returned it to the scabbard and turned to the king for criticism. Instead, the king stood smiling with pride. Peter didn't know what to do next. He sheepishly looked at the king for guidance.

Having pity on Peter the king returned his own blade to its scabbard and motioned for Peter to follow. He did as he was told and followed the king out of the clearing. Within a few minutes, they arrived at another clearing with freshly mown grass and what looked to be a circle in the middle made of ornately carved wooden logs. He pointed for Peter to have a seat and sat himself on one of the logs. Facing one another, they sat, not knowing where to begin the conversation. A smile came back to the king's face, and he sat tall, looking at his student with pride.

Peter looked around the clearing to gain some knowledge of where they might be located. This entire realm remained foreign to him and made him uncomfortable. The inside of the clearing was lit by some unnatural means and as he tried to peer into the woods beyond, they seemed basked in darkness. He bent his head slightly up to view the ceiling of what he assumed to be a large cavern. To his great surprise, the ceiling resembled a night sky. A slight move to the edge of his log gave him a better view of the would-be starry sky. He was mesmerized by the twinkling stars above him.

Taking a moment to focus on the stars above he quickly identified many of the constellations within sight. Peter remained intent on the stars above and didn't hear the king speaking to him. His attention became drawn by the Orion constellation. A feeling of attraction took hold of his body, and he felt a strong tug as he felt himself being lifted toward the constellation. Suddenly around him, the world turned into a swirling mass of lights wrapping around him in a tunnel like structure. He felt himself moving at high speeds as the lights moved swiftly by him. Immediately the lights stopped, and Peter found himself seated on carved logs. Peter looked around, only to see the king was no longer seated with him, and the clearing was gone. In its place stood a large stone courtyard with the same carved logs for seats in a circle.

Jumping to his feet he whirled around to gain his bearings. At first, in the dim light he could only see the faint outline of the stone courtyard. After a few moments, his eyes made out more details of his surroundings, and he was in the middle of a stone compound. His eyes now used to the light, he moved around the courtyard to find signs of life. Silence surrounded him, and he heard only his footsteps echoing on the stones as he moved forward.

Peter felt an icy breeze on his neck and turned to see the cause of the blast. Face to face with a set of ice-cold blue eyes coming from the darkness. He backed up several steps to get a better look at this intruder. The outline of a large, humanlike creature now took form while the blue eyes grew in strength. Fear gripped him, but he couldn't look away from the icy stare. Every muscle in his body cried out to run, but he couldn't get his form to move.

The figure walked forward, emerging from the shadows to reveal his true form. Taller than Peter but other than his height, he didn't look all that different from the human before him. Eyes blazing blue, he stared at Peter but said not a word as he moved forward. When within a few feet of Peter, the strange man stopped and took in the young man before him. Then a very strange thing happened as the man slid a sword from a hidden scabbard and pointed it to the ground, holding the hilt. Without another word, the warrior took a knee and bowed his head in reverence before Peter. Peter knew not what to do and stood unmoving.

A few moments passed before the warrior raised his head slightly and could tell Peter was confused by the unfolding events. He spoke first, "My liege, I'm known as Andre Edgeworld, and I'm your Warden of the Cosmos."

Peter shook his head, trying to wake his mind from the current dream with little success as the figure stood before him. With another swift move, he returned the blade to its hiding place and walked closer to Peter. He reached his hand out to the confused, young man. Before he knew what he was doing, young Sullivan took the arm of the warrior in his and shook. With a little smile, the warrior released and backed away slightly.

He looked to Peter. "My Lord, what's thy bidding?"

Peter responded, "The king is training me, and I assume this is part of the training. However, I have little clue as to where I am or what I should be doing."

A look of sympathy came over the warrior's face. "My Lord, we rarely see our destiny before us until it reveals itself. Know this, you're descended from a long line of remarkable people, and you will do great things yourself. My family serves your family as it has for time out of memory, and I'll be your Warden, if you'll have me?"

"Andre, I can use all the help I can get! Certainly, you could find a more qualified person than myself to be warden for, however. I'm just a young man trying to figure out where I fit in this large universe."

The warrior stood tall. "That, My Lord, is exactly why you're the one! You always look to the benefit of others rather than yourself. No, sir, you will be the one who will put the universe back together."

Peter looked shocked. "Put the universe back together? Andre, I cannot even do my homework right! How am I to lead or help others?"

Andre led the young man back to the logs and sat with him. "My Lord, even the most powerful entities must begin somewhere. Yes, you're a student, but it won't be long before you're the master, teaching others to follow."

He couldn't breath as he listened to Andre speak of becoming a master, a leader, and a student. Not long ago, he hoped not to get beat up on the way to school. Jake came to mind as he sat there alone. His friend was always by his side but here he was facing this unsettling task alone. The thought of doing this without Jake didn't sit well with Peter and began feel anger build inside. Trying to quell the anger he looked at his warden.

He began, "Andre, what exactly is your position and how can you be of service?"

The large warrior came to attention and saluted Peter. "My Lord, I'm the keeper of the keys of travel for the universe. Long ago, it was determined that travel needed to be monitored. Too many abused the ability to travel so freely, causing much damage to worlds, peoples, and time. I am but one of a legion of soldiers whose duty it is to keep the travel lanes clear and safe."

Peter sat up. "Andre, this is all so much to take in, but I think I understand. My grandfather used to tell me all kinds of stories about Earth's astronauts and their exploits. Who knew they were all part of a much larger group of travelers?"

Andre smiled. "My Lord, the universe is indeed quite large and its travelers many but believe it or not, science makes it possible to travel quickly and safely over those long distances. You, sir, are now all the way across your own galaxy. The king summoned me and asked me to visit with you. I'll be here any time you have need of me. When you need my assistance, touch the sword or medallion and call my name."

Peter nodded and stood. "Andre, are the reptilian people as dangerous as everyone thinks?"

A serious look came over the warrior's face. "My Lord, those creatures are the cause of most of the ills in the entire universe. They need to be stopped once and for all! My time with you is short right now, but I assure you I'll be instrumental in your work, bringing these evil beings to justice!"

Peter felt energy building around him, and the warrior took his sword out and held it over his head. A blaze of lightning struck the blade and deflected it into a swirling blend of light and sparks, creating a portal before Peter. He peered into the tunnel-like entrance and remembered traveling here. This was much the same type of tunnel he arrived here in and moved toward the entrance.

He looked to Andre. "When will I see you again?"

The warrior bowed low. "My liege, you will see me very soon! Events on Earth have triggered a chain reaction across the universe. The reptilian people are now free, and their remaining people and allies around the universe have been called to action! Sir, we will be busy very soon!"

Peter nodded. "Thank you for your service, Andre! I'm sure the way is safe with you at the helm. I'm counting on you to keep us all safe!"

Andre saluted. "My Lord, it shall be as you wish! I'll keep the way safe! Until you return, safe travels."

Peter saluted back and walked into the portal. He felt the energy around him engulf him and shoot him through space. Though he heard nothing, he felt the flow of energy and air around him as he traveled home. Within moments, he emerged from the tunnel into the clearing where the king stood waiting. He brought Peter to the logs and motioned him to sit. He did as he was instructed, feeling a little light headed and steadied himself on the log.

The king sensed his turmoil. "Yes, my young friend, all this is a lot to take in, that's for sure. Honestly, that's why most aren't told of the mysteries of the universe. They truly cannot handle the knowledge. Most people want to live a simple and peaceful life."

Peter laughed. "Simple and peaceful! That used to describe my life. How different things look today. My King, please tell me Andre can protect the travel ways."

It took a moment, but the king responded, "For the moment,

everything is sound and safe but with the rise of our enemies, who knows for how long. Honestly, that's why you're here and usually, your family would train you with this information over a long time. You, however, need a crash course in how to use your power and your true nature."

He paused and then continued, "Peter, I know you didn't ask for this and if I could pass it on to someone else, I would gladly do that for you. You and you alone can bring the universe back to the balance it requires. Yes, light and dark have always been and will always be but from time to time the balance needs to be reset. This is one of those times where darkness could take hold across the universe while we waited for you to be born."

Peter shook his head. "My King, I'll learn and use my gifts to help as many as I can!"

Again, the king smiled. "As I've said repeatedly, that's why it is you and has always been you!"

CHAPTER NINETEEN

Michelle gasped as their vehicle crested the hill, drawing them to within sight of the destroyed Zarillion gate. Michelle held back tears of rage while she viewed her people's home. She couldn't bring herself to speak but looked at Derek for assistance. Derek brought the vehicle to the side and parked it behind a rock outcropping. He turned to Michelle whose eyes were tearing up. Without thinking, he reached out and drew her in and engulfed her with a tremendous hug. Michelle allowed herself to be hugged but quickly pushed herself upright. The gleam of duty returned to her eyes, and she grabbed her pack, moving for the door. Derek ran behind, grabbing his gear, and followed her lead.

Both gripped the frozen rock and leaned in to look around the free-standing stones. At first, all they saw was the sheer destruction that was once the main gate. As their eyes darted along the landscape, they noticed scorch marks all over what remained of the gate and the surrounding area. Frozen blood covered the entire hill, making the sight extremely grisly. Michelle searched the ground for the dead but noticed someone did the soldiers the honor of clearing the fallen. They searched for any sign of life without success.

Twisted metal and the remains of the once-proud gate laid strewn across the entrance. At a closer look, someone erected a makeshift gate which closed out the frozen air. Michelle turned to Derek and took out a sidearm, putting it in a ready position. Derek followed suit, and the two left the confines of the frozen rocks, walking forward toward the ruined gate. Michelle walked cautiously, looking from one side to another, expecting an ambush. Derek walked close behind her but kept a view of their rear to make sure they weren't attacked from behind.

The closer they came to the gate, the odder they found it no guard or century stopped them. Michelle walked up to the gate, blocking their way, and stopped looking at Derek. He looked up at the gate and though it wasn't near the strength of the original, he felt the energy coming off the surface of the gate itself. Michelle put her hands up near the gate to feel what type of energy blocked their way forward. It took a few moments, but Michelle backed away and turned to Derek, informing him that no one was getting in this way. She further explained that the gate was sealed with a special energy and nothing she knew would open this gate, short of blowing apart the entire hill itself.

Derek sat with his head leaning back on the frozen wall. As a Seal, he was used to things not going exactly to plan. Even with the best intelligence, things didn't always go the way you drew it up. Thinking about their current situation brought a smile to his face. When this journey began, he envisioned himself defending and bringing the boys to this city, but fate stepped in and delivered the unexpected. He looked fondly at Michelle as this adventure reinforced his feelings for Peter's mother. He remained uncertain how Michelle felt about him, but there was something there. Derek was quite certain they kept things simple for the sake of their boys, but it was becoming apparent that might not work for much longer.

Michelle, as if thinking much the same, came over to him and sat beside him, clasping his hand in hers. Derek responded, creeping closer to her, and she leaned her head on his shoulder. Amid destruction, the two held one another, deciding what should be done now.

Exhaustion set in as they worked on no sleep over the past several days, and they nodded off.

They knew not how long they slept, but a sudden rumble of machinery woke them in a panic. Both were on their feet with weapons drawn as they moved to the entrance of the gate but still covered slightly by the natural opening of the original cavern. In the darkness, a vehicle drove toward them. Michelle thought about running to the side, but the vehicle would easily see them darting out from their hiding place.

She tugged at Derek's sleeve and motioned him to be ready to attack. Derek nodded and checked his weapon. The vehicle continued its trek toward their hiding spot with blaring spotlights. It was a lone vehicle so Michelle considered a quick patrol to make sure the gate was secure, but she couldn't take any chances and stayed hidden. With the lights blazing her way, she simply couldn't tell who was driving or to whom the vehicle belonged. They didn't have to wait for long as it drove within a few feet of the gate, and they crept closer into the recess of rock covering them.

A figure appeared from behind the vehicle, and Derek followed him with his eyes, weapon ready. The figure didn't notice them but went straight for the gate with a small hand-held computer, scanning the gate. Michelle didn't wait and released a stream of energy toward the unsuspecting figure. The energy struck the figure, paralyzing him where he stood. The computer still stuck outward, scanning the gate. Michelle and Derek went to determine what they captured.

Michelle, with flashlight in hand, came up on her prey from behind and flashed her light in his eyes so he couldn't see his captors. At first, she said nothing, letting the light seep into the eyes of the frightened man. Derek stayed right behind her out of sight, looking around to see if he was indeed alone. To his great surprise, no one else came in their direction. Michelle moved forward, grabbing the man by the neck and hauling him up in the air. The show of strength caught Derek by surprise. The fact Michelle wasn't a helpless, weak woman was an interesting development. He smiled inwardly, knowing Michelle could handle herself.

When she held the man in the air, she then noticed he wasn't a reptilian, which made her feel better. Quickly placing him back on the ground, she kept her hand on his collar. Though not extremely tall, Michelle was a good-sized, athletic woman and seemed at home intimidating a prisoner. She now pointed the flashlight in such a way she could see the man's face. A frightened young man's face looked back at her, and she calmed her tone slightly.

She still grasped the man harshly. "Talk! What are you doing here?"

The now-shaking man croaked, "I'm on patrol. The gate is sealed, but we've been tasked with making sure the warding and energy field remain intact."

The young man looked as if he ate a fly and stopped talking. Michelle released the man, still holding the light on him as Derek came forward out of the shadows. The man saw the size of Derek and became rigid, expecting to be attacked. This was no soldier they were dealing with. He was a young scientist tasked with the upkeep of the force field, keeping the gate shut.

Standing before the frightened man, she began, "Whom do you serve?"

The man must have thought the question odd because he looked confused but responded, "I serve the council of elders, or I should say what's left of the council."

Michelle felt a bit of panic at this answer. "What are you talking about? Last I checked, Andrew oversaw the council!"

The man perked up. "Yes, ma'am, that was the case, but since the battle, I'm not even sure who's actually in charge of the council."

"Battle, what battle? Come with me and tell me everything! Are you alone?"

He nodded. "Yes, I'm alone. It's not all that complicated. The reptilians finally found a way to break into our fair city, and they destroyed everything!"

Michelle lost her balance and nearly stumbled as Derek caught her. "Son, take us to your leadership now!"

The young man again nodded, and they followed him to his vehicle. At a close look, the all-terrain vehicle was state of the art. Once inside, they sat comfortably in bucket seats, looking out at the frozen night. The young man alerted them to the fact the gate was secure despite several attempts by the reptilians to breach it. He assured them if the field held, no one could get in that way. He also suggested that each entrance was either imploded to block it or warded and fielded such as this. The gates always held so no one on the council thought about upgrading them to energy fields.

Riding comfortably in the vehicle, they warmed themselves while listening to the man tell them everything he knew about the attack on the city. Michelle gave the man a little knowledge about her being a citizen of the city, which made him more comfortable. When the young man finished his tale, Derek and Michelle sat speechless. Derek, in speaking with Peter's grandfather over the years, knew how formidable the reptilians were, but the Zarillion defenses always held. A sad look came over Michelle's eyes again, worrying about the boys.

The man drove them to the top of another hill, only to see him push a button, and the very ground opened before them. They drove down into a hole in the ice, and the door covered them as they descended further. It took about ten minutes for the vehicle to reach its destination many feet below the surface. He made sure the entrance was secure and closed another gate behind him as they entered yet another cavern. When the vehicle stopped, he motioned them to follow him. Michelle grabbed her gear, and Derek followed form, going to her side.

The young man took the lead. Derek noticed a little too late he was doing something with his small computer. As they turned the corner, they were met by a large contingent of soldiers heavily armed. Michelle went to grab the young man who ran down the hall out of her grasp. Surrounded by the weapons, Michelle and Derek knew the drill and offered them their own. The leader came forward and took them into custody by placing them in irons. Michelle smiled but said not a word as the soldier clasped the cuffs around her wrists. Derek looked to her for a cue, but he could see she was comfortable with the situation and decided against a violent course of action.

They were led through various tunnels and hallways until they stood before a huge, ornate, wooden door. Instructed to wait, the prisoners stood before the door, unspeaking. The leader called into his communicator on his wrist and waited. At first, nothing happened but a minute or two passed, and the door cracked open slightly. The soldier spoke in guarded tones into the crack of the door and waited. Again, a few minutes came and went before the door opened entirely. The prisoners were escorted inside.

Derek's eyes grew larger, looking around the marble covered room. It resembled a throne room to him, and he looked in awe at the grandness of the room with each step he took. They were led to a large, circular table with a recognizable starburst pattern in the middle. There were many empty seats available around the table itself, all but one. A tall woman stood to greet them. She looked vibrant with long, flowing, black hair, and her skin had a smooth olive tone.

The woman held up her hand, and the soldiers stopped. With the flick of her wrist, she dismissed the soldiers. The leader remained behind, but the rest quickly exited the chamber. They were left alone with the woman as the soldier went to the other side of the room to grab a drink of water, keeping an eye on his prisoners. Again, the woman looked at Michelle and Derek but left them bound. Michelle almost strode forward but held her tongue. Again, the woman took a moment to look at Michelle and sat.

From her seat at the table, the woman looked up. "I am Nora Beals and currently, it falls to me to be the first councilor."

Michelle sensed sadness in her announcement. "Nora, please tell me where Andrew is."

Nora stood and looked at Michelle. "How does a human know about Andrew?"

Michelle walked forward and broke the bonds, placing her hands on the table, glaring at Nora. "I'm not human, and I too am a member of this council, though I've never sat at this table! I am Michelle Sullivan, Knight of the Cosmos and daughter of Jerry Sullivan. My son is Peter Sullivan!"

Nora's face looked ghostly white. "Michelle?"

CHAPTER TWENTY

Shooting pain in his head brought him awake. Unsure of his whereabouts, the commander painfully opened his eyes to look at his surroundings. Though his vision was blurry, he could make out the rock ceiling above him. He tried to turn but a blinding pain shot through his left side. With his head back down on the ground, he cursed himself for being in the current situation. Carefully, he tilted his head to one side to study the cave where he lay. From his vantage point, the cave was small, but the temperature inside was comfortable.

The commander listened for signs of life but only heard the wind whistling somewhere outside, away from his view. Frustration set in as he couldn't recall finding this cave or coming in for shelter. He thought back to the battle and his ultimate victory interrupted by Rebecca. He escaped with his life barely but knew the damage was done. The Zarillions' precious city was captured, and his people were free to conquer this world. He knew his people would need his guidance and being stuck in this cave wasn't an option. Again, the commander turned himself so he could move to an upright position, and the pain threatened to tear him apart.

He gritted his teeth in hatred, thinking of Rebecca, and ignored the pain, turning so he was on his hands and knees. With labored breath, he pushed hard, using the wall of the cave for support until he stood. He leaned heavily on the cave wall, taking painful breaths. For the first time, he looked down to see the damage inflicted by that infernal brat Rebecca. His entire left side was ripped apart, and he could see his own rib bones through the damaged skin, with dried blood around the wound. Though he couldn't recall healing himself, looking at the fast-healing attempt. With no one else around, self-healing was the only answer.

The commander took a moment to clear his mind and pushed the pain away, placing his hand on his side. A warm glow emanated from his hand, and he felt the pain subside. Though he couldn't regrow tissue, he could use the energy to temporarily bandage the wound until he could get back to base. With the pain much lessened, he stood unaided and walked around the cave to investigate.

Naturally formed, the cave's walls were smooth, and the floor was stone mixed with dirt. He walked toward the entrance, only to be repelled by a blast of icy-cold air. Despite being free here, he was still stuck in this disgusting cold. Again, rage fueled his thoughts, and he vowed to finish Rebecca and her people once and for all. With a careful spin, he walked back into the protective warmth of the cavern. He continued to stand, knowing if he sat and tried to get up, he could rip the repair to his body.

Peering around the cavern to see if he brought any supplies with him, he remained disappointed to see nothing on the floor or in any of the crevices. He looked down quickly to see if his communicator was still operational and again, met with disappointment. The communicator looked to be scorched and broken with pieces missing. He tore it off his wrist and flung it against the wall, smashing it to bits. With no supplies, communication, or guidance, he would be a goner.

He leaned up against the wall, trying to clear his thoughts to figure a plan of escape. Fatigue riddled his body, but he pushed down the pain to clear his mind. Years of strict military training honed his finely tuned skills of ignoring pain and toil. The commander couldn't help but wonder what happened to his men in this moment of doubt and pain. A true military leader through and through, he rarely gave regard to his men's plight as soldiers. Here he was, a survivor of a large-scale battle and unable to savor the victory. His thoughts moved to the thought of his enemies being in as much pain and agony as he right now.

Breathing was still difficult as he raised himself to his full height and even in his weakened state, he was quite the specimen. He tried to recall his trip to this cave and place his location, but nothing came to mind. Carefully, he worked his way to the cave's entrance, braving the elements. The cold felt like knives entering his body, but he hardened himself and walked into the bleak, frozen terrain. Each step forward caused more pain, but he gritted his teeth and continued using his hatred of Rebecca to fuel his travel.

As he came over the ridge in front of him, he caught sight of a vehicle about a hundred yards away. It made little sense trying to hide as he stuck out like a sore thumb in the middle of this white landscape. Without another thought, he turned slightly and walked straight for the vehicle. When he was within a few feet, it became apparent that it was abandoned. Upon closer investigation, the commander noticed the hull riddled with bullet holes. Peering inside, he saw no signs of life and lifted himself into the driver's seat.

A look at the panel gave him hope as the control panel and mechanics seemed intact. His heart raced as he reached forward and pressed the ignition. At first, the engine groaned but finally let itself come alive. The engine idled extremely rough, and the commander knew not for how long the motor would hold out, so he immediately thrust the vehicle into gear. Using the still working GPS, he located his position and let out a sigh of relief that he wasn't that far from his own base. His luck held as the vehicle rattled along at a quick pace. The commander thought what a triumph it would be to return to the base and find out the lengths of the sheer destruction of the Zarillion.

The damaged vehicle trudged forward as it entered a deeper, softer area of snow. For a moment, the commander thought it would easily move through the snow, only to have the vehicle sink. The commander tried to maneuver himself out of the area but only caused the vehicle to become more stuck in the snow. He looked at the GPS, knowing he was still a few miles out from base. Not that a few miles' hike was anything difficult for the commander but in his current condition and lack of supplies, it might as well be a death sentence.

He rummaged through the inside of the vehicle to see if he could use anything. To his surprise, the med kit and emergency kit were still intact. He found a half-empty backpack and tossed everything into the pack. In the emergency kit, he found a protein bar and opened it, choking down its contents. He wasn't used to this type of food but at this point, he needed something to eat. Pack over his shoulder, he left the vehicle and hopped into the snow, sinking himself up to his waist. Carefully, he waded through until he felt more solid ground beneath him. With better footing, he could move more quickly as he looked up to the sun to gain his bearings. He knew the base was a few miles northwest of his current position.

Turning in the direction of the base, he walked away from the vehicle, cursing his luck. Peering toward the sky, he determined he still could count on several hours of daylight but travel in these conditions could take longer. Nothing could be done about the situation, so he walked as fast as he could in the direction of the base, hoping to make it before the deathly cold temperatures the nighttime brought to this area.

At first, his progress was steady with the sun warming his face, but it was going down faster than anticipated. Shadows lengthened around him, and the temperature dropped significantly. Still, his body was a good temperature, and the exertion of his hike kept him warm. He was still making good time when he heard the explosions. The ground around him shook. He worked his way up to a ridgeline of rock and looked to where the explosions came from.

The commander lay on the ground on his belly, peering out to see what actions transpired. To his great surprise, he found the entrance to his base under fire. Zarillion aircraft pummeled the entrance, and he saw his people sending back fire. He watched as the aircraft came in wave after wave, sending ground-penetrating missiles into the entrance. Though the reptilian soldiers fought back, the commander kept waiting for his own aircraft to storm into the skies and engage the enemy.

He couldn't see any ground troops on either side in any direction. Again, he searched the skies for his own air force, only to see the Zarillion force pound the entrance. The commander saw a clear breach in the entrance, but still no soldiers came out to defend the entrance. As he was about to give up hope, he saw some men setting up tripods with laser weapons mounted to them. The lasers fired at will against the oncoming attacking aircraft. These fierce weapons found their mark and made significant damage to the aircraft.

Zarillion pilots adjusted their course and travelled at a higher elevation and a higher rate of speed to compensate for the new weapons. Again, the aircraft sent missiles directly into the now-open entrance with devastating effect. The craft turned one more time and launched the last of its payload before returning to their own base. Commander Zosa looked on with confusion. His forces overwhelmed the Zarillion forces and decimated their attack capabilities, yet here they were, attacking once more.

With the entrance smoldering in ruin, the commander waited to make sure the aircraft weren't making a return trip before moving off his perch on the rock. When he felt the coast was clear, he began the trek toward the damaged entrance. Smoke and ash still rose in the air as he came within sight of what was once the entrance to his base. The lasers lay in ruin as well as what was once a gate and there stood a huge rent in the earth. He half-expected to see soldiers running out to greet him, yet he ran into not one soldier.

The commander walked right into the rent unmolested and found going quite difficult as everything was destroyed. Rock and concrete lay everywhere, making travel near impossible. Though not at full power, he still knew the strength of many men and thrust rock out of his way. He walked until he found what was left of a tunnel and followed it. Darkness didn't stop him because his finely tuned night vision kicked in. Downward the tunnel led him until he found what was left of his command center. Like the entrance above, the command center was destroyed.

He stood frozen in rage. How could all his wonderful plans be ruined? He was victorious! He saw the Zarillions fall. Sending his fists down on the already broken control panel, he crushed a few more controls. Still, a few emergency lights were on at this point but again, he couldn't locate a soul to report to him on the status of anything. His frustration boiled over when he heard a faint sound.

Through the rubble, he heard movement and looked to see what might be coming his way. It didn't take long before a single soldier crawled through a hole in the wall. The soldier looked to be in rough shape. The commander found the man bleeding from several locations on his body. The soldier also wore a large bandage covering one of his eyes. Making his way through the fallen debris, the soldier didn't even notice the commander standing at the control panel. A few more strides did he come forward before he flinched as he almost ran into the commander.

With his good eye, he looked at the commander. "Sir, I'm sorry I couldn't see you. When we were attacked, I was up near the gate. I lost one of my eyes, and the other I'm having difficulty seeing out of. What are your orders, sir?"

The man tried to stand at attention, but the soldier was barely hanging on at this point. He waved the man to sit on the pile of rubble near him. The soldier complied but was slow in sitting as if every movement was painful. Commander Zosa didn't reprimand the soldier and waited for him to sit.

He began, "Soldier, tell me what happened here!"

The soldier winced. "Sir, we were attacked on two fronts. Our victory at the Zarillion gate was short lived! They attacked our gates, but someone attacked us from inside the compound as well. I'm sorry, sir. I have no idea how that happened. I was up here defending the gate."

Normally, the commander would have the soldier by the scruff of the neck but considering current events, he couldn't help but feel for this lone soldier. His men were highly trained, great fighters. Hoping to gather more intelligence, he allowed the soldier a moment to gather himself. He also looked around to see if any other soldiers may have survived. To his great dismay, not one soldier came into the control room. This devastated the commander. All his planning, all his scheming, and all his rage were poured into this campaign. Victory was his and now, the jaws of defeat were ready to devour him whole.

The soldier leaned heavily forward, propping himself up against some fallen concrete. He looked at his commander, ready to speak but for some reason, looked unsure of what to say. The commander understood, they trained and planned for this moment for such a long time and now, they sat on the edge of disaster. With the soldier still holding himself up, the commander sat next to the soldier. He looked at the lone man with pride. The soldier neared the end but still looked to his commander for orders.

Then the commander did something very uncharacteristic and placed a hand on the man's shoulder and nodded. The soldier looked at the commander with relief and thanks before slumping forward, taking his last breath. Commander Zosa bent down and picked up the man, heading in the direction of the infirmary. Though still a mess, the tunnels here were mostly intact, and he could move a fast clip.

Once inside the infirmary, he saw a grisly sight. The entire room was filled with death. Every area was covered with fallen soldiers, blood, and bandages of all kinds. The stench of blood, medicine, and death filled the commander's nostrils. He looked around the room in disgust and couldn't fathom the situation. Commander Zosa looked to see if there was a spot to place the now-dead soldier but every square inch of the room was covered.

With the soldier still in his arms, he walked out of the dead room. He went to another room across the hall, which many times was used as a lab. Still, much of the space was covered with fallen soldiers, but the commander found a flat area for the soldier, laying him carefully down. Still, not one other soldier was found alive, and the bleak nature of the base caused rage to grow in the commander's mind. His blood boiled as he walked further into the compound in search of survivors.

Smoke filled the tunnels as he made his way to the armory. The rancid smell of burnt and discharged weapons caught his senses.

Though the smoke didn't bother him, he thought about the information the soldier had passed on to him. Attacked on two fronts, the soldier described the attack on the base. How in the world could someone attack them from inside the base itself? There would be no way anyone could get into the base except by the front entrance. Confusion filled his mind, and he walked into the largest of the rooms for his greatest arsenal.

He stood gaping at the fires still raging all around him. Every weapon, vehicle, and aircraft lay in ruin before him. The commander couldn't fathom how even if they were attacked by a good-sized force, it would take more than that to destroy all that stood before him. His legacy destroyed. Rage burned inside and as it did, he sensed something. On the edge of his mind, he thought he could place the energy he sensed. Then, as he turned to go back remembering everything, he growled, "Rebecca!"

CHAPTER TWENTY-ONE

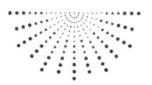

Coming over the last ridge before reaching home, Rebecca could hardly hold her head up as she trudged through the snow. Grace, in no better shape, stumbled several times while trying to prop herself up against Rebecca. The two family members couldn't recall the last time they slept or even rested for that matter. At this point, the only solace they could muster was the wonderful thought of the reptilian base laying in shambles. Though the rage seemed quelled, Rebecca still stewed about the attack on her fair city.

As they approached the damaged gate, Rebecca's footing gave way, and she fell hands out, trying to catch her fall. Her hands slid as she smacked her chin on the mixture of snow and ice. Exhaustion taking hold, she used her last remaining strength to roll over onto her back. The sky was now darkening, and she knew they needed to get inside to avoid the deathly cold. Her eyes watering slightly, she caught her aunt coming to her aid out of the corner of her eye. Grace reached down and with her last bit of strength, pulled Rebecca to her feet.

Once again, the two women, leaning heavily against one another, started forward. As they took their next step, lights blared into their eyes, blinding them. They halted their steps and instinctively put their hands up to block the light. Angry voices came from behind the blinding light, and the ladies could only see shadows moving their way. Blinking her eyes rapidly, Rebecca tried to see the faces of the men coming her way. The lights did their job, and it remained near impossible to see the men as they lay hands on the two women.

Even in her exhausted shape, Rebecca still felt her body gathering energy from the earth around her and prepared to unleash it on her attackers. Her body now felt warm, and she turned with her eyes dancing with energy. One hand was free, and she pointed it toward her captors. Grace saw the look but was a few feet away from her niece. The air around Rebecca crackled and just as she was about to unload the energy, she heard a familiar voice yelling for her to stop.

She heard the voice barking orders, and the lights went out, leaving a few flashlights pointed their way. Still full of power, Rebecca turned to see where the voice originated from. Out of the shadows, she saw one of General Giles' men moving toward them. She tried to recall the man's name and vaguely remembered the general calling him Jon at some point. The soldier approached cautiously as the energy filled the woman before him. With his hands up, trying to disarm the situation, he continued forward. The soldier's eyes were full of fear as he walked to within a foot of her.

Rebecca began, "Jon, I believe?"

The soldier's eyes shot up. "You remember me?"

Rebecca felt the energy powering down and smiled. "Yes, I remember. Now, would you mind telling me where my mother and Holly are at this moment? I have news that cannot wait!"

Again, the soldier's eyes raised. "No one has seen your mother or Holly for some time! The last time anyone saw them, they were travelling with General Giles."

Panic filled her mind. "Take me to the council chambers right away! But first, please tell me you have something to eat? We haven't eaten in days!"

The man came to attention. "Yes, My Lady! Right away!"

Running back the way he came, the soldier barked orders. Another soldier rummaged through a pack. The soldier ran up to her and handed the two ladies a protein bar with something to drink. Rebecca took the food graciously and scoffed it down while following the squad of soldiers back inside the gate. Once inside, the warmth of the city made her smile even though everywhere she looked were signs of battle.

Scorch marks, rubble, blasted holes, and bullet holes invaded the serenity that was once her beautiful city. Sadness took her as people tended to ruined homes. Workers were everywhere trying to repair roads and structures to keep the city up and running. This once-peaceful area now looked to be a military base, and everywhere she looked were soldiers. They were stopped at various checkpoints before being allowed to pass and make their way to the council chambers.

They were greeted with guards everywhere as they approached the council chambers. After a quick conversation, Jon escorted them into the chambers. As the huge doors opened to receive them, Rebecca was shocked to see the chamber a mess, much like the rest of her city. In Andrew's chair, now sat her cousin Nora Beals. Fear gripped Rebecca, not knowing where her mother or Holly were at this moment. She looked around to see if any of the other council members were in attendance, but she only saw Peter's mother and Derek still standing, talking to Nora.

Rebecca felt odd looking at Peter's mother and couldn't bring herself to speak. Since official introductions were yet to be made, she didn't know how Peter's mother would feel about her. Nora stood quickly and smiled at Rebecca, but there was a great sadness behind her smile. Pushing the chair in, she moved to greet the younger member of the gentry. Nora reached out and took Rebecca's hands in hers. Instantly, the chamber appeared different.

As if in a dream, Rebecca saw the chamber, but it was covered in a slight haze. Viewing the chamber from the edge, she saw the council members surrounding Andrew in a panic. Arms waved, and everyone looked hysterical while Andrew tried to no avail to calm their fears. A large banging sound burst from the huge, wooden doors of the chamber. The council looked nervously toward the doors and then again to Andrew.

The doors rattled with each subsequent blow to the wood. Dust and debris fell from the ceiling, but Rebecca saw no cracks forming in the large, stone ceiling. She looked up to see Andrew calling into his wrist for support from the military. Fear gripped his face as the response came back that no other soldiers could be spared at this moment. Andrew growled in the communicator to find General Giles. Again, the response came back that no one could find the general. Andrew's face grew red as the chamber doors burst in with a blast of air.

At the front of the squad of reptilian soldiers, Michael stood with an evil smile covering his face. Andrew sent a blast of energy in Michael's direction. The evil, wraithlike creature deflected the blow, easily returning one of his own directly into Andrew's chest. The council president took the full brunt of the blast to his upper chest, throwing him many feet into the air. A cackling laugh rang in the chamber as Michael watched the Zarillion leader in a heap on the floor of the chamber. Andrew lay unmoving while the reptilian soldiers fanned out and slaughtered everyone in the room. Rebecca thought she might be sick watching people she loved and knew being cut down by these evil creatures.

The battle was over in short order with Michael sitting now in Andrew's chair with his feet up on the circular table. A huge smile crossed Michael's face as he turned and looked at Andrew's fallen body. For good measure, Michael sent another blast of energy at the lifeless body. This time, the body caught fire and blazed what remained quickly. Rebecca felt her own anger raging inside but knew there would be nothing she could do from her vantage point.

Rebecca took a moment to scan the room, only to see the sheer destruction of the entire council. She felt terrible for these good people. A shot of hope entered her thoughts while she looked around the entire room. Though Andrew lay dead, Rebecca knew Holly and General Giles weren't here, which made her feel much better. Out of the corner of her eye, she caught a minor movement on the floor. The soldiers, satisfied with their work, left the chamber with Michael still taking residence in Andrew's chair. His smug look was enough to get Rebecca's blood to boil. One thing was for sure, if they ever met again, she would put an end to this scourge.

Now, the vision wavered with the image of the chamber dissipating. Before the final image melted away, Rebecca saw the still-moving body of Nora on the floor, covered by debris. She felt the breath start in her body as Nora released her hands. Rebecca stepped back, surprise covering her face. Nora put a calm hand on her cheek. Rebecca whirled around, trying to use the right words to describe the vision.

She looked at Nora. "Are you all that's left?"

Sad eyes met hers. "Rebecca, as far as I know, no one can get in contact with Holly or General Giles. At this point, until either return, yes, I am all that's left!"

Rebecca, with gritted teeth, continued, "And Michael?"

"Gone!"

A quick turn to face the now Zarillion leader, she started, "Nora, this is Holly's sister Grace! I know there's little time for pleasantries, but it would be wonderful to welcome her home with better than this situation."

Nora embraced Grace. "My Lady, you're most welcomed home! I wasn't yet on the council when you left, but I do remember the stir your disappearance caused."

Grace took the hug in stride while choosing not to say anything about her alleged disappearance. She held Nora at arm's length before releasing her and having a seat at the table. Rebecca joined her and, for the first time since entering the chamber, thought of Peter. She nearly jumped up out of her seat with hands firmly grasping the arms of her chair. Nora saw her terror but allowed her to sit.

Rebecca's hands turned white, gripping the arms of her chair as tight as she could. "Peter? Nora, is he all right?"

Nora smiled. "My dear, the young man is well protected. Jake went with him and at last check, they were still in the garden."

A wave of relief came over her face. "Thank you! I need to go to him, but I cannot while the city remains in danger. What is the status?"

Nora stood. "My Lady Rebecca, you go see that young man! We're out of danger for the moment, but those evil scum will be back for more!"

Rebecca rose herself. "Nora, I'll be at the garden, but if you need me for anything, please alert me at once. Also, if any word of Holly and my mother come to your ears, please let me know."

Nora nodded as Rebecca, followed by Grace, left the confines of the council chamber. Her pace quickened, walking through the streets until they reached the outskirts of the city. She felt great relief to look around her and see the nature around her undisturbed. Her mother walked with her many a day on these paths, telling her one day she would be walking this path for a much different reason. Now, she knew what premonition her mother spoke about. Grace kept pace with her but said no word. She too looked around at the untamed beauty, recalling the many times she too as a young lady walked these very paths.

A clear trail laid before her, and she followed its winding path until the large castle structure loomed before them. Both Grace and Rebecca stood at the castle gate waiting to be greeted by guards. A few minutes passed with no sign of life. She waved for Grace to come with her, and they walked around to the entrance to the garden itself. Rebecca turned the corner, her heart nearly leaping out of her chest. There standing guard with a host of other soldiers was Jake, looking every bit the part of soldier.

Without another thought, Rebecca ran to Jake, grabbing him and nearly knocking them both over. Jake, with a sheepish grin on his face, looked at the lovely young lady accosting him. Rebecca released the young man, still smiling. Still holding him at arm's length, Grace came up behind with a questioning look on her face. Rebecca smiled again, touching Grace on the shoulder.

She looked at Jake. "Jake, I'm Rebecca! I'm so honored to meet you!"

Jake stood straight and looked into Rebecca's eyes. "Rebecca? Oh my God! Pete is going to kill me!!"

With a confused look, Rebecca raised an eyebrow. "Jake, what are you talking about?"

Jake laughed. "Rebecca, do you have any idea how mad Peter will be when he finds out I met the love of his life first!"

Blushing, Rebecca started, "I know, Jake! It hasn't been easy for either of us. I hope he'll understand and not be angry with me."

Again, he burst into laughter. "Angry, Pete, not with you but me, on the other hand, that's something altogether different. No, I wouldn't be surprised if he doesn't know what to say to you. He's the kind of person that doesn't like to mess anything up."

A large smile came across her face. "He won't mess this up. Where is he, Jake? I've travelled through danger and peril around every corner to be here with him."

"He's still in the garden and has been for weeks."

She saw by Jake's face he was concerned for his friend. He relayed to Rebecca that he trained every day with the soldiers and with General Giles when he was available. This made Rebecca happy as she knew Jake's importance to their mission and very lives. He went on to explain that after training, he guarded the garden entrance every day, waiting for his friend's return. She felt a great deal of pride listening to Jake speak about looking after his friend in this way. Someday, she would have to explain to Jake that his position with Peter was preordained through space and time long ago. For the time being, it was necessary to let Jake train to be the soldier they would all need.

Jake further described to Rebecca how Holly could somehow tell that Peter was completely safe inside and was training himself. She took all the information in stride, soaking up every bit she could. Now, so close to her love, she could no longer wait to be with him. Jake was still talking when she stood, walking right past him and Grace. Jake waved off the guards who would now intercept her before she reached the garden. Paying no attention, she walked past everyone standing, looking at the large hedge covering the whole outside of the garden.

She turned to Jake. "Where's the entrance? There used to be a gated entrance that was guarded here."

Jake frowned. "When Peter entered the garden, it sealed itself, not letting anything in or out!"

Rebecca, with ultimate determination, walked forward, placing a hand on the hedge. "It will open for me!"

CHAPTER TWENTY-TWO

Holly stared at Helena waiting for an in-depth explanation of her last statement. She couldn't help but wonder what type of help the dead could provide. Never having been to this place, she tried to think back to council discussions to remember any information that might help her figure Helena's motives. Her strength returned quickly, and she reached up caressing General Giles cheek letting him know she was well enough to be under her own power. Straightening herself she walked over to Helena ready to open a serious dialogue.

As if Helena read her mind, she reached up with a broad smile, placing a gentle hand on Holly's shoulder for reassurance. Rather than respond, Helena calmly grasped Holly's hand and led them to the entrance to the stone castle. Holly followed, eyeballing the castle suspiciously as they moved inside to the courtyard. Though nothing noteworthy, the castle seemed made in traditional fashion. Holly sensed something on the edge of her memory but couldn't grab hold of it at this moment.

Michael still looked to be in a trance as they continued forward. This pleased Holly, but she still couldn't recall his capture. Helena now moved away from them and walked over to the stone family crest on the wall. Holly watched as her family member glowed, placing her hand on the starburst pattern in the middle of the crest. Immediately, the entire structure around them changed from the ancient stone structure to that of an ultramodern military building. As soon as the structure changed, Holly looked and laughed aloud. This military compound was created long ago in case of an enemy incursion. As a council member, she was privy to this information, but no one in memory besides maybe Andrew would remember this place.

General Giles heard Holly's laughter and looked her way for an explanation. She smiled brightly and walked over, grabbing his arm in hers. He took her arm and lovingly looked into her eyes. Holly turned him toward the door on the far side of the room. Helena already walked into the next room with the lights coming on for her as she entered. She tugged at Michael's chains and forced him to sit in a metal chair off to the side of the room. A quick turn saw her place herself in front of a large computer screen.

Her hands moved quickly over the keyboard, and the computer screen sprang to life. She peered over her shoulder to see if Holly and the general were now watching, which they were indeed. On the computer screen, a grainy image of another control center came into view. They all stared at the screen to see a lone figure making his way through the rubble. Holly felt Ryan's muscles tighten as he viewed a ragged Commander Zosa. He felt no sympathy for his enemy. Again, they watched as a soldier stumbled into the room.

The soldier, in obviously rough shape, could barely stand and struggled to breathe. Though they couldn't hear the conversation, the gist was apparent. Someone retaliated against the reptilians and destroyed their base. A feeling of justice entered the general's mind but also a sense of disappointment. He always felt it would be he to destroy the commander. On the screen, the soldier now leaning heavily against the wall didn't have much time, and they all watched in horror as the man expired. The reality of war known to all in this room still caused much sorrow. Strange to his nature, the general saluted the fallen soldier. Holly nodded, and they turned back to the screen as the huge commander unexpectedly picked up the soldier's body and left the room after a salute.

Their small party still stood surprised, looking at the destroyed base of the reptilian people. Obviously, someone or something unknown to them attacked and were quite successful in their campaign. Helena watched with her friends for a few more minutes for signs of life but saw nothing. With the commander gone, no one else showed up on screen. She punched a few keys on the computer to see other areas of the base, only to see destruction and no life. After a few more moments of exploration, Helena turned to her friends.

Helena composed herself. "General, could you explain that scene to me? From what I understand, our military capability to this point is limited. What I just saw, there isn't anything we could have pulled off right now!"

The general raised an eyebrow. "Helena, I honestly have no idea. We barely repelled the breach at the gate, and I still have no idea how many reptilian soldiers are in the city right now!"

Holly came forward. "Helena, when we arrived at the council chambers, that was to save as many of you as we could. From our vantage point, the city seemed fallen. As Ryan stated, we don't know the extent of the damage or if indeed the entire city is fallen."

Helena nodded and punched more keys on the computer. The screen again jumped to life, this time showing different views of the city. To their great surprise, they found little reptilian presence in the city. A few small pockets of reptilian soldiers here and there but overall, the Zarillions maintained control over their fair city. Bright faces looked at the screen as each scene gave them more hope.

A sigh of relief left Helena's lips. "It would appear as if we avoided disaster, my friends! I'm still very puzzled by the reptilian base. Our allies are awaiting our call for assistance. They wouldn't strike without coordinating with us. I'm not sure the humans could do that type of destruction to the reptilian base without our help."

A quick glance by the general knew she was correct in her assessment. Their human allies were ready to come to their aid, but the attack happened so suddenly, communication with the humans wasn't made. He was even unsure if the human leadership knew of the attack yet. The general usually shared a great deal with his human counterparts but lately, he spent more time keeping tabs on the reptilians. Since they were now free, the humans were in dire need of assistance from his people. Of course, that depended on his capability to help both. His current situation would warrant communication to the human leadership.

Holly spoke up, "Well, my friends, what's our next move? For the moment, our city is safe but even with the reptilian base destroyed, we know that will only stall them. Commander Zosa is free, we have no idea if any of his soldiers remain. They will bring reinforcements. For eons, they were unable to communicate with their home world, but that's all changed."

Helena perked up. "Holly is right. We aren't out of the woods yet. We know the enemy now can enter our city. It's imperative we coordinate with the humans. Also, the gates need to be opened!"

General Giles rushed forward. "No, Helena! Those gates must remain closed! We don't know what lies out beyond this planet any longer. Honestly, we barely escaped to this world and were able to close the gates at a heavy toll to our people!"

"I understand your trepidation but, Ryan, those gates were never meant to be shut in the first place. It is our task to keep those gates safe and secure. Like you say, we have no idea what things look like outside this world now!"

General Giles looked at Helena. "Helena, you and I know Rebecca isn't close to ready! Peter is being trained but right now, his own power is in its infancy. In theory, it may be time to open the gates but without those two ready, opening them would be suicide for us!"

Rebecca's mother frowned. "I know, Ryan. I know they aren't ready but now that our enemies are free, it won't be long before they are on our doorstep! This time, we may not be as lucky to repel them. The humans are honorable and will fight to the last, but I'm afraid if we don't open the gates, that may happen. We vowed to protect both peoples. That is the reason we went underground. We changed our entire existence to save both peoples."

Holly piped in, "Helena, I agree with your assessment of the current situation but opening those gates will in all likelihood be our ultimate downfall!"

Helena looked at her fellow council members and friends with great pride. She knew them to be unselfish, honorable people and could count on them to make the right decision. With the push of a button, the screen went black. Helena walked briskly toward the door on the opposite side of the room. Again, the others followed into a long hallway lit in bright light. They could barely see a small door at the end, and no one spoke until she reached it.

As they entered the next room, General Giles stopped in his tracks as he viewed the large semi-circle of stone before him. He thought he knew of all the star gates throughout their kingdom, but this was foreign to him. All along the stone structure, he discovered various runes and at the very top, sat the starburst pattern he was so familiar with. Helena already was working on another pattern of runes on the wall of the rock cavern in which they now stood.

The runes glowed a sparkling, reddish tint. General Giles ran forward to intercept Helena before she completed the sequence. Helena held up her hand, stopping the general in his tracks. A feeling of an invisible wall surrounded him, and he found himself unable to move. Rage filled his mind as he knew once the gates were opened, it would be near impossible to shut them. He recalled the last time the gates were open. His people were ripped from their homes and casted from their world by the very reptilian people who hunted them now. The general was amounting the men tasked with the closing of the gates when they reached planet Earth. Wave after wave of reptilian soldiers followed them through the gates. General Giles repelled the reptilian soldiers, and all seemed to be in his favor until Commander Zosa stepped out of the gate.

Commander Zosa and the general were locked in mortal combat before one of the gates, while Holly and Helena used their abilities to close the gates here on Earth. Bodies lay piled around the gate as many other reptilian soldiers streamed out. Holly sent wave after wave to their deaths, but even her strength wasn't enough. Helena worked furiously to close the gates and received a grievance wound to her head for her efforts. Bleeding profusely from her head, she punched in the last sequence just as a large contingent of reptilian soldiers made it through the gate.

Blood filling her eyes, she used her own ability to save the day. Her friends, surrounded by soldiers, wouldn't survive without intervention. She wiped the blood from her eyes and touched one of the extremely large reptilian soldiers near her. She unleashed her power into the creature until its eyes turned white. The man then turned to her, and she ordered him to protect those surrounded. A wave of grisly death and destruction took place before her while she watched her creature cut a path to her friends.

Helena took up her station next to Holly and fought side by side until they all were drained. The reptilian soldier came to her as she fell over in exhaustion. Feet planted around his fallen mistress, he fell any soldier within view. In the end, Holly, Ryan, and Helena were the only Zarillion people alive at the gate. Helena learned later that when she used the proper sequence at one gate, it would close all. She also learned she would become the only person alive who could open them again.

When Holly, Ryan, and Helena found the rest of her people at various points around the planet, they learned many reptilian people also made it through to this world. A huge civil war for the planet ensued, and the Zarillion people needed to save the fledgling human race at the same time. When the dust settled, the Zarillion people were successful in their exile of the reptilian people into the heart of the earth. In the end, they needed to exile themselves in much the same way to allow the humans to grow into a civilization unmolested. The reptilians, although prisoners in the earth, could use their own powers of persuasion to corrupt the humans.

With the gates closed, the Zarillion people were also cut off from their home world as well as other allies around the cosmos. Their new mission of colonizing this planet and watching the humans went south quickly. As soon as they learned of the reptilian interference, they spent much time countering the schemes of those like

Commander Zosa. So much time was spent trying to keep the humans safe, they nearly lost the planet when a large scouting party of reptilians found their way to the planet, unaware their own people were prisoners below their very feet.

Again, a large skirmish took place, and they were triumphant. They then decided they should hide themselves as well, in hopes not to draw unwanted attention on the humans. The hope was the humans would grow into a civilization much like their own, who could defend themselves from the likes of evil races such as the reptilian. After this, Earth knew a peaceful time of growth and knowledge until a devastating plague wiped out much of the human population.

Though the Zarillions could do little to assist during this time because the plague spread quickly and through human contact, they did what they could to slow the spread. When the humans were deemed healthy, they had lost much of their gained knowledge, putting them back centuries in terms of advancement. Again, the Zarillions would leak knowledge to them in hopes of them catching up, but things went extremely slow. All the while, the reptilian people were in the background, working to undermine every advancement the humans made.

As the humans showed signs of growth and peace, the reptilians would influence one group or another and cause unrest, which led to large-scale wars raging across the world, nearly wiping out the humans. Through their vigilance, the Zarillions were able to, from the shadows, help the humans get to a point where they would be ready to join them as allies. Contact was made, and alliances formed. Now, those bonds would be tested to their limits.

Helena turned to her friends. "I must do this! I'll travel and get help for us. I'll take this scum Michael with me as well! Maybe I'll drop him in a black hole."

Holly moved forward. "Helena, surely you cannot do this alone!"

Helena smiled. "I'm the one who can open and close the gates. I'll open it for now, get rid of this parasite, and go for help. Once the reptilians reestablish communication with their own world, this world may very well be doomed!"

General Giles reluctantly stated, "Holly, she may have a point. She can close the gates once she arrives. At this point, we have few options."

Holly turned to the general. "Our mission is the humans, along with Rebecca and Peter right now! If those gates are opened, how are we supposed to defend ourselves? We barely survived this attack! The humans don't even know what's happening yet."

He moved again to stop Helena but was too late, as she stepped into the now-glowing semi-circle. She stood glimmering for a moment and vanished. The star gate remained glowing with Holly and Ryan staring at the gate, hoping Helena would come back. Their hopes were dashed when several minutes later, the gate went dark, and the runes went back to stone.

Holly turned to the general. "Now what?"

CHAPTER TWENTY-THREE

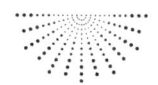

Peter's eyes sprang open to behold the smiling face of the king staring down at him while sleeping. Though completely odd, Peter made nothing of the king waking him. He jumped out of the cozy bed, throwing the down comforter out of his way, placing his bare feet on the cool floor. The wood felt firm and strong on his toes as he leaned over on his hands slightly. He popped up and dressed quickly, excited about the day's upcoming training. He couldn't remember exactly how long he trained with the king, but each day found him more skilled.

Training today was a mystery, but the king warned him to be careful and guard himself against everything. He didn't understand the king's warning. Still rubbing sleep from his eyes, he walked over to the basin of water on his bureau, digging his hands into the water. Cupping his hands, he threw water on his face, gasping a little at the cold nature of the water. Reaching for the towel, he pat dried his face and quickly tossed on his shirt. Peter didn't even look at the king while he grabbed his backpack. The king nodded and led the way out into the training yard.

Morning training consisted of Peter sparring with the king. This came to be Peter's favorite part of the day. Although he viewed himself as a modern-day explorer, he was quite fascinated by the sword, dagger, and staff as weapons. Each day, the king trained him with these weapons until his arms could no longer be raised to defend himself. Peter wore many bruise trophies to show for his efforts. Every day, he became faster, stronger, and more skilled wielding the weapons. The king complimented him, telling him becoming a weapons master would be as important for him as learning to wield his own power. Time after time, the king would hammer home to Peter how any blade or staff could kill just as easily as his power.

Feeling much like an ancient knight, he showed pride each evening by oiling and cleaning his weapons as any true weapons master would. Today, the king marched him up a large hill. Peter didn't recognize the path. When the king stopped, he pointed Peter up the path. He looked to where the king pointed, seeing the beginnings of a gravel path. At first, something in the back of his mind told him not to move forward, but he could see the serious look on the king's face. Without another word, he did as the king instructed, walking the path alone. The gravel under his feet crunched and made travel slow, slipping under his feet with each step.

At first, the path went forward in a straight fashion but within a few minutes, the path became a dusty, dirt trail, winding around very rocky areas. Peter found it difficult to go forth because the light grew very dim, causing him to stumble more than once. Instinctively, he drew his sword, placing it in front of him in a defensive posture. Darkness surrounded him, and he could barely see a foot in front of his face.

Suddenly, he heard the whoosh of a blade sailing toward his head. He ducked out of the way just in time to see a flaming sword flying by his head. Peter bent his knees and brought his sword up to defend himself. The flaming sword came to rest in front of his attacker's face just enough for Peter to see who assailed him. A scream erupted from his throat, seeing the face looking back at him.

In the flames, the red, evil face that smiled back at him was that of his best friend Jake Andrews. Confusion, anger, and uncertainty clouded his mind as the evil Jake swung the blade at him. Again, Peter blocked the blade, causing fire and sparks to fly everywhere. Peter flinched as one of the flames licked his bare arm. Rage now filled Peter, and he brought his own sword coming up to attack. His blade turned a blinding white and came down on Jake's blade. The strike caused the evil Jake to fall to one knee.

Jake punched Peter in the stomach, catching him off guard. Peter, hardened by the king's training, took the blow in stride, and continued his own assault upon the new enemy. He launched into a series of swings, kicks, and punches of his own. Though his enemy was strong beyond measure, Peter kept on the offensive. He put his blade in front of his own face, lighting up the area around him in brilliant white light.

Jake put his arm up to one side with his own flaming blade, watching his opponent carefully. Through the dim light, both men flexed their muscles, looking to one another for the next series of blows. Sweat poured down their faces, giving them an eerie look in the light of their swords. They circled one another, waiting for the other to make the first move.

Jake stopped midstride. "Peter, I see you're surprised to see me!"

Peter shook his head. "Jake, that's an understatement! Where have you been?"

"You went into the garden and didn't return! You left me on my own with enemies swirling all around me. I was captured by the reptilians and tortured!"

Peter looked up in horror. "How long have I been gone? I just got here! Jake, I'm so sorry! I never should have left you."

"You will be sorry! I'll take every torture session out on your hide. After I'm done with you, I'll turn what's left over to the commander!"

Peter stood in shock as Jake jumped at him, flailing the red-flaming blade toward him. Again, he blocked the shot. He knew the only way to stop Jake was to disarm him. With a series of moves, he knew Jake wouldn't know he switched up his attack from left to right, taking Jake by surprise. Jake tried but couldn't keep up with Peter's attack and as Peter came swinging up, he caught Jake's blade, sending it flying into the air.

With quick hands, he reached up and grabbed Jake's blade, holding both gleaming blades before him. Jake, rather than stop, launched himself with hatred toward Peter's mid-section. He caught Jake in the face with the hilt of his sword, dropping him to his knees. Through the flame light, Peter looked down into the hate-filled eyes of his friend. Blood streamed down his face from the gash caused by the hilt, but Jake still looked fresh.

He glared at Peter. "Do it! What are you waiting for? I'm already dead! You left me to die in the hands of those butchers! It should have been you, Peter! I trusted you. I followed you here."

Guilt came over Peter in a wave. "Jake, I'm so sorry! You're right, it should have been me!" He took both blades down into the ground and knelt before Jake. "What would you have me do to atone?"

Jake stood in front of Peter, smiling. "You must die!"

A dagger flew Peter's way from behind Jake. As the blade came down, Peter didn't move, expecting death. As the blade was to find its mark, another gleaming blade intercepted the dagger, blocking the blow. Peter looked up to see the king wave his hand, and the image of Jake disappeared. Peter looked up at the king and fell to his knees, breaking down in tears.

Hands on his face with tears freely flowing, he felt the hand of the king on his shoulder. Stopping to look at the king, he saw concern on his face. Struggling to his feet, Peter still held both blades, glowing brightly. He thrust them both into the ground. The blades immediately went dark. As if on cue, the light grew around them until daylight. The king motioned him to sit on the ground.

Doing as asked, his tear-stained face looked to the king for answers. The king frowned. "Not easy being a leader and a friend! There will be many decisions you will make in your lifetime that will affect those around you. Your loved ones will always be in the crosshairs. Think of Jake, your mom, and Rebecca. Imagine any one of those dear ones captured or worse, killed by our enemies."

Tears beginning anew, Peter started, "My King, how could I live with any of those people being hurt or worse under my watch? I would die!"

Again, the king looked on his charge with sympathy. "I understand, I really do but, in our case, the universe is our responsibility as well. This is the most important part of your training. You're an extremely unselfish person, and that will serve you well during your reign. I'm here to help you understand that even the most important ones to us can be casualties of this fight."

Gritting his teeth, Peter blurted out, "Casualties! How can you talk that way! I saw you die with your love by your side. You would die for each other! As would I!"

The king nodded. "Yes, my young friend, and that's actually why we're here now. I couldn't do what I'm trying to teach you! You must sometimes sacrifice those you love to stop ultimate evil."

Peter's eyes shot up. "You know I cannot do that! I would rather die than see those I love hurt! It will always be that way."

Sadness came over the king's face. "Then I've failed, and we'll all perish. Peter, I don't do this out of spite, I do this out of love. You're my ancestor, and I would gladly give my life over again for any of you. That, my friend, is our bane of existence. We care too much for those whom we love."

"My King, you haven't failed. What you see as a weakness, I see as our greatest gift to the universe. In my mind, there's no greater power than love! I've yet to meet Rebecca, but I tell you this, I love that woman, and we'll bring these evil beings to their knees!"

The king's eyes brightened. "Peter, I know how you feel. Each time we're able to stop evil in its tracks, we choose to save the ones we love first. Then the cycle starts over again. Our ancestors have been playing the same sequence of events repeatedly for time out of memory. I was hoping with you, things would be different. You have more ability than any of us, and you're the smartest of us."

Peter knelt before the king. "My Lord, I won't fail you! Together, Rebecca and I will find a way to put things right. We'll do what's needed to bring the universe to peace."

A large hand landed on his shoulder. Peter caught a hint of a smile coming from the king. They walked back down the path toward their cabin. The path now easy to follow, they came down the hillside until they reached a grove of trees. For some reason, Peter felt a chill go up his spine as he looked at the gnarled, ancient, dark trees. These trees, he sensed, were much different than the tree of life he saw when he first arrived in the garden. Hatred emanated from them with each passing footstep.

Suddenly, Peter stopped as if drawn by the trees. He felt his feet moving now toward the trees. Cold struck his body with each footstep. Peter shivered, and it brought him out of his little trance. Looking to the king in panic, he saw the king waving him inward. Again, he looked at the deep, thick bark of the trees, and he noticed how dark it was inside the grove. Before he entered, he spun to the king, looking to see if this was necessary.

A serious look came over the king's face. "Peter, you're strong, fast, and smart. You've passed every test I can throw at you, but there's one final test I must give you. Please know I do this to help you."

With that statement, the king vanished, leaving Peter cold and alone. He walked ahead and moved by the first set of trees. Once beyond the first trees, the temperature drastically changed. It felt stifling and very humid inside the grove. He felt as if the air was being sucked out of the atmosphere. Now, he was sweating with each step. Heat built, and he finally came to the center of the grove.

Sun blared down on him or at least it felt like sunlight and nothing grew in the middle of grove. Though the grass wasn't scorched, it seemed long dead and mostly straw. Peter adjusted his eyes as two figures walked out from behind the trees. One figure was captor to the other. As they came into view, Peter noticed Rebecca with a collar around her neck, being led by Commander Zosa. The commander noticed Peter and sneered at him.

He glared at Peter. "Well met, my young friend. I warned you about this. I told you I would have Rebecca. Your little temper tantrum is over! The city is fallen, and it belongs to me, along with everything in it, and her."

The commander pushed Rebecca down onto the ground, causing her to fall and roll to the ground. As she tried to rise, he yanked her back by the neck. Rebecca lay on her back, choking. Peter's rage took hold, and he went forward to strike at the commander. To his surprise, he stopped in his tracks and could no longer move. He watched as the commander picked Rebecca up by the neck choking her in front of him. Fear gripped him as he watched her face turn purple.

Though he couldn't move, he could still speak, "Stop! Please, let her go! Take me instead! I beg of you!"

Commander Zosa laughed and threw Rebecca to the ground barely alive. He cackled. "Peter, do you think this is part of the king's stupid training? Oh no, this is reality! You won't be walking away from this. I'll have you both."

Something in the way the commander spoke told Peter he was speaking true. Did the king know about this? Was that why he disappeared? Could he not help Peter this time? He knew he couldn't walk forward so he thought about what he might be able to do from this vantage point. Trying to move his arms, he found that he did have limited movement. Moving his hand over so he could grab the hilt of his sword, he wrapped his hands around it. Immediately, he felt the warmth of the sword and its power entering his own body.

The commander noticed this and laughed. "That silly sword cannot help you now. No, this is your end. I'm really going to savor this. Today, my wishes all come true. In a few moments, you both will cease to exist, and I'll rule the universe as should be."

Again, he reached down and grabbed Rebecca, pulling her up to her feet. This time, Peter noticed Rebecca's tear-stained face, lined with dried blood, mouthing to him, "Sorry." Tears came to his own face and streamed freely. Again, he let the rage take hold of his body. Mixed with the sword's own power, he felt something crack. After the sound of the crack, he felt his foot move forward slightly. Taking his sword, he pulled it forward, cutting through what was left of the energy field the commander created.

The commander, no longer smiling, grabbed Rebecca by the neck and held her up in front of Peter. Without another word, he threatened to snap her neck. Peter stopped in his tracks. Instead, the commander waved a dagger in front of Peter and swung it around until it entered Rebecca's side. Peter fell to his knees in agony, holding his own side. He didn't understand as the commander brandished the weapon. Commander Zosa, smiling, cut the outside of Rebecca's arm.

Peter grabbed his own arm, looking down to see blood seeping through his clothes on his side and arm. Pain taking hold, he struggled to his feet, rage again taking hold. This time, the blade turned a brilliant blue, and Peter felt his wounds healing as he strode forward. There was no way the commander would leave this grove alive. To the commander, he quickened his pace.

Commander Zosa, now with his own sword in his hand, swung at Peter. Peter caught the blow and countered with amazing speed. The blade bit deep into the commander's side. A scream of pain broke the silence. Then the commander cried swinging his blade upward trying to stab Peter's face. He missed, and Peter swung with frightening speed before the commander could counter. Peter's blade found flesh and cut across the arm of his assailant. He could smell the blood and his rage now took hold of him. Peter would finish this once and for all.

Standing over his enemy, Peter turned his blade downward for a death blow, only to see the commander smiling. The blade stopped mid-strike as he saw a globe now in front of the commander. The scene showed Peter explosive devices planted around this city and various others around the world. The commander smiled and raised his arm to show Peter a wrist device. He knew at once if the commander pressed the button, all those places would be destroyed.

His enemy, now on his feet, looked his way. "I told you I will have you both today! You're mine, along with this world you love. Today, your world; tomorrow, the universe. There's nothing you can do. This device is tied to my life force. Strike me down and kill everyone!"

The blade slumped to Peter's side, and he peered down to a fast-fading Rebecca. She barely stayed upright, leaning on her arms. Her eyes almost closed, she looked to Peter and nodded for him to let her go. Peter's heart felt terror grip it as she nodded. He couldn't choose between her and the world. The king tried to teach him. Falling to his knees, he laid the blade on the ground and placed his hands out in front of him.

Laughter caught his ears. "Well now, finally some proper respect. Since you bow to me, I'll make you deal the life of your love for the lives of this world."

Peter couldn't see through the tears coming in his eyes. "What assurances do I have you will honor your word?"

Sneering, the commander started, "You don't! However, I'm a man of my word. You will have your little world, for now. I'll leave it now that I'm free. There are so many worlds to conquer. I'll be back someday, but I'll leave this world to you in the meantime, but you must choose!"

Peter couldn't breathe. "You win! Spare my world!"

"One more thing, Peter. You will take her life! Those are my terms. Do we have an accord?"

Peter looked to Rebecca, who now slumped forward, almost expired. Knowing he couldn't save her, he crawled to her with the blade scraping the dirt. Once next to her, he reached out and drew her into his body, holding her tight. She looked up into his eyes and broke out into a smile. Something inside him broke as he started crying uncontrollably. He picked up the blade and put it to Rebecca's sternum with the blade still a brilliant blue.

As he was about to thrust, Rebecca grabbed him, kissing him passionately. He took her lips to his and kissed her back, tasting blood and tears. The two kissed for what seemed like an eternity until Peter felt Rebecca's limp body fall in his arms. He looked down to see her dead body holding a dagger, thrust by Rebecca herself into her heart.

Peter cried, "No!"

CHAPTER TWENTY-FOUR

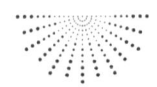

Jake felt goosebumps running up his arms as Rebecca placed her hands on the hedge, keeping her from her beloved. He felt the heat rising from her body, and an electric charge hummed in the air. Eyes raised, he moved back slightly, watching cautiously. Rebecca, a tall, strong woman in her own right, grew in size and stature before the garden. Jake knew the garden needed to open, or Rebecca would destroy it. A sly smile came to his face while thinking of anyone ever trying to keep Peter and Rebecca apart.

The air still crackled with electricity, and Rebecca's hands now glowed with energy ready to be released. As Rebecca was about release her full force on the garden, Jake heard the rustle of leaves. With a whoosh of stale air, the hedge slowly gave way revealing an opening large enough for Rebecca to fit into. She spun to face Jake, asking him to continue to guard the garden. He assured her no one else would be allowed in. Then, by surprise, the young lady reached over to Jake, planting a small kiss on his cheek. Feeling his cheek buzz from a small jolt of Rebecca's power, he blushed and went back to his post with renewed rigor.

Rebecca walked briskly into the opening, not knowing what way to go or what to expect upon entering. The air around her felt dry and stale as she moved onto the gravel path. All she heard was the crunch of the small rocks under her shoes. Behind her, the rustle of leaves let her know the hedge closed. Not even looking back, her determination to find Peter took hold, and she followed the path. Turning the corner, the air became fresher. Pungent fragrances from the multitudes of flowers struck her nostrils, bringing on memories of being with her mother in the flower gardens outside the council chambers.

More than once, Rebecca's mother found her playing in the garden, only to be scolded because it was off limits. Her mother would lecture her about this type of beauty being for all eyes and not for her simple pleasure of picking the flowers. Then her mother would laugh while picking a flower, placing it in her daughter's hair. Nature always called to Rebecca. The animals loved her and came to her naturally. Now, as if in a dream, the garden felt much more inviting. Reaching out, she touched the flowers and knelt to smell one rose which she loved as a child.

A soft chuckle behind her made her stiffen. Cautiously, she turned to see the intruder on her solitude. The image came into focus, leaving Rebecca speechless. A tall man walked out of the shadows of the trees to stand within a foot of the crouching young woman. He looked at the scene of a young woman enjoying a beautiful garden with a smile of delight. Now on her feet, she walked to the man, reaching up with a finger to poke him to see if he were indeed real. Her hand jumped back when her finger touched only air. Panic now struck her eyes as she expected something evil happening.

Again, a smile came to the man's face. "My dear Rebecca, I'm here but not in the form you would expect. I really don't have time to explain exactly how that is but let me assure you, I am real. My time with you is short so please listen carefully to all I have to say."

Biting her lip, she looked at the man. "Mr. Sullivan? I don't mean to sound insensitive but are you not dead?"

A sad look came over his face. "Yes, my dear, my time in a body has now passed, but I'm not allowed to move on yet. There remains unfinished business that must be addressed. I'm a sworn knight and protection of my family doesn't end in death!"

"Mr. Sullivan, is Peter all right? Please tell me he is here!"

His face lit up. "Yes, Rebecca, my grandson is here! He is quite smitten with you! I almost needed to shackle him to train him. All he wanted to do was find you!"

Her face grew red and warm. "Believe me, Mr. Sullivan, the feeling is mutual. I'm almost ready to blast you into oblivion unless you take me to him!"

A surprised look came over his face. "I have no doubt you would, but you need not worry. Your meeting is preordained by forces much more powerful than I. Your love's training is nearing its completion, but the training needed to be sped up. Measures were extreme!"

"Extreme! You didn't hurt him?" Rebecca looked as if she would blast the image into nothingness.

The elder Sullivan held up his hands as if to ward off the blow. "No, my dear! I would never let anything happen to my grandson. That doesn't mean his training isn't harsh. Rebecca, you spend much time watching over Peter. He is an amazing young man with a heart of gold but that, some would say, is his ultimate weakness. There will be a time soon in which he will need to make the decision to sacrifice someone important to him."

Grinding her teeth, she glared at the man. "What did you do?"

He responded, "I know, Rebecca. I insulated him his whole life to allow him to grow as he is now. The genuine, loving person that he is will remain an important strength, however, his destiny will require more than love, I'm afraid. I know he will travel the universe for you!"

She couldn't stand this any longer. "Mr. Sullivan, please take me to him!"

Again, a warm smile came to his face. "It would be my honor to make formal introductions. I always thought I would be doing this in the council chamber under pomp and circumstance, but this will have to do."

Unbidden she jumped to her feet. "Where is he?"

He reached out his hand to her. "I'll take you to him."

Rebecca reached for the hand cautiously, half-expecting nothing to be there. To her surprise, she grasped a semi-solid hand. Mr. Sullivan clasped his hand around hers and instantly, the image of the garden faded from view. Swirling lights surrounded her as if she were in a vortex. They were thrown out of the lights into a dark grove of trees. At first, Rebecca saw nothing but as her eyes became accustomed to the dim light, the images of people came into view. A large, muscular image standing in front of one tree appeared, sneering in triumph at two images on the ground.

From her vantage point, it was difficult to see who lay on the ground and who held the fallen figure, but the commander appeared in plain view. A hand held her in place, and she looked down to see Peter's grandfather holding her at bay. Panic rose in her, and she looked back to the kneeling image on the ground. Now, she saw a dirty, grungy, and tear-stained Peter holding the limp body of a young woman.

At first, she thought it might be his mother, and her heart sank. Again, her eyes adjusted in the light, and horror took over her body as she saw the face of the fallen woman. She too sank to her knees with her face in her hands, sobbing. The scene was too much to bear, and she couldn't control her primal scream coming from her soul. Before the elder Sullivan could do anything, the energy from her scream waved out in a semi-circle, blowing apart anything in its way. The sneering commander was torn to shreds along with half the grove as splinters flew everywhere.

Rebecca rose, holding onto the power with her hands out down by her sides, ready to raise more power to punish anyone responsible for this travesty. Rage beyond control held her, and power consumed her body at an unbelievable rate. Terror shone in Mr. Sullivan's eyes, but he knew he hadn't the power to stop her. As the power seemed ready to consume her, she looked down to see Peter's face gazing up into her eyes.

Power now danced in his own eyes as he stood to face his love. Standing and facing one another, they reached out, simultaneously clasping each other's hands. The crackle of power shot out from their now-touching bodies. Lightning struck around them, and power filled the two beings. Eyes, bodies, and hands glowing, they looked into each other's eyes. Peter reached up, cupping her face gently, and tilted his head slightly, allowing his lips to reach for hers.

Even before their lips touched, the charges danced off their lips onto one another's. Peter took her lips into his, and a blast of white light set off around them, blasting out as if a star exploded. Waves of energy pulsated as the two figures were bathed in the white light. A kiss of passion continued, and the two became intertwined as the elder Sullivan looked on. To him, it seemed as if the two bodies became one.

In a booming voice, he looked to the sky. "Let all be warned within my hearing that today, destiny is fulfilled! Those that stand in destiny's wake will be wiped from existence! Those of the darkness, be it known that you will be swallowed by the light!"

He then looked to his charges and couldn't help but feel a wave of warmth as he took in the scene before him. Rather than interrupt, he allowed the moment to finish naturally, standing to one side, grinning from ear to ear. Unaware of the duration of the kiss, he sat on one of the now-fallen trees that littered the ground. A great sense of accomplishment took hold in that moment, and his mission of bringing the two young people was now complete. Mr. Sullivan knew the meaning of this finite task but allowed nothing but happiness to enter his mind.

Eons of preparation washed over his soul, watching the two young people hold one another, intertwined. Thankfulness summed up this moment. When the commander's men found them and attacked the Sullivans' home while Peter was at school and Michelle at work, he fought with everything he was. Though his foe didn't capture him, the damage was done as the fight left Jerry Sullivan clinging to life when Peter's mother arrived home that day. Sadness came over him as he thought of his time ending and not having the ability to say goodbye to his beloved daughter.

Michelle would take his mantle of Knight of the Cosmos and was well trained being ready for the position. He always envisioned the two travelling the stars, making the universe safe for peace-loving people. Fate now stepped in and would leave her alone. Such a daunting position needed a person of remarkable abilities and strength, all which Michelle had. Pride swelled up in his heart thinking of another Sullivan taking on the Knighthood. His pride reached an apex as he watched the young couple kiss one another.

He knew he would leave this world as it should have been prior to his death, in the hands of the light. Finally, the two released one another in a haze of glowing light, lightning, and radiance they walked toward Mr. Sullivan hand in hand. The two glowing beings stood in front of him with wide smiles. Without another word, the knight fell to one knee, offering a sword to the two standing before him. Rebecca reached forth and took the sword.

Peter bent down and lifted his grandfather to his feet, smiling the entire time. Warmly, he hugged him. "Grandfather, thank you!"

Rebecca touched his cheek. "My knight, your task is fulfilled! Be at peace!"

The light surrounding Rebecca and Peter transferred onto the body of Jerry Sullivan. The two watched as the light entered his body, causing him to look almost invisible. The image of Peter's grandfather hovered now in the air, looking fondly at the two young people. Rather than whisk away he seemed comfortable to stay a while longer.

Rebecca looked to Peter and nodded. Peter let his hand leave hers and walk to his grandfather's image. Standing before his grandfather, he couldn't speak. The two looked at one another with love.

Peter spoke first, "My whole life you've watched over me. Thank you! I cannot begin to imagine the trials that await me, but I promise you this, I'll make you proud."

Jerry tearfully smiled. "You're by far the best man I've ever known! Let all the lessons taught and yet to come be your guide. Always look to others in the darkness. Light will always find a way!"

Tears fell on Peter's cheeks. "Will I ever see you again? Now that your mission is complete?"

Peter's grandfather looked uncertain. "I would like to think so, but

I simply don't know the answer to that. It's true my time here is at an end, but you will learn that death is only the beginning."

He looked at his grandfather. "I'll find you again! I promise!"

Jerry reached out and engulfed the young man in a white glowing hug. "Please tell your mother I love her and will miss her. Look after her and Rebecca."

"Grandfather, you will never have to worry about that. I'll never let anything happen to either!"

Mr. Sullivan knelt. "My King! Thank you for your faith in me. Know I love you and will keep watch over you."

The glowing light faded, and the image of the old knight vanished. Peter stood weeping. He felt the warmth of a hand clasp his and gripped Rebecca's hand firmly. She leaned in, placing her head on his shoulder and rubbing his arm. Peter took her, hugging her close to him. He was still looking to where his grandfather stood.

For the first time since his training began, he felt safe and looked around him at the destroyed grove. The devastation, frightening to behold, caused him to blink. Not one tree in the semi-circle remained intact for a least a hundred yards. The ground looked sandblasted with chunks of wood and splinters sticking out of the ground like some unnatural porcupine. There was no sign of the commander or the fallen Rebecca. He couldn't fathom the amount of power released into the grove but was glad beyond imagining to be here with Rebecca in this moment.

Unspeaking, they reached for one another's hand and walked together out of the dark grove. They followed the path without interruption until they arrived at the main flower garden. Standing in the crossroads, Rebecca stopped Peter and looked into his eyes. He felt his cheeks warming and looked down at his feet. A gentle hand lifted his face until his lips were within an inch of hers. No electricity, no lightning, and no power this time, just a young woman's beautiful lips right there for him. Peter backed away slightly.

Rebecca laughed. "I told you, Peter Sullivan. You're going to be nothing but trouble!"

Peter shook his head. "I've thought of this moment almost every night since I first saw you and now, I have no idea what to say!"

She pulled him close and let her lips interlock with his, kissing him as passionately as when they were in the glowing light.

Peter sheepishly whispered, "This is my first kiss!"

Rebecca slyly snickered. "My love, it won't be your last!"

CHAPTER TWENTY-FIVE

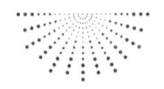

A look of dismay and uncertainty crossed Nora's face as she contemplated her next move. For her part, the council member knew very well who Jerry Sullivan was and vaguely recalled Michelle in her early years. True, Michelle never attended any council meetings in Nora's recollection. Jerry, though not often present, was viewed as an extremely important member of the council. Her thoughts moved to a time where Jerry stood before the council, alerting them to the impending danger about to fall upon his people.

Argued for years at the council table, the plight of humanity came up time and time again. Jerry pleaded with the council to become more involved with the molding of humanity. His lead argument being the reptilians already controlled much of what went on in human society. Though the council saw serious merit in his argument, their policy remained one of observation. Observation continued throughout much of the human's history until the reptilian people helped the humans upgrade their technology. As the technology progressed, so did the human society at an alarming rate.

Still, the Zarillion people watched as the humans used the technology to build a war machine. Time and time again, the war machine would threaten to wipe out what many on the council felt was a promising human race. Again, Jerry approached the council, calling for action, and again, the council rebuffed his request. The exchange became quite heated, and Jerry said he vacated his seat at the table, leaving the council to its own designs. His last words to the council were a warning for them to digest regarding the lack of assistance to the humans. Jerry warned and quite accurately, the reptilian influence would boil over into their own world. His warning didn't end there as he sternly spoke to the council that their lack of involvement would directly doom their own society.

Nora thought back to the firestorm Jerry's departure had on the entire council. The council became splintered that day as many of the council members believed as Jerry did that their own fates were directly tied to that of the humans. In hindsight, Jerry couldn't have been more correct. The void Jerry left by leaving the council caused a large rift and much political maneuvering throughout the council and city. It became even more so as Jerry's warning looked to be coming true.

Adding insult to injury, Jerry's daughter Michelle, a Knight of the Cosmos herself, went into exile with her father, leaving the council without two of its most powerful allies. Unrest further took place when Michelle married a human and gave birth to a hybrid in her son Peter. The council begged Jerry to return with his family, but he refused, stating he would raise the young man himself, training and preparing him on his own. The council went into panic as they found out Peter was indeed the one they were waiting for to bring their society into balance. Knowing Rebecca's abilities and knowing Peter was out of their reach, caused much anger on the council. Andrew ordered Peter to be taken and brought back to Antarctica.

In the end, the council wisely succumbed to Jerry's wishes and watched from afar as the boy grew. When it became apparent Jerry had been correct all along, the council changed its tune. This happened a little too late as Michael already dug his claws deep into the council and even deeper into the politics of the city. As Jerry predicted, their lack of action caused devastating effects on their own society.

In his exile, Jerry kept in contact with few of the members of the council. His focus to prepare Peter and keep him safe took all his strength. He even went so far as to cloak his home and family from prying eyes to keep them all safe. What Jerry didn't count on was the reptilian's prison field to weaken and fall. Once the field failed, the reptilians could use more of their influence to search for Jerry.

Nora pondered all this as she eyed Michelle. The council member aware of Michelle's station understood if she so chose Michelle could take over the council by right. Rising to her feet she faced Michelle and Derek. The man, clearly military, made matters even more unsettling. Not only did Michelle have the right to take over the council, looking at Derek's prowess, she offered little in the way of resistance at this point. Her thought to tread lightly could be the only play at this time.

Nora smiled. "Michelle, welcome. As you stated, it has been awhile. Things haven't gone well for us as of late, but we will survive as always."

Michelle replied, "Nora, I only really want one thing at this moment. Where is my son?"

A wave of relief washed over her. "Your boy is training in the Royal Garden. I'll take you to him."

She walked over across the floor. "Follow me, and I'll have you there in short order."

Derek and Michelle fell in behind Nora, following her through the chamber out into the hallway beyond. Derek, used to structures such as this from his tours in Afghanistan, moved quickly. Michelle, anxious to see her boy, followed Nora, not looking around her. She recalled the city but didn't want to see it at this point. The only thing on her mind now was seeing Peter.

Nora, well aware of Michelle's need to see her son, took advantage of the mother's hurried state. Turning one corner quickly, she punched a few quick commands into her wrist communicator. The dimly lit hallway allowed her to keep Michelle and Derek off balance.

She continued for several minutes until they walked into a small cavern with no exits. Nora feigned ignorance, trying to offer her apologies but still didn't turn back.

Derek's military training kicked in, and he spun just in enough time to see soldiers coming his way with drawn swords. The first man tried to stick Derek in the chest and received a hilt to the face for his trouble. Derek, no stranger to close quarters combat, took out his own long military knife. Facing his attackers, he entered the fray with full force. The Zarillion soldiers, trained to follow orders, knew not who they were attacking. Derek dispatched soldier after soldier, only to look over his shoulder at Michelle seeking her safety.

Again, Michelle wielded her own sword, cutting through the outmatched soldiers. Another soldier came at Derek, this time with dual swords cutting a crossing swath in front of his face. He reached down quickly, grabbing a short sword dropped by a fallen soldier and brought his own blade up with his newly found blade to block the blows. The soldier's skill matched their fine weapons, but years of hard fighting were on Derek's side. He dispatched wave after wave of soldier until he and Michelle stood together facing Nora alone.

Michelle's eyes danced with power as her blade now glowed a brilliant white. "Nora, what's the meaning of this?"

Nora chuckled. "Welcome home! What, did you expect a warm welcome? There are many on the council that blame you and your family for everything that happened to us. I for one do!"

Michelle moved forward to intercept Nora but stopped abruptly as if running into an invisible wall. She put her hands up to move or push something away, only to feel a force field blocking her way. Derek moved to her side and struck out at the field with his sword. The sword struck the field, bouncing off it, sending sparks through the air. She shook her head, telling Derek it was no use. The knight took a few steps back to look at her captor.

Nora smiled as she turned to look back. "Enjoy your new home! Don't worry, I'll take great care of Peter. When he finds out his mom met with an accident on her way to see him, well, he's going to be devastated!"

Michelle remained calm as Nora truly knew little about the Knights of the Cosmos. Derek, on the other hand, looked ready to chew through the rock to strangle the council member. Taking her hand, she placed it on his shoulder and whispered for him to sit with her. He took one look at her serene face and followed her lead as she sat legs folded on the stone floor.

They watched as Nora walked away, disappearing around the corner. Around them lay fallen soldiers with communicators and weapons littered the cavern. A smile came across Derek's face as reached down, picking up a light assault rifle. Checking the weapon, he slung it on his shoulder and rummaged through the pockets of the soldiers, taking anything useful. Michelle still sat on the floor, unmoving with her eyes closed. He took a bite of a confiscated protein bar, watching Michelle carefully.

Her body nice and calm, she let her mind search the cavern for unseen exits or weaknesses in the field. Upon inspection, the cavern seemed solid with a few crevices here and there but no true exits. Taking a moment to let her mind probe the field itself, she was disappointed to find no weak spots. Discouraged, Michelle thought of some other way to break through the field.

Again, she allowed her mind to reach out but this time, she looked around the outside edge of where the field met the rock face of cavern itself. A great sense of triumph entered her mind while she saw in a few places where the rock wall was its most jagged there were weak spots. The field did indeed end at the wall but in a few places, the jagged walls caused rifts in the energy field. The rifts couldn't be seen, but she felt them. Her mind looked around the cavern until Michelle was satisfied she had found their escape route.

Derek looked very relieved when her eyes popped open. She smiled brightly at him and rose to her feet. He looked to her for an answer to his unasked question. Towards the back of the cavern stood an outcropping with some low-lying rocks on the floor. These rocks made great seats, and Michelle sat comfortably upon one. Derek kept looking toward the door anxiously for more soldiers to arrive. No soldiers came, and Nora stayed away.

In hushed tones, Michelle called out, "Derek, come sit. Nora will leave us here. No one is coming here."

"Michelle, we cannot stay here! We must find the boys!"

Michelle clasped his hands. "My dear Derek, have no worries. I'll seek out the boys. Trust me, I can break us out of here any moment. Honestly, right now, I need a safe place to be to make contact. Nora unwillingly gave me such a space. No one will bother us here."

Derek still don't look convinced. "I have every confidence in you, but what do you have up your sleeve?"

She looked slyly at Derek. "Well, considering what we know about the council right now, it has become apparent that Nora doesn't want any competition for the top position right now."

Derek shrugged. "Isn't she the only one left?"

Michelle responded, "That makes even more sense. She now is the only game in town. By right, the position would fall to my father but in his absence, it would then go to me. I'm the rightful leader of the Zarillions now."

Derek's eyes brightened. "Are you a queen?"

Michelle smacked him. "You wish! No. I'm what you would consider the head of the council. Our society doesn't use kings and queens any longer. The council is supposed to be made up of diverse members of the society to work for the good of all."

He laughed. "Michelle, this isn't much of a diverse group. Tell me why we're staying here though?"

"It will allow me to move around undetected while you watch my back."

A wide smile came to his face. "I don't mind watching your back!"

Michelle smacked him again. "You're terrible. Seriously though, I'll need you to keep me safe while I do this. It's like what you would call an out of body experience. It won't take me long, but I'll find out where the boys are."

CHAPTER TWENTY-SIX

Fury reached every fiber of his being walking through the devastation that was once his home. Everywhere he turned looked to be a scorched nightmare. The eerie silence added to his angst while he pondered his next move. High Commander Zosa, the leader of the reptilian people, now stood alone and free of his prison, yet he still felt captive. Eons of living below ground on this miserable planet gave him much time to plot his revenge. That revenge was served and in the wake of his triumph, everything turned to tragedy.

The entire compound seemed abandoned except for the corpses of his fallen people littering the floor around him. The smell of blood, fire, and roasted flesh still hung in the air, giving the commander more fuel for his rage. Each step forward caused actual pain, thinking of how close he came to realize his dream of the sheer destruction of his enemy. One chance remained for him to reach his goal and that hinged on being able to contact his people off world.

A great advantage to his freedom was his ability to attempt to contact his people. The real issue remained, would anyone pick up the signal. Also, he knew not the state of the reptilian people throughout the cosmos. When they were imprisoned, the reptilians had conquered many star systems. His hope remained that the reptilian people still maintained control over a vast empire, giving him the needed support to finish his mission on this world.

Stopping midstride, he spun his heals, snapping them together while nearly running back toward the exit. Images of death and destruction of the Zarillions filled his thoughts as he wormed his way through the rubble. He stopped at what was once his office to see if anything remained intact. Luckily, the office itself didn't suffer too much damage. His desk now in pieces covered what he was looking for, and he swiped it out of the way. Kneeling, he brushed away the debris to reveal what looked like a stone floor.

Letting power flow to his hand, he positioned his hand as a blade and thrust it down into the rock floor. Working his hand into the floor, he moved around until he found what he was looking for and grabbed it. Pulling his hand from the floor, he looked at his prize. In his palm, he saw a large medallion made of gold with the image of a reptilian ancestor molded into the front. Commander Zosa wrapped his fingers around the medallion, nodded his head, and continued his journey toward the exit.

Once again braving the elements, he looked to the sky, laughing. He walked a good distance from the gate so there was nothing within sight that could affect his transmission. Feeling satisfied this location would work, he held the medallion up to the sky. In a few moments, he felt an energy building in his hand. A warm, tingly feeling grew down his arm, and a brilliant light formed around his hand. As the energy in his hand built, he smiled when he felt it release into the air above him. He watched as the brilliant light went forth into the clouds up into space, searching for any reptilian people monitoring the skies.

The light beam never wavered and only stopped when the commander's arm was exhausted. When he finally brought his arm down by his side, it felt numb. He switched the medallion to his other hand and raised it to the sky, allowing it to try to make contact. Again, the commander held onto the medallion until he nearly fell over from exhaustion. His only hope now was that someone heard his message.

With his hand still tingling with power, he placed the medallion in his pocket and searched the horizon for any sign.

Pink, orange, red, and purple colors swirled in the evening sky. The commander knew he would need to move back indoors soon or freeze to death. His footsteps seemed very heavy in the newly fallen snow as he sank into the snow with a crunch for each footfall. His disdain for this area knew no bounds and tomorrow, he would search for new accommodations. Taking one last look over his shoulder at the darkening sky, he saw a glint off to the right of his position.

His military instinct kicked in, and he thought the worst. The enemy wasn't done with them. With his sidearm raised, he looked around for cover. The ruined gate made the best cover, and he used the rubble and fallen stone to hide behind. From this position, he could monitor his enemy's movements. Even in the coming darkness, he saw the outlines of a large group of soldiers making their way toward the gate.

Commander Zosa held his weapon pointed in the direction of the first soldiers in the front of the group. One soldier against many was never good odds, but the commander knew many situations such as this over his long career. He maintained a silent vigil but was ready to engage if needed. As the group came closer to the gate, the commander heard more muffled voices. At first, he heard a mixture of wind and low voices but as they came closer, the voices became clearer.

He couldn't fathom why an attacking force would be so loud or coming straight for the gate. This strategy puzzled the highly seasoned military man. As the voices became clearer, he could make out they were soldiers talking about typical things one would do returning home from a battle. Again, he couldn't understand the lack of military bearing on the part of this group of soldiers. The last rays of light moved behind the horizon when the soldiers were close enough for him to get a look at his attackers.

As he prepared to open fire, he saw a familiar soldier come into view. Relief entered his body as he saw the force were reptilian soldiers. Though they returned from battle, having various injuries and looking worn, they were mostly intact. Not a large force but better than the nothingness he thought he would be dealing with, gave him hope. Moving from the shadows, he approached the unsuspecting soldiers. At first, the soldiers drew their weapons, intending to engage, only to see their commander alive.

They spoke briefly at the gate but decided the conversation needed to continue inside. Once safely inside, the commander informed the soldiers that not much was left, but it was warm. He ordered them to tend to the wounded and to look for any working weapons, along with food. Having a group to command made the leader of the reptilians feel whole. This ragtag group may be all he could muster, but he could do a lot with such a determined group.

When the soldiers were settled and tended to, he met with the remaining leadership to grill them on the events leading them to this moment. According to the soldiers' accounts, this group of soldiers only survived because they were the last wave of soldiers assigned to invade the Zarillion city. Upon their advance, many in their unit were wiped out right at the gate. One soldier described how a blast of energy came out of the gate, leveling everything in its path. Their group happened to be coming up over a small ridge, moving toward the gate to not come directly in front of the gate. That move saved their lives.

By the time they arrived at the gate as destroyed as it was, they were barred from entry by a new force field. One soldier listed the ways they attempted to get in and were unsuccessful. The commander was pleased with their dedication to their mission. He listened to them as they talked about looking for another way into the city and being attacked by another small force of Zarillions.

The Zarillions cornered them, pinning them down in a small ravine. A grisly fight ensued, leaving the already small force of reptilians decimated. He couldn't help but be impressed by their courage as they fought their way out of the ravine. According to the soldiers' accounts, the Zarillions gave way grudgingly, leaving the reptilian force out in the cold to deal with the elements. Their small force marched for days, finding shelter in rock outcroppings and small caves. They also alerted the commander of losses on the trek home due to injury and exposure.

When done with the tale, the commander sat back, looking at the soldiers sitting before him with pride. Though he wasn't their actual instructor, he felt a great deal of pride in their military training, which helped them survive such a fight and flight. The soldiers respectfully asked the commander about the abandoned base. He caught them up on events and alerted them to his request for help from the reptilian people off world. The soldiers listened intently, but the commander noticed the concern in their eyes. He assured them help would arrive, and their mission would be seen through.

With the soldiers safely inside and tended to, he ordered them to take turns on watch. He left them to get some much-needed rest and found a room that wasn't destroyed to use for the time being. At this time, he realized how tired he was and wasted no time lying down. His eyes closed quickly, and sleep took him just as fast. Dreams took hold as soon as he was in deep sleep.

The images of Rebecca came back into his mind. Her attack on the base still baffled him as she didn't come in through the front gate. He knew her power was immense, but he didn't think she could transport herself yet. Someone let her in, and he would find out how this invasion took place. Those responsible would be punished severely. He thought for a moment about the small force of his soldier's left. He couldn't help but wonder if one of their own allowed Rebecca into the base. That might remain unknown as there were so few remaining soldiers. Still, this invasion destroyed all his planning in an instant.

Rebecca remained his largest concern. Peter was raw and unskilled, but Rebecca was another matter altogether. Her skill and training aside, her power was beyond anything she even knew. Many a time, he knew he should do away with her, but something in the back of his mind always told him to wait. If he could capture and use her or at least turn her, his own power would go unchallenged in the universe. His current mood changed all that, and he was bent on destruction. He wouldn't be happy until everything she held dear lay in ruin and destroyed. The key would be Peter, and he would make the boy suffer untold tortures while she watched. The commander would find comfort in the fact her love was broken in front of her very eyes.

His dreams then took a different turn, and he saw Rebecca, but the scene was dark. She stood at the edge of the sea with the sky above full of bright stars, holding a bundle. The commander couldn't see the bundle, but he did see Rebecca hand it to another person covered in a large cloak. The mysterious person took the bundle and for the first time, the commander saw slight movement out of the bundle. At that moment, he knew it to be something of importance.

Rebecca now turned toward the commander with tears streaming down her face. She reached down at her feet, picking up a backpack, and handed it to the strange figure. The figure didn't speak and took the pack unbidden. The commander watched with curiosity as the figure walked with the bundle to a small craft waiting on the edge of the water. The craft seemed not a boat but more of a spaceship. As the figure was about to enter the craft, Rebecca ran to the ship with her arms out.

She reached the figure and grabbed the bundle, holding it to her face. He heard her cry, "I'm sorry! We'll find you one day! Know we love you beyond measure!"

The strange figure took the now-squirming bundle from Rebecca and entered the craft, closing the door behind. Rebecca watched as the craft made its way out into the ocean. As the craft was about to leave view, she fell to her knees, wailing. Reaching out, she grabbed the sand with both hands and looked to the sky, screaming. Again, she looked to the water to see a beam of light go straight up into the sky.

Rebecca, now on all fours, bent her head and looked up with gritted teeth. "They will pay! I'll destroy every one of them in the universe. None of them will be safe from me!"

The commander's dreams changed, and he saw himself on another planet much like his home. He now stood before a council of his own people surrounded by angered faces. As he looked around the room, he didn't recognize anyone looking back at him. He turned to the leader and again, he didn't know this person either. He found himself asking, "Where is the emperor?"

Laughter filled the room. "You've been gone a long time! Time flows much differently on that planet. The emperor is no longer in power. We rule here, and you report to us!"

Commander Zosa continued, "Is that so? Well, my friends, there's much to discuss but at this current time, I'm within a whisker of taking over this world!"

Again, laughter erupted. "You are! My intelligence tells me you're a prisoner on that world."

He held back his rage. "Who are you to question me? I'm second in command to the emperor and by all rights, if the emperor is no longer, I rule!"

The once-laughing faces now looked concerned as the leader responded, "Commander Zosa, that may have been true at one time but as I stated, you've been gone for a long time. For our part, you've been dead or missing for all that time. Are we to sit leaderless while you're a prisoner?"

Again, rage flared, but he controlled it. "Your point is well taken. However, as you can see, I am quite alive, and I rule by right. I'm not here to take your position. This planet is perfect for our new home world."

Again, odd looks came across the council's eyes as the leader spoke, "My dear Commander, we're currently on our new home world. As I've stated, you were gone for a long time, and many expeditions went out to find a new world. This one was chosen after you went missing."

Commander Zosa paused. "Fine! Come get me, and we'll obliterate this world! I'll be glad to rid myself of this human-filled cesspool."

The council nodded, and the leader continued, "Commander, things are much different from when you left us. We have our home world and our colonies, but our mission of conquering the universe that you and the emperor hatched, caused us nothing but death and destruction! No, Commander, you will remain on that planet and turn it into another colony for us. As far as your right to rule, you've been stripped of your title and now, you're just a soldier!"

Before the commander could respond, the image went black, and he shot up from sleep. Sitting up in bed drenched in sweat, he looked around the room, ready to strike someone. He was furious at the council. They couldn't strip him of anything. Those petty politicians would all be destroyed as well. Stuck on this planet with no resources put him in a bind but there were other allies waiting to help.

As if on cue, a globe glowed in front of him. As the globe glowed brighter, he could make out an image in the middle of the globe. He nearly doubled over in laughter as he saw the image of his emperor in the globe. When the globe was directly in front of the commander's face, the emperor glared at him.

The emperor spat, "Commander Zosa, so nice to see you alive!"

CHAPTER TWENTY-SEVEN

Derek's muscles tightened as he watched Michelle fall into a trance. His nerves on edge, he saw Michelle's eyes roll back into her head, leaving nothing but the whites of her eyes showing. Her body now completely rigid, Derek knew enough not to touch her but hoped she wouldn't fall over. To his great surprise, Michelle sat upright, unmoving, and her body emitted a glowing light. The glow formed around her entire body while Derek watched with raised eyebrows.

Once Michelle's entire body glowed, Derek noticed a whitish, wispy smoke rise from her body. The white smoke pooled over Michelle's head, forming a cloud above her. At first, the cloud hovered and then moved quickly toward the force field covering the cavern. Derek looked to Michelle then to the cloud, not knowing what he should do next. As the cloud neared the force field, Derek thought he saw the cloud take the shape of Michelle for a split second.

The cloud moved to the edge of the cavern entrance and now wormed its way through the weakened area along the edge until it stood on the opposite side of the field. Once again, the cloud gained the form of Michelle, looked at Derek and proceeded down the tunnel out of sight. He looked to where Michelle sat unmoving to make sure she looked well. Besides the white eyes staring back at him, she seemed fine. Rather than sit doing nothing, Derek thought he should try probing the field in case he needed to exit quickly.

The expanse of the cavern door seemed very solid at first inspection. The Navy Seal chose to use a stick found on the ground to probe the field as not to shock himself. Frustration mounted as there seemed no weaknesses in the field that he could exploit. As Michelle did, he moved to the edges of the cavern where the rock stood very jagged in spots. The smooth areas stood strong, but the jagged areas, Derek could put his stick through the field in many places. Hope filled his mind as he thrust the stick into multiple areas within his reach that he could put the stick into.

Out of sheer curiosity, Derek reached forth, grabbing what looked to be some loose stones at the edge of the cavern. Careful not to touch the field, he wormed his fingers into small pieces of the stones, prying them from the wall. He looked down at the pieces of the wall he easily took out with his bare hands. Swinging around, he searched the floor for larger sticks or thicker rocks he might use as tools. Luckily, both sat on the floor nearby, and he grabbed both. Without a moment to lose, Derek hacked away with a solid piece of stone, sending small pieces of the cavern wall flying.

Dust built around him, and a small cloud of his own formed. Unconcerned, he worked until sweat formed on his brow. As the sweat moved down his face, he used his now dust-filled sleeve to wipe his forehead. Derek reached forward and carefully tested the open area he created with another stick. A smile crossed his face as the stick went unhindered through the opening. He reached through, touching the outer cavern wall.

Pulling his hand back into the cavern, he picked up the rock he used as a tool with renewed vigor, chopping away at the remaining wall. Stopping only periodically to make sure Michelle wasn't in distress, he worked much of the next hour until he could pull himself through if needed. By this time, his hands were raw, and cuts covered his knuckles, but their escape route would be available when needed.

Dusting himself off, he searched through the field to see if his noise caused any issues. To his great delight, Michelle was correct about Nora leaving them here to rot. Derek was sure no one would be coming to check on them, but he still cleaned up the area in question just in case. To leave nothing to chance, he placed a few larger stones from the ground into the cavity he created, making it look to be part of the wall. When he fell back a few feet to see his handiwork, it looked quite natural.

Returning to Michelle, she still showed no signs of moving, so he reached up to check her breathing with his hand. Her shallow breaths touched the backside of his hand, making him confident Michelle still knew no danger. Derek found a nice nook within a few feet of Michelle, which he chose to lean back against to rest. A sweat-soaked shirt clung to his chest, which felt cool on his body. Leaning back to get comfortable, he let his head rest on the wall, thinking of their next move. Images of the boys came into his brain. They appeared to be running from something. Derek wasn't surprised.

His head shot off the cavern wall, startled from sleep. Jumping to his feet, hands ready for combat, he stood with legs apart in a prepared defensive stance. Eyes fixed on Michelle, he knew not how long he dozed, but he saw something wrong. Michelle's body convulsed violently before him. Blood now appeared from her nose, running down her face. Her hands shook at a rapid rate, threatening to hit herself. Derek ran over, trying to wake her, only to be repelled by her own protective field around her shaking body.

The military man dusted himself off and again looked around the room for help. Against the wall on the far end of the cave stood a large branch of some forgotten tree. He lifted the heavy branch from the wall, running back to his still-shaking friend. Michelle now spat up blood, and Derek knew he needed to wake her soon. Taking the small log, he carefully put it against Michelle's shoulder and pushed her over onto her side. At first, the convulsing continued, but he poked her again with the branch, and the shaking stopped.

Her body lay on the floor silent and unmoving while Derek tried to move her. Reaching under her, he felt hope as her field faded around her, and he propped her up against him. Talking into her ear, he hoped to wake her, but nothing worked. Checking her breathing again, he could still feel her breath, but this time it was very shallow. Wiping the blood from her lips and nose, he then held her tight.

A good problem solver, the Navy Seal knew they needed to escape this cavern and soon. Now calm, Michelle breathed much more regular now and was no longer coughing up blood. Still, despite his best efforts, he couldn't raise her from her self-induced slumber. Though she seemed out of danger, he knew not where she was or how to help her out of her current state. Carefully, he laid her against the back wall. Before rising himself, he knelt, taking Michelle's face in his hands, and kissed her softly on the lips. Half-expecting her to wake, he sat back until he was sure she was still somewhere else.

A quick move to the far wall allowed him to go to the edge of the cavern and still watch outside for intruders. Still, no one showed them any interest. He grabbed the rocks from his makeshift wall, tossing them to the side. With great care, he wormed his way into the hole until he could pry himself out onto the floor. Lying on his back, he looked up to the ceiling, letting himself breathe more freely. Turning onto his hands and knees, he thrust himself to his feet. Derek took a few moments to examine the cavern from this side. At first, he thought Nora created some field out of her own magic, until he noticed an odd-colored rock.

Letting his hand run over the odd-colored rock, it felt artificial. Pulling the panel to one side revealed an entire control panel. This excited Derek, and he knew leaving Michelle wouldn't be an option. Looking at the panel, he determined which button to push and soon saw the field lower, allowing him to retrieve Michelle. Still unawake, Michelle sat on Derek's shoulder in a fireman's carry as he moved back down the tunnel the way they originally came.

At first, they made good time but as the tunnels became more lit, Derek took it more slowly to not run into anyone from Nora's camp. A large crossroad stalled him, and he kept looking at each tunnel, hoping to figure which one would lead to freedom. Panic rose in his throat at the sound of voices coming from one of the darker tunnels. Looking around, Derek found a doorway near him. He placed

Michelle leaning against the door and took out his knife. Standing prepared for battle, he awaited the voices.

Two people quickly appeared into the light. One stood very tall with a white, flowing dress. These tall women looked regal, and her skin glowed. The man, muscular, tall, and fit led the way and seemed not concerned as they walked down the tunnel. Derek thought he could hear them speaking about a star gate. Standing protectively in front of Michelle, he spread his legs out, preparing to fight. The man stopped and instinctively wielded his own sword. A gleaming blade looked down at Derek. Unfazed, he readied himself for attack.

Again, the muscular man waved his sword in the air, taunting Derek. He didn't take the bait and maintained his vigil over the fallen Michelle. Now, the man attacked with a strike from above that Derek easily deflected. He returned a strike of his own with his knife which was also deflected. Both men went through a series of moves, only to be rebuffed constantly by one another. After a few minutes of back and forth fighting, both men paused and looked to one another in a sign of respect.

As the man prepared to attack Derek again, he heard the woman yell to cease. The man did as he was instructed and looked questioningly at the tall, stoic woman. As he did, she pointed to the floor at the fallen woman. A surprised look came across the man's face. Placing his sword back in its scabbard, he glared suspiciously at Derek. Derek stayed in front of Michelle protectively. The woman now moved in front of the military man and walked toward Derek with concern on her face.

She whisked by Derek without permission and knelt by the fallen woman, feeling her head. Derek was about to stop her, but something inside him told him she meant no harm. The tall woman now took Michelle's head in her hands chanting some odd words. He now knelt next to Michelle hoping the woman could help. He could tell Michelle's breathing was now more regular. Still holding her head, the tall woman chanted until Michelle's eyes popped open.

Michelle sat up. "Nora! Nora has taken control of the council!"

Derek watched as Michelle fell against the other woman, shutting her eyes. The woman in white looked even more concerned. She turned to her military man who nodded and stood, waiting for her instructions. She looked to Derek and rose to her feet.

As tall as Derek, she exuded power, and he knew fighting her would be worthless.

She looked calmly at him. "Derek, I presume?"

Derek looked shocked. "How do you know that?"

She almost laughed. "Well, Derek, you're with Michelle. According to our intelligence, you and Michelle were on a mission of some importance. I take it you were successful?"

He still looked unsure. "Who are you that you have access to that type of information?"

The woman stood tall. "Derek, I am Holly Cheric, Zarillion council member, and this is General Giles, Supreme Commander of the Zarillion forces. We're your allies, Derek, and Michelle is family!"

He looked at her with hope. "Can you help her?"

"Yes, I can but not here. We must get somewhere safe. We're going to get your boys."

For the first time, Derek looked happy at the mention of his boy. "Are they okay?"

General Giles stepped forward, leading with his hand. "Derek, well met! Now I know who trained your son! He is quite the soldier! You must be proud!"

A prideful father, Derek took the man's hand. "Thank you. He is quite the young man but honestly, I cannot take all the credit. Sometimes I think his fate isn't in my hands as if some other unseen force is guiding him."

Holly and the general looked at one another while Holly spoke again. "It is odd that you say that. We will speak more of this at some other time but for now, we need to get to the boys. Now tell me more about Michelle and Nora!"

Derek did as requested, telling Holly about their encounter with Nora and their ultimate capture. Holly listened, not interrupting until Derek finished the entire story. She reached over and touched his shoulder, nodding it would be okay. She informed him when they reached the boys, she could recall Michelle but wouldn't say any more about it. Derek wanted to question her but thought better of it. He knew how important it was to get to the boys. He followed Holly and General Giles with Michelle still on his shoulders.

The general volunteered to assist Derek but saw that wasn't needed. The small group moved forward through the tunnels without running into any other issues. Holly guided them expertly and before long, they were walking on the regular city roads. Some people gave Derek some odd looks as they looked at the woman over his shoulder but said nothing. Holly waved them on and continued forward. The pace picked up, and Derek could tell the general wanted to get to the boys but was trying not to add more of a burden to Derek. The Navy Seal said not a word and maintained the pace.

General Giles looked back several times to make sure Derek was okay, only to smile and stare at the staunch military man with great reverence. Travel went smoothly, and they now moved into a different part of the city. Derek saw the landscape change quickly, and they went from a cityscape to that of a country scene. Trees became more frequent, and the smells of flowers, plants, and cut grass now came across his nose.

Even the air seemed fresher and less stale with each step. A calmness settled in the area, and Derek felt comfortable in these woods. The light of the city went by the wayside, but they could see using their own night vision. Holly decided to give them more light and created a glowing globe to guide them. The globe floated in front revealing the way forward. Their steps became easier, and they moved quickly until they came out of the woods into an opening.

Holly, still leading the way, came into the clearing, first walking to the guards watching the gates of the large garden before them. Derek looked at the huge hedge before him and then to the castle to the side of the garden. As they came into the light, he saw the guards. In the dim light, he caught the view of Jake. Without another word, he gently handed Michelle to the general who took her carefully.

Moving from behind the general and Holly, he strode forward to meet his son. "Jake, my boy, you're safe!"

He ran to the young man, swallowing him in a bear hug. Jake allowed the hug, before separating from him. He returned to his post. His father noticed this and backed up slightly in understanding.

He smiled. "A soldier indeed!"

Jake's face was stern. "Sir, it's wonderful to see you!"

He snapped a salute to his father, which Derek returned quickly. "Where's Peter?"

CHAPTER TWENTY-EIGHT

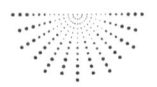

Hand in hand, arms intertwined, Rebecca and Peter clung to one another as they made their way along the wooden path. They looked in wonder at the full face of nature on display, along with the gentle beauty surrounding them. The fragrant air added a mystical feel to the garden. With each step, the garden almost felt as though it approved of the pairing between the two young people. There was no feeling of malice, and a jovial feeling built while they walked to the exit.

As they turned the corner, the huge tree Peter found himself beneath when he first arrived in the garden stood tall and mighty before them. Peter couldn't help but be in awe of the magnificent, ageless tree. Out of the blue, taking out his gleaming blade, he turned it point down while kneeling before the tree. Rebecca looked at Peter but questioned not his action and followed his lead, kneeling reverently. The two kneeling figures bowed their heads in respect.

The air now surrounded them in swirling fashion, whipping their hair everywhere. Rather than move, they maintained their current posture, waiting patiently. The circling air built around them. Then, a brilliant light flared upward toward the heavens. Peter now looked up to see the light shooting upward. He reached over, grasping Rebecca's hand. Hands clasped, they looked quickly to the tree. The tree itself glowed a whitish soft light. Both young people watched as a glowing unidentifiable figure came forth out of the light. Though the figure glowed with brilliant light, Peter saw her soft facial features.

He stood, shocked to see the face looking at him. The glowing figure stopped in front of Peter and Rebecca, placing an invisible hand on each of their shoulders. Peter felt the bristle of charged energy touching his skin but didn't sense any danger. Warmth filled his mind, and peace came over his body. As if in a dream, the woman's image became sharper and lifelike until a full woman stood before him.

She looked down at Peter smiling warmly. "Yes, Peter, Rebecca and I are kin. There are so many things I must tell you both, but that will have to wait for now. You're both in grave danger! An ancient evil has been unleashed, even darker than the reptilian people. We did stave off the darkness for the moment, but the evil coming for us now threatens to swallow the entire universe!"

Peter blinked his eyes, furiously looking for Rebecca but could only see the woman standing in front of him. "My Lady! What is it you would have us do?"

Her smile widened. "Peter, you continue to impress! It is true that you and Rebecca will become the ultimate power in the universe but only if you pass the trials set forth by the King of Monsters."

Again, he looked up with questions in his eyes. "King of Monsters? Up to this moment, I was hoping to make it safely to this city! My Lady, I'll do what you need of me if it is within my power or die trying!"

She laughed. "The King of Monsters revealed himself after eons in hiding. Many felt he was lost, but those of us who can feel his very evil knew better. Just know he can take many forms and is also the King of Falsehood. He goes by many names, but the names matter not. It is the monster itself that must be stopped."

Peter asked, "What form is he currently taking? Is there a way to track him and what can I do to stop him?"

Her hand came off his shoulder. "My young friend, it won't be you alone assigned this task. You will go with a circle of allies to complete your tasks. The dangers will be many, and no one can see all ends, but I'll tell you this, I am confident in your abilities."

He sheepishly looked her way. "My Lady, what do I call you?"

"I go by many names in many realms, but here on this blue planet, I am known as Mother Earth."

He bowed. "Mother, how should I address you?"

Once again, she smiled. "Peter, we're family. For now, call me Mother. When we meet next, I'll discuss with you my true name and reason for still being on this planet."

"Where is Rebecca? Is she all right?"

"She is well. I'm speaking with her now as well as you. My conversation with her will be brief as she knows of me already. Her family and I are connected in many ways."

He looked down to see himself still kneeling but couldn't feel any pain or discomfort. Again, he looked around him for Rebecca but could only see the glowing white light surrounding Mother and himself. The resemblance frightened him as he could be looking right at Rebecca. There was little doubt of ancestry between his beloved and this creature. Still, as he looked at Mother, he felt safe and warm with her glow surrounding them.

He started, "Mother, I understand you have confidence in me but right now, I'm no better than a novice. My power lay untapped and much to the king's chagrin, untrained."

She stood tall. "My boy, I watched all of your training, and I tell you this, there are few in this universe with your gifts and even fewer who can wield them properly. You, my friend, are a rare jewel, and a time will come where many current enemies will see this and rally to your cause."

"Enemies as allies?"

"Yes, enemies as allies. This surprises you, does it? Many who may consider you an enemy now may be swayed by the right ruler. You, Peter, are that ruler and each day will prove your leadership qualities. Any other leader of their people who doesn't see this will perish in your wake."

Peter now stood before the figure and still seemed dwarfed by her.

"My Lady, how am I, just a boy, to rally experienced leaders to my cause? Until now, I couldn't even get a lab partner to follow me."

She patted him on the shoulder. "Is that how Jake responds to you?"

"Jake? He is my oldest and dearest friend! Our connection is special and different. How can I expect those types of connections with strangers?"

Laughing she put her hand around his shoulders. "Humble beyond measure! That is why you will succeed where others fail!"

Still holding his shoulder, she guided him to the base of the tree motioning him to sit. He did as bid, sitting close to the huge trunk of the ancient tree. She moved to the side of the tree and placed her own hands on the still-glowing trunk. Peter saw the figure meld with the tree and in a matter of moments, the figure vanished into the tree. He sat alone, still watching the glowing tree cover him in light.

From somewhere in the tree, he heard a voice, "My boy, be secure in your abilities as a person. Those are the most important gifts you own. Many with great power have no character, causing great damage to all they touch. Your character is beyond that of all your ancestors. I say it here and send it out to the universe, you are my son, by right and deed! Let all hear me, Peter and Rebecca are my voice and hand. None shall stand against them!"

Peter felt the earth tremble beneath him as the light faded from the tree. He saw the bark and branches now but still felt life pulsating from the tree. Even in the clearing picture, he panicked as he still couldn't see Rebecca. The air around him felt cooler, and the fragrances from the garden made their way to his nose. Backing up slightly, he walked cautiously around the trunk of the tree. As he came to the other side of the tree, his heart filled with relief to see Rebecca.

Her eyes danced with the same brilliant light the tree gave off, and she seemed in a trance. Peter moved to her but thought better of touching her when in this state. Standing guard, he protectively looked around to make sure no one interrupted her meditation. Over the next few minutes, Rebecca seemed comfortable but didn't move or speak. Every now and again, he would peer at her face to see if the energy faded.

Finally, he saw the color of her beautiful blue eyes return. Quickly moving to her in case she stumbled, he stood ready to catch his beloved. At first, she seemed not to recognize him as he noticed her trying to focus her eyes. After a few blinks, she smiled at Peter, taking his hand, letting herself be led away from the tree. The two walked a few feet from the tree, sitting on a log seat looking at one another.

Rebecca spoke first, "Peter, Mother has one final message for you. She says beware false empires. I'm not sure what that means, but she said when the time comes, you will. She is sorry that her time with us is short but communicating in person as she did, takes tremendous power and even she cannot hold it for long."

Peter warmly held her hand. "Rebecca, what form did she take when speaking to you?"

Rebecca looked oddly at him. "This is very curious, Peter, but to me, she looked just like me!"

He smirked. "So, I'm not crazy. According to her, you're related, much like the king and I."

"Peter, I know much of this seems out of our control, but please let me assure you. My feelings for you are genuine and beyond measure!"

He looked at her red faced. "Rebecca, my feelings for you are beyond comprehension, and I feel nothing pushing on us to be together. I know everyone says we're destined to be together and that may be true, but I know how I feel. No one can make me feel this way!"

She reached over, engulfing him in a hug. "I understand. I too feel as if nothing can come between us!"

Peter stood, holding his hand to Rebecca. "Shall we go tell everyone else what's going on or stay here?"

With a sly grin on her face, she pushed his shoulder playfully. "As much as I could stay here with you forever, there are bigger concerns we must face."

He shrugged his shoulders. "Can't blame a guy for trying!"

She shook her head. "Trouble, Peter! You are sheer trouble!"

This time, Rebecca grabbed his hand and led them down the rubble path. She felt a slight tug as Peter stopped for a moment to look back at the tree. He smiled and bowed before turning to follow Rebecca. With the nod of her head, she started forward, skillfully guiding them to the hedge where they entered the garden. Coming around the corner, he half-expected to see his grandfather but, to his disappointment, only the hedge greeted them.

Both looked at the hedge, but the entire length appeared the same. There were simply no edges or divides where an exit might be waiting. Rebecca walked back and forth, inspecting the hedge to see if they might be missing something. Peter did the same in the other direction to no avail. Discouraged, they walked back to one another with arms up, not knowing what to do. Rebecca thought for a moment and walked to the hedge, placing her hands as she did to enter. Nothing happened as she released power into the hedge. The hedge absorbed the energy like food, almost swelling before her eyes.

Peter tried his hand at the hedge with much the same results. Once he returned to Rebecca, the two young people stood dumbfounded. Peter recalled how easily the hedge opened to let him in and couldn't understand what would be required to exit. Rebecca's thoughts were much the same. She wouldn't be denied entry and willed herself inside the garden. Over the next hour, they walked back and forth, looking at the entire area of the hedge where they entered, hoping to find something that might help.

Peter looked upward to see if they could scale the hedge and escape over the top. Nothing around him would allow them to climb the hedge as most of the larger trees were far from the hedge. The only things growing near the hedge were beds of beautiful wild flowers. The hedge itself looked to be a good twenty feet high and unclimbable. Again, they were at a stalemate with the hedge getting the best of them.

Rather than get upset, Peter led Rebecca to a waiting bench near one of the beds of wild flowers. They stared at one another, waiting for each to suggest a solution. Nothing came to mind as they held each other's hands. Looking into Rebecca's eyes, Peter didn't want to leave but knew what was at stake. Rebecca, for her part, didn't want to leave either but much like Peter, had a great sense of duty. The two sat for several minutes, trying to wrack their brains.

All at once, Peter shot up to his feet, nearly running to the hedge with a huge smile on his face. He turned, waving Rebecca to join him. She didn't question him and moved over to him. Peter seemed anxious but sure of himself and took a few breaths, gaining his thoughts. He licked his lips and rather than say a word, he gently clasped Rebecca's hand and placed them on the hedge.

At first, nothing happened, but Peter nodded to Rebecca, and she knew what he meant. They needed to do it together. Both invoked their power, releasing it into the hedge together. Again, the hedge absorbed the power, but Peter could hear a cracking sound. The hedge slowly gave way and opened an archway to allow them to exit.

Hand in hand, the two watched with relief as the hedge gave way. Leaves fell to the ground, and dust formed around the now exit. Rebecca and Peter released their hands at once, moving toward the opening. Making their way through the dust into the outer cavern beyond them, they saw shadowy images taking shape. Unsure of what to expect, each held onto their power to defend themselves, if it came to that. Walking forward, the dust moved from their view to reveal a familiar face.

Jake ran to Peter and grabbed him, sweeping him up in a bear hug. Peter, too excited to say anything, just hugged him back. An overwhelming sense of joy and love filled his heart in that moment. After his trials in the garden, to see his friend so happy to see him made the entire ordeal worth every struggle. Once Jake let him down, he looked at him strange and punched him in the shoulder.

Peter flinched. "Ow, man! What's that for?"

Jake growled, "I'm never leaving your side again!"

Peter smiled. "That, my friend, would be most welcome!"

CHAPTER TWENTY-NINE

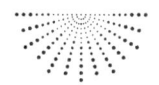

High Commander Zosa stood proud and tall, staring toward the supreme leader of his people. The emperor, as he called himself, waited for the commander to prostrate himself before him. The commander relented but didn't bend a knee and turned to face his once master. Energy danced between each of their eyes, threatening to incinerate the other. Though the globe separated them, the commander still felt the energy emanating from the emperor. A standoff of will ensued, and the commander stood strong despite a small amount of hesitation on his part.

Taking a moment to think of the visions of the ruling council full of politicians rather than warriors was worrisome. The commander powered himself down and looked at the emperor waiting for an explanation. At first, the emperor seemed quite content with launching an attack on the commander, but he too needed allies. With a flick of his hand, the energy dissipated, and the globe returned to a crystal clear. Although the emperor let go of the building energy, the commander felt at any moment the evil man would strike him down. Again, the two iron wills struggled for control of the situation.

The emperor opened the dialogue, "Commander Zosa, much has transpired since you went in search of a new home world."

"My Lord, how is it you're no longer in control?"

A low growl came from the emperor. "My friend, I've been in power for a long time. Leadership always creates enemies, but those from within are always the most dangerous. My second learned too well from me and didn't have anyone like you to challenge him, so he grew in power."

The commander shook his head. "I don't even recognize him. Who is he? I know I've been gone for a long time, but surely I would know someone like that who could rise to power."

"He was but a lad when you left. He belongs to a small noble family all but destroyed by you years ago!"

The commander cackled. "Well, that explains a lot! Still, My Lord, how is it you were ousted?"

"I underestimated my opponent! It won't happen again! Yes, at first, I thought of nothing but his utter destruction, but I have bigger aspirations. He can have his petty little council. You and I want the universe!"

Again, the commander cackled with a wide smile. "Now, My Lord, you're speaking my language. Tell me, sir, what do you have in mind?"

The emperor paused briefly. "First, I must make my way to you. According to my calculations, it won't take long but thirty of your Earth days for me to make the trip. Once I arrive, we will coordinate our efforts to bring that world to heal. When that world is under control, we will launch our efforts on a much larger scale."

Again, the commander smiled. "Emperor, this world is on the brink of its own destruction. We may not even have to do anything. It is quite possible when you arrive that you will do so to a ruined planet ready for our own inhabitants."

A sly look came over the emperor's face. "What fun would that be? I do love a good conquest!"

Commander Zosa took a seat and listened to the emperor outline his plans for the conquest of Earth and the universe. Though his own plans were much the same, he took exception to another leader getting in the way of his own plans. He listened with keen attention but kept thinking of how things were simpler before he knew of the emperor's existence.

Emperor Conswane, as he called himself, droned on about his eternal rule as the commander grew weary quickly. He tried with great difficulty to maintain some semblance of attention but nearly got up and walked away. The emperor sensed his loss of attention and changed the subject quickly. He now offered details of his own forces and how they could help the commander win control of Earth.

The commander perked up hearing about a fresh new set of forces at his disposal. Thinking of the still-lurking German forces waiting to take control of the earth's surface. Still, he needed to round up what remained of his own people to get a good idea of what he could add to the emperor's forces. As much as he detested the Germans, they were steadfast in their conviction, and he could count on them to finish the job. The Nazis, as they called themselves, infiltrated every government on the face of the earth. Operating from the shadows for a century, they worked their magic, bringing people to their cause.

He leaned back in his seat, slightly recalling meeting with Colonel Whilhelm's predecessor. The commander automatically liked the leader's moxie and felt he could use this man to attain his own goals. Though the man served the reptilian people faithfully, he got himself killed during an incursion. When the colonel took over, he was worried, but the colonel made himself valuable immediately.

Colonel Whilhelm, for all his bravado, was a very accomplished military tactician. Time after time, he watched as the colonel turned defeat into victory. That was where the angst toward the man came since it was the commander who wished for the victories himself. While the commander ranted on and on, the colonel maintained his military bearing. This may also have something to do with the hatred toward the man as he kept himself composed.

With everything taking place now, he would have to reestablish contact with the colonel if he remained viable. The emperor finished his pitch as the commander sat up straight in his chair. Long years of rule hardened the commander beyond measure, but he could recall a time when the emperor took him under his wing, schooling him in the art of leadership. Much like the commander, the emperor was bent on world domination. Like his mentor, the commander wouldn't be content with one world. The emperor did surprise him with his thought that domination was good for a people. Under his guidance, he felt people needed to be ruled and too much freedom created ultimate chaos.

The idea of ultimate rule appealed to the commander, but he felt a society should be under the boot of its leader. He wanted complete control and didn't care for anyone but himself. His teacher shared his thoughts with him, and he always kept his own thoughts to himself. When he left for this world, he did take all the emperor's teachings, using them to create a structured rule of his people on this planet.

He did soften much from his original stance of ultimate leadership, watching his people struggle with his harsh rule at first. The very nature of his people living and working as a collective did allow for a certain hard rule, but he needed to allow them to be a part of it as well. Early on, as his people grew to except their new planet and prison, they looked to him for guidance. Once they were safe and established, he needed to have a ruling council much like home where he still maintained control.

When it became apparent his people were stuck behind the force field, he needed to make use of their gifts to find a way out. His science officers worked diligently year after year with little success, but they never gave up. All his people never lost faith, and this impressed him greatly, causing him to re-evaluate his rule over his people. Now, listening to his mentor spouting the same things he had learned first thing as a ruler, made him smile inwardly.

There was little doubt humanity could handle the collective type of rule. They were a weak-minded people and very selfish in nature. He knew he would have no choice but to rule them completely. Maybe after he molded them in his image, he could get them to develop like his own people, but from what he observed of these people, they would just as soon die than live together. Freedom was valued above any money in the human's eyes. Although in theory, he agreed with them, he knew better if they were to survive as a lasting species.

As an interstellar traveler, he came upon many societies who valued freedom this way, only to see them flame out fast. Freedom was constant work and needed to be fed into constantly with an ever-changing need for something new. In his experience, consistency was what made a society last, and working in conjunction with all people made for strong people. He looked at the emperor, and the wheels turned. Normally, he would hatch a plan to dispose of this new threat to his rule, but something made him quell his heart.

A calm emperor looked at his student and saw the man weighing his choices carefully. He trained the commander well and was quite upset to find his protégé disappeared. After so many years of hunting throughout the galaxies, he finally found his student. He knew what a powerful leader and warrior the commander could be, so he knew gaining his trust again would be the key to success. Even more important to the emperor would be implementation of his own brand of rule on the weak-minded people of Earth.

Both men took a moment to review their thoughts before renewing their conversation. Each weighing their current options and their own needs. After a few minutes of silence, it was the emperor who took control of the conversation. He looked to his protégé with a serious expression and waited.

He began, "I understand your trepidation. Here you've become a revered ruler on your own and a successful one at that. You must be, to survive what you've endured."

Commander Zosa cleared his throat. "My Lord, I used all your lessons and ruled the best I could for my people. We went through some difficult times, only to come out of it even stronger!"

A genuine smile grew across the emperor's face. "I see they are lessons well learned. Again, I would trust none other than you with this task."

"My Lord, I mean this with no disrespect but once Earth is under our control, what becomes of us?"

With his eyebrow raised, he looked at the commander. "Well, my boy, as much as I love to rule, I'm much like you and know I cannot do everything myself. I'm sure there will be plenty to rule and new worlds to conquer as always."

A nod of the head by the commander. "Yes, sir. I as ruler wouldn't want to step on your toes and cause unwanted friction between us."

"A politician as well." The emperor grinned.

Frowning, he looked up. "Yes, My Lord. I'm not a fan of the politicians, but I've come to understand their worth. As you stated, you cannot do everything on your own!"

The emperor started, "My student, listen well because we will have use of an ancient force that once dominated the planet you're on. This force will then be used on any other planet we wish."

A questioning look came over the commander's face. "What force are you referring to, My Lord?"

"That, my son, remains to be seen but if my research is correct, it will be a formidable force that will bring many people to their knees. Though the force I refer to isn't native to Earth, it has remained hidden for eons and will be brought out of the shadows soon enough."

Again, the two exchanged glances, and the commander moved back in his chair. What kind of force could the emperor be referring? True, he couldn't do much searching while imprisoned, but he knew a great deal about the planet and to his knowledge, he knew of no force like described by the emperor. Now free, he could do his due diligence to get up to speed using the emperor's own research.

The emperor described his travel plans to the commander. In turn, the commander went into detail as to the nature of the humans he would encounter. He went into great length, telling the emperor of all the relevant intelligence to make his encounter easier. As always, the emperor was impressed with the commander and his preparedness. He listened to the commander not wanting to miss any details. Once finished, he felt the commander prepared him completely for his forces to invade Earth.

He always felt in control but after digesting the commander's information, he had little doubt the humans would give little resistance. His mind made up, he ended the conversation with the commander alerting him he would contact him during his journey to Earth. The commander nodded and watched as the image of his teacher slowly faded away, leaving him alone in his seat.

Standing, he paced around the room, wrestling with all he learned at the hands of his teacher today. First, the fact his emperor lived was comforting if not confusing from a ruler's standpoint. Then he needed to adjust his thinking as he stood alone to conquer Earth, yet here was the emperor ready to invade and now take over the planet. Though he revered the emperor, he couldn't help feeling a pang of selfishness come over him. All his years of scheming to make the Zarillions pay for their imprisonment of his people. That was when he sat back down.

The emperor didn't mention the Zarillion people once in his entire conversation. He couldn't fathom that and now, with the emperor gone, he couldn't help wondering what caused this oversight. The mysterious force he mentioned bothered him. What force and could they contain this force to their own will. As the commander knew well, working with a mercenary force did have its advantages but still many more issues than they were worth.

As he chewed on all the information given to him by his mentor, a soldier interrupted him. The man saluted him and alerted him to another force making for their location. He stood and walked with the man over to a barely working computer. While the screen was cracked all over, he could make out shadowy figures walking this way.

The commander ordered what was left of his own force prepare for battle. He looked around the room, and his ragtag group put their game faces on while preparing to fight. A thought occurred to him that the Zarillions were in a position to crush them while they were in their weakened state. When his men were ready, they stood by the gate, waiting for the order.

Viewing the screen, he waited. If he allowed this meager force to be attacked, and they lost, he would have no one left. In pure military fashion, he straightened himself and prepared to order his men to battle. He wouldn't surrender, and he would die in glorious battle as should be proper. As he was about to press the button and give the order, one of his soldiers shouted out to look at the screen.

There on the cracked computer screen, he saw a new force of his own people walking this way. The way they walked, and the shape of the heads gave them away. He couldn't help but feel a sense of relief. The force wasn't exceptionally large, but it would help swell the ranks of what he knew to this point. With great vigor, he pressed the button and went to welcome back his troops. A great pride came over him as he walked to the gate.

CHAPTER THIRTY

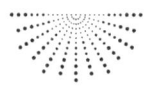

Silence hovered over the entire council chamber. Stoic, thoughtful, and cautious faces peered across the circular table at each other, hoping someone else would speak first. Eyes darted from person to person, wondering how to begin the conversation. To everyone's surprise, Peter rose from his chair and placed two hands on the table, slightly leaning forward. Light surrounded him as his mouth opened to speak. Those seated felt vibrations in the air but remained in their chairs.

Peter's eyes blazed a glowing blue, and he stood tall, seeming to grow in stature before the council's eyes. Despite these events, no one at the table felt any danger and calmly waited for Peter to speak. Again, Peter looked at his assembled family old and new before speaking.

A bright smile crossed his face. "My children, to see you all gathered here at last brings me joy beyond measure! As I explained to Peter a short time ago, I'm known by many as Mother Earth. My actual name is of little relevance but know we're related in all the most important ways possible."

The small group remained silent and waited for Peter to continue. Jake was the only one who seemed a little nervous, looking at his best friend's body taken over by another entity. He looked around from face to face, only to see calm and collected gazes looking back at Peter. They all looked to be under a spell of some sort. He couldn't help but wonder why he wasn't still in a trance such as his friends were in now.

Peter turned to Jake. "Jake, I'll answer your questions, but I need to speak to you alone. You may have begun to realize you're much more than Peter's friend. Your position as his friend, guide, and bodyguard has been preordained long before you were born. Make no mistake, you have free will as we all do, and you could walk away at any time."

Jake coughed. "Preordained? I am Peter's friend by choice, and I don't need any force telling me my duty toward my best friend. I would give my life for him because that's what he would do for me!"

The smile on Peter's face brightened. "That, Jake, is exactly why I'm talking to you now. You developed your friendship naturally and as a result, you share a bond none could have foreseen. It is of that bond I would now speak to you."

"If you know our bond is natural, why would you want to question it?"

Peter continued, "You mistake my intention. I don't question! I implore. It's that bond I want you to use and always look to. Your journey is just beginning and even I cannot see all ends, but I'll tell you the road is long being filled with danger!"

Jake retorted, "Danger. Well, what else is new? Peter and I made it here through untold dangers. He is the most loyal, smart, and cunning person I know. We will do what's asked of us."

"I know you will. Although I cannot tell you all, I'll say you'll need to make the ultimate decision soon. When the time comes, I feel you may leave Peter's side. It is for that reason we're speaking now. You must promise me you won't leave Peter for anything!"

Jake felt a jolt of energy surge through his body, and his eyes immediately shot to his father sitting next to him. There was little doubt in his mind, this was what the entity was referring to. Now, uncertainty filled his mind as he took in his military father sitting next to him. Looking at the stoic military figure made him feel better, and he looked at Peter.

He licked his lips. "I promise to never leave Peter, if I can help it!"

Peter looked at Jake. "Promise made, now it must be a promise kept!"

In the blink of an eye, Jake looked up at Peter, whose eyes still glowed blue, but he found himself seated. The entity spoke to the group about the many choices facing them. She led the conversation, sharing information they knew along with some they didn't expect. Although aware of the reptilian defeat, they were unaware of the survivors regrouping and reforming an army. Though informing them more danger lay in waiting, she didn't elaborate on the nature of the new challenges awaiting them.

All sat looking to Peter. "My major reason for breaking my silence is twofold. First, you're all that stands in the way of ultimate darkness in the cosmos! There was a time when many of your kind existed but now, my knights are few and flung throughout space. Each of you comes from a long line of knights in service to me going back eons. These knights have gone by many names, including Templar, Knights of the Round Table, and Magi. No matter what name they've taken, their task is always to fight to keep the dark from overtaking the light."

Michelle now stood. "My Lady, I understand your calling as I'm one of your trained knights, and I'll assist in any way you need me!"

Peter smiled. "Yes, you're a true knight, and I'm extremely glad of your service. I want you all to know that even though you lack numbers, there are those among you that account for entire armies. Yes, the fate of many depend upon you, and I have ultimate faith of your victory!"

Holly spoke from a seated position. "My Lady, what would you have us do?"

"Holly, right to the point. I would have you bring the seven kingdoms of earth together and prepare to defend this planet. To defend other worlds, this one must be secured first. The reasons for that can be discussed another time, just know this world is the key to everything else."

Holly stood quickly. "The seven kingdoms? We're all that's left of the seven kingdoms. They all died out long ago!"

Peter chuckled. "My dear Holly, much like your civilization, they remain hidden, but the time is now for them to reunite. You have all the tools to find the realms and bring them together. It's this task for which I've come to you today. You must reestablish contact with the kingdoms and prepare the defense of this planet. A great ancient evil is about to be released upon this planet, and only the combined might of the seven can combat the evil to come!"

Rebecca interjected, "Holly, I contacted the lost kingdom of Atlantis. I'll give you more detail after this, but I can assure you, their society is flourishing. If that's the case, we could find and work with the others."

The council's eyes moved toward Rebecca. They looked for more information. As she was about to offer more, Peter raised a hand asking for them to wait. All sat and waited for the entity to speak to them.

"Rebecca is correct. The Atlantians are alive and well. I'll provide you with clues and what information I can, but you will have to find the others on your own. My time with you is short as I need to prepare other worlds for the impending struggle that's to come. Just know that, in Rebecca and Peter, you have two beings who are the closest to me in abilities."

Peter reached out and clasped Rebecca's hand, raising her to stand next to him. The glowing blue light surrounding Peter now engulfed Rebecca as well. The entire company at the table sat in awe of the two beings emanating such raw and beautiful power. To an innocent bystander, they would see the two almost melded into one being as the blue glow intensified.

Peter raised his and Rebecca's hand into the air and in a huge booming voice, yelled, "Let all hear me now! The union foretold is now complete. Anyone who tries to come between that union will do so at their own doom!"

A blue beam of light shot into the air, along with crackling lightning and thunder. The group watched as the beam moved into the sky above them, leaving a small sapling tree with platinum-colored leaves sitting carefully on the round table before them. Each member looked at the beautiful tree in wonder without reaching out to touch it.

In a whisper, Peter heard, "My son, you must go into the garden and plant this tree in the Grove of Kings. You will know it when you see it. Let the tree be your guide. Only you and Rebecca can do this. You will be safe, but I have another task for Jake at this time. He will only leave you for a short time, but he needs to contact one of the kingdoms, and they only understand warriors. He is both a warrior and very diplomatic, so he must go."

Peter whispered back, "It will be as you ask, My Lady!"

As the blue light was about faded in the sky, Jake heard a voice, "Jake, I know you and I discussed not leaving Peter ever again, but I do have one task that only you can accomplish. If Peter and Rebecca were to go with you right now, it might cause outright war with a potential ally. You're a supreme warrior but an even better person. That's why you're being asked to accomplish this mission."

Jake, in his mind, whispered back, "What would you have me do?"

"Take Michelle and Derek with you. She has the items you'll need to accomplish your mission. Beyond the garden is an ancient set of caverns that no one will go near because they think it's haunted. You must go there as this is one of the entrances to the ancient dwarf kingdom of Earth. The talismans Michelle has will allow you safe passage. Just remember this, the dwarves respect warriors but value friends and family above all others. Good luck, my son!"

Jake came awake with shock in his eyes. "A dwarf kingdom!"

Everyone looked at Jake in surprise. Peter ran over to his friend, who put his hand up to let him know he was all right. Each person wrestled with the events that took place. Peter wondered if everyone had a visit from the strange Mother Earth. Jake shook his head, trying to decide if his message was real. Holly grabbed General Giles by the shoulder and looked deep into his eyes. Michelle, already on her feet, was the only one comfortable with the messages. Derek followed behind Michelle as she moved to the seat vacated by Andrew's demise. She looked down at it and then to her friends.

She stood behind the chair now, looking out at her friends for guidance. Holly saw her conflict and moved around the table to speak with her. Derek still stood close but let Holly move over to Michelle. General Giles stood on the other side, keeping an eye on both powerful women. Peter and Rebecca, still holding one another's hand, moved to a position in front of the council president's chair.

Michelle cleared her throat. "My friends, I'm a Knight of the Cosmos as are you, but I'm also next in line to lead our people. I find myself in a difficult position as a warrior, where I've been given a direct task by Mother, yet that would leave our people without a leader."

Holly reached out and placed a reassuring hand on her shoulder. "I understand the magnitude of this decision all too well."

Michelle looked up. "Holly, would you accept the position? I'm a warrior and couldn't lead from a chair. You have much experience here in the council and with our people."

Holly let her hand glide down Michelle's arm to her hand, allowing herself to sit in the council president's chair. "Michelle, I too am a warrior, but you're correct that we have need of someone with experience and understanding. If it is the will of those in this room, I'll fill the role until such time as the real rulers of our people return."

Everyone looked up at Holly and nodded with the decision to lead the council. The mood immediately became more comfortable, and they all returned to the circular table to discuss their strategy. At first, no one seemed ready to discuss the strange events with Mother Earth, but Peter oddly took control. He stood and looked at his friends.

"I'm probably the last person who should be addressing this council, but I feel as I'm sure many of you do, Mother gave me a task to complete."

Each member nodded, thinking of the individual task given them. Holly was asked to lead the council along with General Giles continuing his defense of the city. Michelle and Derek were given their orders. Rebecca and Peter were to plant the little sapling, while Jake was to become ambassador to the dwarf kingdom.

Peter continued, "As Mother stated, we have much to do to save this world, among others. We each have our tasks, and the sooner we accomplish these, the sooner we can reassemble to defend this planet."

Holly responded, "Yes, Peter's right. We must act quickly. Mother gave us some information but not all we needed. It will fall to us to prepare and be ready to defend our home. We also need to prepare the rest of the world to assist in its defense!"

Derek rose. "Holly, I would be glad to assist in that area. I do have a task assigned by Mother first and then, I'll contact government officials. Did they have an open dialogue with your people?"

Holly winced. "Not for some time, unfortunately. After the Americans went to the moon and found one of our old colonies still there, they became very standoffish."

Derek nodded. "Understood. I'll work on it. You'll be surprised by how much information they actually have on your people, even though they really don't understand it."

Peter announced, "Rebecca and I have a small but important task to accomplish, but we'll be back in no time to assist all of you!"

Michelle walked over to Jake and spoke to the young man quickly. Jake nodded but didn't say anything as he listened to Michelle's instructions. When finished, Jake spoke to Michelle, adding to her instructions based on what Mother asked him to do. Derek patted Jake's back and smiled. As a military man and father, he couldn't be prouder of his son. Father and son stood in the glowing light of one of the large lamps. To an outside viewer, it would have occurred to them that a torch was being passed from one generation to the next in that very moment.

Holly pulled General Giles to one side of the council chambers. "Ryan, I understand everyone was given assignments, but that may leave the city at our enemy's mercy?"

General Giles spoke, "Normally, I would say yes, but my intelligence says the reptilian people are scattered all over the surface. Even if some can make it back to their compound, I'm not sure they'll survive. Rebecca destroyed the whole compound. I don't know if they were able to shut it enough to keep the cold out. The cold is their greatest enemy now. At least the force field shielded them from the weather."

Holly, showing great concern, advised, "Ryan, the commander is still out there! Never underestimate that bastard! Besides, he and I have some unfinished business!"

CHAPTER THIRTY-ONE

Cradling the tiny sapling gingerly in his hands, Peter and Rebecca approached the garden entrance. Peter recalled his last trip to the garden and its dusty, dry feel. As they came up on the gate, the garden seemed more vibrant and inviting, as if a fresh spring rain left it teeming with life. The hedge around the garden looked soft and plush. When he entered the first time, the hedge seemed angry and defensive. Even the air around the garden smelled fresh and fragrant.

He noticed for the first time, other life around the garden as a squirrel squeezed out from beneath the hedge. Peter and Rebecca watched with great interest as the little creature scampered within a few inches of them. They smiled while the squirrel looked up at them and bowed before scurrying into the woods. Birds sang a song of joy and welcome. Insects rubbed their wings together in great concert. The amount of life swirling around the garden made them feel welcome.

Once again, Peter went to the gate and without hesitation, it opened before him. When the gate did close behind them, it didn't close itself off behind the hedge as before. They saw the gate shut, but the outside remained. Feeling more confident about not being a prisoner, Peter walked forward. His steps quickly brought him to the place where Rebecca and he kissed for the first time. Without a word, he turned and planted a soft kiss on Rebecca's cheek.

She smiled and turned to him. "What was that for?"

He looked a bit unsure of himself. "Rebecca, I don't know what adventures await us, but I'm so happy to be with you here at the beginning!"

Reaching out, she cradled his shoulder. "You're sweet! I too am glad beyond measure of our opportunity to be together. I cannot begin to explain how meeting you has filled a huge void in my life!"

Peter blushed. "Honestly, I still cannot believe how beautiful you are in person! Each time I look at you, it takes my breath away!"

This time, it was Rebecca's turn to blush. "You're too kind! I have to tell you, Peter, you're quite the handsome young man yourself!"

They laughed but continued down the path, looking from side to side, hoping to find where they should plant the sapling. The further they marched into the garden, the less life they saw. Now, the garden looked more like some of the barren areas they walked past on the way to this location. The terrain was now much rockier and more devoid of life. Peter turned, looking to Rebecca because he felt they must have traveled too far. She looked at him with the same questioning eyes.

"My love, I know not where we are? As we already discussed, this garden is an ancient mystery to my people. No one within memory has been allowed into the garden. All we know from our lore is only members of the royal family are allowed access."

Peter shrugged. "It looks as if we went too far off the path."

"It does look quite barren!"

He looked down at the little sapling whose leaves glistened. A strange light now emanated from the small tree. Peter felt his own power come to life inside him as the tree's light grew in strength. He felt a small tug on him as the tree's light glowed. The light was a beacon for them to follow as it cut through the dim light, pointing in the direction of a barely visible hill in the distance.

They walked at a brisk pace, following the light of the tree. Peter saw the light growing as they approached the hill and the tug from the tree almost driving him forward. When at the foot of the hill, Peter looked up into the dark air but couldn't see the top of the hill itself. Again, Peter felt the tug from the tree but this time, a flash of light sent out by the tree itself flared toward the top of the hill. Both young people looked up toward the light but still couldn't see the top.

A quick glance down revealed an ancient footpath leading upward. Moving forward, they found the path easy to follow. Though steep, the walk up wasn't too strenuous. It took the better part of two hours to climb the hill. When they broke the crest of the hill, the little tree flared to life, sending a beam of light into the air. The beam reached the stone roof, and a large globe roared to life with brilliant light. At first, Rebecca and Peter needed to shield their eyes until they became accustomed to the light.

Still blinking their eyes, they couldn't believe the sight now laid out before them. A well-groomed path laid straight ahead of them with burial mound after burial mound. Both couldn't tell how many were interred here, but the site was nonetheless impressive. Above them, the globe acted as a sun, and the light allowed them to see down the path. They continued their journey down the path, looking from side to side at each burial mound as they passed. Stone doors covered each entrance to the tombs, and they saw runes on each.

Peter laughed as he could read many of the symbols from his work with his grandfather's journal. The messages on the doorways were ones of hope and finding peace. As the two moved down, the rows of tombs they saw what looked to be a grove of trees ahead. Entering the grove, Peter found the trees held no leaves yet didn't look dead—more in a winter slumber. The air in the grove felt stagnant and stale but didn't make Peter or Rebecca feel welcome. They moved forward through the grove until the path wound around to the right behind many of the trees.

At the end of the path on a flattened stone, two thrones made of interlaced tree branches stood, as if someone weaved the branches together with magic. Peter felt the tug from the tree pulling him toward the thrones. He relented and walked toward the tree-made seats of power. Rebecca, grabbing his elbow, followed close behind. When they approached within a few feet of the thrones, the tree flared out a beam of light, revealing an old withered tree standing behind the thrones. Peter could tell this tree wasn't like the others, and the life force no longer was in this tree. Again, he felt the tug toward the old tree. He brought the little tree over to the withered one, placing it on the ground.

Without being told, he went to the old tree, wrapped his hands around the trunk, and pulled it from the ground. He couldn't believe how light it was, even though it was a tree of significant size. Walking carefully to the edge of the grove, he saw an open space where another tree stood. He gingerly placed the tree in the open spot. The tree rested in its new place of honor, and Peter walked back over, taking up the little sapling. Placing the small tree in the spot formerly held by the ancient tree, he knelt, pulling dirt around the tree to plant it.

As soon as the dirt covered the small tree's roots, Peter stood back to see the light build. This time, the light seeped into the ground, and he saw it moving from the roots into the ground. Each of the trees in the grove glistened with light, and leaves spread out on the branches of all. The ground came to life as beautiful, green, lush grasses and wild flowers bloomed everywhere.

The stale air grew in freshness while the fragrances of the newly growing objects engulfed the air. Rebecca moved to Peter's side and held his hand, watching the rebirth of the grove happen before their eyes. Though Peter felt similar when he first entered the garden, now he felt a completeness enter his heart. The grove, now teeming with life, looked royal in every way. As the two young people soaked up every second of the rebirth, they couldn't help but be held in wonder of Mother Nature's magnificence.

When the transformation stood complete, the grove shimmered in light and power. The small sapling, though not bigger in size, oozed light and power. After a few minutes, the power and light ebbed from the leaves and branches as Peter saw the last remaining issues of light seep into the ground. Now, the little tree stood alone as a newly growing one in a beautiful grove.

Feeling they were being watched, both in unison turned to see the intruder on their solitude. Peter nearly laughed as he looked into the face of himself. The king that trained him in the garden stood before him. Rebecca looked to Peter as he nodded it was all right to her. Without a word, he motioned for them to join him at a circle of stump chairs off to the side. Following close behind, he and Rebecca took a seat across from the king.

A bright smile came across the king's face. "Peter, you continue to amaze me! Even when we were training, I knew you to be an amazing person, but your gentle, kind nature is refreshing!"

Peter knelt before the king. "My Lord, what would you have us do?"

The king stood. "Rise, my boy! You bow to no one! I've been granted a small amount of time with you. Just know that Mother will be watching over you!"

Rebecca addressed the king, "My Lord, Mother asked us to perform this task. Can you explain its significance to us? I don't mean to sound rude or ungrateful but if the world is in as much danger as we're being told, why are we still in the garden?"

He looked at Rebecca. "My dear young lady, that's a valid question and one that deserves an answer. I'll explain what I can."

Peter sat. "My Lord, what is this place?"

Leaning back, the king looked pleased. "This, my boy, is a special place for your family. Though the garden is a special place for the royal family, only the kings and queens may enter this area. This is King's Grove, a place of reflection and of recharging one's gifts. It is here that you two will find your peace, and a place to cure most ills."

Rebecca chimed in, "I do feel invigorated! This place is so peaceful and beautiful. Why, My King, were we asked to come here?"

He looked at Peter and Rebecca. "Your mission, though you may think it insignificant, was a most important one. This sapling is the last of its kind in existence. It isn't just a tree, however; it's a conduit from the earth to you. Rebecca, you of all people will understand this."

Rebecca looked at the king. "So, when I gather power from everywhere, this is one of those places?"

A sly smile came over his face. "You're a fast study, my dear! Yes, our power comes from the very earth itself, and we can use the magnetic fields of the earth for various things."

Peter rose. "My King, the grove seemed to be in a state of slumber when we arrived."

"Yes, the last tree as you can see, lost its power which can happen if one isn't careful. We're beings of great power but like anything else, we have limits. I thought I could go beyond those limits, and it cost me and our people everything!"

"What happened?"

"In my final conflict with the reptilian people, I used all my power to imprison them on this world. I wasn't smart about it. After fighting them around the cosmos, I felt they needed to be stopped at all costs. Holly, among others, helped me imprison them but at great cost to myself and our people. So much of our power went into the force field holding them at bay, our own power was diminished. That might not seem like a big deal, but we needed to hide ourselves for fear of retribution from other species."

Rebecca stood. "So, that's the real reason we went underground!"

The king replied, "Yes and no. We were already planning on it as some of our ancestors lived on this planet, creating underground colonies before us. This sped up the process. Also, we became a very secluded people whereas before, we helped other species."

Peter asked, "My Lord, what do you need us to do now?"

"My son, I need you to put an end to this reptilian threat once and for all!"

Peter shook his head. "I do understand that, sir, but what exactly do you need me to do?"

The king stood to his full height and in a booming voice, called out, "You're my heir! You're our hope and our dreams! You will do what's needed to succeed. I cannot tell you exactly what the road will look like but know we're all with you!"

Peter was shocked. "All with me?"

The king pointed behind Peter. He turned, looking into the grove. Visions of other former kings and queens walked from behind the trees, standing around the thrones. They stood in silent vigil as Peter and Rebecca saw the looks of pride on their faces. Peter felt the swell of love and guidance emanating from these visions.

Speaking the king offered, "They are here to bear witness to the making of history. You two are history. The cosmos tries hard to bring balance to the universe and in you both that balance is achieved! Now, you must use your gifts to bring peace and prosperity back to the universe."

Rebecca added, "The universe is a large place, My Lord!"

"Indeed, it is, but I have every confidence in you both that your task will be accomplished. Together, you're the most powerful entity this universe has ever seen! Speaking of which, it's now time you claimed your birthright."

He strode to the two thrones, waving for Peter and Rebecca to sit. The two looked at one another before doing as they were bidden and walked forward. Still, they stood in front of the two woven, wooden thrones and waited for instructions. The king stood in front of them and motioned them to sit. They did as they were instructed and sat one in each seat. Peter could now see all the kings and queens surrounding them with bright smiles. The king produced woven branchlike crowns and placed one on Rebecca's head and one on Peter's.

The king then looked to the sky. "The universe has spoken and given us the answer to our prayers. We're here to guide them in their quest and counsel them in their hour of need. Here now, let me present Lord Peter and My Lady Rebecca as King and Queen of the Cosmos!"

CHAPTER THIRTY-TWO

Jake stopped midstride and looked back at Peter and Rebecca, his heart torn in two. His grief not only for leaving Peter but the heavy feeling in his heart that he may not see Peter again. Growing up Jake could always read people and situations well. This situation seemed no different, and the lump in his throat kept telling him not to leave Peter's side. Duty pushed him forward, yet he looked at his friend with uncertainty in his eyes. The two friends bonded for life nodded to one another, and Jake turned to follow the path leading out of the city.

Head down, each step away from his friends, seemed harder with each passing stride. Derek moved alongside his son, putting a reassuring hand on his shoulder. This made Jake feel much better, and he peered into his father's eyes for guidance. Derek squeezed his shoulder with love and nodded to keep moving forward. His entire life seemed dedicated to duty and here given the assignment of a lifetime, he should be proud of the confidence shown to him by others. Instead, all he could think of was Peter. The actual dread of not seeing his friend again almost made him sick but then Peter's mother came from behind and engulfed him in a loving hug.

The embrace said volumes as she too must have felt the anger and fear of leaving her son behind. Jake looked at Michelle and smiled, disarming the entire mood. Standing in the middle of the path still locked in an embrace, Derek smiled. The two most important people in his life were with him in that very moment, but he sensed the struggle of both Michelle along with his son. He watched his son grow in love for his friend Peter from the youngest of ages as the two were inseparable. He couldn't help feeling for his son but also knew the dire situation they all found themselves at this moment.

For years during his military service, he caught wind of various situations and reports of this type of clandestine operation. Derek always knew being on a need to know basis would be his people's downfall. As a military man, he struggled at times with the need for secrecy over sharing intel with those who really should have important information. Knowing too much could also be dangerous, and information spread out amongst a team helped lessen the burden. Here and now, the knowledge of the Zarillion people in full bloom seemed overwhelming. In his military capacity, he was privy to some knowledge of the people they shared the planet with but now, working with them seemed surreal.

The trio, still huddled close, continued up the path toward the ancient caverns. Mother gave them specific instructions on how to enter the caverns and to beware of the illusions they would see upon entering. Derek pressed forward, taking the lead, moving back into military mode. His thoughts still on his son, he quickened his steps, hoping the faster they completed their mission, the faster he could reunite Peter and Jake. His son sensed this and sped up to keep pace with his father.

Michelle inwardly smiled as she watched father and son determined to complete their mission. She knew duty well and thought back to a time before Peter was born in which she decided to live a normal existence. Her father came to her with tidings of dread, explaining to his daughter their need to hide in the human world. Michelle's world of leadership, and her warrior status now gave way to a simple domestic life. At first, she struggled with the mundane existence but when she met Peter's father, that all changed.

Growing up with her father, everything revolved around the duty to and protection of her people. He taught her every aspect of rule and military engagement. When her father was satisfied her training with him was complete, he passed her along to General Giles to complete the next phase. The general, the mightiest warrior in their midst, was also among the wisest and trained her to be a Knight of the Cosmos. Ryan, early on, saw her potential and shared with her ancient texts no one else could master.

When her training concluded, it became apparent that Michelle was a special knight. Her combination of power, intuition, and wisdom put her in a realm of her own. Ryan trained many knights but couldn't believe the ease with which Michelle served in her capacity. Every task she received from the council was completed without question and in record time. Her service to her people didn't go unnoticed, and she was soon next in line for a council seat. Once seated, she used her wisdom and diplomacy to enhance the council's effectiveness.

The council itself promoted her quickly, and she was about to be named head of the council when her father informed her, they must leave. The news devastated her but as always, duty came first. She left without complaint and learned to live a simple life. Peter's father was a large, vibrant man but human in every way. Michelle felt terrible keeping secrets from her husband but knew the danger that surrounded her family. Her father was aware of the Nazi involvement with the reptilian people which made things even more complex. The Nazis were free to roam the earth while having their puppet strings pulled by the reptilians.

Still, she learned to love her life with her father and the man she came to love. On the eve of her son's birth, her husband brought her flowers and made her a large dinner. He explained it to be a custom in his family to help the baby come into the world quickly and safely. Finishing the dinner, he took her on a long walk, saying it would speed up the process. Amazingly, it worked, and Michelle went into labor that night. Several hours later, Peter was in her arms, looking into the face of his loving mother.

It was then Michelle first noticed Peter's power. While holding him, she saw the telltale energy dancing in his precious eyes. She said nothing and enjoyed the day with her entire family. Many days after the loss of her husband, she thought back to that perfect day. A day of love, tenderness, and joy. Her loss weighed heavy on her for years as Peter grew. Peter's grandfather did the best he could in the father role, but Michelle knew nothing would take the place of Peter's father. Watching Peter and Jake grow together as children encouraged her that her son was doing well despite the absence of his father.

Derek, from the moment Michelle met him, felt a connection to him. Both militarily trained and minded, they made an instant connection. Over the years, it became much more than that, but both never acted on their feelings as they feared a relationship would jeopardize their sons' relationship with each other. As the boys became older, it became apparent that the feelings Michelle and Derek felt for one another weren't going away. Still, the two kept a working relationship. All that changed during this adventure, and the connection between the two grew with each step.

Derek and Michelle looked into each other's eyes while pushing forward with a distinct glow. Jake noticed but said nothing. On many occasions, he approached his father about his obvious caring for Peter's mom. Derek was always respectful and told Jake the time wasn't right. Now, amid their current situation, Jake understood why his father remained at a distance from Michelle. He couldn't help but feel happy for his father. He was aware of the loss of a parent such as in Peter's case. That very fact cemented their relationship from the moment they met and allowed them to grow together, filling the void.

The path laid before them was easy to follow with nothing but silence. Their footsteps echoed, and they listened for signs of life. This far from the city wasn't visited much by anyone. The idea of haunted caverns kept most nosy folks away, but the occasional daring lad or two would venture into the caverns, only to come back with tales of dread. Now, the air around them became cold, and Jake shivered but kept stride. As they came around the bend, there looming over them was the entrance to the haunted caverns.

Jake investigated the dark entrance, which sucked all light into it, with no air moving here. Michelle strode forward, raising her hand with the starburst medallion over her head. It blazed to life with a brilliant white light and pierced the darkness. The entrance now resembled that of any of the other caverns they traveled in, with the occasional drip of water welcoming them as they entered. Michelle took the lead but already brandished her sword while Derek, sidearm in hand, moved to her side.

Jake held the rod Michelle gave him and felt the balance of it, thinking it would make a great weapon in a pinch. He stayed close to his dad, gripping the rod a little tighter. The path led them deeper into the cavern and before long, they arrived at a decaying wooden door. Large cracks along with missing pieces of the door suggested many trying to get beyond it by any means necessary. Michelle approached the door cautiously, using the light of the medallion to examine the damage. She then peered through the holes in the door to catch a glimpse of what laid beyond it.

Looking into the next room, she discovered a defined tunnel, comprised of intricate stone work. She immediately knew they were in the right place. Growing up, Michelle listened to many stories of the dwarf kingdom and their adventures. Most of all, her grandfather would tell her about the tremendous cities of stone built by these master builders. He would tell her of the dwarves' precise nature and how no detail was overlooked during construction.

Like the Zarillion people, the dwarf race immigrated to this planet to escape the reptilian people. The reptilian people shared the dwarves' love for living underground and wanted the many resources they mined. Greed always the great motivator for imperial races was the ultimate motivator for the reptilians. Due to their collective outlook on life, they felt other races should supply them with the necessary materials to live. They felt they were superior to any other race.

Michelle thought of this as she reached out to touch the broken doors. As her hand was about to touch them, she felt an energy surrounding the door. Immediately, she flared her own energy around her and grasped the door handle. At first, nothing happened but, in a moment, they heard the door groan as it reluctantly opened outward. When they moved inside, the door shut instantly, and all light went out. She raised her hand, showing the light from the medallion down the tunnel. With each step forward, they felt malice building around them.

Michelle led the way, and Jake stood next to his father. Jake heard whispers growing around him, and he swiped at imaginary bugs he thought swarming around his head. The whispers grew with each step, and the temperature increased, making them perspire. Even each breath they took seemed labored. The trio moved forward, struggling to see the tunnel ahead. Vibrations now made their vision blurry. They all now couldn't see where they were walking as the vibrations grew in strength.

Again, Michelle released her energy into the tunnel, hoping to drive the vibrations away. At first, her solution seemed to work until the vibrations started anew with more power behind them. The strength of the vibrations now drew them to their knees. Hands on their ears for fear of losing their hearing, they were frozen in the tunnel. Jake felt his own anger building as this foolishness kept him from accomplishing his mission and from his friend. With a strength he didn't know he possessed, he stood, holding the rod, and drove it into the ground.

The rod struck the stone floor with a deafening sound, and soundwaves blew outward, dispersing the vibrations. Michelle and Derek looked at Jake. Rather than talk, they followed one another into the tunnel. Now, globes of lights like the ones in their own kingdom littered the walls, allowing them to see comfortably. Michelle put the medallion inside her shirt and led the group forward.

For what seemed like hours, they strode forward, looking at the stonework in envy. The intricate carvings making up the walls and ceiling were beyond description. They approached a bend in the tunnel and came face to face with an immense doorway blocking their way. The door itself was a mix of a golden wood with scrollwork made of metal. Faces of people covered the doors, and runes marked the top and bottom.

Michelle read the doors, "Here lies the ancient dwarf kingdom of gold. Only the true of heart and soul may enter."

Jake whispered, "Kingdom of Gold?"

She laughed. "The humans know it as El Dorado!"

Jake spat, "El Dorado! That's a myth!"

"Jake, does this look like a myth?"

CHAPTER THIRTY-THREE

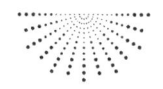

Holly sat in complete contemplation, not even hearing General Giles enter the council chambers. Her people on the brink of a monumental shift in protocol. After eons of little or no interference by them regarding their human counterparts, it was decided to share their knowledge and protection. Normally, the room would be abuzz with debate in this matter but since the latest attack from the reptilian people left the council barren, Holly and General Giles were the only original members of the council left.

A heavy hand propping up her head from exhaustion, she peered around the round table with a deep sense of sadness. These people were her friends, contemporaries, and confidants. The emptiness grew inside her as she thought of each member of the council and their gifts. Even Michael, for all his greed and scheming, still did much for the Zarillion people. Replacing the council would be paramount at this time but who should they choose going forward would be a daunting task. Her mind reached out to Rebecca to see what she was doing at this very moment, but she couldn't locate her. Nervousness ran through her body, which in turn woke her from her thoughts.

General Giles reached forth a comforting hand towards his love.

Holly quickly came back to herself, taking his hand and rising to her feet to greet the general. Without a word, they took in the empty table and, looking at one another, nodded, knowing their responsibility in that very moment. Hand in hand, they walked around the table as if trying to picture their perfect candidate for each chair.

When they stopped at Michael's chair, a dark look came over each of their faces. Here sat one of the most prosperous financial persons in the history of their people. Yet in secret over a period of many years, Michael schemed to destroy the council and take over rule for himself. The two stood over the chair, trying to grasp the devastation caused by this man so deep in their own councils. Holly blamed herself as she could read people better than most but over the last few centuries, she was so concerned about the prison of the reptilian people failing, she let Michael be.

Her oversight cost many lives and her entire society. Michelle requested she take the seat of high council member to keep it warm for her, and she reluctantly agreed. Holly couldn't help but feel she wasn't the best candidate for the position, but what other choice did she have? Michelle was the most qualified and trained for the position, but her role as a Knight of the Cosmos trumped the council position. Holly would be sure to build a council they all would be proud of upon their return from their respective missions.

Holly sadly blurted, "Ryan, where do we begin? When everyone returns, we may have a few more members, but something tells me we won't be together for a long time."

General Giles looked concerned. "My love, what have you seen?"

"It isn't what I've seen, more a feeling of dread I have! Jake going to the dwarf kingdom! Ryan no one has heard from them in centuries. The other kingdoms no longer exist. How are we to fulfill Mother's missions?"

The general spoke in a hushed tone, "I suspect, much like Peter and Rebecca finding each other, the other kingdoms will be found as is needed. Each kingdom decided on its own to break from the accords, if you remember. They also decided that a time would come where they would be called upon once more."

She looked into his eyes. "My dear, I hope you're right! I can't help but feel the reptilians are far from finished. We must prepare ourselves as well as the humans for an all-out assault."

"My love, we'll be ready to defend this world and others. Do not underestimate Michelle, she will call upon the other knights to return. Also, Peter and Rebecca are coming into their own. Trust me when I say this, now that those two are together, I fear for anyone who goes against them! I've seen them close up, separately but together, that's scary!"

Holly smiled. "Yes, I'm sure they will surprise many! The only thing that concerns me is their total lack of understanding of how much power they wield. You're right that whoever challenges them will be in for a rude awakening. I want to see the commander's face when those two come face to face with him."

"That, my dear, I would love to see as well. It isn't just their power though; it's their genuine caring for one another that will turn out to be their greatest strength or their greatest weakness. You and I developed a love unmatched over many years of learning about one another, but those two are cosmic magnets! I say this now; their love will know no rival."

She reached over and playfully smacked his shoulder. "No one can match our love!"

He grasped her hand lovingly. "Of course! How could I dare suggest otherwise!"

The two strode from the council chambers, still chatting about their young charges. They stopped and left instructions that the chamber be sealed until their return. The centuries closed the huge doors and with a combination of Holly's power and special locks, the council chamber couldn't be entered until they opened it. She stopped and looked at the empty chamber, thinking of her studies. As a young lady, she studied the history of her people vigorously. In her recollection, the council chamber never was sealed. The thought of no one guarding the council chambers sent a shiver down her spine. The general led her forward gently, and she allowed herself to follow.

They agreed that one person should be approached about the

vacant council positions. Nathan Alls, Holly's mentor growing up, taught her everything she knew about rule and the diplomacy needed on a council such as theirs. Holly thought back to a time when, at the height of his powers on the council, he suddenly announced he would step down from the council. Council members did occasionally leave their seats for other endeavors but in Nathan's case, the departure was scandalous.

She remembered watching the huge man silently pushing his seat back, and he walked out of the council chamber without a word. Andrew Olin, the head of the council, was furious, demanding Nathan take his seat. Nathan paused for a moment and glared at Andrew. "I'll never again step foot in this cesspool! You're all doomed!"

The exchange between Nathan and Andrew stood frozen in her memory. Though she made many attempts over the years to reestablish a relationship with Nathan, the elder statesman refused to see her. After a while, she relented and moved on with her life, but the void left by her mentor's absence still haunted her to this day. Only after the urging of Ryan did she even entertain the idea of going to see Nathan.

From all accounts, the reclusive Nathan still maintained a residence near the haunted caverns at the entrance to dwarf kingdom. As she recalled, he was the last leader to have direct contact with the dwarves. They quickened their pace, hoping to arrive at Nathan's compound before anyone noticed their absence. Along the road, they passed a few people going about their business, but no one paid them much mind.

As they left the city proper, they noticed a change in temperature. A cold chill surrounded them as they closed in on Nathan's home. Approaching the darkened compound, they nearly turned around. The entire area seemed abandoned and overgrown. Something scratched at the back of Holly's mind about Nathan. When she was a child, Nathan taught her about appearances. He droned on and on about how, with the right set of circumstances, one could make anyone see anything they wanted them to see.

Fury took hold of her in that moment as she walked up to the rusted gate. She let the power fill her and was about to release it, blowing the door inward when she heard a click. The large wooden door encased in iron creaked loudly open. Still, everything inside laid dark. Holly's anger grew, and she threw the door open the rest of the way. Nearly yanking the general's arm out of his socket, she pulled him inside the door.

Once inside, the door slammed shut, secured by several magical locks. Standing in the darkness caused Holly to lose her temper. Gathering as much power as she could safely handle, she glowed until she was a burning, white globe. The light emanating from her reached forth, clearing away any darkness near them. Shadows hid from the light, and they saw an intricate and beautiful courtyard. Even in the darkness, the area looked well-tended, unlike anything outside.

Power aiding her anger, she yelled forth, "Nathan, enough of this madness! I have neither the time nor the patience for your games! Show yourself, or I'll level this place to the ground and place you under arrest for treason!"

Her words rang against the stone structures that made up Nathan's compound, but no response came. Holly motioned Ryan to move back toward the gate. She walked calmly to the first structure and raised her hands to release her power into the building. Power sparkling from her fingertips, she readied herself to watch the power dismantle the stones.

She yelled at the silence, "Nathan, you leave me no choice!"

As she was about the lose the power, a voice came from somewhere within, "Who is it that has the audacity to disturb my solace?"

Lights appeared in places around the compound. Still, Holly held the power and moved even closer to ensure the most damage. Raising her hands, she funneled the power from her body, focusing it all to her arms. They now glowed so bright, anyone looking at her might lose their own sight. With determination, she let all the power gather into a molten ball of fire between her hands. Taking it into one hand, she threatened to throw the ball at the building.

From somewhere within, she heard, "Wait! Do not hurt a single thing in my home!"

Still holding the molten ball of power, she playfully tossed it up and down in her hand. "Nathan, you're testing my patience! Show yourself!"

Stepping into the light provided from the ball, an extremely large man appeared. He was easily seven feet tall, but his height didn't make him intimidating. His face was strong looking, made even more so by a well-groomed salt and pepper beard. Steel eyes peered down at Holly, who, in her own right, was a large person. In the glowing light, his prowess radiated. Even though he wore baggy clothing, his muscles were still visible, and his thick neck bulged with his own anger looking at Holly. The heat generated between the two threatened to set the courtyard ablaze.

For what seemed an eternity, the two brooded at one another. The general was afraid one would strike the other, and he thought he would have to get in the middle. To his great relief, the large man relaxed his stance and waited for Holly to do the same. Holly still held the globe, and the general saw the anger in her eyes not lessening. He walked to her without touching her, stepping between her and Nathan. If her anger could increase, it looked if that were the case for a moment, but then she looked at her love.

With a scream, she threw the globe several hundred feet into the air outside the compound, striking the side of the cavern and melting a large hole in the wall. With the power dissipated, she growled, looking toward Nathan. General Giles took her hand in his gently, and she looked calmly at him, holding her rage back. Then, from out of nowhere, tears streamed down her cheeks, and she sobbed uncontrollably. He took her into his shoulder to comfort her and looked to Nathan. The huge man now looked concerned and moved over to the two council members.

Holly pushed her face away from his shoulder, yelling, "He left me! I was all alone! How could you leave me? Nothing! No explanation! You wouldn't even see me!"

Nathan looked genuinely unnerved at these accusations. He motioned Ryan to bring her inside. He did as bid and led her inside the first stone building. From the outside, it didn't look any different than any other Zarillion structure but once inside, the warm light greeted them to a wondrous view. The plain stone work outside made way for polished and highly intricate stone from all over the planet. Holly easily noticed the dwarven work everywhere she looked. Not just carving, but the actual walls showed unmatched craftsmanship. Pillars reaching to the tall ceiling made the inside of the building look more like a castle rather than a simple building.

He led them to a smaller room with a large circular fire roaring in the middle of the room. Books laid strewn everywhere, and he took some off a few chairs. He cleared another chair for himself and sat first, looking at them with a sympathetic expression. They followed suit and sat, waiting for the large man to speak. It took a few moments and a few throat-clears for Nathan to get the courage to speak.

His eyes moistened as he spoke, "Leaving you was the hardest thing I've ever had to endure! I can never expect you to forgive me, but please know I couldn't stay. Because I couldn't stay, I could no longer be your teacher. It remains my biggest regret to this day not having you in my life!"

Holly's eyes were now red and puffy. "You destroyed me! For years afterward, I thought it was my fault you left. I thought because I was a poor student, you were disgusted with me and needed to leave!"

He nearly choked on his next words, "Disgusted? In you? Never! You were honestly the only reason I stayed as long as I did. My disgust was directed at the council itself and its refusal to help the humans protect this planet. Time and time again, our enemies sank their teeth into this fledgling people and every time we balked at the opportunity to help. We always used the excuse of too much interference, but these people are no different than us in so many ways."

She looked shocked. "Nathan, members have left the council before, but you left our society! You wouldn't even see me!"

"I know! I'm ashamed of my treatment of you. I'm not sure what I can do to make amends, but I'll do what I can. Holly, what is it exactly you want from me?"

Holly stood and pointed directly at Nathan. "It's time for you to stand with me! Our people require your services, and your voice will be heard! You have my word."

Nathan stood a head above her but nodded. "Yes, it would seem I have much to pay for. I cannot go back into that chamber! I'll never again enter that accursed room."

She barked at him, "Then you don't go into that room! That room isn't the council, we are. Right now, I could care less if you ever return to that room. I have need of you, and we have much work to do to prepare our people against ultimate evil!"

He asked her to explain. Holly went into detail about the reptilian attacks and how the last succeeded thanks in large part to Michael. Nathan shot up with rage in his eyes. He explained to Holly that this was one of main reasons he decided to leave. According to Nathan, he alerted Andrew to Michael's indiscretions, but Andrew looked past them because of the financial prosperity Michael afforded them. Nathan couldn't believe the trouble caused by this man.

Holly further explained how they repelled the attacks, but it left them vulnerable. General Giles listened but thought it odd that Holly didn't mention Peter or Rebecca at all. Nathan asked a few more questions about the reptilian activity and leaned back to let it all sink in. He then leaned forward and asked the general for his assessment. The general went on to tell Nathan of the current state of the defenses and how they planned to repel the next attack. Nathan seemed comfortable with the general's plan.

Unexpectedly, he reached forth, clasping Holly's hand in his huge hands. "My dear Holly, please know that even though I wasn't there in person, I watched you from afar. There wasn't a day I didn't check in on you or think about you!"

She looked with teary eyes at him. "I needed you! I felt so lost without you. I was so incomplete and knew not how to control my power. There were many times I thought the power would consume me, and sometimes I wished it would."

Nathan rubbed her hands gently. "I know you won't accept this but one day, I'll tell you more about why I couldn't be with you. Now doesn't seem like it matters, but then it did. I'm yours now, and I won't leave you unless you ask that of me."

Holly lunged at Nathan and engulfed the man in a hug. "I've waited a lifetime to hear that! I'll hold you to that promise! If ever you leave me again, there will be no place you can hide from me!"

"Of that, I have no doubt. For now, you and Ryan stay here for the night, and we'll talk more in the morning. I must find out some information for myself, but I promise I'll only be gone for the evening. I'll see you both in the morning. Good night! Sleep well! Holly, it's wonderful to see you."

Holly smiled. "Thank you for the hospitality. We will sleep well, and I'll see you in the morning!"

CHAPTER THIRTY-FOUR

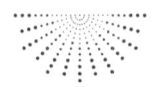

A huge sense of calm, pride, and strength surrounded Peter and Rebecca as they walked away from the hillside. The vision of the beautiful sapling taking root into the magical ground stood fresh in their minds. Many adventures befell them on their way to this moment, but meeting with their ancestors brought about a new sense of duty toward their planet. The two young leaders walked for quite some time locked in their own thoughts. Each struggled with the expectations now heaped upon them by those same ancestors.

Rebecca grew up watching the council bicker and use their own political aspirations, causing nothing but heartache for her people. Now, here she stood, thrust into the same political arena. Up until now, her only thoughts were of reaching Peter. Now that the two stood side by side, the magnetism pulling her towards Peter swiftly made her feel whole. For months on end, she couldn't fill the hole in her mind and soul. Finally meeting Peter, she felt as if the two became instantly interlocked.

She felt a deep sorrow for Peter being forced into a world alien to his young mind. Despite the sorrow, a sense of pride also swelled inside her at the way he responded to everything. He didn't complain but instead, took every challenge head on and thought of others first. His unselfish nature brought her even closer to him with every passing moment. During the entire ordeal, she pictured herself teaching Peter about her society, only to have him thrust deep into the middle of unfolding events.

Peter, on the other hand, couldn't fathom the events swirling around him but knew so many depended upon him, he couldn't fail. His mother always schooled him to never put things off and handle problems head on. He smiled inwardly, thinking of his grandfather guiding him time and time again but never letting him off easy. Both his guardians knew what lay ahead of him and wouldn't allow him to falter. He spent a life in training and knew their teachings would follow him always.

The two walked side by side, holding one another's hand in silence. The power and warmth of their ancestors now turned to a colder, drier air surrounding them. Peter felt Rebecca shiver, and he too felt the cold seeping into his bones. Drawing her closer to him, the two leaned against one another for warmth. The path before them darkened, and they walked toward the city.

As they approached the city, a feeling of dread overtook them. Though they couldn't place its source, they knew something was amiss. Immediately, Rebecca perked up and allowed the energy to fill her body. Peter saw her back straighten, and he reached to his side, allowing the gilded sword the slip out of the scabbard to gleam in the dim light. Holding it before him, he stepped in front of Rebecca protectively.

Out of the darkness stepped a group of four figures gripping weapons and spread out in an attacking position. Peter let his eyes follow each member of the group, and anger built as he now saw the features of these would-be assailants. Reptilian faces peered back at him with murderous grins. Each reptilian member carried a firearm and pointed them directly at Peter.

Peter ground his feet into the soft dirt under him in a defensive stance as the king taught him. His attackers seemed amused at the sight of such a simple weapon. Without another thought, Peter took the flat of the blade and placed it gently to his forehead. Lifting it slightly away from his head, he allowed the energy to fill himself and work its way into the blade. The blade glowed, and he could now feel heat rising from the blade itself.

His attackers took a step back and looked at one another with uncertainty. The largest, seeming to be the leader, stepped forward with a scowl on his face, pointing his weapon directly at Peter's heart. He released an energy bolt from the weapon, and it screamed across the distance right at Peter. Peter moved the blade ever so slightly and caught the bolt directly taking the energy into his blade. The blade seemed grateful and glowed even more brightly.

Again, the reptilians backed up slightly. Their leader, undaunted, reached behind him and pulled out a large, curved blade of his own. After flipping the blade in the air in a series of calculated movements, he grinned at Peter. The rest of his group followed suit, pulling out their own blades. They all inched their way closer toward Peter who stood his ground. These fools didn't understand their foe and continued forward.

The leader launched himself at Peter with his blade high overhead, hoping to come down directly into Peter's skull. A simple defensive swing from Peter disarmed the reptilian quickly. His other companions, seeing their leader in trouble, jumped at Peter to defend their man. Skills took hold of the once-peaceful young man, and he ducked and dodged each swing of the knife. No blade came close to touching his flesh, and he allowed his enemy to think they had a chance. After a few minutes of toying with his opponents, he stepped back and held the sword in front of his face.

Again, the four reptilian soldiers looked to one another for guidance. Rage filled the leader's eyes, and he came at Peter with his knife flashing through the air. Peter swiftly let the man come into his space and turned his own blade downward to turn and swing right back at the man. Blade spinning toward him, he saw it make its way downward as anticipated. Peter blocked it and this time, punched the man with the pommel of the sword.

Taking the brunt of the blow directly to his face, Peter felt bone shatter, and the man slumped to the ground in pain. Peter gave them a chance but now, the rage took hold of him, and he moved on the remaining assailants. The reptilians were no match for his skill, and the first two received severe wounds as their reward. The remaining man, unfazed by his comrade's failure, straightened himself and prepared for battle. This one seemed different and much more controlled. He held his blade differently behind his hand and had a good fighting stance. Peter immediately knew he was dealing with a seasoned warrior. The two combatants circled each other, measuring the other for weaknesses.

Each unleashed a series of thrusts and strikes, hoping to draw first blood. Peter worked his sword with little use of energy. The reptilian breathed heavy, and Peter took advantage, sending a quick thrust under the defense of the man striking him in the side. The man gasped in pain but held his ground, bringing up his knife to counter. Again, Peter deflected the blow and swung the pommel toward the man's head. This time, the man ducked and swung his leg to catch Peter off guard.

Peter moved out of the way and again arced his blade, coming down upon the man's head. A quick, desperate lift of his knife upward saved his life and caught the blow. He rolled to the ground and looked at the sword master for the first time, slightly panicked. Peter used this to his advantage and launched his own attack. With a series of moves that took his opponent by surprise, he went inside and outside, lacing his attacker with many small wounds. Though the wounds weren't mortal, his opponent stood before him bleeding in many places.

A blind rage took over the bleeding man, and he launched himself at Peter, blindly hacking away. Quickly countering each strike, Peter couldn't believe how with each swing of the attacker's knife, it seemed as though Peter could anticipate each blow. Again, Peter defended himself and caught the man in both legs, causing several deep gashes in each leg. The man now went down to one knee and tried to push himself back up without success.

Peter quickly looked around to see if any of the man's companions were still ready to fight. The two wounded men still lay on the ground, holding various wounds. An angry leader rose knife in hand. Face disfigured, he hid the pain and advanced on Peter. Without thinking, Peter whisked inside the man's defenses and ended his suffering, landing his blade directly in the middle of the man's chest. He pulled the blade out and turned to finish off the remainder of the attackers.

Both wounded soldiers waited for the sword master and paid for their bravery with their very lives. Peter, in the throes of battle, blazed with anger of his own and looked for the final reptilian soldier to finish the threat once and for all. The soldier stood before him, bleeding from multiple wounds but looked ready to do battle. Anger still in his eyes, Peter advanced and swung ready to strike, only to see the reptilian soldier reach forth with his blade up toward Peter. The blade immediately stopped its track and fell to Peter's side.

The soldier offered the blade to Peter. "My Lord, I'm a soldier of many campaigns, and I've never been bested in one-on-one combat! If you spare me, I will be your man. The only thing I ask is you teach me so I will never again lose to an opponent!"

Peter, taken back immediately, looked to his side to see Rebecca smiling, catching him off guard. Here was an enemy who until a moment ago was quite intent upon killing them both. Something inside him stayed his hand, and he calmly brought the sword back into the scabbard. The soldier barely could keep himself upright. Peter noticed the wounds taking their toll on the warrior. As the man stumbled forward, he reached out to grab hold of him.

The soldier leaned weakly upon Peter and slid downward. Guiding the man softly to the ground, he looked into the soldier's eyes to see fear staring back at him. Kneeling, he took the man's head in his lap and looked to Rebecca, who was already moving to join Peter next to the soldier. Her eyes still danced with electricity, and she reached out to touch the man's chest. At first, Peter thought she might be killing the man as his chest thrust into the air in convulsions.

After a moment, the thrashing stopped, and the man's breathing took a more even pace. The fear, once in the man's eyes, now held a thankfulness to them as he looked back at his captors. A great sense of relief washed over Peter as he watched the soldier's strength return. After a few minutes, the man sat unaided against a rock. Though the cuts remained, the bleeding stopped, and the drained life force refreshed.

He peered up at the two young leaders. "My Lord and Lady, I'm your humble servant! I owe you my life!"

Rebecca leaned in. "I'm not sure you understand what that means to be in my service but if you're true, your service will be welcome. Know this though, if you ever betray me, my love will finish his job and think nothing of leaving you to die in the dark alone!"

A look of panic came over the man. "My Lady, I understand and will be a true warrior for you!"

Peter chimed in, "How can you make this offer when you know that if the commander ever finds out you're a deserter, he will come for you?"

In a calm voice, he blurted out, "The commander is the reason I am here alone with what's left of my unit. No, My Lord, he won't be back for me. I'm here alone, left to die. I chose life and if that costs me my very life, so be it!"

Again, Rebecca smiled. "I accept your service, but you will have to prove yourself!"

"It will be my honor, my lady!"

Peter looked uncertain but knew he must trust in Rebecca's decision. She was more skilled in politics than he was. He could guess her thought was to find out what she could from this soldier and use him to her advantage. Though this seemed the right thing, something wasn't quite right about this situation. In every encounter with the reptilians, they were taught to fight to the death.

His lady looked at him and nodded, understanding his trepidation. As soon as he looked into her eyes, he knew there was a master plan. Of course, he knew they couldn't discuss it at this moment but what would they do with this man in the meantime. He leaned down and pulled the man to his feet. Rebecca came over and touched the man's hands, leaving a glowing set of bonds holding his hands fast. The man looked down but said nothing and allowed himself to be led away toward the city.

Walking at a slow pace, they came upon the council doors blocked by the guards an hour later. The guards alerted her to Holly's orders and informed her that they would remain locked until her return. She looked at Peter and then to their captive before leading the soldier forward. In a few minutes, they came upon the prison doors. Though the prison wasn't used often since the attack, a few cells were occupied with reptilian soldiers being interrogated for information.

The soldier again said not a word and allowed himself to be placed in a cell. When safely locked behind bars, Rebecca released his bonds. She looked sympathetically at the man but didn't make a move to release him. After a quick discussion with the guards where she informed them to take good care of the man and tend to his remaining wounds, the guards saluted and went back to their business. As she walked away, a pang of guilt took her, but she walked up the stairs with Peter in tow.

When they came up into the street, Rebecca began, "I know he entered into my service but right now, I cannot have him running around."

Peter clasped her hand. "You have to explain nothing to me! Your mercy stayed my hand. It may very well be that mercy that will be repaid to us someday."

Rebecca looked back at Peter like he knew something. "Wise words, my love, wise words. Where do we go from here? You heard the guards. Holly and General Giles left to go find her mentor. The only thing I know about Nathan is he's a hermit that lives near the dwarf kingdom entrance!"

Peter's ears perked up. "Let's follow them! Maybe we can catch up with Jake!"

Rebecca warmly grabbed Peter's hand. "My love, I'm sure we will see Jake soon! In the meantime, let's find Holly. I'm interested to meet Nathan, the man who betrayed Holly! That is if she hasn't turned him to ash!"

CHAPTER THIRTY-FIVE

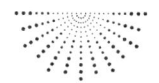

Silence met Jake as he stared at the frozen shut entrance to the dwarf kingdom. He felt the presence of Michelle and Derek moving behind him as he still held the rod. Taking in every inch of the door, he wracked his brain about how he should prove his worth to enter the kingdom. To his sight, the door looked ancient but otherwise made of normal materials, yet he sensed something else keeping the way shut.

Reaching forth, he allowed his hand to brush along the lines made by the runes inviting the pure of heart into the kingdom. Though the door didn't repel him, he felt a type of energy surrounding the entrance. Still touching the door, he looked down at the rod in his other hand, only to see it glowing. Without thinking, he touched the rod to the ancient wooden door. At first, nothing happened, but he held the rod to the door and closed his eyes, concentrating. He felt energy surrounding him starting at his fingertips and slowly moving throughout his body. When his whole body felt on fire, he opened his eyes to see the runes on the door glowing as well.

The letters blazed as a flame until the letters could no longer be seen. A series of clicks and clangs sounded as if someone behind the door unlocked the many bolts holding the door fast. A large, dark crack opened, splitting the doors open slightly. Stale air shot from behind the door making them cough. In a few moments, the air leveled off and Michelle along with Derek moved toward the door. Jake still held the rod which glowed slightly, but the energy seemed nearly spent.

He turned to look at his companions, only to have Michelle look at him with great wonder. Derek, with a look of great pride, grabbed his son by the shoulder and squeezed slightly for reassurance. The three swung to face the now-open gate thinking of what course of action they would take. Jake swiftly handed the rod back to Michelle who stared at the artifact. Taking it, she tucked it away in her pack and moved toward the door taking the lead role.

Holding one hand up, Jake saw it glow brighter with each passing moment. As they approached the crack in the door, Michelle reached forth, pulling the door on the left open enough for them to travel through comfortably. Once inside, the light Michelle gave off illuminated a pathway directly in front of them. The amount of dust on the stone path in front of them told them no one traveled this way in a long time. Once a few steps inside the door and on the path, the doors automatically closed again, locking behind them.

Jake didn't even turn around, and he knew to get out; they needed to go forward. Michelle moved her hand a little higher to show more of the tunnel. Derek moved to her side and held his firearm at the ready in case of ambush. The trio continued forward at a good clip, hoping to notice any signs of life. To their great dismay, they traveled most of the day and into the night without any signs anyone ever existed in this realm. For the first time since entering, they felt their bodies becoming tired and looked for a comfortable place out of the way to rest.

Around a corner, they found a nice niche with a few low rocks to act as seats. Each member of the troop searched through their packs for a few things to eat. After a meager meal, they all sat up, looking at one another, wondering whether to continue or turn back. Jake could almost feel his companion's thoughts, but he also felt an uncanny tug pulling him forward. He stood, looking into the darkness.

Michelle stood. "Jake, what is it?"

Jake turned slightly. "I'm not sure. Something is calling to me! We need to continue. Something tells me we aren't that far from our destination."

Derek strode forward. "Son, are you sure?"

He looked confidently at his father. "I'm very sure. It's hard to describe, but I feel as though I'm being led forward. We're on the right track."

Michelle nodded. "Lead the way!"

Jake turned, following the light Michelle provided back into the tunnel. With each step, Jake felt the tug on his heart strengthen. He quickened his step, and the others followed right behind. Michelle pointed to the ground as they saw the cobblestone path giving way to a flatter, finished stonework. Even the tunnel walls showed a much different architecture with different types of stone that sparkled in the glowing light of Michelle's hand.

As they turned another corner, they stopped abruptly, staring at long lances, and swords pointed at their heads. In the dim light, they saw dark figures holding the weapons but couldn't see any features of their assailants. Derek aimed his firearm, only to have Michelle put her hand on his arm, indicating he should put the weapon down. The strange figures surrounded them, but Michelle still showed no signs of panic.

Jake moved slightly to show the figures he was unarmed. A stocky, well-muscled man came into view. He stood a head below Jake but looked like any other human except for a braided beard going well down the front of his chest. His clothing looked very well-tended and clean. Coming within a few inches of Jake, he looked the large young man up and down. The figure raised his hand, and the lances and blades backed away from Jake's friends.

The stout figure turned to Jake. "Well met, Mr. Andrews! We have been expecting you. You passed the first test at the gate but now comes the true test. As stated, only those true of heart may enter our kingdom. Ancient law states anyone entering our kingdom must pass our tests for admission."

Jake raised his hands. "More tests? With all due respect, the Mother of all has sent me on a mission of great importance and every second we stand here wasting time, could mean the difference between life and death."

The power behind his words made the figure uncomfortable, but he stood his ground. "Jake, that may be so, but the law is the law. You must submit to our tests of your own free will. Will you allow it to be so?"

He looked at Michelle, who, with a sparkle in her eye, nodded. Jake moved closer to the figure. "What's your test?"

The figure smiled brightly. "Trial by combat!"

With that sentence, the strong figure reached behind his shoulder, releasing a wicked-looking, double-edged battle axe. He swung it in his hands with little trouble and took a very combative stance, waiting for Jake. Anger awoke in Jake. He was sent here as Mother's emissary, and this little man stood in his way. Without another thought, he grabbed his own sword and pulled it from its scabbard, letting the ring of metal hang in the air. The blade itself almost looked as long as the man was tall. Jake didn't fool around, and he too bent his knees into a strong stance.

The two soldiers walked carefully around one another, measuring for weaknesses. After a few passes, Jake could wait no more and launched into a series of strikes and thrusts to test the man's defenses. The man was spry and quick, blocking each strike easily. The smaller man took matters into his own hands and launched his own assault. Jake just as easily blocked each strike, and the two backed up slightly, thinking of their next moves.

Surprisingly, the smaller man led with his shoulder and slammed into Jake's chest, causing him to lose his balance. Though he didn't fall, he was nearly beheaded by the sharp blade of the axe arcing down on his head. A quick step to the side saved his life, and he spun, swinging his own weapon at the man's back. Jake felt his blade go through some clothing but didn't bite flesh. The man flashed a grin as he turned to face Jake, swinging his axe right at his chest.

Jake dodged the strike and felt his own anger building. He knew many were counting on him to finish this mission. Peter and Rebecca came into his mind, sending him over the edge. There was no way in hell he would disappoint them, and he needed to complete this mission to return to them. He promised Peter he would never leave his side again, but Mother insisted he complete this mission. Jake, always the good soldier, understood the need to complete missions for the good of others. He turned with an angry glare in his eyes. This needed to end.

He stepped in and out, flashing the blade with swift strikes, learning the man's own style with each blow. Soon, he visualized in his mind the way the man fought, and he adjusted accordingly. The smaller man wanted him to try to get inside so he could use Jake's size against him. Jake moved away slightly and swung with arcing movements, keeping a larger distance away from his opponent. The strategy paid off as the man faltered against Jake's heavier blows. The large battle axe took the brunt of the strikes, but they took its toll.

Jake, a young man whose energy never seemed to waver, hacked at the smaller man until he was down on one knee. Seeing his chance, Jake continued his assault in the hopes of ending this test here and now. He spun and swung a death blow upon the man who looked frightened as the blade crashed down upon him. The blade stopped midstride, causing Jake to look at his blade stuck in the air with his hands still around the pommel with confusion.

From the shadows, he heard a voice boom, "Enough of this! Jake, put away your sword. My people, put away your weapons! These are our guests."

Immediately, the weapons disappeared, and the soldier lifted his axe and bowed to Jake in respect. Jake, not knowing what to do, nodded slightly and held his weapon still in front of him, waiting for another assault. Derek reached out, placing his hand on his son's arm. Jake looked at his father and released anger, dropping his sword. With a swift move, he returned the sword to his scabbard.

His eyes blinked as lights sprang to life around him. As his eyes grew accustomed to the light, he saw built stone structures surrounding him. They looked abandoned, but the craftsmanship and stonework were amazing. Now that he could see his would-be captors, he acknowledged they were very much like him, just slightly shorter. Everyone sported a well-groomed beard with long hair and bushy eyebrows. Their faces looked hardened, but the light in their eyes told Jake they were quite jovial when needed.

From behind the ring of soldiers walked a dignified-looking older man. His clothes looked quite rich with silver and gold needlework throughout the entire outfit. His beard reached his chest with braids capped with gold at the ends. A large, gold necklace hung from his neck, and he oozed reverence as his men formed a protective ring around him. The man stopped in front of Jake, looking up into the young man's eyes. He held Jake's gaze for what seemed an eternity until he backed away slightly.

He turned and nodded to Michelle, who nodded back before he looked at Jake. "Jake, well met! You're indeed a warrior worthy of entrance into our kingdom. You've met the criteria for entrance and as such, those you deem worthy may enter with you. What say you? Shall you enter the ancient dwarf kingdom of El Dorado?"

Jake softened his stance. "My Lord, I thought you would never ask. My companions and I are here on a mission of the most importance. The Mother of all sent me here to you in the hopes of reuniting you with the Zarillion people. The world is at the precipice and without your help, we have little hope of surviving the evil to come!"

The noble-looking man came forward, offering his hand. Jake stepped and met the man's hand with his own in a firm handshake. As strong as Jake was, the smaller man's hand seemed made of rock with a grip to match. Jake held onto the shake for a moment and then let go. He looked at the man and waited for their next move. His men were in a more relaxed line behind their leader. In the light, Jake could see his party numbered seven. He looked around to each of the smaller men's eyes as each had a different appearance to them.

Some seemed wise, while others seemed strong, and still others seemed guarded. Living in a soldier's world his entire life, he could appreciate the different skills each soldier brought to the battlefield. His dad always instructed him that a man's unit was only as strong as the last man. Derek taught him that every soldier came with something to enhance the strength of the unit. Jake saw this first hand on their escapade to make it to Antarctica. Jake protected Peter his entire life, but there were many times Peter returned the favor on their way to the South Pole.

Michelle stepped forward. "My Lord, Thomas, if it would please you, could we continue this conversation in a more secure location, preferably with some food?"

The nobleman raised an eyebrow of recognition. "Michelle, it has indeed been a long time. Are things that bad to cause a Knight of the Cosmos to seek our help?"

"My Lord, things are worse than you could imagine! I'll explain once we're safely behind sealed doors."

He nodded. "Michelle, it will be as you say. Follow me, and we will speak further."

The regal man turned and gave orders to form a protective circle around his guests as they made their way into the city. Michelle moved to the nobleman's side and spoke in hushed tones to him as they strode forward. Derek walked beside his son. Jake looked to his side to see the soldier he fought right by his side. The man gave him a look of respect and then looked forward to keep an eye out for any danger. The small group continued forward down the well-laid path, and the lights shone on everything around them. Signs of life showed themselves as the plants became a lush green, and the smell of cooking met their noses. The welcome smell caused their hearts to soar as they looked forward to a nice meal.

CHAPTER THIRTY-SIX

Commander Zosa walked with large strides of purpose. His head bent slightly forward, he didn't look anywhere but straight ahead. His master gave him specific instructions not to mention his plan with anyone else. That notion brought a small smile to the commander's face. Hardly any of his beloved force remained after Rebecca nearly leveled their compound to the ground. The thought of an adolescent child almost bringing them to their knees brought an even stronger sense of commitment to his mind. He quickened his pace through the maze of ancient tunnels below his people's compound.

For as long as the commander led his people, he couldn't remember coming down in these tunnels. The very entrance was a mystery and if not for information granted to him by the emperor, he may have never found it. The commander even questioned himself as he approached the rocky wall before him. All he saw and felt was rough stone.

According to the emperor, he would find a star-like pattern etched in the floor to the right of the tunnel. Finding the pattern proved more difficult than he anticipated as the floor itself was filled with rubble and a layer of dirt. He did as he was instructed, looking for the star-like pattern and after an hour of searching, there it shown in the floor. A great sense of relief washed over him, and he backed away from the wall. Raising his hands, he recited the incantation the emperor drilled into his head. At first, nothing happened but as he turned to leave, a heavy cracking and ripping sound broke the silence.

Commander Zosa laughed aloud and proceeded forward into the rift standing before him. Never one to fear anything as he walked into the dark tunnel, even he felt a chill run down his spine. Proceeding with caution, he brightened the glow coming from his hands to see more of the mysterious tunnel surrounding him. At first, the tunnel resembled those about him as he traveled down to this level. Without another thought, he plunged into the tunnel and again livened his pace.

With each passing step, the heat in the tunnel rose until even he, the great reptilian commander, stood uncomfortable. Sweat poured down his face and again, a chill ran down his spine. His head whipped around from side to side as he felt a presence searching his surroundings. Slowing down, he cautiously continued forward, looking this way and that, anticipating an unseen attack.

Sword in hand, he raised it in front of his face, ready to strike at a moment's notice. A feeling of dread permeated the air, but he wouldn't be daunted. Willing himself forward, his feet felt as though shackled with leg irons. The emperor, in his head, instructed him about the many things he may see or hear in this strange underground cavern. His sword at the ready as he moved forward, he saw the walls change. The once-rough and nature-hewn stone became a smoother and handmade tunnel system. Though he knew no one traveled this tunnel in his memory, it looked as fresh and new as ever. Glittering walls shown all the many natural minerals reflecting at him from the light.

Staring at the walls, he couldn't help but be in awe. Something about the stonework, and the carved symbols piqued some ancient memory, but it was gone as soon as it came. Still, the sense of dread built with each step. Again, the sound of the emperor's voice rang in his head, and he made his way down the tunnel until it opened into a huge cavern. Commander Zosa poured more energy into his hands in the hope of gaining enough light to see the entire cavern.

In the available light, he could see the closest wall looked exactly like someone's home, carved right into the actual stone of the earth. He moved to get a better look at the residence. Again, something looked familiar, but he simply couldn't place the memory. Clearly abandoned, he opened one of the decaying wooden doors. It reluctantly opened with a loud groan. Inside looked even more ornate than the façade. Intricate wood carving made up much of the inside décor. Though the outside showed signs of wear, the inside looked untouched by time.

Upon entering, the globes on the wall glowed dim at first until they brightened to show the entire ground floor. It took a few minutes for the commander's eyes to get used to the light. When his eyes stopped watering, he laughed when he walked into an adjoining room. Inside stood a large forge with various metal working tools hanging everywhere. Though the forge stood stone cold, he could picture the fire raging and corded arm muscles working the metal, willing it into shape.

Now standing facing the forge, he knew where the memories came from. Dwarves, he stood in an ancient dwarf kingdom. According to all his intelligence, the dwarves became extinct centuries ago. The thought of the dwarves no longer on this earth made him smile greatly. In typical soldier fashion, he searched the bottom floor in the hopes of finding booty. The legend of the dwarves' wealth in the back of his mind, he searched every nook and cranny, only to find a few odd trinkets but nothing of value.

A search of the entire complex revealed much of the same. The structures themselves looked well-tended despite the abandonment. What he truly hoped to find was the armory so he could have his men raid the stash. His hopes were dashed when he couldn't even find a small knife. When he was satisfied he would find nothing else, he followed his master's orders, going to the north end of the settlement. He found a well-defined path as the emperor described.

Looking back slowly, he half-expected to be attacked by his

ancient nemesis, the dwarves. No attack came, and he turned to his mission at hand. The path led him upward into what looked like a valley of some kind. His own light only allowed him to see little into the distance. He followed the path until he stood in front of the sheer face of a rock wall. Immediately, he looked to the ground to find the star-like pattern. He was relieved to find the symbol quickly and again uttered the incantation, allowing the doorway to open.

White light showed in the form of very thin lines running along the stone face, until a clear doorway shown in the rock. The door slid open inward in silence. He needed to crouch down to enter this tunnel. Using his hands to guide him along the wall, he descended, feeling the sense of dread build. A glow of light peered back at him from the end of the tunnel. The going was slow as the tunnel went downward at a steep clip.

At the end of the tunnel, the commander peered out to make sure it was safe. When comfortable no attack awaited him, he pulled himself from the tunnel. Straightening to his full height, he looked around to inspect his surroundings. A feast of wealth stared back at him. Gold, jewels, statues, armor, and precious items of every description littered the floor in heaps so large, he couldn't see some of the tops. His eyes nearly popped out of his head. Not that his people ever had any use for such wealth and were well beyond this earthly greed, he knew very well its implications.

Walking among the heaps of the unimaginable wealth, he couldn't help but feel triumphant. So many eons, the dwarves turned up their noses at the reptilian people. There was a time the two people were allies, but the reptilian people evolved into a society not relying on wealth. The dwarves couldn't give up their precious possessions, and it cost them everything. Their wealth made them a target for many greedy civilizations. In the end, the reptilian people left the dwarves to their own end.

Upon arriving on the planet, he recalled meeting a dwarf prince by the name of Edward Elon. The two befriended one another right away. They trained side by side on many occasions, fighting the dreaded Dark Elves for control of the planet. The two people developed quite the relationship with one another being both warrior races. That was until the Zarillion people intervened and caused an irreversible rift. The dwarves all but abandoned the reptilian people. With the Dark Elves driven from the planet, the Zarillion people wanted peace for all to build a new home.

The major issue remained that the Zarillion people and reptilians were lifelong enemies. The dwarves ended up having more in common with the Zarillions, and the reptilians chose to put an end to the dwarves for good. During a costly and lengthy war, the dwarves and Zarillions banished the reptilians into the earth behind a force field. During their imprisonment, the Dark Elves returned and with the reptilian people no longer available to repel the evil race, the dwarves were slaughtered.

He couldn't help but be impressed with the immense wealth surrounding him. This could help his people in other ways. The Germans were always trying to build up their own wealth in the hopes of increasing their own war machine. The war machine he could appreciate and know he wasn't a prisoner, he could better understand the Germans. Plus, they did do everything he requested to help the reptilian people in their struggle against the Zarillions.

Still in a trance, thinking of the wealth before him, he nearly stumbled into a large golden rock formation. He took a step backward and looked upward. To his great surprise, the formation was indeed made of gold, but he took it in until his eyes followed it to its apex. He nearly ran back behind one of the gold piles. Staring back at him were a large set of hot, evil eyes. A closer look revealed a large shape towering up into the cavern, sitting atop a large mound of melted gold.

The golden shape turned out to be an animal he thought to be nothing but a bedtime fairytale. Huge wings frozen in time smelted with gold rose into the air as if the animal was cast into gold in an instant. An open mouth looked ready to devour him with fangs of gold larger than his own body. His eyes took in the entire shape of the strong beast. Back legs of bulging muscles with smaller front legs. Scales covered the animal all the way up into the neck area. The head resembled his own in many ways with a reptilian look. Shock but reverence took hold of him. The commander backed up to take in the entire beast. He, in all his long life, never witnessed such strength and beauty in an animal.

Silence surrounded him as he took the time to appreciate the majesty of the animal before him. Strength and power were his calling so seeing such a powerful animal before him gave him goosebumps down his arm. Looking at the gold covering the entire beast, a multitude of questions arose in his mind. *How did this magnificent animal become frozen like this? How long has it stood here? Is this what I think it is? Do these animals exist?*

Standing before the animal, he raised his hands and allowed the light to brighten to the point of seeing the sight in its full view. The light hit every facet of the golden animal until it again came to the animal's eyes. To his great surprise, the eyes moved slightly. Once again, he stepped back while blinking, thinking he was seeing things. Again, he moved slightly forward to see the eyes and again, they moved following his own movements.

He grabbed his head as shooting pain forced him to his knees. "So, you have questions, do you? Well, to begin with, I do exist and much of what you've heard in legend is true!"

As the pain lessened, he rose and retorted, "How is it you're still alive though encased in gold?"

The boom from the voice in his head nearly forced him down again. "The fact is you and I have the same enemy. Together, we will make the Zarillions pay for their insolence!"

CHAPTER THIRTY-SEVEN

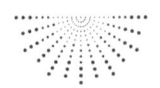

Throwing their packs on their backs, Rebecca and Peter practically sprinted down the road in the hopes of chasing down Holly. A look of sheer determination lined Rebecca's face, and Peter joined her side and could still not believe a few short months ago, he worried about school. Thoughts of being late for class and normal everyday issues seemed so far away. He gazed at the look of concentration on his beloved's face and bore down, trying to stay in stride. The two ran as one, and Peter hardly noticed the rapidly passing homes. When they came to the outskirts of the city, Rebecca finally slowed.

She stopped briefly and raised her nose in the air almost as if sniffing for Holly. After a few moments, she looked down the right branch of the split path and ran again to the right. Peter turned quickly to follow her and nearly slipped in the rubble but righted himself. Again, the two glided through the dim light. Those looking out their windows would only see the wisp of the wind in the night. Peter marveled at the stamina of his lovely lady, and a sense of pride swelled inside. For what seemed another hour, they jogged the path until Rebecca came to near a screeching halt.

Peter stood by her side, wiping the sweat from his brow and for the first time, realized he was quite tired. He leaned over, placing his hands on his knees, trying to gain his breath. Rebecca stood in the dim light, glistening and searching for something. She took a few strides to the left and then back to the right before stopping again. Turning to Peter, she looked a little confused.

Peter looked at her quickly. "What is it?"

"Peter, something isn't right! Holly and General Giles stood exactly where we are, but someone tried to magically wipe away any traces of them!"

Peter paused. "Could it be Holly trying to cover her tracks? She may not be expecting us. We were given a different task by Mother."

She looked relieved. "Peter, that must be it! Holly wouldn't want anyone knowing her business. She must have tried to hide her tracks."

He smiled. "Are we close then?"

She returned the smile. "Yes, we are indeed. Follow me."

Again, she turned and walked briskly down the path, followed by Peter. After twenty minutes, she stopped, holding up her hand to indicate they should move off the path. Peter dove behind a tree off the path while Rebecca crouched behind a large boulder, peering out onto the path. They moved just in time as a small group of six figures, in formation, marched by them, going toward Nathan's abode. From their vantage point, it was difficult to see and identify the figures. Peter felt something was indeed not right and waited for Rebecca to let him know the coast was clear.

After several minutes, Rebecca waved him on, and he followed her forward. Keeping to the edge of the path out of the light, he witnessed Rebecca's experience in hunting. They moved carefully forward but didn't run into the mysterious group of figures. This disturbed Rebecca as she stopped and looked around cautiously.

Peter felt the attack and responded with the ring of steel hurling through the air. His blade intercepted the strike intended for Rebecca. She turned to see the blade deflect, and she immediately took in as much energy as she could. Out of the shadows jumped the other five figures with blades of their own waving in the dim light. Rebecca released a bolt of energy toward two of the figures. The bolt struck the two directly in the chest, nearly blowing them apart. Peter saw the figures fly and land ten feet away sprawled upon the rocky terrain, unmoving.

He turned to engage the original attacker who was joined by another of the figures. Peering to his right, he saw Rebecca squaring off with the remaining two attackers. The two combatants ran forward, brandishing their blades in thirst for blood. Peter crouched slightly and planted his feet in a defensive posture. The first figure swung high, and Peter met the blade quickly and deflected the blow easily. From behind, he heard the whistle of steel coming for him and turned to meet blade on blade. Sparks flew in all directions.

Meanwhile, Rebecca faced the two blade-wielding enemies and still held her power with eyes blazing. For a moment, the two looked at her eyes and paused. Then one of the attackers ran right at her, swinging his blade toward her chest. Spinning, she let the man's momentum carry him, spinning to the ground. His comrade looked angry and went into a series of moves with his sword, hoping to intimidate his opponent. Rebecca smiled and released another blast of energy into the ground in front of her attacker.

The blast struck the ground with complete devastation. Splinters of rock along with small pebbles acting as shot riddled the man's body, tearing holes the size of larger-caliber weapons. The wounds were deadly, and the man sank to the ground, examining his ravaged legs that now looked like hamburger. Blood pooled on the ground, and the man keeled over, grabbing at his destroyed legs.

She turned to face the remaining man, hoping to dispatch him quickly as she felt her own strength waning. Seeing his fallen comrade on the ground, the man went into a rage, swinging the blade so fast, it looked like a fan creating a large breeze. Spinning toward her head, she ducked and lashed out with a quick punch aided by her remaining power. The blow landed on the man's chin, dropping him where he stood. Her own rage building, she reached down and picked the man up by the neck, ready to snap it at a moment's notice.

Peter spun, locked in combat of his own, trading blow for blow with his two attackers. The combatants lashed out in frustration as

Peter countered every move they made as if toying with them. Peter confirmed Rebecca was in control of her own attackers and turned to end this nonsense. He allowed his own anger to build and launched his own offensive. At first, the two enemies defended themselves well until Peter let the anger take control. Now, his blows seemed superhuman, and one swing snapped one of his opponent's sword in half. The blow was so strong, it also flew into the man's skull, taking a huge chunk off the top.

The one remaining opponent looked nervous but faced Peter with his blade to finish things. Peter didn't even wait and picked up his blade, holding it like a spear and threw it directly into the man's chest, ending the threat then and there. He quickly ran over and retrieved his blade from the man's chest while cleaning it on his clothing. Swiftly turning to assist Rebecca, he saw the lone man high in the air above Rebecca. Rebecca's eyes blazed with electricity.

Before he could stop her, Rebecca squeezed too tight, snapping the man's neck. He heard the crack of bones and then saw the limp body still up in the air, held by his beloved. Peter took a moment to look around to make sure no other attackers were coming at them. When he was satisfied, he turned to Rebecca. Her eyes were now normal color, and she released the man's limp body. It fell to the ground with a thud. Rebecca used her remaining energy to light up the area to thoroughly inspect her attackers.

At first, Peter thought they might be Germans but upon further inspection, these figures were much thinner with almost ghostly white skin, and their pure black eyes were missing pupils. Peter took a step back and noticed one of the attacker's ears, specifically a slight point to the ears. Peter immediately thought of elves but how could they be elves? Then again, here he was in search of another magical being.

Rebecca grabbed his hand and made him look at the man before her feet. "Peter, we're in a lot of trouble! These aren't ordinary people, these are Dark Elves!"

Peter's eyebrows shot up. "Dark Elves! What's a Dark Elf?"

"As evil as the reptilian people are, the Dark Elves make them look like puppies! They are the evilest beings in the universe! They were supposed to be extinct! My people made sure of it. We didn't have a choice, they chased us across space, trying to destroy us."

Peter said, "We need to find Holly!"

She nodded. "Yes, my love, we must hurry! Come now!"

Again, she sprinted down the path, and Peter ran this time behind her. He was fast, but Rebecca grew stronger with each stride. After about ten minutes, she stopped before an ancient, worn, wooden door. Peter sprang to her side, and they looked at the ancient door, hoping it would automatically open. At first, nothing happened, and Peter decided to push on it. He reached out to touch the door, and a pulse of energy shot through his body, causing him to fall back onto the ground. Shaking his head, Rebecca sprang to his side, helping him up.

She croaked, "The doors are protected. Sorry, I should have said something as I felt the energy coming from the door. I'll teach you how to do that."

He stood, shaking the dust from his pants, trying not to look embarrassed. "Yes, that was quite the jolt! Next time, I'll have you check the doors first. What do we do now?"

"Now, I'll summon Nathan!"

Rebecca moved Peter behind her and allowed the energy to fill her. After a few moments, she raised her hands and sent what amounted to a sonic boom at the door. The blast wasn't enough to blow the door in, but the entire mountain shook, and the door buckled. She backed up slightly and waited. When nothing happened, she raised her hands.

Before releasing the energy, her voice boomed, "Nathan, I have neither the time nor energy to play these games! Open this door immediately, before I turn this entire mountain into rubble!"

Again, she waited. Still, silence greeted her. She raised her hands and allowed her wrath to fill her. Peter, afraid she might destroy the mountain, burying them in rock, reached out to touch her arm. He felt the charge of energy, but it didn't harm him. He could almost see her thoughts. He felt her anger and her nervousness about finding Holly. Without thinking, Peter reached into her mind and asked her to stop. Inside her mind, Rebecca looked into Peter's, seeing his concern.

Rebecca's eyes popped open, looking into Peter's. "Peter, I'm so sorry! I cannot believe those evil beings still exist. We need to find Holly now!"

Peter warmly embraced her. "I know! I know!"

He walked forward, taking his sword from its scabbard and placed the blade downward while holding the pommel. With a thrust, he rammed the blade into the ground, and a pulse of energy waved outward toward the wooden door. The energy struck the door and rather than destroy it, the door absorbed the energy. At first, nothing happened but within a few seconds, Peter heard a click, and the door opened slightly.

Rebecca held her hands up, allowing the light to lead the way. Entering the doorway, they could see three figures approaching them. Without thinking, Rebecca and Peter immediately went into a defensive posture. Rebecca raised her hands to unleash her power at the new threats, only to see at the last minute, the glinting eyes of her mentor.

Rebecca ran full stride to Holly, nearly knocking her over with a huge hug. General Giles met Peter with a warm handshake. The two held the shake for a moment, but the general noticed the look of concern on Peter's face. He waved the other figure to close the door which he did quickly, muttering another incantation of some kind. The door clicked and glowed from the inside this time.

Holly quickly gathered her friends and led them inside the compound. Peter followed, standing next to the general, looking up at the large man on the other side. Peter realized he was a powerful man, but he had a hidden wisdom below the surface. It was hard for him to determine the man's age as his beard was salt and pepper, but his eyes seemed young. The small group went into the first building, shutting out the night.

Once inside, Peter sensed security he didn't know for some time. The structure inside, though made of wood, seemed indestructible. The fire raging in the hearth threatened to consume any intruders.

The group walked into a large dining room, and they all collapsed into the carved wooden chairs.

Rebecca and Peter looked much disheveled. Holly looked at the two in grave concern. Holly read Rebecca's mind but said nothing, waiting for the young woman to explain herself. It took Rebecca a few breaths to think of what she would say. Peter almost started the conversation, but Holly held up a hand, alerting him not to interfere. He leaned back in his seat, waiting for Rebecca to tell Holly of their adventure. General Giles sat slightly forward as if waiting for a briefing from one of his soldiers.

Rebecca stood, leaning heavily on her arms. "Holly, we're in a lot of trouble! The Dark Elves have returned!"

Holly shot up, and her face turned deathly white. "Are you sure? We hunted them to extinction."

Rebecca nodded. "Yes, My Lady, I fought them myself! Peter and I were ambushed by them! They were Dark Elves. There's no mistaking them!"

General Giles interjected, "This is indeed mind-altering news! How many attacked you?"

Peter responded, "My Lord, we were attacked by a small squad of six, but I'm sure there are more where they came from. They definitely didn't seem to be a rogue group as they were well dressed and equipped."

The general sat back. "Holly, this must be the help the reptilians were referring too!"

Holly's face turned to steel. "I hunted them down once, and I'll do so again! This time, both species will end!"

CHAPTER THIRTY-EIGHT

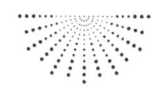

The sound of the huge gate being magically sealed made Jake feel more secure. Dwarves surrounded them, looking with very curious eyes at the odd strangers invading their daily routine. At first, the dark looks made Jake feel nervous, but he watched his father and Michelle walk unconcerned with the dwarf lord. He hastened his pace and caught up to his father, who turned and flashed a small smile in the direction of his son. The dwarf lord gave orders they be left alone, and the remaining crowd dispersed immediately.

A few guards dressed in heavy armor with the crest of a large tree took up posts on either side of Thomas. He didn't notice and walked at a brisk pace, waving his guests onward. Michelle nodded and walked that much closer to the large dwarf. In a few minutes, they came upon a small stone building resembling a tomb. Without explanation, the dwarf opened the heavy metal gate and entered. Michelle and Derek followed while Jake turned to look around, only to see he was the only member of the group still outside. With a quick turn, he dashed into the tombs gate.

Once inside, the clang of metal sounded ominous. The smell of dank air met Jake's nostrils, and he moved to the right side of his father who looked straight at Thomas. The dwarf lord stood in front of what looked like a large sarcophagus. Raising his hands, he chanted some strange language as Jake watched the large stone box scrape across the floor to reveal a hidden stair. Thomas stepped down into the dark hole and as he did, light sprung up, surrounding him. The others followed him down into another smaller, naturally stone-hewn chamber.

Globes mounted on the walls provided the light, and Jake noticed the room to be empty except for a few stone seats. Thomas took one of the seats and waved his hands, asking his guests to do the same. When everyone was seated, he again chanted in the same strange language. The large stone box returned to its original position with a click. When Thomas was satisfied the room was secure, he rose to his feet to address his guests.

Thomas, with a serious tone, said, "My friends, things have reached our ears that cause us much anxiety. For many eons, we have lived in relative peace, but that peace is being put to the test."

Michelle looked at Thomas. "My Lord, what are you referring too?"

Again, Thomas looked serious. "My lady, it's better if I show you!"

In that moment, Thomas again raised his hands but this time, he released what looked to be smoke into the air. At first, the smoke seemed a wisp but within minutes the smoke resembled a cloud. The cloud became a brilliant white and seemed almost solid. Hovering at eye level, the seated figures noticed images on the cloud. As the images came into view, Jake nearly leapt up, gripping the pommel of his sword. Derek held his son at bay with his arm. Jake took his seat again to see the image of the reptilian commander surrounded by immense wealth. Everyone viewing this scene held their breath and watched it unfold.

Jake gritted his teeth at the sight of the commander and wished to put an end to the evil once and for all. Michelle watched in awe as the commander stopped before what looked to be a massive golden statue. At first glance, it was difficult to make out what type of animal the statue looked like, but Jake walked forward ready to speak. Again, his father held him at bay.

Thomas noticed the young man's interest. "Yes, Jake, it is exactly as you guessed. The beast is a dragon!"

Jake spat, "A dragon! They're real?"

Thomas answered, "Like much in this world, they were real and thought to be extinct. This beast was thought to be destroyed. The cavern you're viewing is one of ours, thought to be lost to time. A few hours ago, this image came into my mind, and I'm sharing it with you!"

Michelle stood. "My Lord, do you mean to tell me we have a living dragon to deal with?"

Thomas nodded. "Michelle, I sent my best scribes and historians to find out as much as they could about this situation. My mind isn't what it once was but if memory serves me right my great grandfather magically encased the dragon in gold to imprison him. As you may know, according to legend, the only thing more important to a dragon other than slaughter is gold. My ancestor turned the tables on the monster and imprisoned him in the thing he wanted the most!"

Jake came forward. "My Lord, can the commander release the dragon?"

Thomas turned to Jake. "No, he doesn't possess the tools or skill to reverse the spell. The commander isn't what concerns me. I'm feeling another presence surrounding the commander that I haven't felt in eons!"

Michelle chimed in, "Thomas, what presence?"

"That, my dear, is what has me vexed the most! I cannot place the energy reaching out to him. Whoever it is, doesn't want to be known. They're masking themselves very well."

Michelle moved forward. "My Lord, do you know where this chamber is? Can we get there and make sure the dragon isn't released?"

Thomas frowned. "That is what I'm telling you, my dear. That chamber was lost long ago. I have no idea how the commander got in and found it in the first place!"

"I wish Holly were here! She could help me reach out and read the commander's mind."

Thomas spoke not a word while walking directly to Michelle. The dwarf reached forth with both hands, touching slightly Michelle's temples. Immediately, the image of the commander flared into Michelle's own mind. She could almost reach out and touch the commander. Heat surrounded her, and she felt nothing but wrath filling the room about her. The commander strode closer to the immense golden-covered beast. Michelle wanted to strike him down where he stood but knew not to do anything to reveal herself.

The commander raised his head, looking up at the golden maw. "You still haven't answered my question. How is it you're still alive?"

The room shook, and a booming voice rolled through the entire cavern, "I'm a magical being and like you, I get much of my own energy from the very earth. No, the dwarves used a magic I didn't know they possessed to entomb me here. It wasn't until my messages were received was I able to summon you here."

The commander laughed. "Summon me! You didn't summon me, I was sent."

The golden dragon rumbled a low, growling laugh of his own. "You were sent because I summoned you! You don't have the magic I need to release me, but you do have other talents I need. Part of my imprisonment made me sleep but a few weeks ago, a power of some sort must have been released, causing that part of the spell to be lifted. When I awoke, I immediately sent out messages to my people but couldn't contact one of my people. I communicated with your emperor, and he assured me he could release me."

Commander Zosa nodded. "He told me much the same. What's it you think I can do for you? Honestly at this point it is I that need help from you. My forces are all but destroyed. The emperor thinks he's coming to this planet in a blaze of glory but from where I stand, he may come too late."

The dragon rumbled, "The emperor will return with what you need but in the mean time you need to find a talisman for me. It is a special medallion that should be in this cavern. Though I cannot move, I still can send out my own energy a short distance, and the talisman isn't here. Someone has taken it from the room, and it must be found to release me."

Again, the commander looked puzzled. "You want me to find something that spent eons in this room and is gone? You have to know that trying to find this talisman will prove near impossible."

Booming, the dragon growled, "That again is why you're here! Without that medallion, I'll be forever locked in this golden prison."

The commander looked up. "Medallion? What does it look like?"

"It resembles any other medallion, but it is made of a special metal that allows the wearer to be imperious to magic. It also can draw magic into it or cancel out other's magic. It has an intricate starburst pattern on the front."

At the description of the medallion, the commander spat, "I know the very medallion you describe! I too have sought this talisman. It now resides in the hands of our enemy!"

A near scream came from the dragon, "Then go get it!"

The commander grew angry. "You presume to command me! I'll get the talisman but right now, I need an army. Without that, I can attain nothing for anyone!"

Another bout of laughter rang in the air. "Well, Commander, I sense a little fight left in you after all. Worry not about your army. One beyond your wildest dreams is on its way. Trust me when I say this, the dwarves, humans, and Zarillions will perish in waves of fire!"

Raising his eyebrows, the commander spoke, "Waves of fire?"

"Yes, waves of fire. Worry not about the army. I have another request of you. To clear the way for this army, you must open the gate that's hidden somewhere in this city. I cannot find it. The dwarves hid it well, but I'm sure you will find it. When you find the gate, prepare it to receive your army."

The commander's eyes blazed. "There's a Gate of the Cosmos here? Much like you, I thought all of them were destroyed. If what you say is correct, that could be a game changer."

The dragon responded, "Truly a game changer. Yes, the gate still exists but must be found."

Michelle felt her strength waning as she opened her eyes to see Derek moving to catch her. He let her lean into him, and she looked into his kind eyes. Thomas nearly stumbled to the ground in exhaustion, only to be propped up by one of his men. The group waited for the two to regain their strength with concerned eyes. After fifteen minutes, both spoke freely and began their tale.

Thomas went first, sharing the encounter between the dragon and the commander. Michelle nodded many times but didn't interrupt as the dwarf described every detail of the dragon's plan to be released. He spent a great deal of time talking about the medallion and the gate of the cosmos. Each member of the group listened intently, not wanting to interrupt, but each wanted to ask questions.

When Thomas finished his tale, he leaned back slightly, looking at his audience, allowing the story to sink in a bit. Each member of the group chewed on the information in their own minds. Michelle couldn't wait to say something but allowed her companions to think on the information. Derek looked at Jake and then at Michelle, only to see her looking off in another direction, contemplating her own thoughts. Thomas witnessed each member wrestling with what needed to be done next to protect their own realms from this new danger.

Michelle finally could take it no longer and rose. "My friends, the dragon will never be released as long as I have breath in my lungs!"

At that, she raised a medallion high in the air. "This is what they are looking for, and it's an heirloom of my house! They will never get their hands on it!"

The power in her voice made Derek step back. He looked at her with pride. Her strength and power were on full display. Thomas smiled as though he knew what Michelle would do next. Jake knew of the medallion and his father's involvement in its retrieval from the Nazis. Derek moved over to Michelle, standing next to her. Once again, Michelle looked at her group and then sat.

Thomas moved slightly forward. "Michelle, I didn't know the medallion found its way out of the hoard in that room. I know it is from your house but for time out of imagining, it has been used by many in the defense of all that's good. I'm glad to know it is where it should be!"

Michelle looked concerned. "My Lord, it isn't my intent to place blame on anyone! My only goal is to stop evil from winning the day! I won't allow my people, your people, or Derek's people to suffer any longer at the hands of evil!"

Thomas responded, "Spoken like a true warrior. My Lady, worry not about all our peoples. The time is for us to rise together!"

Jake rose to his feet, having said nothing to this point. "My Lords and Lady, I'm a young warrior, but what I have is yours to command! I will rise with you!"

He offered his sword to the small group. Thomas strode forward and took the sword, looking it up and down. He turned, showing the sword to his own men. They all nodded and looked at Jake with great respect.

Thomas spoke, "Jake, my men tell me you bested one of my greatest warriors. That isn't something to be taken lightly. In this world, a warrior is held in the greatest regard. You haven't only earned entrance into our kingdom, you've earned a place with us."

He returned the blade. "We will indeed rise to meet this evil, together!"

CHAPTER THIRTY-NINE

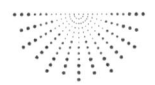

Nathan stood in silence, hand on his chin, staring into the glowing embers of the roaring fire. All the years of solitude and study with nothing to show for his efforts caused him to regret many of those decisions. Leaving Holly behind wrenched at his heart, and he needed to make amends. A chance for redemption, a chance to right many wrongs stood within his reach. He caught sight of the bluest ember near the middle of the fire, and the image of a great winged dragon came forth.

The dragon moved toward him stopping at the edge of the fire. "Nathan, the time has come to pay for your sins! When I'm released, I'll come for you and nothing in this world will save you from my wrath!"

Stepping back as if struck by a blow, Nathan shook his head, blinking his eyes to focus again on the fire. This time, he saw only fire, and the blue ember looked yellow. Sweat on his brow beading up, he turned to see the eyes of Holly meeting his with worry on her own face. Nathan offered a curt smile and turned back to the fire, too ashamed to look into her eyes. If the dragon awoke, they all were in more danger than initially thought. The Dark Elves were one thing and difficult to deal with, but the dragons devour worlds. If the dragons return, they would destroy the planet and move on to another world.

The dragons were the more pressing of the two threats. He spun and waved to Holly to join him as he walked briskly toward the exit. Holly up on her feet sprinted to his side. General Giles ran to meet her but paused when she looked at him with her hand up telling him to stand down. He returned to his spot around the fire glancing up to see Peter and Rebecca also ready to follow Holly.

Watching Holly walk away with her mentor gave him mixed thoughts. Here was the man who taught Holly to control her immense power and feel as a normal person. Until Nathan, Holly felt much like her power would consume her. She frightened herself anytime she was near a loved one for fear of releasing her power harming them. Nathan calmed the storm and taught her much about life, wisdom, and friendship. The general recalled the day Nathan walked out on Holly. He was nearly scorched to death when Holly accidentally unleashed a primal scream that nearly destroyed the council chambers. Everyone on the council needed every bit of their own power to keep Holly's at bay.

For years following Nathan's exit, Holly spent much of her time trying to track him down, hoping for an explanation that never came. Eventually, Holly moved on and returned to her position on the council, but her brooding bothered the other members. Ryan finally broke through to her, not making her feel bad about her behavior but rather, he focused on her nature to help others. Holly, from a small child, always stood for those less fortunate and weaker. Around this time, Rebecca showed signs of her own power growing. Ryan suggested Holly help the young woman hone her skills. At first, Holly resisted, thinking herself not worthy to be Rebecca's teacher. That changed when one day, Holly witnessed Rebecca's power firsthand. It was as if a door opened in her mind, screaming for her to stop feeling sorry for herself. From that point on, Holly and Rebecca were inseparable.

Ryan held back his own emotions toward the man who caused so much pain in his love's life. He knew Peter and Rebecca would need him focused if they were able to succeed in their quest to save the world. Still, it was hard to quell his anger, seeing the two walk off on their own. The general would have his hide if he hurt her again.

Letting his emotions go, he turned to Peter. "If he hurts her again, I'll skin him alive!"

Rebecca chuckled. "General, something tells me that it will be Holly that skins him. I cannot tell you how many conversations about this very subject I endured over the years. No, Ryan, if Nathan steps out of line even a little, he will have to answer to her and her alone. I don't want to be anywhere near Nathan if that ever happens."

"General, what's our next move? Do we go after Jake and company?"

The general looked at Peter. "Right now, my friend, we need to make sure our own borders are protected. If the Dark Elves are indeed back, we have to fortify our city first."

Peter looked worried. "What about Jake?"

He nodded in Peter's direction. "When Holly returns, I'll see if she can reach out to determine how our young warrior is faring in his quest to find the dwarves."

Rebecca walked over to Peter and reached out, touching her hands to his head. Her hands were warm and in an instant, he felt energy seeping into his mind. At first, he could only see what looked to be a white light. Though the light didn't hurt his head, he felt it surrounding him as images formed. Jake's smiling face emerged from the light, and a scene of a stone building with a great fire came into view. Peter could see Jake was comfortable and then, he caught sight of his mother.

Peter shuddered. She stood tall and was in conversation with a noble-looking, bearded man. A warm sense of pride seeing his mother brought him to his senses. He searched for Jake, who was speaking with his father. Peter couldn't help but look around the room and into the faces of those other bearded men surrounding the large, blazing fire.

Seeing Jake surrounded by his family members comforted Peter, and he smiled as Rebecca released him. He reached up with a large hug threatening to smother her. She accepted the hug and returned one of her own before holding him at arm's length, nodding. He knew everything with Jake was going to plan.

Peter looked at the general. "My Lord, Jake is with the dwarves and is joined by Derek and my mom. I would say things are going as planned."

General Giles smacked Peter on the back. "This is indeed terrific news. I was worried the dwarves may have left the planet or ceased to exist. We have heard nothing from or about them in eons."

Rebecca interceded, "General, do you really think the Dark Elves are truly back, or is this a surviving pocket?"

"That, my dear, is the ultimate question, isn't it? We cannot take any chances and must be prepared for anything!"

Peter chimed in, "General, should we grab Jake and the others first? According to Nathan, the entrance to the dwarves' kingdom isn't that far from here."

General Giles winked. "I know you want your family back in the worst way, but Mother sent them there for an important mission. They will be back in short order. You can see for yourself they are doing well."

Feeling embarrassed about allowing his feelings to get in the way of the mission, he moved back a bit. The general noticed this and placed a hand on his shoulder for reassurance. General Giles felt for the young man. As a military leader, he knew very well what the young man felt. Training and fighting with many young men in his own army in much the same situation gave him a more sympathetic view of Peter. He also knew that Peter grew up much in the last few months, much too fast.

Holly sped up to catch up to her mentor, who at this point was running out the door. Nathan didn't look back to see where his student was in relation to himself. He moved through the door and led her into another large room, spinning to face her with a look of dread. The two stared at one another, not knowing what to say.

Holly broke the ice, "Nathan, what is it?"

He glanced down at her. "The Dark Elves aren't our only problem!"

She waited. "Well, spit it out!"

"The dragons, Holly! The dragons!"

She winced. "Nathan, the dragons are no more! You turned the last one into a huge, golden statue!"

"I turned it into gold, but I couldn't take its life force. All I could do was put it to sleep forever. I'm afraid it's awake now!"

Holly spat, "Nathan, what do you mean it's awake?"

"When Peter and Rebecca came into their power, they unlocked many closed doors in the cosmos! I'm not blaming them. It's their destiny, but it is tied to many unfinished tales. Things we have chosen to avoid or prolong are coming home to roost."

She glared at her mentor. "If this creature is awake, is there any chance it can summon others to its side?"

A look of panic struck Nathan's face. "Let's hope not! I, however, need to find a way to put it to sleep or now that Peter and Rebecca are here, maybe they can destroy it!"

"Nathan, they aren't ready to face such a foe! The magic the dragons possess is both complex and far reaching! I'm not sure even together, they can compete with that!"

Nathan laughed. "My dear Holly, don't sell those two short. I've dealt with the dragons and bested them, with help of course. Trust me when I say this, the power those two possess will bring this universe to its knees! We have to keep them focused on the right path."

Holly eyes shot up. "What have you seen? Are the young ones in danger?"

He raised his hands. "You know as well as I that the flow of time is both ever changing and hard to read. I'm just saying that power is a great burden, and with that burden comes challenges to stay on the right path."

"You don't know these two very well but let me say this. Peter and Rebecca are two of the purest creatures I've ever come across! They will stay true!"

Nathan looked uncertain. "Holly, I trust in you and your assessment but know even the purest hearts can be swayed in the right situation!"

She looked angrily at Nathan. "We will speak no more of this! What do we need to do to put the dragon back to sleep?"

He brought her to a door and opened it, stepping in and waving his hand to light their way. Inside, it looked like a library of some sort with stacks of books coming up from the floor. Without a word, he moved across the room, reaching out to grab hold of one of the lamps on the wall. He pulled, and the wall opened before him. Waving to Holly, he disappeared into the wall. Holly followed, ducking into the next room.

The room beyond held other volumes of books with scrolls all neat and catalogued on clean shelves. He motioned her to come over a large table that held a large ancient volume that looked as if it would fall apart at the touch. Holly leaned over the volume, looking at the text with great curiosity. Nathan gingerly turned the pages until he came to the passage he searched for and pointed to the page. Holly read and nodded. When she looked up, Nathan looked confident but wary.

Holly blurted out, "We need Michelle! We need her now!"

Nathan shook his head. "Holly, we do need her, but they must complete their mission first. If they fail, having Michelle here won't matter in the least!"

Holly twisted her head. "Nathan, what are you talking about? They did complete their mission. The dwarf kingdom has been found and relations reestablished!"

Nathan leaned forward heavily on his arms. "That's only the beginning. Making contact is the first step! You know yourself how long it took for our people to listen to you. I tried for a lifetime to get them to listen to me, to no avail. Jake has much the same issue before him. He must make the dwarves remember their oaths."

Holly retorted, "The dwarves are loyal and trustworthy people. They will rise with us!"

Nathan shook his head. "That they are but so are we and look, it almost cost us our lives. Hopefully, Jake can get them onboard before it's too late!"

"Jake is a special young man, and I'm sure Mother wouldn't have sent him if he couldn't sway the dwarves."

Nathan nodded. "I'm sure you're right. The dwarves are especially stubborn, and it takes an act of God for them to do anything. I'm afraid they'll be too late."

"Nathan, what do you know? What are you not telling me?"

He looked sheepishly at her. "I could never hide anything from you. Jake will have difficulty because the dwarves are lost!"

Holly shouted, "Lost! Jake found them!"

"He found the royal family or what's left of it! The dwarf people are nowhere to be found! The very people we need to rally to our cause are gone. There was a struggle for power long ago when they decided to break away from us. The ruling faction wanted to honor their oaths while another faction wanted to greedily build their own world around gold."

"So, Mother sent Jake to find the dwarf people and bind them to us. He's a fantastic warrior, but what does he know of politics?"

Nathan laughed. "Holly, maybe a politician isn't what's needed!"

CHAPTER FORTY

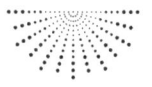

Echoes of the pain still buzzed in his mind as he walked out of the cavern. Still trying to come to grips with the existence of dragons made the pain intensify. Shaking his head in hopes to clear it quickly, he walked briskly back the way he came. The day began with such extreme disappointment, only to turn into a near triumph. His displaced and ruined army would soon be replenished. Still, he couldn't help but wonder what reinforcements the emperor referred to in their conversation.

As soon as he was clear of the presence of the dragon, his mind cleared. He tried his communicator on his wrist several times but while in the dwarf kingdom, it didn't work. Exiting into tunnels he recognized, he tried to hail his people. Finally, a voice came over the speaker, sounding relieved the commander was safe. Commander Zosa kept his military bearing but nearly smiled at the soldier's attempt to sound concerned. He alerted the soldier that he would meet immediately with his high command upon his return.

When he signed off, he smirked to himself, thinking of passing on his newfound information. His entrance to the compound was met with brisk salutes and happy eyes. He looked his soldiers up and down with pride. Each soldier stood tall, dressed and pressed, despite their lengthy campaign. The resilience of his soldiers never ceased to amaze him. On his way to command, he briefed a few underlings of items he wanted attended to and darted into the room.

Already seated awaiting his arrival, the soldiers spread out around the large wooden table jumped to their feet, saluting the commander. He waved them to sit and quickly grabbed the nearest seat. Not waiting for pleasantries, he began his tale with great haste. He watched as the eyes of his command grew wider and wider with each breath. The same sense of renewed hope showed in each man's face as he finished his tale.

The barrage of questions shook the room as he attempted to answer as many as he could in short order. Normally a man of little patience, he smiled as he explained the new strategy to conquer the earth's surface. At the end of the question and answer session, he dismissed all but one of his colonels. The officers exited to a new bustle and energy to their step.

The colonel looked nervous as the commander looked his way. "Colonel, where are we with the Nazi stooges?"

Squirming a bit, the colonel responded, "Sir, the Nazis haven't answered any of our communications. With our limited resources, I was unsure how you wanted us to handle their insolence."

The commander pondered his next answer for a moment. "They are uncertain as many of you were until this very moment."

He let the sentence sink in for a moment. "It's understandable, Colonel. We spent so much time and energy planning the downfall of the humans along with the Zarillions, we never built a contingency plan."

The colonel looked down at the floor with an embarrassed look. Commander Zosa, a few days ago, would have wrung this soldier's neck, but things changed with their defeat. Without telling his subordinates of his own uncertainty, he thought carefully of his next words.

"Colonel, we were rocked to our core but even in defeat, threads of triumph remain. Our anxious nature to escape our prison and ruination of our enemies almost cost us everything. Mark my words, it won't happen again!"

The colonel's eyes rose with conviction. "My Lord, we will turn this to our advantage. What would you have me do?"

He motioned the colonel to take a seat. Once comfortable, the commander went into his instructions for bringing the Nazis into the fold. He would use their greed and need for technology to bring them to their knees. The colonel was given the task of bringing diplomatic relations to bear. Once the colonel was up to speed, he dismissed him, leaving the room completely empty of a living being other than himself.

Silence surrounded him and as many times as he would have loved to strangle or destroy many of his officers, he couldn't help but feel remorse for their loss. The Nazis would come around with the dangling of new war technology; he would soon have them eating out of his hand. Sitting in the empty room, he never even considered all the Nazis lost during this campaign. In his blindness for revenge, many suffered at his hands.

Thus, was the responsibility of a military leader, he told himself often. Now at defeat's door, he understood the loss his plans inflicted. He would make things right and be the most powerful man in the universe. With the emperor's new force and his new relationship with the dragon, no one would stop him.

Thinking about the dragon made him shudder and pressed his temples as if they still throbbed from the dragon's torture. He shook his head slightly and pictured the huge golden dragon. The sheer size of the beast was enough to bring the most fearless warrior to his knees. In his briefing of his high command, he did utter a word of his own mission to obtain the medallion. With the thought of squeezing the life from Michelle, he rose from the table, leaving the silence of the room behind.

Once in his quarters, he packed items he would need for a quick journey. He anticipated dealing with Michelle and company in short order. If his intelligence were correct, Michelle went in search of the dwarves. Commander Zosa laughed inwardly because he was aware of what Michelle would find. Nothing but a few stray groups of the dwarves existed in large part because of their own greed and the commander's raids. Centuries ago the dwarves were needed for many resources the commander needed. Trade between the two cultures worked well for a time, but the dwarves' love of gold caused a large rift. Before the reptilian people were imprisoned, the commander launched a large attack on the dwarves' main city while negotiating a new trade partnership. The traitorous reptilians wiped out the dwarves while what was left fled into the inner earth.

The only issue standing in the commander's way would be the magic used to seal the dwarf kingdom. Over the centuries it was learned that the dwarves sealed away their kingdom so no one could plunder their riches. He laughed because a legend spoke of a great young warrior solving the mystery of the seal, and the dwarf kingdom would be reborn.

Now that he was free, he would test his own meddle against the dwarf seal. Throwing a few more weapons into his pack, he threw it over his shoulder and walked out. Without speaking another word to anyone, he left the compound with the ringing message of the dragon in the back of his mind. He would find the medallion and return to release the dragon. With such a powerful entity by his side, no one would ever challenge his supremacy again.

Shifting his pack to a more comfortable location on his shoulders, he bore down and sped up his steps. The entrance to the dwarf kingdom was a several days' trip due to his limited transportation. Most of his vehicles were destroyed in the fight so he could only walk or jog to his destination. Jogging at a nice clip, he bounded off in the direction of the sealed kingdom. The faster he arrived, the faster he could return with his new prize.

Only the singular thought of destroying Michelle spurred him on, and he quickened his pace. A hardened warrior, it felt good to be running again toward a battle. Too long it was that he ordered others into battle from the confines of the compound. He felt the rush of energy with each stride as his body temperature rose, making him feel even that much stronger.

As he came closer to the Zarillion lands, he knew which paths to take to enter undetected. He slowed and carefully chose each path.

Slowed by stealth he knew the price of foolishness and kept to the shadows. Caution guided each step, but he also couldn't help but wonder why he saw zero signs of his enemy even though this territory usually teemed with activity. Looking around, he moved from tree to tree, waiting for an ambush. Nothing happened, and he made decent time.

Leaving the Zarillions behind him, he now recognized the old dwarf paths leading to the kingdom. Dark as the paths were, he saw signs of recent travel. He smiled inwardly, knowing this to be the correct path. Within sight of the sealed gate, he sensed something to be wrong. Quickly ducking behind one of the large boulders just off the path, he watched as a small group of figures approached the gate. In the dim light, he couldn't see or recognize the nature of the persons at the gate.

Curious, he pressed himself onto the boulder, straining to see what the group was about. Speech was difficult to pick up as the person spoke in hushed tones. One of the group members came forward, pointing a weapon at the gate, and released a bolt of energy into the gate. At first, the gate seemed to be blasted into oblivion until the energy from the weapon dissipated, leaving the door unharmed.

Again, another member of the group came forth with a larger weapon that he mounted on a tripod on the ground. He unleashed the weapon against the gate as his counterpart before him with the same result. Commander Zosa couldn't hear what they said, but frustration was mounting. Another person approached the door, this time with a simple torch. The man raised the hand with the torch and breathed some words until the flame grew and shot toward the gate. The flames licked the door and engulfed it with yellow, red, and blue flames. No damage again to the gate as the flames subsided.

Sitting behind the boulder, he couldn't help but like the group's resilience as they bombarded the gate with everything they could think of. An argument ensued among the group. The commander watched as their frustration brimmed over. After a few more attempts, they cursed the door and turned to one another for new ideas. When the gate wouldn't give up its secret, they packed up their things and disappeared into the darkness of the rocks off the path to their right.

Commander Zosa waited and patiently watched for ten minutes, anticipating their return. He was disappointed when the group showed no signs of coming back to finish the job. When he felt the coast was clear, he peeled himself from the rocky hiding place, slinking out onto the path. Again, checking around him, there were no signs of life. As he approached the gate, he was surprised to see not a scratch on the heavy, magically sealed gate. He couldn't help but chuckle, looking at the gate keeping him from his mission.

Reaching out, he touched the wooden gate, only to feel a jolt of electricity shoot through his body sending him flying. Landing with a thud he spun around glaring at the door mocking his own stupidity. Dusting himself off he moved again to the front of the gate and this time allowed energy to fill himself from the very earth around him. As the energy approached its apex, he raised his hands to unleash his own weapon upon the sealed door.

A shooting pain in the back of his neck caused him to lose concentration, and he lost his grip on the energy. The energy went back harmlessly into the earth as he reached up to find out the cause of his pain. His hand came upon a type of dart, and he pulled it from his neck. Looking at the dart, he saw the point itself was covered in a dark, sticky substance. Taking some of the substance into his fingers, he smeared it around his fingers, only to feel drowsiness take a hold of him. Turning to look for his attackers, he found no one, and his eyes grew heavier by the second.

Blinking his eyes rapidly he reached for his sword letting the ring of metal break the silence. He stood his ground with blade in hand waving it in front of him defensively. Still, he could see no one. His eyes could hardly stay open, but he refused to go down. Another dart struck the side of his neck and still another in his shoulder. This time, the poison worked quicker, and his muscles failed. He couldn't move and felt himself starting to waver. Though he couldn't feel himself fall, he saw through heavy eyes the ground coming up to meet him. Dust and dirt entered his mouth, but he could do nothing. Now he could hear voices gathering around him. The muffled voices whispered to one another, and he could barely feel himself being turned over.

As his eyes were about the close for good, he thought he saw a few of his captors. He couldn't place the persons, but they were not Zarillion or dwarf. The shapes looked familiar, but he couldn't place them in his muddled state. Looking at the back of his eyelids, he felt himself going to sleep. Drifting off he could still hear the voices speaking around him in a fog.

He barely heard someone say, "We will take him to the king! He will know what to do with this traitor!"

CHAPTER FORTY-ONE

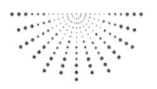

Lord Thomas stared into the flames, unmoving. Michelle and Jake moved to either shoulder of the dwarven lord, waiting for the man to speak. Michelle, along with the entire group, learned of the existence of a living dragon, albeit a golden dragon. Flames from the large fire licked the remaining logs showing colors of red, orange, and some blue. Derek stayed back a few feet, scanning the area for any intruders in good soldier fashion. The remaining dwarves were seated, quietly munching on hard cookies. One of the dwarves offered Derek one which he gratefully accepted.

Thomas sharply turned to look deep into Michelle's eyes. Without speaking directly, he reached out to her in his mind. "Michelle, you're a Knight of the Cosmos. Only you can open the gate!"

She reached back with his mind. "My Lord, the gates were all destroyed!"

"My dear, you and I know the gates cannot be destroyed. We wanted our enemies to have that information. I won't ask you about your gate, but I'll say we need to protect our gate! From what we have heard, the reptilians are making for our gate to open it for evil purposes! I won't allow that to happen."

Michelle didn't mention the Zarillion gate. "I'm sure that's why

Mother sent us here! She wanted us to bring the kingdoms together and defend each other."

Thomas responded, "Michelle, what do you know of Jake? He is more than he seems. There's no way a normal human could best my men. Who is he really?"

Michelle was taken back by the question. "My Lord, he's a normal young man. Growing up in a military family, he has turned into quite the warrior. But I can see as you that he is special!"

"Mark my words, that boy is more than we see! I wouldn't be surprised to see him chosen by the knights themselves."

Again, Michelle said nothing about the knights. "Thomas, how do we guard the gate? I'm but one knight?"

Thomas broke the silence, announcing his plans, "My friends, we need to find our kin, and we need to do it now!"

Jake strode forward. "Lead the way, My Lord! The sooner we find your people, the sooner I can get back to Peter and Rebecca."

The dwarf lord looked fondly at Jake. "Yes, Jake. I'm sure they will have need of your skills very soon."

He drew them all close to him around the fire and outlined for them the road to the other dwarves would be hard and dangerous. In no uncertain terms, he also let them know that he himself didn't know whether they lived still or not. The last communication with the other dwarves he could remember took place over three hundred years ago. Jake looked concerned at this news. For him, if this turned into a long expedition, it would be months before he saw his friends again. The image of Mother formed in his brain assuring him this mission was of the utmost importance. Without hesitation, he listened to Thomas' plans for the group.

When finished, Thomas returned to looking into the fire without another word, leaving Michelle and the others to themselves. Jake ushered his father to one side of the room and looked questioningly to him for guidance. The elder Andrews took his son in a big embrace, pulling him close. Jake never knew his father to be so affectionate, but he could tell this was new territory for the military man. Derek held his son at arm's length, telling him he would be there every step of his journey. Knowing his father had his back made him feel more confident. Having a Navy Seal covering his six would be Jake's best scenario.

Michelle stood in front of Derek. "We must find these dwarves, and we have to find them now! The enemy is making a move on this kingdom and if it isn't able to defend itself, we're all in grave danger."

Derek reached out clasping her hand in his. "What do you need of us? Jake and I are ready."

She smiled. "Of that, I have no doubt, Mr. Andrews!"

Jake moved over to Michelle's side. "My Lady, what are our orders?"

She marveled at the two military men before her. "Thomas is worried of what we may find when we continue our search. According to him, his group lost contact with the other dwarves over three hundred years ago!"

Jake interrupted, "Are we even sure the dwarves are still there?"

Michelle nodded. "Jake, a valid question. Thomas seems confident the group is hidden and can be found. He will take us along the path and show us the way."

Jake turned away from Michelle and walked quickly to Thomas. "My Lord, with all due respect, we need to make haste! Let us leave now please."

Normally, Thomas would reprimand such a brash statement by one of his men, but he held his wrath. "Yes, Jake, I understand the need for haste. We will be ready within the hour."

A wave of relief flowed over Jake, and he bowed. "Thank you, My Lord! Every minute I'm sitting here, Peter goes unprotected."

Thomas placed a hand on his shoulder. "My dear boy, you do realize that Peter and Rebecca are among the strongest beings in the universe, right?"

Jake looked at the dwarf lord with a stone-cold face. "My Lord, they can just as easily be slain by a knife or sword."

Jake spoke the truth and Thomas knew it all too well. "Yes, you're absolutely correct. I hope Peter knows how good a friend he has in you!"

"We watch each other's backsides. Peter and I would do anything for each other!"

Thomas smiled. "Of that, I have little doubt, Jake! That is a rare quality. Loyalty is a knightly quality."

He waved to his men, and the dwarves scattered to get things ready for the expedition. Leading Michelle, Derek, and Jake out of the room, they followed quickly behind until he stopped them before a large steel door. Muttering a chant, the door glowed, and it opened silently. Thomas brought them inside, and they all marveled at the array of weapons before them. Each wall stood lined with uncounted weapons of all kinds. Swords of the most magnificent craftsmanship and ornate battle axes to accompany them stood ready to be wielded.

Suits of armor stood in each corner of the room with helmets of pure gold. The gleaming suits stood as if ready to fight anyone who would take the weapons. Jake went as if drawn to the far wall where he looked up on the wall about six feet high to where a gleaming sword waited for him. Without asking for permission, he reached for the ornate blade. The leather felt warm in his hand, and the weight of the blade seemed minimal. He raised the blade to look at it in the light. Runes went up and down the blade. Though he couldn't read the runes, he ran his fingertips over the raised letters in hopes of learning their meaning.

Jake felt a hand on his shoulder, and he spun to see who interrupted his solitude. The smiling face of Thomas met his and nodded. Thomas reached his hand forward, asking to see the blade Jake so coveted. Hesitantly, he handed the blade over to the dwarf lord. Thomas took the sword reverently and held it up, working the blade into the air. Jake watched as he moved to the middle of the room and moved into a dance with the blade. Jake marveled at the speed and quickness that the blade moved through the air, wielded by the dwarf lord. Arcing through the air, the blade looked more like a torch moving in the air rather than a blade.

Sweat on his brow, the dwarf lord moved toward Jake and offered the sword, "This is no ordinary sword, Jake, as you're no ordinary human! It's no wonder to me that the two of you found each other.

This sword is an heirloom of my house. My family brought into many a battle, including perhaps the greatest warrior my people have ever known, my grandfather Alric."

Jake held the blade gingerly and handed it back to Thomas. "My pardon, My Lord! I should have asked before touching anything. It was as if it were calling to me."

Thomas laughed, not taking the sword. "As I said, I'm not surprised you found one another. The bond between sword and wielder is extremely important. Some would say the two need to become one. No, Jake, the blade did call to you and is yours now with my blessings."

Jake stood shaking his head. "My Lord, I cannot take something like this, not from your family!"

Thomas looked lordly. "The gift is already given, young man, and if you will do my family a great honor by bringing that blade once more to battle."

Again, Jake went to one knee. "My Lord, I'm not worthy of such trust, but I swear to you, I'll make you proud."

Rising, he unlocked his own blade and placed it on one of the racks. As he turned, he saw Thomas with a very ornate and well-constructed scabbard. He handed it the Jake, and he hooked it on his waist. The leather felt as if it were there all his life and wouldn't encumber him in the least. Still holding the sword, he looked to Thomas. The elder dwarf nodded as Jake slid the blade home into the scabbard with no sound. Jake marveled at how light the blade felt on his hip. His own blade heavy and cumbersome took some time to get used to, but this blade felt right.

Jake turned to Thomas. "My Lord, I've heard all great blades have names, is this blade any different?"

Thomas looked fondly upon Jake. "You are indeed correct; every great blade is named. This blade is known as The Serpent's Bane. This blade has indeed been the undoing of many reptilian enemies. Our two people have been fighting the reptilians for many generations."

Without another word, Jake turned to see Michelle and his father fitted with their own weapons. Jake couldn't help but feel such pride as he saw his father dressed as a knight of old with chain mail and helm. Michelle, on the other hand, looked like a mighty queen warrior. Her armor was much different from the dwarf armor. It was sleek and lightweight with different runes all over. She gleamed as much as any weapon in the armory. When he turned to look into Thomas' face, who stood with a dazzling chain mail in his arms, Thomas offered the mail to Jake, who took it without question. Again, he was amazed at how light and easy it was to put on. With the chain mail and leather chest plate given to him, he looked every bit the part of a knight.

Thomas nodded. "The mail goes with the blade, and they are both made of the same material. It is a type of metal not found on this world. The metal is known as Arcanium and is only found on one world many light years from here. It is such a rare metal, it was all mined long ago. There's little of it left in the known universe. Keep them both safe. If anyone knew what you had, they would do anything to take them. They are both priceless!"

Again, Jake looked down at the blade in awe. This was all too much for him, but he knew his mission must be fulfilled. Once fitted, they all walked back out into the tunnel while Thomas chanted again to lock the steel door behind them. He led them through the tunnels until they came upon a large kitchen. Jake looked around at the vast nature of the kitchen. Such a place could feed thousands of dwarves, but he could tell only a small portion of the kitchen remained in use.

The dwarves hustled around, grabbing all the provisions they could pack and handed the rest to Jake. Jake stuffed everything into his own pack. Michelle and Derek moved over to his side, following Thomas out the door. True to his word, the small group was underway within an hour. Thomas led them down into more tunnels with great skill and haste. Jake felt the temperature increase, and the air felt stale. The dwarves marched along, speaking to one another softly. Michelle spoke in hushed tones to Derek about what they would do if they encountered the old dwarves.

Jake wondered much the same. He couldn't help but wonder what caused such a rift between Thomas and his people. There were many times his father and he fought over trivial things, but they always found a way to make things work out. He and his father were lucky though because he knew many other families that couldn't forgive one another, causing irreparable damage. Whatever happened to the dwarves must have been quite bad for such a split. He knew bringing the two factions together would be his greatest test to date.

Again, Thomas drove them into another tunnel but this time, there were no lights. The other dwarves lit torches and passed one to Jake. Even with them, travel slowed because the light was much dimmer. Thomas still skillfully guided them in the right direction. They all continued for many hours until Thomas made them stop. He halted them in front of what looked to be a gate like the one Jake opened to enter Thomas' kingdom.

Thomas walked up to the door and again chanted, expecting the door to open, to no avail. After a while, a very frustrated dwarf lord approached Jake and Michelle.

He looked directly at Jake. "You're up!"

CHAPTER FORTY-TWO

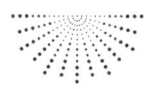

Muffled voices clanged in his hazy mind, and he felt himself moving unaided somehow. He blinked his eyes in hopes of clearing the cloudiness impairing his vision with little success. A shooting pain struck his back and electrical current spread over his entire backside. The commander felt his body instinctively lurch forward, and he thrust his hands out to steady himself. While bringing his hands back down, he found they were bound in some way. Shaking his head, he tried to clear his thoughts, only to feel a blunt instrument strike the back of his head. Rage built inside the commander, but he wanted to see where this game of cat and mouse led him.

Holding the rage deep down, he focused and listened to his surroundings closely. The once-muffled voices became clear, but the commander did his best to hide his knowledge. His captors spoke of a king eagerly awaiting the prisoner. The conversation revolved around what the king would do with the commander once in his presence. As far as he could tell, there were a total of five captors, and each offered their take on the king's wishes for the commander. One thought torture until death, while two others agreed that the king would like to meet his enemy in a fight to the death. Yet another laughed and said the commander was more important left alive. The final voice told them they were all idiots and alerted them to the fact the commander was powerful in magic which the king would use.

Inside, the commander smiled at the banter of the soldiers. Having served and commanded in so many campaigns, he knew soldiers when he heard them. Still, he knew them not to be dwarf or human. Then it hit him, the Dark Elves! They were destroyed, or so he thought, and he was the cause of their demise. Many eons ago, the Dark Elves thought themselves above the reptilian people, causing the commander to find them all and eliminate them. He hunted them on this and other planets until he was certain none remained. He was quite mistaken and missed some.

The Dark Elves were his allies for a time out of imagining and as much as it pained him to destroy them, it was either his people or theirs. He recalled a time when he routed for the Zarillions as they hunted down the Dark Elves as well. The commander also knew the Zarillion strength to be a fraction of what it once was even then, but they remained a force to reckon with. Thinking back to his encounter with Rebecca, he shivered, thinking of the young woman's ability. Gaining access to that power would have to wait as it seemed he would have to dispatch some Dark Elves.

Steps were more measured, and he heard the rushing of water. Commander Zosa felt the cold mist of water being thrown into the air from an underground waterfall. His own feet felt the moist and rocky floor moving forward. His captors led him carefully and didn't poke or prod him, letting him know this part of the journey would be tricky at best. Hands gripped his bound arms and guided him over wet rocks. Water rushed over his scaled skin. Frigid, the water made his body shudder as his body temperature needed to be high to function properly. Any sudden change in body temperature could be deadly for him in the right situation. He shook uncontrollably as more water rushed over his body.

All at once, the rushing of water ceased, but his body was in shock. Convulsions took over, and he felt himself fall to the ground. Shaking, he felt the sharp prick of rocks penetrating his freezing-cold skin.

Frantic voices around him erupted with panic of failure to deliver the prisoner. Still shaking and writhing on the ground, he felt a blanket covering him. A growling voice yelled at the men to get a fire going.

He felt his body temperature slowly coming back but still, he couldn't stop shaking. A harsh smell of chemicals mixing to cause a flame penetrated his nostrils. Within a few minutes, the Dark Elves made a fire big enough to warm the commander to the point of comfort. When his captors realized he was no longer in danger, they all breathed a sigh of relief and pushed the commander to his feet.

He now felt a smoother path, as if they were traveling along a dried-up riverbed. After another hour of travel, they halted and stopped the commander, making him sit on a large rock. They heard whispers, but the commander couldn't make out what they spoke of. Within a few more minutes, new voices questioned his captors about the prisoner. One elf was extremely interested in the prisoner and grabbed the commander, yanking him up to his feet with great strength.

A few words were incanted and within a second, the commander's eyesight returned. At first, he could only see shadows but within a few minutes, he could make out a small encampment tucked into a cavern that once held a large underground river. He turned to the elf who returned his sight and thought he recognized him. For his recognition, the commander received a blow to the face. He took it in stride and laughed at his assailant. The next strike never happened as the commander returned one right to the nose of the offending elf.

Blood sprayed into the air as the Dark Elf fell backwards onto the smooth rock. His comrades coming to his aid pummeled the commander until he heard the boom of a voice telling them to stop. A muscular elf emerged from the shadows, throwing his soldiers away from the commander. Angry, the commander rose to his full height, towering over his new opponent. Though much taller, the commander didn't have the muscle stature of the elf facing him. Even in the dim light, the corded muscles rippled, threatening to lash out at him at any moment.

The combatants circled one another, trying to measure the other.

Mid-stride, the commander stopped and looked shocked. "Ramious, you live?"

For his sarcasm, the commander took a shot to the chest that threatened to crush his insides. "Yes, Zosa! I live! No thanks to you!"

Commander Zosa, still a young officer at the time, was assigned to take out a pocket of remaining elves near the reptilian border. In good form, the commander wiped out the elves in short order, all for one, Ramious. The elf refused to die and fought with such bravery, the commander captured him, bringing him back as a gift for his precise emperor. Amused, the emperor threw the elf in the deepest, darkest dungeon the reptilians could find, forgetting about the soldier.

When the dust settled, and the elves were all destroyed, the reptilians turned their sights to the Zarillion menace. The commander never saw Ramious again until now. He backed up to gain more air in his lungs so he could return a blow of his own, while his assailant lunged at him with a blade in his hand. The commander ducked in time to save his head from being separated from his shoulders. He quickly swung around to face Ramious, looking around for a weapon of any kind. With nothing in sight, he chose to grasp at the earth magic, only to have nothing happen.

The elf stopped mid-stride and laughed. "Something the matter, Zosa?"

Panic set in. "What did you do to me?"

"Oh, it's a little remedy I learned from your people while I was in captivity."

Commander Zosa nodded. "Nothing like using one's own remedies against them. Then, if we're going to fight to the death, I would like to request a blade to fight warrior to warrior."

An angered and twisted look came over the well-muscled elf, and he lunged. "You left me to rot! Warrior to warrior! I lived off bugs and lichen. No, Zosa, you will die at my hand."

Again, the commander moved just in time to save his skin. This time, he swung his leg swiftly around, catching the elf by surprise, buckling the attacker's leg. Ramious' leg gave out, and he fell to the ground, dropping his sword with a loud clanging sound. Now, the commander looked to see if he could grab the sword, only to see he was surrounded by a ring of other Dark Elves. They sneered at him, looking as if they wanted his blood, but they knew this was Ramious' fight and stayed back. One of the elves kicked the sword over to the fallen elf. Ramious grabbed it and pulled himself up to fight.

Again, the two circled one another until the elf went into a series of flowing movements with the sword. The commander knew he needed to do something; the elf remembered all his military training and let his rage wane. If the elf focused, he could slice the commander to bits. Out of the corner of his eye, he saw an elf looking back over his shoulder at something other than the fight. While the soldier wasn't paying attention, the commander swiftly grabbed a dagger from his belt. Now with a blade of his own, he turned with a smile toward Ramious.

Each warrior nodded toward one another and launched themselves into a dance of thrusts and strikes to rival any sword master. Ramious ducked in and sliced at the commander's mid-section, only to be thwarted. He received a quick slice to his arm for his trouble, drawing first blood. He backed up slightly, looking down at his arm, and nodded, going back for more. Ramious twirled his blade in various positions until he sliced into the commander's leg. Though not a mortal wound, it found its mark deep in the flesh of the commander. The Dark Elf saw the big reptilian go down to one knee and went in for the kill.

The commander pushed with all his might to gain his footing, but the wound cut deep, preventing him from rising to his feet. He lifted his dagger just in time to deflect the death blow from the Dark Elf. Ramious reached around and swung quickly, this time catching the triceps of the commander. Unable to get to his feet to get his blood flowing, caused the commander to panic. He still held his own dagger, deflecting blows the best he could, but his strength waned from loss of blood. Strength leaving him, he thought he would need to do something crazy to get out of this one. As he saw Ramious come around for another blow, he put his hand quickly under his wounded arm, cupping his hand to collect the flowing blood. With one motion, he sucked the blood into his mouth and, as the blade came around again, he spat the blood into the elf's eyes.

The blood did its job and filled the eyes of the elf, causing him to back off his attack. Commander Zosa rolled on the ground and used his good leg to smash into Ramious' knee. He missed doing great damage, but it did stun the elf, causing him to go down himself. The elf swung his blade, looking to thrust it into the reptilian's heart this time. As the blade made its way, another one diverted it. Ramious glared up at the new intruder, only to put his blade to his side and stand at attention before the new elf.

Standing before him was an elf of great importance and dressed in wealthy attire. A light crown sat atop his head. With dignity, he waited for the reptilian to gain his knees before glaring down upon his prisoner. Blinking his eyes, the commander thought he was seeing a ghost. Mathious, the King of the Dark Elves, stood before him in the flesh. As with Ramious, he thought Mathious long dead. The emperor himself claimed the death of Mathious. He could tell the king was quite pleased with himself.

The king began, "Yes, Commander, you've seen a ghost or what your emperor told you is a ghost. I, like Ramious, escaped and spent much time rebuilding the society you nearly caused to go extinct!"

Commander Zosa retorted, "It wasn't from lack of trying. I certainly thought I caused your extinction! I should have known. You're all like cockroaches."

Again, the king smiled. "Yes, Commander, you caused much pain among my people. You and those scum Zarillions! You both will pay! From what my spies tell me, you both have all but destroyed one another. You, Commander, have no force left, and the Zarillions are a shell of their former self."

Commander Zosa struggled to his feet, staggering before the king. "Just kill me now and get it over with! You bore me!"

A cackle came from the king. "That would be too easy. No, you have much to pay for, and I have use for you. When I'm finished with you, I may grant your request but until then, you're mine to do with as I please."

Struggling to hold himself up, he nearly went down to one knee but held too much pride to show weakness in front of the king. "What's it you want? As you already pointed out, my military capabilities are limited."

The king looked more regal. "What I need from you is your knowledge of the Zarillions. True, they aren't what they once were, but they will still be a formidable opponent. They bested you!"

An angry look came over the commander's face. "I wasn't bested! I was nearly destroyed by a force I or you have never faced."

Again, the king looked serious. "Ah yes, Rebecca. We know about her, but my spies tell me her equal has been found, and they are now joined. Is this true?"

"It is true. A young man by the name of Peter is her equal, and they are indeed joined by Mother herself!"

"Mother?" said the king. "That is grievous news!"

"Yes, Mother! You're going to need a substantial force to take down the likes of those two. I've never seen anything the likes of Rebecca's power, and she is now coupled with someone every bit as powerful as she!"

"Commander, you have no idea the force I have at my command! We will defeat them all! When I'm finished with this planet, it will be but a pile of rubble!"

Commander Zosa, feeling lightheaded, continued, "I thought as much myself, going up against only Rebecca. She laid waste to my entire base by herself, without breaking a sweat! No, Mathious, you won't win this one! Better tuck tail and run before she comes after you too!"

"I'll be prepared for Rebecca. You forget, my people know how to render their powers useless, much like we did here with you!"

The commander felt himself falling. Before going black, he whispered, "It will be at your own peril."

CHAPTER FORTY-THREE

Nathan led a fast pace through the maze of tunnels ever moving downward. Peter and Rebecca in tow moved as fast as they could through the failing light of Nathan's staff. The curious man said little to them before leaving, only that this next mission would determine much of what would transpire in the days to come. Though such a large man, he moved through the tunnels as if he were a mole, not stopping to check anything along the journey. Checking over his shoulder to make sure Peter and Rebecca were still following, he whipped around and doubled his pace forward.

Peter nor Rebecca said a word but looked at each other and ducked again, trying to quicken their own pace. Rebecca thought to herself how curious that Holly chose not to come with them as she re-established relations with Nathan. Peter followed behind her, and they nearly ran at this point to maintain sight of Nathan. As they turned the next corner, both saw a glowing light emanating from ahead.

Rebecca nearly ran into Nathan who stood still, looking at the large cavern entrance before them. Peter came to a screeching halt, trying to catch his breath. He laughed as he looked at Rebecca and Nathan, who looked as fresh as daisies, while his lungs felt afire.

Nathan held up his hand, and both stood still. The large man cautiously moved toward the entrance and moved to the very edge, barely peering inside the large cavern. Peter saw this was where the golden light came from. He waited patiently, but Nathan didn't show any signs of entering the cavern or allowing them to follow.

A rumbling from inside the cavern made them all jump back. "Are you all going to stand there like cowards?"

The loud, hoarse voice shocked them, but Nathan almost laughed. "Is that how you speak to your captor?"

Nathan shook his head and entered the cavern with a full head of steam. Rebecca followed, grabbing Peter's hand, dragging him behind. With a scowl on his face, the large man looked not the least bit intimidated by the strange voice. He led them through the large chamber, looking in awe at the piles of wealth strewn everywhere. Nathan walked with great purpose and stopped before an enormous statue of gold. Peter looked up in shock as he took in the golden dragon standing before him.

Peter did a double take as the golden statue blinked. He looked to make sure his eyes weren't failing him and again, the eyes blinked. The eyes weren't of a person but more of a reptile and without lids. It was as if the inside of the eye itself blinked. They all watched, waiting for the strange voice to address them. For what seemed like hours, the huge golden statue stayed silent.

Finally, a booming voice broke the silence. "Well, Peter and Rebecca, I presume! Well met, my friends!!"

Nathan held Peter and Rebecca back with his hand while moving forward. "No, scourge, you won't have them for another of your treasures."

Laughter filled the cavern. "Nathan, you, for all your power, still know nothing of me! You chose to imprison me rather than befriend me! It is you that should be my treasure."

The big man looked unsure. "You're pure evil! The only master you serve is the one that sees everything before you destroyed!"

A strong, angry voice almost sent them to the ground. "Evil! You dare to call me evil! Who was it that destroyed the elves to near extinction? Who was it that destroyed all the dragons? Who was it that imprisoned the reptilian people because they wouldn't live the way you wanted them to?"

Nathan, with an angry look of this own, shouted, "You dare to question my people! They defended themselves against the likes of your allies that they would see all free people in chains! No, it is you that should be destroyed! For that very reason, I've brought your doom with me! Look upon the universe's knights!"

Nathan pointed to Peter and Rebecca while waiting for a response. Peter stood dumbfounded at the new title given to him. A knight of the universe now, he could barely handle being a regular young man. Rebecca smiled at Peter's anguish while clasping his hand. Her smooth, warm hand, as it always had, comforted him, and calmed his nerves. She moved out of Nathan's shadow, coming within sight of the dragon.

A calm, soothing, magical voice broke the air. "My dear, come closer. Let me look at you. I've dreamt of you for eons! It is you, isn't it?"

Rebecca ignored Nathan as he tried to keep her back. "My Lord, I know of you, and I too have dreamt of you my whole life."

The statue laughed. "Then, you know I was wrongfully imprisoned!"

She moved even closer. "How is it you were wrongfully imprisoned? You led an army against my people?"

The dragon became more subdued. "Yes, my dear, something I deeply regret! Much like you, I was misled. Like you, my people were in danger, and we allied with the wrong people, as happens in these situations."

Rebecca continued, "My Lord, I know of what you speak, the Dark Elves misled many. They are the true enemies of all people."

The dragon spoke in a hushed tone, "Though I cannot deny the elves care little for others, I would find it hard to blame them entirely. Your people oversaw their destruction. I say this to you, My Queen, you need to look deeper to find the truth."

"What truth is that?"

The dragon remained silent for a moment. "My Lady, it's a little more complicated than we were all led to believe. Being here, locked in this frozen body, I've spent much time searching for the truth. I know this much… your people have a lot more in common with the elves than you care to admit."

Rebecca stood strong. "My Lord, you would have me believe the Dark Elves were innocent in the slaughter of countless people throughout the cosmos! No, I cannot and won't hear any more of this nonsense. Entire populations were wiped out by the elves!"

The booming voice returned, "It's true, the elves retaliated against many! They grew terribly angry over many slights from other races. They also felt in grave danger by those same races and fought to preserve their own kind."

Rebecca, rather than continue this banter, chose another approach. "My Lord, why have you brought us here?"

Again, laughter filled the room. "My Queen, you're amazing, but it wasn't me that brought you here. No, something tells me Mother had a little to do with it!"

"Mother, what do you know of Mother?"

In a whisper, the dragon responded, "You, my dear, are perhaps her equal in many ways but now that Peter is yours, you must watch out for Mother."

Rebecca retorted, "How dare you speak ill of Mother! One more comment like that, and I'll melt you where you stand. I may not be able to kill you, but I'll make sure you never speak to anyone ever again!"

"My Queen, please accept my apology as I meant no offense. For most of history, Mother was the only one with the type of power you and Peter possess. All I'm saying is watch your back. Power of all kind corrupts even the purest heart!"

Rebecca looked questioningly. "What is it you think you know?"

"I am, like you, a humble servant of Mother but like you, I'm responsible for the fates of others. No, My Queen, we're tied together in ways even Mother hasn't seen!"

"My Lord, again, I ask you what is it you want from me?"

A whisper came from the dragon, "Free me!"

Nathan stepped in front of Rebecca. "Over my dead body will you be released! We've heard enough of these lies and deceit. Rebecca, My Lady, let us destroy this evil once and for all!"

A hand reached up and grabbed Nathan's shoulder. He looked, thinking it to be Rebecca, but Peter strode forward, glowing full of light. Nathan tried to stop him but was repelled by an unseen power. Without a word, he reached for Rebecca's hand. The two clasped hands and immediately, Rebecca felt power enter her body. At first, she felt a little nervous, but the warmth that filled her calmed her nerves.

An image took shape in her mind and spoke, "Be at peace, my child. Peter is my vessel in this. You will have need of this creature with the danger that's to come. As powerful as you and Peter are, you will continue to need the help of those who surround you."

Peter looked into her eyes, and she immediately felt peace. The image of Mother still fresh in her mind, she looked up at the golden dragon. Peter moved even closer to the dragon, and Rebecca felt herself gathering power from her surroundings. The two glowed so bright, Rebecca saw Nathan hiding his eyes and backing away in fear. Still holding her hand, Peter moved so close he could touch the golden foot of the dragon.

Like many times before, Rebecca felt the unlimited power continuing to fill her body. Peter seemed so calm, it made her fell a little uncertain, but she knew Peter would never do anything to harm her. The warm feeling surrounded her but this time, the power felt different somehow, as if it weren't from the very earth but from somewhere else. She let herself be led to the foot of the dragon and saw Peter smile.

Peter looked up at the dragon. "For your crimes, you deserve death, how plead you?"

The dragon responded, "Mother, I throw myself at your mercy! My crime was only the protection of my people! For this, am I to be destroyed? If that's your will, let it be done!"

Peter's mouth opened but without his own voice. "If your life is spared, will you serve the king and queen to your death?"

A hush fell over the room. "My Lady, I knew this day would come! I planned to give myself over to the king and queen long before this day! My fate is tied to theirs as is my people's! I will serve."

Bright light surrounded the golden statue. "Then let it be known across the universe that Gemini is tied to the king and queen by their very life force!"

A boom radiated out from the golden dragon, and particles of gold-like dust entered the air. The particles formed a large cloud above the dragon. With each passing moment, more and more of the scales of the original dragon appeared. Overhead, the cloud swirled around in the shape of a large circle. When the entire dragon stood free of gold, the particles still swirling fell like snow around the entire cabin.

Peter's voice boomed, "The spell is lifted and can never again be brought upon this creature! Let all who would harm this creature have fare warning they will deal with me!"

Still glowing, Peter and Rebecca felt the power leaving them, and the haze of light surrounding them lessened. Holding one another's hand, they turned, looking into each other's eyes with a wide smile. Peter reached forth, pulling her in for a huge hug. Rebecca embraced Peter, holding him to her tightly. When they released one another, Nathan fumed with anger, looking at them.

Peter spoke first, "Nathan, Gemini is now tied to our life force and is ours to command. She is of her own royal family and as such, it is fitting we should be linked."

Nathan stood in awe. "My Lord, forgive me. I only wish to serve Mother. It was upon her orders, I imprisoned the dragon long ago."

Peter smiled. "Yes, Nathan, I'm aware. Mother didn't want her destroyed and held her in stasis until needed. I cannot begin to understand your frustration, just know Mother has need of Gemini."

Nathan accepted the explanation and backed away, only to look at the awaiting dragon with uncertainty. Rebecca led Peter to the front of the living, breathing dragon. Scales glistened in the glowing light, and Peter saw how stunning the creature before him was in real life. Nobility showed in the entire length of the beautiful creature. He couldn't help but admire the strength, nobility, and wisdom emanating from the ancient creature before him.

Rebecca, still holding his hand, looked up into the eyes of the awaiting creature. The dragon stiffly rose to its full height, filling the entire cavern and nearly bumping its head. They all watched as the dragon slowly spread its wings while pumping them to see if they still worked. The wind created by the wings sent the gold dust flying in all directions, and Peter heard the clanking of coins being thrown into the air. Rushing throughout the cavern, the wind swirled around Rebecca and Peter.

At first, Nathan almost sent power into the dragon but quickly changed his mind as the dragon made no attempt to harm anyone. Now, the air surrounding Peter and Rebecca lifted them both into the air. Both felt themselves moving upward into the air. Still holding hands, they looked up into the eyes of the dragon.

Gemini spoke when both were so close, they felt her breath, "My King and Queen, I am yours. Command me!"

Rebecca slowly touched the snout of the dragon. Rough but not yet soft, the skin felt moist without being wet. Underneath her hand, she felt the rhythm of the dragon's breathing, and heat emanating from the beast. A warmth surrounded her, but it was the type one would feel when tucked together for warmth in a large blanket. The beast didn't move and allowed the touch to continue. Peter joined Rebecca's hand, and he too felt the warmth fill him as well.

"My Lord and Lady, I've waited for this moment for time out of memory! I vow in this very moment, I'll protect your life with my very own. You shall not fret with me by your side."

Peter looked into the eyes of the dragon. "My first command is to place us on the ground carefully."

A short burst of laughter erupted. "Whatever My Lord wishes."

The wind dispersed, and Peter felt himself being slowly brought to the ground. Once safely with two feet on the ground, Peter felt more comfortable. Rebecca put a reassuring hand on his shoulder, and the two watched as the dragon moved. Careful not to harm his charges, Gemini moved away from the two and, once in a clear area, she crouched. Nathan moved in front of Rebecca to protect her, but she held him at bay. Gemini knelt on one knee, bowing to Rebecca.

"My Lady and Lord, thank you for my freedom! I'll spend my life making sure your trust in me is well earned. Nathan, I understand why you did so, but please understand, I did what I needed to help my own people."

Rebecca and Peter, in one breath, replied, "My Lady, your service is accepted. Please rise!"

CHAPTER FORTY-FOUR

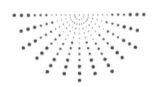

Anguish spread across Derek's face as Michelle announced her intentions to leave the group to protect the Dwarves Gate. Derek pleaded with her in hopes to change her mind, but the Knight of the Cosmos stood duty bound and wouldn't be swayed. Torn between the two most important people in his life, he spun to look at Jake. His son moved to within a few inches of his father and clasped his arm. The two embraced and when they released, Jake walked in the opposite direction of where his father stood. Jake waved to Thomas, indicating they needed to be on their way.

Derek slung his pack up high on his shoulders and put on his Navy Seal face. Michelle moved down the tunnel as Thomas directed. The two spoke in depth about the way to the gate, but Michelle assured Thomas she felt the gate's power and would have little problems finding it. Little was said as Derek peered over his shoulder as they were about to round the first corner to catch one final glimpse of his beloved son. Michelle noticed but chose not to comment and led the way forward down the tunnel.

Jake watched as his father turned the corner and once out of sight, he secured his own pack while looking to Thomas for the next leg of their journey. Thomas nodded and pointed to the awaiting door. Jake, without another word, removed the rod from his belt and slammed it into the ground before the door. The earth beneath rumbled and cracked before the force of the magic rod, sending waves of energy into the surrounding area. Waves of energy moved toward the door while Jake watched as it absorbed that force, but nothing happened.

A look of disgust came over Jake's face as he was about to take his newly obtained sword to the door when he heard a metal bolt unlock. Though the door stayed fast, Jake walked forward, pushing it inward. With determination, he entered the darkness of the awaiting tunnel. Thomas' soldiers ran ahead of him with torches, and Thomas walked beside Jake. Thomas instructed Jake to hold his position for a minute while his soldiers inspected the area to ensure their safety. Jake, being very impatient, relented, waiting for the soldiers to clear the path. Jake needed to get back to Peter and each second he stood here, doing nothing, could be time watching Peter's back.

One soldier came up to Thomas, whispering something Jake couldn't hear into his leader's ear. The dwarf leader nodded and slapped Jake on the back with a wide smile. With renewed energy, Thomas moved to the front, taking the lead from his soldiers. Jake rushed to catch up while staying slightly behind the dwarf leader. He looked around at his surroundings while moving forward. Though the tunnel looked well kept, nothing he saw would suggest the presence of life.

Jake sensed the attack first. He felt the ripple in the air as the arrow made for his head. One quick movement of his own to the side, ducking the arrow, he swung Serpent's Bane high in the air to deflect anything else that may come his way. Thomas' soldiers already knocked their own arrows ready to return fire while surrounding their leader protectively. Jake, already on the move, saw his attackers with their own blades drawn, moving to intercept him.

A spinning kick knocked the first attacker clear back into the darkness of the tunnel. Another would-be attacker received a blade across his arm for his trouble. Jake, hot with anger, crouched, looking for his next opponent, only to see himself surrounded by shiny blades.

He widened his stance, waiting for the next attack. At first, no one made a move, trying to see what Jake would do. He didn't have to wait long as two of the unknown people leapt at Jake with blades up in the air. Jake caught the first blade and twisted his wrist, sending his opponent's blade into the air. He punched the bladeless man in the face, dropping the man in his place.

The other man met Jake's blade stride for stride. Jake knew he was up against a seasoned fighter as the man didn't exert too much energy with his thrusts. After a few minutes of hacking at each other, they circled each other, trying to regroup. Jake couldn't help but let his anger grow as a vision of Peter needing his help entered his mind. Fueled by his anger, he launched his own offensive which proved too much for his attacker. The larger boy used his strength and quickness to his advantage, striking the smaller man several times in the arm. The man backed off while blood poured from his wounds. Rage filled Jake's mind, and he went in to finish this man, keeping him from his friend.

Raising his blade for a death blow, swinging it downward, he knew the man was done. Before the blade struck the man, another blade crossed in front of Jake's, deflecting the stroke. Surprise took Jake as he looked quickly to see who spoiled his victory. He looked in confusion as in the dim light, he saw Thomas' bright blade still in the air, holding Jake's. Thomas' eyes told him to stop his attack, but his anger wasn't suppressed.

Lights popped up around them, showing more of the tunnel. For the first time, Jake saw those who attacked them and to his great surprise, they were dwarves. Thomas let his blade down, holding up his hand for the soldiers to put their own away. The soldiers followed suit, but Jake moved back into a defensive posture, waiting for another attack. This didn't go unnoticed by the new dwarves, who still looked cautiously at the huge young man.

The dwarven leader moved in front of Jake. "My kin, I am Thomas Radclif. Who is your lord?"

One dwarf with a noble air to him moved from the group approaching Thomas. "I am Prince Aaron of the Elder Dwarf Kingdom! If you truly are Thomas Radclif, I should run you through where you stand!"

Jake moved quickly in front of Thomas with his blade pointed at the prince. "You move one more inch, and I'll slice you to pieces!"

The noble dwarf smirked, looking at Jake. "Of that, young warrior, I have no doubt! You bested some of my best. Although, some other time, you will have to explain to me how an outsider came into possession of Serpent's Bane!"

Thomas responded, "The blade found its next warrior. The gift was earned before given to be sure. Aaron, I would do as he asks. You really don't want to see him angry."

Aaron backed up slightly. "It is true the king's weapon always chooses its own warrior. Thomas, we're in strange times. Why is it you, a traitor, is in our midst?"

Thomas took the barb in stride. "If I'm a traitor, your people are rebels! Do you speak for your people?"

The noble dwarf thought a moment. "I do speak for my people, and we have nothing to say to you! Now leave before the rest of my soldiers arrive, and I put an end to all of you."

Anger took control of Jake as he leaned forward, grabbing the smaller dwarf by the scruff of the neck, lifting him in the air. "Enough of this dwarf nonsense! Do you want to die right here, right now?"

The other soldiers drove forward with their blades pointed at Jake, ready to strike to protect their leader. Aaron put his hand up to stop their advance. "Stand down! What do you want, young warrior? I can see in your eyes you're on a mission of great importance. Put me down, and I'll listen, though I cannot guarantee my army will still not kill you for placing your hands on me!"

This comment made Jake even madder. "I thought my people were stubborn! You dwarves make me so mad. The world around you is falling apart and yet, you still sit here doing nothing! I should leave you all to your fate."

With his last statement, he placed the dwarf down and glared at Thomas. "My best friend could be in grave danger at this very moment, and I'm here playing with children!"

Thomas, with a sad look, spoke, "Aaron, we're at the end of all things. If we don't forget our quarrels, all our people will be destroyed! A great evil is on its way to this world and while we're arguing, it could already be here. Would you please take us to the council of elders so we can explain our plight to them?"

Aaron rubbed his neck, still looking up at Jake. "Thomas, do you still not even know who I am?"

Thomas blinked, trying to look at the dwarf and gain memory of him. "Your face looks familiar. You're my kin, that much I know. Why?"

Aaron smiled. "Kin, indeed. I am your cousin, Aaron Radclif!"

Thomas laughed. "Of course! When last I saw you, the whiskers of your beard were just coming in. I'm sorry, my cousin. I didn't recognize you as I'm under great distress."

Aaron waved his hand, and his soldiers moved into a squad ready to travel. He waved for Thomas and company to follow. Jake hesitantly followed as he felt something was still not right about these dwarves. Thomas patted him on the shoulder, assuring him all would be well when they spoke to the council. Once again, Jake put on his military bearing look and followed Thomas. Very alert, he watched every move the soldiers made, but nothing seemed out of the ordinary. The soldiers even seemed comfortable with the other dwarves following.

The tunnel turned around a sharp corner and before him, opened a large cavern with warm light streaming out to meet them. Though a comforting sight, Jake still was skeptical and kept his eyes peeled for anything out of the ordinary. Entering the light, it took a few moments for his eyes to adjust. Blinking several times, his eyes focused on the beautiful stone homes greeting him. Unlike the barren tunnels they emerged from, this part of the city stood very inviting. The city seemed to reach everywhere his eye turned as Jake saw no end in sight. Everywhere he looked, he saw buildings.

Not just the buildings caught his eye as he walked forward. There were dwarves everywhere. Teeming with life, the dwarves bustled about here and there, taking little notice of the soldiers and their guests. When another group of soldiers met Aaron along the way, people noticed the large human in their midst. With Serpent's Bane still in hand, the large young man with his chain mail looked every bit the intimidating warrior. Aaron told his men to escort them to the council chambers and quickly.

They worked their way up through the streets until they stood atop a great hill, looking down upon the city. Jake took a moment to stand in awe at the overall size of the city. The largest cities he was used to seeing on the surface would be rivaled by this sprawling landscape. The architecture caught his eye as every building seemed finished to perfection. He saw not one detail missed, down to the designs in the very bricks that made up many of the buildings. Cleanliness surprised Jake. He was used to seeing trash and dirty alleys all over the surface cities but here everything looked meticulous.

Aaron led them to a large set of plain wooden doors. Unlike the Zarillion council chambers, the doors were very plain and inside, he saw simple furniture to match the doors. Jake said not a word as Aaron led them inside, only to be joined by a few of his trusted soldiers. He walked around a round wooden table and pulled out a seat, motioning Thomas to sit as well. Thomas nodded to Jake, but the young man put his sword in its scabbard but took up a guarding position behind Thomas. This brought some raised eyebrows, but Aaron let it stand.

A few moments later, the wall opened, revealing a hidden door, to allow other dwarves to enter unnoticed. Eight dwarves sat at the table, along with Aaron, Thomas, and a standing Jake. The sitting dwarves took notice of the young warrior but said nothing, waiting for Aaron to speak. The dwarven leader took a moment to look at his kin before standing.

Leaning heavily on his arms, he looked seriously at his friends. "We have avoided this day for a very long time, but our past sins have caught up to us."

He pointed to Jake. "Jake, show them!"

Jake stepped forward, taking the sword from its scabbard with a metallic ring in the air. He placed it first onto the wooden table. The remaining council members' eyes shot up, looking at the famous blade. The large warrior stood, looking at the council, waiting for someone to speak. All at once, the room erupted in chaotic voices. Jake took the blade from the table and slid it home into the scabbard, returning to his vigil behind Thomas who looked a bit amused at this point.

Aaron banged his hands down on the table and waited for silence. "Serpent's Bane is risen once more; all of you know that means the coming of the end!"

Silence came over the room, and Thomas stood. "Elders, please hear me!"

An ancient-looking dwarf immediately interrupted Thomas, "Thomas, sit down. This council has nothing to say to you or your people. As far as we're concerned, you're an outlaw and should be treated as such!"

Aaron tried to interject, but the older dwarf spoke again, "Aaron, what right do you have to bring these outlaws before this council?"

Aaron tried to keep calm but even Jake witnessed the dwarf's anger building. Jake then without thinking, as if the blade almost had a mind of its own, he found the blade in his hands. With all the force he could muster, he swung the Serpent's Bane over his head and came down upon the wooden table slicing it right down the middle. Splinters and pieces of wood sprayed everywhere sending the shocked dwarves running for cover. Jake grew in that moment and in the light, looked to be towing over the cowering dwarves.

Anger still dancing in his eyes, Jake spoke, "You will all listen, or I'll drop you all where you stand! I care little for your petty family squabbles. I've been sent here by Mother herself for one reason and that's to mobilize the dwarven people to do their part to save this planet. If you choose to sit here and bicker, I can lay waste to you all right here and now! What's it going to be?"

Thomas came to Jake's side. "I can see why Mother sent you!"

CHAPTER FORTY-FIVE

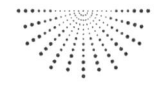

Holly Cheric, defacto ruler of the Zarillion people, paced the highly polished floor, stopping periodically in hope General Giles would file in and give her a report of the city's defenses. Her mind sought out her protégé Rebecca, and she nearly shrieked as the large head of a dragon came into view. The view became clearer, and she saw the delicate soft hand of Rebecca touching the snout of the calm dragon. Though still taken back, she could almost feel the scales as Rebecca stroked the beautiful creature's face.

As Rebecca retracted her hand, a sparkle shone in the dragon's eyes, and it then kneeled to Rebecca and Peter. The nobility of this powerful creature fascinated Holly. Her only interactions with dragons before this was her running for her life and using her power to defend herself from dragon fire. Watching the dragon return to a seated position, she couldn't help but notice how beautiful the beast was, yet how dangerous this was for Rebecca.

Peter held Rebecca's hand as the two looked into each other's eyes with nothing but love and trust. Holly knew from the moment Rebecca spoke to her of Peter, this young man would be the one her people searched for during countless years of waiting. The amount of power wielded by Peter and Rebecca scared Holly. Rebecca alone was near impossible to control when her power engulfed her body. Now, Rebecca met her equal in Peter and together, they held power unlike anything the universe could fathom.

Feeling better as she heard Nathan's voice telling the young couple they needed to return to Holly right away, she looked to the council door. Sensing the general, she moved to intercept her love as he opened the door with great purpose. Despite his usual military gruffness, she engulfed the powerfully built man in a huge hug. The general's military bearing melted temporarily as he welcomed the hug and returned the favor with a quick kiss. Holding Holly at arm's length, he looked into her eyes, and she could tell right away the news wouldn't be good.

His stern face returned. "My love, the scouts are coming in, and the reports are very disturbing. Several of the scouts remain unaccounted for, and the ones that did make it back continue to report our borders are being watched. The soldiers I spoke to couldn't identify the spies as they seemed to melt into the darkness before they could be confronted. Also, evidence of attempts to breach some of the lesser gates are happening with great frequency."

Holly responded, "Ryan, it couldn't be the reptilians. They are very few now. Could it be the Nazis?"

"Holly, the Nazis are good soldiers, but there's no possibility they could avoid my soldiers! No, my dear, I fear it is as we thought. The Dark Elves have returned. Only they can disappear so quickly, and their magic easily rivals our own."

Panic appeared on Holly's face. "Ryan, please tell me the gate is being guarded right now!"

He reached over and took her hand. "The gate is being guarded by some of my best men. No one will be able to breach the gate from this side."

Holly's voice cracked. "It isn't this side I'm worried about. Ryan, Nathan warned us when Rebecca and Peter joined forces, their union sent shockwaves across the universe. Things long thought in slumber are now awake! Thanks to Rebecca and Peter, at least one dragon is on our side, but who knows what else they disturbed!"

The door then flew open and in ran a ragged-looking soldier, followed by two upset guards. The two embarrassed guards looked to the general with apologies in their eyes. The general raised his hand, dismissing the two guards back to their posts. The haggard-looking soldier nearly collapsed into the general's arm but straightened up to report to his commander. General Giles reached out, supporting the exhausted man.

The grateful man gathered himself. "My Lord, someone broke into the archive! I'm not sure what, if anything, was taken, but my men were cut down as if they were ragdolls. I couldn't even see what I was fighting. It almost looked like a dark cloud with no shape."

Holly gripped the general's arm to the point of nearly breaking the skin. "The archive! Ryan, the artifacts contained there are precious beyond measure. Not only are they rare, but they are also extremely dangerous in the wrong hands! We need to get down there and find out what, if anything, was taken."

General Giles brought the tired soldier to the guards, ordering them to get him medical attention. Securing the council chamber with warding, he clasped Holly's hand, leading her down the hall toward the archive. He only hoped nothing extremely important was from the precious collection. Running through tunnel after tunnel, the two didn't look at anyone as they passed by in a blur.

Finally, the general stopped before the archive doors. He investigated the area around the doors very thoroughly before entering the archive itself. Once sure the doors were secure, he ordered the three soldiers joining them in the room to guard the doors. Carefully, he opened one of the doors, peering into the darkened room. Holly nearly knocked him over as she barreled into the room with her hand raised, glowing with white light to lead their way. He learned over the years not to get in her way when she was on a mission.

A quick view of the lesser collections revealed nothing missing. As they went down into the lower halls, they almost breathed a sigh of relief as nothing of great value seemed missing. Holly spent many a night with Rebecca in the archive, looking for things in their people's history, hoping to come up with a solution to the reptilian threat. Most of the history revealed time after time, the reptilian people defeating the Zarillions with huge numbers. Rebecca marveled at the sheer numbers their enemy always enjoyed when attacking her people. Holly instructed her about this, telling her it was always that way, no matter where they met the reptilians in combat. Holly shared the fact that during the days before the reptilians were locked away behind the shield wall, they were able to multiply rapidly. One huge benefit to their imprisonment in the Antarctic was the temperature didn't allow for good breeding conditions. Almost no children were born to the reptilian people while in captivity.

Rebecca also learned, though the population of the reptilians may be finite, they were no less dangerous. Holly led the general to the rarest collections and spent her most time investigating this area. Everywhere she looked, nothing seemed disturbed. Even in the hidden archive, which she needed to use special magic to open the stone door, showed nothing touched or moved. She looked around in surprise as not one thing of value looked to be gone or moved. The two Zarillion leaders looked at each other with uncertain eyes.

Holly looked puzzled. "Ryan, nothing has been touched! Why would someone go through all the trouble of attacking this area and take nothing? The warding on everything of significance remains intact."

The general shook his head. "It makes no sense!"

Immediately, they looked at each other, repeating in stereo, "A diversion!"

No sooner than the words left their lips, they felt a great rumbling under their feet. The vibrations that followed sounded more like the soft humming of music. The two leaders made their way back up to the entrance to the archive. Once into the main hall, they ran at full speed toward the exit, only to be greeted with the doors barred shut from the other side. This was very puzzling as the doors opened inward and were therefore warded against entry from inside. Only those with the knowledge to open the doors were allowed in the archive.

The general grabbed the handles, hoping to yank them open, but nothing happened. They yelled for the guards, but they couldn't even hear any movement on the other side. Holly, now getting quite mad, built up energy around her to release into the doors. Ryan looked at her but could tell she would blast the doors into toothpicks rather than stand here any longer.

Holly waved the general out of the way, and he relented, moving over to the side. He watched as her whole body became engulfed in yellow light. The aura coming off her smooth skin threatened to burn anything it encountered. He could also hear the sizzle and crackle of energy oozing from her skin. With her full power, she sent the blast of energy hurling into the unsuspecting wooden doors. Without even so much as a groan, the doors repelled the energy blast, striking Holly in the process.

The general went to the doors, which didn't even feel hot and tried to open them without success. Holly grabbed energy from the earth, this time calming her mind. If she couldn't blast the doors open, she would have to try another tactic. Keeping the vision of the outside door knobs in her mind, she allowed her mind to see what might be holding the doors shut. To her great surprise, she determined it to be a powerful but reversible spell. Holly couldn't think of anyone besides herself and Rebecca in the city who could conjure this type of spell.

Continuing to concentrate, she let threads of power weave their way under the door and attach themselves to the existing spell. Immediately, Holly felt the spell unravel. Again, she thought to herself, *this was too easy*. If this was a diversion, this was a stalling technique for their unknown guests. Releasing the energy, she backed up, motioning Ryan to try the doors. Grabbing both doors, the general easily swung them wide open, rushing out with sword in hand, ready for battle.

Rather than be greeted by attackers, General Giles saw his soldiers sprawled upon the stone floor outside the doorway. He ran to see if the first man lived. His heart jumped when he felt a pulse. As he turned to look at the two soldiers, he saw them stir. Holly checked on the two coming to and gave the general a thumbs up to assure him the men would be fine. Again, nothing dangerous but still holding them up.

Another rumble moved below their feet, and the humming continued. Holly looked to Ryan. "They're going for the gate!! Hurry, Ryan, and gather all the men you can. I'll meet you at the gate."

"Holly, wait!"

Before he could stop her, the tall woman sped off in the direction of the Gate of the Cosmos. She knew this to be the most valued commodity the Zarillions possessed. The gate itself was shut after the war with the reptilians, in hopes it would never be needed again. For many eons, it looked as though it wouldn't be needed but today, someone was trying to open the gate. Ryan quickly ran toward Holly, barking orders to every soldier he met along the way to follow him.

By the time he neared the gate, he already gathered quite the nice squad of soldiers to his side. They all ran around the corner, only to see Holly locked in combat with another magic wielder. Two glowing figures grasping at each other's necks swung around in front of the gate itself. Though the gate resembled the surface of the cavern in which it stood, Ryan saw the white outline of the magically induced doorway coming into view.

All around him now, he saw other figures running toward him and his men, wielding weapons of their own. The general's men met the oncoming attackers in a huge slam of bodies, nearly crushing one another. A huge melee ensued with the Zarillion soldiers fighting others nearly resembling themselves. The only noticeable difference was the skin of the attackers had a slightly whiter pigment. Knives, swords, and axes flew, creating a bloody battle scene before the Gate of the Cosmos. The battle raged on for what seemed an hour before coming to a head.

Though the attackers were quite skilled, the Zarillions luckily still outnumbered them and took the battle. General Giles, still fighting two attackers, swung his sword in an upward arching motion to go underneath his attacker. The soldier deflected the blade while the other thrust his blade at the general's chest. The open side would have been pierced if not for the quick sword work by Holly joining the fray. She met the oncoming sword and twisted hers while flicking her wrist, causing the attacker's sword to fly in the air. While the sword flew, Holly ran the combatant through with her own. Spitting up blood, he grabbed for her but with no strength left, he slid off her blade to the ground.

A hacking soldier still swung at the general in hopes of catching him off guard. Though the soldier was as strong as he was, he couldn't muster enough skill for the general who sliced him with several cuts to the arms and legs. Bleeding from multiple cuts, his opponent tried valiantly to defend himself but with speed no longer with him, the general easily dispatched the man. He and Holly stood back to back, looking for the next wave of attackers. To their surprise, not one of the attackers remained on their feet and very few of the general's people seemed hurt.

As they were about to congratulate themselves on their victory, they noticed another figure standing before the gate. The figure stood before the door, hands raised, chanting in some unknown language. The chalk-white lines creating the gate doorway glowed brightly in a white-blue hue. Again, the ground rumbled, and another round of vibrations overtook the cavern around them. As the figure chanted, the lines around the door became more pronounced, threatening to open right on the spot.

Holly rushed toward the figure, gathering her own power as she ran. Fingertips crackling with energy, she hurled a lightning bolt at the man trying to open the gate. Reaching back with one hand, the man deflected the lightning and nearly struck the general. Ryan ducked just in time as the bolt struck the wall next to him, sending shards and fragments of rock spraying everywhere. Holly gathered more power, ready to strike, when the man turned, sending his own blue bolt at Holly.

Holly, rather than deflect, chose to absorb the energy and took it into herself. "You shall not open that gate! It is closed to the likes of you and will remain that way!"

The figure cackled with evil laughter. "You're too late!"

CHAPTER FORTY-SIX

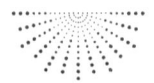

Blade still trembling in his hand after dispatching the dwarf council table, he turned to Aaron with a scowl on his face. Anger brimming over, he nearly stepped forward to finish the leader of the elder dwarf kingdom. Thomas placed a hand on his chest as Jake whipped his head around to see the calm face of the dwarf lord. He felt his anger traveling down his arms into the sword as if it absorbed the energy. Vibrations took hold of his arms, traveling the length of both arms until they stood flexed for battle.

Thomas spoke calmly, "The weapon is answering the call of battle. It is responding to its new master, but you truly must master the blade itself. You must find control, or the rage will take over in battle, and only slaughter will follow!"

Jake pulled the glorious blade up straight in front of him, viewing its ornate scrollwork. "Thomas, maybe only a true king can use this sword. I can barely lead myself, let alone control a kingly weapon such as this."

The dwarf lord smiled. "That is exactly why the sword chose you! You're the humblest warrior I've ever encountered. Judgement is key when involved in any battle. There are times aggression is needed but other times, discretion is called for along with mercy. You, my friend, have a compassion for life unlike any I've met."

Jake slid the sword back into its scabbard and bowed to Aaron. "Forgive my outburst, My Lord. I'll build you a new table if needed. My friend is in dire need of my assistance, and I'm here fighting a family battle I have no idea how to solve."

Aaron moved forward, looking to Thomas and then to Jake. "You are, my young friend. You are thrust into quite the family feud. I can only imagine the fortitude you needed to leave your own family to complete Mother's task. I'll table my wrath with my kin and listen to your plight."

He felt relief wash over his body. "Thank you, My Lord. Mother sent us to alert the dwarf people of the danger to the entire planet. In this, all free people are in dire need of allying to survive. Mother described the evil to come as unlike anything ever seen before. Her tone of haste with me is what drove me to you. Now, My Lord, you must decide, will you continue to hide behind your hidden gate, or will you come forth and stand with us for freedom?"

The dwarf lord stood in awe of the audacity of the young warrior. "Young man, I will excuse your lack of protocol and chalk it up to inexperience. Along the road, I may find time to school you on the finer points of speaking to others of station."

Turning to leave, Jake, still looking at the dwarf leader, walked over to the expanding group of gathering dwarves. Many still looked at the young warrior as if he were a barbarian. Aaron fell into heavy animated conversation with the group huddled around him. Jake detected by the angry looks that the dwarven leader would have a hard time convincing his kin of the dire nature in which they all found themselves. Thomas and his dwarfs stood behind Jake but chose not to disturb the young man during his vigil.

Voices rose to a fever pitch, and Aaron's arms waved in the air as to demonstrate the need for action. Finally, he nodded his head and strode toward the waiting Jake. A look of uncertainty showed on his face as he drew closer to the other dwarves. Thomas could see the look but said nothing and allowed Aaron to address Jake.

Aaron stepped a few feet from Jake's group. "Though I completely understand your need for haste, I would ask for a certain amount of patience on your part. You're asking a people who chose to leave all the woes of the surface and its dwellers behind long ago. Jake, my people care little for the plight of others, and they have suffered much in their own right."

Jake stood in disbelief at the decision of Aaron's people. "So, My Lord, your people will allow innocent blood to be spilt while you hide in your tucked-away land?"

Thomas nearly stepped in, but Aaron responded, "As I said, a little patience is needed. This will need to be handled in a delicate manner. I'm already with you and no matter what my people's decision, I'll bring those I can with me."

"My Lord, I appreciate your kind words, but Mother was quite adamant. The entirety of the dwarven people would be needed to defend the planet!"

Again, Aaron looked uncertain. "I wish I could make them come to your aid, but it's simply not that easy. My young friend, one wrong move, and I could be the only one traveling with you."

Jake felt in his heart the urgency with which he was needed back at Peter's side. "I cannot wait, My Lord. Mother sent me to find the dwarves, and I've done that. If they choose to do nothing, I cannot be responsible for their failures."

The dwarf leader stood, unmoving. "I know the mission given to you is extremely important, but I can also tell your loyalty to your friend is weighing heavily upon your heart."

Jake walked away. "My Lord, Aaron, tell your people one final thing for me. If by some miracle my people survive the evil to come, I'll be back, and the broken table will be the least of your worries!"

Thomas even looked at Jake in surprise. "Jake, please, even I know Aaron will do all he can to get his people to see your cause, but he's right about it being a delicate matter."

"Thomas, the only delicate matter I care about right now is that Peter is without me at his back, and evil is stalking him."

With his shoulders slightly arched forward from the weight of the entire situation, he moved away from the group of dwarves still looking at him. Stooping to pick up his pack, he slung it upon his shoulders without breaking stride. Footsteps of determination took him out of sight of the dwarf nation he was tasked to find. Turning around a corner, he found the path leading away from the city, back toward the magic gate.

At the gate, he looked at the ancient door and laughed at how he, only a few short months ago, was worried about homework. Now, as he reached forth to push the door open, his work was about to begin. Touching the door, he paused for a moment as he felt the blade pushing into his side. Jake reached down, grabbing the pommel, and again felt a vibration much like that when he destroyed the council table. The blade communicated with him, and he turned, looking back to where he had left the dwarven people.

He nearly ran back the way he came. Out of breath, he saw the dwarves taking out their own blades to defend themselves. Aaron stepped in front of them, telling them to stand down. Blades came down, but not one made it back into a scabbard as if waiting for combat. Jake, towering above the awaiting dwarves, reached for his own blade. Ringing in the air, the blade glowed a brilliant white, lighting up the scared dwarven faces.

Jake placed the blade in front of his face, lighting it in an ominous, ghostly hue. "Listen to me and listen closely. I'm not leaving without the dwarven people. Mother sends me to bring you to my side. Your sword chose me, Thomas chose me, and Aaron chose me! Legends say the dwarves are a race of loyal, strong, and determined people. I say we'll need every bit of that loyalty, strength, and determination in the fight to come!"

Faces looked uncertain as they glared at one another to see what their kin's decision would be. Aaron moved to the front. "My kin, the young man speaks the truth. I, among all of you, have the gift to tell when someone is untruthful. Jake is a true warrior and has demonstrated his own gifts worthy of the Serpent's Bane. There isn't one among you who can boast this and as such, needs to pay heed to the calling of the blade."

Jake looked to the viewing faces. "I promise you this, I'll fight by your side and will honor your ancestors. I know little of what awaits us, but I do know we won't be alone. I do know Peter and Rebecca are among the most powerful beings this universe has ever seen, but they're just flesh and can still be struck down. They'll need the might of the dwarf people to be their shield in their fight against evil. We cannot let evil triumph!"

One dwarf soldier came from the shadows. "I'll fight with you!"

Thomas smiled as another and then another offered their swords to Jake. Aaron came to Thomas, taking his hand and shaking it in front of the rest of the dwarves. As soon as the others saw this gesture, all descent left the dwarves. In a matter of minutes, Jake stood surrounded by hooting dwarves offering oaths of loyalty. Thomas and Aaron watched with great pride as their people instantly stood together united.

Aaron came over and patted Jake on the back. "Well done, my young friend! Honestly, I'm glad you came back. Nothing I could have said would sway their thought process, it needed to be you. Still, we need to mobilize our strength, and that could take days."

Jake looked panicked. "I cannot wait that long, My Lord. I feel in my soul that something is about to happen, and Peter will need me!"

The dwarf lord nodded. "I know, and I'll send those I can with you as you leave now."

A wave of relief came over Jake. "Thank you, My Lord, for your understanding. I'm sure the dwarves will find their way to us."

"No, my young friend, you won't have to worry about that. Though we have kept to the shadows, we also have kept tabs on the Zarillion people. We'll be there in short order. For now, give me a few hours, and I'll have a nice force assembled for you."

Again, he nodded in gratitude, replacing the sword in its scabbard. Feeling weak from exhaustion and lack of food, he sat upon the nearest chair. Aaron, noticing, hailed a young dwarf standing near, telling him to bring food and ale for their guests. Thomas and his men took up places around Jake, showing the same signs of hunger. Food arrived quickly and within minutes, the group felt refreshed. The dwarves broke into song, praising some forgotten warrior, and Jake marveled the tune. He sat back, listening to the harmony and resting his head on the wall. He closed his eyes, only to meet a yellow fire, causing him to surge forward. Thomas grabbed him, calming him. "Jake, what is it?"

"Yellow eyes of fire! A face of an enormous serpent!"

Thomas waved to Aaron, who knew what to do. He disappeared for a few minutes, only to return to tell Jake they could be off within the hour. Jake thanked the dwarf lord. He returned his pack to his shoulders and made ready to travel, taking a few more bites of a soft cake given to him. Thomas already barked orders to his men, and they were ready within minutes. Jake, along with Thomas, went from man to man to see if they needed any supplies while they were still in the city. When the men were stocked and packed, they awaited their kin so they could travel on their way.

Aaron, true to his word, gathered quite the force and all told, they were a formidable group of five hundred strong. Seeing the large force lightened Jake's heart, making him feel more confident his mission fulfilled. As promised, within the hour, they were underway. Passing the magic gate, they stopped, hearing the ominous clang of the door and the magic locks. Once confident the locks would hold, they made their way toward Thomas' homeland. Thomas assured them they could gather more men and supplies once there. The road was true, and they quickly arrived at Thomas' city. Aaron and his dwarves looked upon the city with longing but said nothing. Jake could tell a great healing would need to take place for the dwarves to be truly at peace with one another.

Anxious to continue, Jake took little food and looked to the road. Thomas hurried, gathering what men he could, and they moved out as quick as could be expected. Now, both groups ready, Thomas took the lead through the quickest tunnels, hoping to get to the Zarillion city early the next day. Jake pushed the group, and he marveled at the hearty nature of the dwarves. They tired little and maintained a great pace all night. Jake grew weary come morning, nearly stumbling to the ground. Thomas begged him to rest, and he relented, taking a quick nap on the rocky ground.

He knew not how long he slept as the rumbling and shaking of the cavern woke him from his slumber. Jake jumped to his feet and saw dwarves running to get their packs on, getting ready to move out. Thomas grabbed him, telling him the rumbling just started. Once again, the group moved in the direction of the Zarillion city. The closer they came to the city, the rumbling became more intense, with more frequency. Overhead, rocks fell, and he, along with his friends, found themselves dodging falling debris.

Thomas quickened his pace, and they moved into the city limits, only to be met by centuries. Seeing Jake, they were allowed to pass, and the host moved into the city proper, following Jake this time. He led them forward but now, he almost sensed Peter. Using his senses, he led the host downward through tunnels until they came to an ancient part of the undercity. Jake nearly ran at this point with the vision of the yellow-eyed monster in his mind. He didn't want to arrive too late.

Again, the rumbling caused them to duck out of the way of falling rocks. Now, the tunnels, although large, were littered with fallen debris, making travel more difficult, especially for such a large force. They made their way forward as fast as possible. Aaron told them not to wait for his force; they would follow his trail and find him. Jake quickened his pace, with Thomas in tow. Much of the force kept pace, and they turned a corner, only to come face to face with a huge monster staring down at them.

Jake, already with his sword ringing through the air, ran forward, yelling, "You shall not have them! I'll smite you where you stand!"

CHAPTER FORTY-SEVEN

Eyes sparkling with energy and anger, Jake leapt into the cavern with blade drawn, looking for blood. Gleaming sword brandished in front of his face, no one in their right mind would confront the young warrior. Wild with thoughts of protection, Jake stood only in defensive mode, ready to cut down any attacker between him and his lord. Raising the sword, he didn't even think of the size of the enormous beast before him and ran forward to attack.

Blade blazing a white flame, even the dragon before him backed up slightly. Jake covered the distance between him and the beast in mere seconds. He jumped in the air with the blade arced, with his shoulder holding it fast for a deep thrust into the dragon. The eyes of the dragon showed anger of their own, and the young warrior saw the beast sucking in air for a strike of its own.

As the blade was to strike the scaled skin of the waiting dragon, Jake felt himself stop short, as if running into an invisible wall. Bouncing off the unseen wall, he found himself on the ground, looking up at the now-advancing dragon. The dragon possessed exactly the flaming yellow eyes he saw in his vision. Thrusting himself to his feet, he raised the magical blade before him to deflect any strike from the dragon. He braced his body for a heavy, strong strike from the beast, but nothing struck his blade.

A booming voice broke the silence. "Stop this nonsense!"

The voice ringing in his ears was that of a woman. "Jake, stop! She's our friend! The dragon won't harm you!"

Jake stood looking up at the glaring dragon, unconvinced. "I saw her attacking in a vision! Rebecca, she isn't our ally! We must dispatch her immediately!"

He felt a strong hand on his shoulder, only to turn to see the bright, smiling face of his friend Peter. "Dude, we got this! The dragon is with us!"

Seeing Peter, he let out a huge sigh and ran to embrace the young man. He grabbed Peter so hard in a bear hug, Peter thought his friend would break his back. Jake pulled Peter's head back slightly, holding it in front of his, looking over his friend to make sure he was sound and in one piece. When satisfied, he released him, nearly dropping him on the ground. Once back with both feet on the ground, Peter smiled from ear to ear, slapping his best friend on the shoulder.

Another hand grabbed his shoulder, and he spun to take in the beauty that was Rebecca. Her eyes reached into his soul, taking hold of his heart. Every time he looked into her eyes, he felt embarrassed as if he weren't worthy to look upon her. He felt his face becoming red and hot. Her warm, genuine smile disarmed him, and he took her embrace without delay. The hug lasted only a few seconds but, in that time, Jake felt as if all the anxiety of being away from Peter melted away instantly. As Rebecca let go of Jake, she held him at arm's length and gave him a quick wink.

Shaking his head to bring himself back from the haze that beholding Rebecca always caused him, he looked up at the majestic creature before him in awe. Taking in the sheer size of the dragon, he nearly laughed, thinking of the sheer folly of trying to attack her with a mere blade. As his eyes made their way upward to the snout, he shivered slightly when his eyes caught sight of the razor-sharp teeth gleaming in the light of the cavern. Each tooth looked to be larger than he stood and then, he noticed the yellow eyes while backing up.

In his vision, those eyes attacked, breathing fire but here, the creature seemed at peace.

Looking down to see Peter okay, he turned back to Rebecca with questions in his eyes. She giggled and grabbed his hand, pulling him forward, closer to the dragon. At first, every muscle in his body screamed not one more step closer, but Rebecca's power overwhelmed him. He found himself stroking the scales of the dragon's ankle. Surprisingly, the flesh felt like that of a lizard but softer. Jake felt the scales and sensed the softness but expected it to feel oily. As he lifted his hand, bringing it close to his face to inspect it, he expected to see oily residue, nothing appeared. He looked up at the dragon, only to see the creature smile his way.

Jake, realizing he still held the blade in one hand, returned it to the scabbard quickly. He then turned to the dragon, bowing slightly in apology. The massive head met his bow with a nod of understanding and then looked to Rebecca for orders. Jake followed suit as a large rumble came through the cavern, knocking them all to the ground. Scrambling to their feet, they all looked into one another's eyes, only to see the dragon already moving out of the cavern.

The dragon peered over her shoulder. "Stay behind me, and I'll deflect any debris. They're going for the Gate!"

Rebecca called up, "What gate?"

The dragon looked downward. "My Queen, they're trying to open the Gate of the Cosmos! They must not be allowed to succeed. If they open that gate, we'll all perish!"

Rebecca rushed forward. "Lead on, My Lady!"

Rebecca grabbed Peter, and they ran behind the dragon with Jake on their right-hand side. For the first time, Peter noticed Jake wasn't alone. A large group of soldiers pulled into formation behind Jake. He glanced over his shoulder, trying to get a better look at the soldiers. Peter could tell the men were shorter than he but much stouter in stature. Thoughts rushed into his mind, telling him Jake was successful in his mission to find the dwarves. Smiling slightly, he spun quickly, moving with Rebecca as they made their way through the awaiting tunnels.

The rumbling more violent, they found themselves nearly jumping over large pieces of fallen rock. Gemini told them to walk closer to her, and they were underneath the dragon as they went forward. The dwarf army held strong shields above them as they advanced. Within a few minutes, they heard shouting coming from somewhere nearby, telling them they must be close. Rebecca, with panic in her eyes, sprinted out from the protection of the dragon, making for the awaiting cavern ahead.

Peter took off after her, trying to catch her to bring her back, but she was already running into the cavern. They nearly skidded into one another when Rebecca stopped short, witnessing the carnage before her. Bodies lay strewn everywhere, and she panicked, looking for the voice she recognized. Seeing Holly, she again sprinted toward her mentor. Off to their left, Peter saw an odd figure standing before a stone wall with its hands raised to the sky. He looked at the wall, only to see the white outline of a door of some kind.

Rebecca yelled, "Holly!"

Holly paused for a moment but didn't look back at Rebecca. She brought more power to her and released it in the direction of the waiting figure before the wall. The blast struck the figure, sending him flying until it crashed into the opposite wall. The small man hit the rock wall with such force, Peter could hear the crack of bone and ripping of flesh. Landing on the floor, the man didn't move, and Peter ran forward to intercept Rebecca.

Holly turned to greet her protégé with a grim look. The rumbling began anew, and they all looked toward the now-cracking wall with the white outline. The outline more defined, started to split, revealing a clear doorway. A spiraling wave of energy moved inward in a type of vortex. A brilliant white light emanated from the middle of the vortex.

Holly ran forward with her hands and arms glowing their own brilliant white light, sending a blast of power into the doorway. Nothing happened as the doorway sucked the power into itself. General Giles barked orders to his remaining men to guard the entrance with their lives. The dwarf army took up positions in front of the opening to not let anything out of the vortex. Behind them all stood the golden dragon. Gemini awaited anything coming out of the doorway, sucking in air to breathe fire.

Sparks flew from the now-spinning vortex shooting into the cavern. The brilliant white light gave way to an almost TV-like picture. Peter peered into the doorway, and it looked to him to be another world, one of darkness and fire. He discovered volcanoes spewing lava into the air, and his eyes shot up as he saw the vastness of the awaiting army standing ready to attack. Not taking his eyes off the force, he caught movement from the corner of his eye. Holly stood in front of them with her power forming.

Again, she shot forth a bolt of energy into the now-open doorway. The bolt found its mark, obliterating the soldiers standing outside the door. She watched as body parts flew into soldiers still standing, ready to march. The general waved his forces to follow him, but Holly put her hand up to halt them where they stood. Her face stoic, she gathered power to her, only to take a bolt from a crossbow in her shoulder. Nearly falling over, she gathered herself, forcing her bolt of energy into the opening. Again, the bolt found its mark, creating chaos on the other side of the door.

Grabbing her shoulder, she turned slightly to find the general who already stood within feet of her. Again, a bolt found her, this time in the left leg. General Giles picked her up as she fell and pulled her close to him, running away from the doorway. Jake, without being told, waved to his force of dwarves and led them forward. The dwarves followed closely with shields in front of them. Jake had both shield and blazing sword in front of him as he ran forward.

In front of the door, he ordered his archers to release. The dwarves sent a volley of arrows into the doorway. Again, the soldiers on the other side were struck and scattered. Peter looked to Rebecca as they witnessed the vast numbers still forming, despite their efforts. Volley after volley, the dwarves sent into the breach, only to see more and more soldiers moving toward the door.

Peter heard a rumbling behind them as the dragon asked them to move. Rebecca grabbed Peter and moved to the side, allowing the dragon to come forward before the door. With a large sucking sound, they heard massive amounts of air filling the dragon's lungs. Without a sound, the dragon launched a huge fireball into the breach. Peter looked with horror as the flames lapped the soldiers and instantly incinerated them. Rebecca pointed as the void filled with soldiers and again, the dragon breathed fire into the doorway.

Hundreds of arrows flew through from the other side, bouncing off the dragon's protective scales. Gemini laughed and breathed another blast into the door. Surprisingly, another bolt came from inside the door. This bolt was extremely large and struck the dragon in the leg, biting flesh with bone. A booming yelp filled the air as the dragon stumbled back, using her tail to take the bolt from her leg. Pain riddled her leg, and she told Rebecca the bolt was poisoned.

Rebecca strode forward with an uncontrollable angry look on her face. With arms straight out and arched back, she took as much energy as she could gather from the earth in those few moments. A quick flick of her wrist sent the wave of energy into the doorway, leveling everything within sight. Relief spread across everyone's face as Rebecca turned to her friends. Peter surmised she felt strong, but the look on her face told him she was very worried about Holly.

Peter looked hastily around the cavern for signs of the general. He quickly found him beyond the door to the cavern itself, looking down on Holly, tending to her wounds. The general's face was distraught. Peter thought to himself what the dragon pronounced about the bolt being poisoned. Rebecca was already running to the fallen Holly, hands glowing with energy. She nearly fell over her mentor's body with tears flowing freely. Holly, unmoving, showed little signs of life, and the general announced they needed to find a way to help Holly. They could all tell the poison to be fast acting, and Rebecca couldn't stop crying.

Peter knelt by his beloved. "Rebecca, we'll heal her together!"

Without another word, Peter clasped Rebecca's hand and felt her energy building. He closed his eyes and let the energy build up inside himself as well. Within moments, the two were in a trance, holding the energy ready to release a stream of it into Holly to counteract the poison. Both reached down and took a hand of Holly's into theirs. Peter felt the effects of the poison running through Holly's body immediately. His hand felt cold, almost freezing, as if the poison was trying to freeze Holly completely. He knew this was no ordinary poison and had aspects of magic to it.

Rebecca and Peter released a nice, warm flow of energy into Holly's hands, letting it move throughout her body. At first, nothing happened, and the general looked manic. After a few moments, some color returned to Holly's skin, and she breathed a little more evenly. Rebecca and Peter let energy make its way into Holly's ravaged body. Opening their eyes, they saw General Giles looking at them in awe through tear-stained eyes.

A blast came from behind them, striking the rock wall on the other side of the gate, sending shards of rock spraying everywhere. The dwarf army, smart enough to raise their shields, remained unharmed, but it did get Peter's attention. Peter looked at Rebecca and then to the general. General Giles nodded, telling them Holly was out of danger, but they needed to tend to the gate. Peter ran over to her and pointed to the fallen dragon, knowing they couldn't leave her injured.

Rebecca stood in front of the gate and released another blast of energy into it, clearing the way for the moment. She then ran to the dragon where Peter was already calling the energy to himself as she grabbed his hand to join him. As she did, boom after boom exploded from the still-smoking gate. Rebecca knew they needed to close the gate, but she couldn't let the dragon die. Again, she and Peter let their energy find its way into the dragon to fight the poison. They felt the poison leaving the dragon's body.

Over their heads, another blast rang out from the gate. The booms were rhythmic, like drums but different. Peter heard shouting, and he peered toward the gate. Large hands gripped the edge of the gate, and Peter's eyes bulged at the grotesque head he saw coming through the doorway. It resembled a man, but the face was hugely disfigured with scars over the entire face. He looked down at the wounded dragon and then to Rebecca for guidance.

CHAPTER FORTY-EIGHT

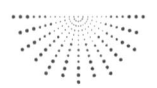

Michelle, running at full speed with her sword waving before her, moved through the tunnels. No one in their right mind would bar her way as she felt the danger rising to her son in her gut. Though a Knight of the Cosmos, nothing came before her son, and she ran with reckless abandon to her son's side. Beads of sweat ran down her face, showing the intense exertion of her quest to join her son. Darting up one of the tunnels, she heard a deep, booming sound, and the tunnel shook around them. Putting her head down, she quickened her pace, understanding her son to be in peril didn't sit well with her.

Derek said not a word, running behind Michelle to protect her backside. He peered quickly over his shoulder, nodding at the dwarf force covering his own six. Silently, with deadly precision, the large force moved through the tunnels, ready to defend their newly formed alliance with the humans. Stout figures covered in chain mail, and, even in heavy boots, they made not a sound as they covered the ground before them in search of Jake. Boom after boom burst, telling them they were close to the danger ahead. Each soldier viewed the tunnel ahead, waiting to be ambushed at any moment.

The ambush never came, but the booms intensified with each step, as did the shaking of the tunnel itself. Dust and debris formed in the air, impairing their vision. Michelle, undaunted, moved through the dust with laser focus, keeping the vision of her son before the Gate in her mind's eye. She needed to get to Peter as fast as possible. The sharp image of Jake doing battle with a dragon made her step even faster. She knew Jake wouldn't let anything happen to Peter, but they needed her assistance at this point to close the gate. Derek pulled up on her shoulder, and the feeling warmed her heart to know the soldier fought by her side.

In her mind, she reached out to Peter and saw the image of a fallen dragon over which Peter bent. Though hard to see everything around him, she saw Rebecca bent over the dragon as well. Questions swirled around her mind as to why Peter would help the dragon until she watched Peter's head sharply bend toward the gate. In her mind, she watched in horror as an enormous Space Troll pulled itself through the gate, barely squeezing into the cavern.

With a blazing white sword, Jake joined Peter, who brandished his own sword. Rebecca stood at his right, eyes sparkling with energy. Michelle understood no power in the universe could stand before those three, but she also knew them to be just as easily struck down by a stray arrow. The troll stood to its full height as the trio moved forward to intercept the creature without hesitation. A great feeling of pride swelled deep within Michelle to see her boy becoming a man. Her father would be extremely proud to see what a royal figure Peter cut as he moved forward to combat the troll.

Rebecca launched the first strike unleashing her bolt of energy into the torso of the beast. The blast caught the creature full on and sent it crashing into the cavern wall, sending shards of rock spewing into the air. At first, the troll slumped on the floor but then stirred, shaking its head. Pulling itself to its full height, the huge creature roared so loud, everyone covered their ears.

Again, a blast of energy planted the troll on the ground. While still on hands and knees, it looked at Rebecca. While smiling through broken teeth, it sent a huge boulder hurling her way. Peter quickly jumped to push Rebecca out of the way while the boulder crashed to the ground harmlessly. Peter and Rebecca scrambled to their feet, only to see another boulder sailing through the air at them. Peter released a blast of energy into the boulder, shattering it into a million shards of sharp rock.

Peter marveled as the shards took the form of a rock cloud and sailed straight for the unsuspecting troll. The shards ripped into the flesh of the troll, renting great tears in the creature's torso. Blood sprayed onto the opposite wall as the creature wailed but didn't fall. Instead, the troll became angrier, and an unseen whip appeared in its hand. Snapping the large whip into the air, it struck the top of the cavern with a noisy crack.

The troll stood with the whip by its side with blood streaming down the front of its body, making a gruesome sight. With the already scarred face, blood, and dim light, the creature made for a frightening sight. With the flick of the wrist, the whip flew, aimed directly for Rebecca's head. The blow never came as a streak of white light entered the scene as Jake jumped in front of Rebecca, catching the whip midair and slicing it in half with his blade. Jake spun with the blazing blade arced behind his back, waiting for another strike.

Again, Michelle couldn't feel prouder looking at the boy that, in many ways, was now her defacto son. Jake swung his magnificent blade around, spinning it multiple times in front of himself, warning the troll this would be his last campaign. Moving with terrific speed, Jake dipped under the legs of the huge troll and sliced at one of its Achilles tendons. The blade found its mark, and the molten blade sizzled as it burned through the troll's flesh. An agonizing cry emanated from the troll as it fell forward, crashing to the ground, causing the entire cavern to shake.

Jake's face covered in sweat, showed no mercy as he jumped onto the troll's leg. Continuing to run up the length of the creature at the shoulders, launched himself into the air, arching his back with his blade pointed down in a killing blow. The young warrior flew with the blade hissing as it found its mark in the back of the troll's head. Michelle nearly lost her connection as she watched the blade slide deeply into the troll's skull. She watched in horror as Jake snapped the blade first to the left and then to the right, scrambling the beast's brains.

A primal scream came from the entrance of the gate as everyone spun to see the new threat. Michelle knew they were all in trouble as the large skull of a dazzling silver dragon appeared in the gate. She heard voices around her as she let the image in her mind falter. She knew they didn't have much time, and the gate needed to be shut. Turning the corner, she and Derek entered the cavern in time to see the dragon squeezing into the gate. Michelle unleashed a blast of energy of her own into the face of the dragon. Stunned, the dragon halted for a moment. Regaining its composure, the dragon pulled itself through.

Derek stood shoulder to shoulder with his son as Michelle stood with Peter. Clasping Rebecca's hand, Peter joined her in building more energy together for a death blow to the dragon. Again, Michelle blasted the dragon, causing it to fall back into the gate. Michelle motioned to Peter to release their energy. As they were about to unleash the energy, a huge blast of fire coursed through the gate aimed at Peter and Rebecca. Michelle met the blast with her own energy just in time to create a boundary around Peter and Rebecca, protecting them from the flames.

The flames deflected off Michelle's boundary and flew in all directions, missing the couple. Michelle wasn't quite so lucky. As she tried to send up more energy to protect herself, the flames slammed into her, sending her crashing into the cavern wall. Peter screamed as he watched his mother sail into the wall, lying on the ground unmoving. He released Rebecca's hand, running to his mother. Sliding to the ground, he cradled her head in his hands. As he looked down, he noticed her hair slightly singed, but nothing else seemed wrong. It took a moment, but Michelle opened her eyes to behold her son, and she smiled painfully.

A sigh of relief washed over Peter as he held his mother close to his chest. Holding her head carefully before him, she reached up to hand him a medallion. Seeing the starburst pattern in the middle, he nearly laughed as she placed it in his hand. As soon as the pattern touched his hand, it glowed, and the outlines of the starburst pattern turned a brilliant white. He held the medallion in front of him and immediately knew what he needed to do. Pushing himself to his feet, he watched as Rebecca took his place tending to Michelle, and he turned to the gate.

He heard a hoarse voice shout behind him, "You must hurry! The gate cannot stay open! You must not let the dragon enter this realm!"

With the voice of his mother ringing in his head, he walked to the gate with the medallion raised before him. Heat surrounded him as he felt himself gathering energy, but this was different. The medallion sent the brilliant light into his body, adding to his own power. As he prepared to unleash the power to seal the gate, he couldn't help but look to his friends first. They all looked into his eyes with gratitude.

Another blast of fire screamed through the breech but flew around him as he stood protected by his magic. However, screams from Rebecca threw off his concentration, and he spun to see her distraught, thinking the flames would destroy Peter. Not looking at the gate, he released the energy into the gate to close it but didn't see the tail coming for him. The energy hit the gate and again, the white vortex spun, ready to close the breech.

He turned just in time to see the dragon's tail curl around his waist. Still holding the medallion, he let the energy do its job to close the gate. The tail constricted around him, but he didn't relent, using every ounce of energy he had to close the gate. Peter saw the vortex closing around the large tail, and he thought the gate would sever it in two. Screaming, Rebecca ran toward Peter, and he saw her own energy dancing in her eyes, ready to strike the tail.

Legs spread apart in a power stance, the energy danced in her eyes. She wouldn't allow anything to hurt her beloved. Raising her hands to release a blast of energy, she watched in horror as the tail quickly retracted, dragging Peter with it into the closing gate. Peter nearly bent in half at the quickness with which the tail pulled itself into the vortex. With a last-ditch effort, he threw the medallion at Jake. Jake caught it but looked helpless, running toward him with blade drawn.

Rebecca watched in horror as the love of her life was sucked into the now-closed vortex, "Peter, my love, no!"

CALL TO ACTION

Thank you for purchasing Rise.

If you have five minutes, please leave a review and make sure to sign up for my mailing list at www.cpaniccia.com.

ABOUT THE AUTHOR

Christopher Paniccia was born in Providence, RI. He grew up in East Providence, RI and Rehoboth, MA.

For over twenty years he has been an educator at the elementary and college levels in the Boston area. As an author and illustrator his goal continues to be one of inspiring others to follow their dreams.

His student's remain a huge inspiration to him and directly inspired his first book, "Gridiron Conspiracy." The Gridiron Conspiracy Trilogy continues to expand its reach to all types and ages of readers.

He is a Veteran of the United States Air Force, where he was a Combat Medic.

He lives with his family in the Boston area.

Made in the USA
Middletown, DE
28 June 2025